The Stoneware Monkey

&

The Penrose Mystery

TWO DR. THORNDYKE NOVELS
by R. Austin Freeman

With a new Introduction by
E. F. BLEILER

DOVER PUBLICATIONS, INC.
NEW YORK

This Dover edition, first published in 1973, contains
the unabridged texts of American editions of the
following novels:

The Stoneware Monkey, as published by Grosset &
Dunlap, New York, in 1939.

The Penrose Mystery, as published by Dodd Mead
& Company, New York, in 1936.

A new Introduction has been written specially for the
present edition by E. F. Bleiler.

International Standard Book Number: 0–486–22963–7
Library of Congress Catalog Card Number: 72–82073

Manufactured in the United States of America
Dover Publications, Inc.
180 Varick Street,
New York, N.Y. 10014

INTRODUCTION TO THE DOVER EDITION

Whenever one turns to the detective stories of the period between 1905 and 1925 or so, a single name is preeminent. That is Richard Austin Freeman (1862–1943), the British doctor who turned to mystery fiction for a living. His work was accepted by his peers and the readers of the day as the best; and his stories are among the few from this era that can still be read with enjoyment and some profit.

They may not be read for the same reasons that they were read two generations ago, since they are not likely to be puzzling as mysteries, nor are they likely to serve as sources for technical information in criminology, as they were originally intended, in part at least. But they have achieved a classical status in that they were written, as Vincent Starrett once put it, by a man "with a touch." They have served as a permanent rebuttal to the hardboiled critics who have sneered at the British problem detective as too far removed from life to be vital. Indeed, Raymond Chandler, who led the onslaught against the British form, in private correspondence to Hamish Hamilton once commented, "This man Austin Freeman is a wonderful performer. He has no equal in his genre."

Just what is Freeman's genre? Although it may not have been what Chandler had in mind, Freeman has always been considered the foremost practitioner of the scientific detective story, a story where the detective is a scientific worker, a story where the insights and techniques of science are used for the solution of a mystery. In Freeman's case this has meant microscopic analysis of blood samples to determine corpuscle size or shape or the presence of bloodstream parasites; or the symptomology of rare African diseases; or identification of dust grains under the microscope; or racial characteristics as determined from cross-section of the hair; or anthropological characteristics of skeletal material; or identification of neolithic pottery . . . all in addition to the standard pharmacological tests used in medical criminology. Freeman took great pride in accuracy in these areas, and it was also something of a small delight to him that he had anticipated the professional police in many tests and techniques.

Strangely enough, there have never been many good scientific detective writers. One could even say, without too much exaggeration, that the form has had only one noteworthy practitioner, Freeman himself. During his lifetime, the term was applied to several other writers, notably to Arthur Reeve, the American writer, whose Craig Kennedy stories were written somewhat in the manner of Freeman, but the rivalry was more in sales than quality. In America there was once an attempt to establish the scientific detective story as a permanent form, when Hugo Gernsback, the so-called father of science-fiction, launched a magazine entitled *Scientific Detective Stories* and *Amazing Detective Stories*. It was not very viable.

Freeman was apparently impelled to write the sort of stories he did in reaction to the low-grade "scientific" detective fiction that was being written around him, and he had strong feelings about both the aim and the technique of the story. In general, his mode was realism, with reasonable crimes committed for valid motives, and his stress was on the intellectual side of the puzzle story. In his well-known essay, "The Art of the Detective Story," which is really the great summation of the classical form, he makes the following points:

> It is a work of imagination, demanding the creative artistic faculty; on the other hand, it is a work of ratiocination, demanding the power of logical analysis and subtle and acute reasoning, and added to these inherent qualities, there must be a somewhat extensive outfit of special knowledge . . . the distinctive quality of a detective story, in which it differs from all other types of fiction, is that the satisfaction that it offers to the reader is primarily intellectual. . . .

> There is the story, with its dramatic interest, and enclosed in it, so to speak, is the logical problem; and the climax of the former may leave the latter apparently unsolved. It is then the duty of the author, through the medium of the investigator, to prove the solution, by an analysis and exposition. . . . If it is satisfactorily done, this is to the critical reader usually the most interesting part of the book; and it is the part by which he—very properly— judges the quality of the whole work.

All this, strangely enough, involves a paradox. Freeman set out to create the most cerebral detective stories, and yet the reason that his work is read today is most certainly not for the factors that he rated most highly. The modern reader, who has come through the even more cerebral stories of Nicholas Blake and the Coles, the plot intricacies of J. D. Carr and Ellery Queen, the romantic realism of Hammett and Chandler, and the psychological brilliancies of T. S. Stribling is apt to marvel at Freeman's blind spot about what he was accomplishing, even in his own day.

Historically speaking, Freeman might be characterized as the antithesis to the work of Doyle, despite some superficial resemblances between the stories of the two men. Even more, Freeman embodied a reaction against the school of Doyle, such men and women as Richard Marsh, L. T. Meade and Robert Eustace, M. P. Shiel, B. Fletcher Robinson and the many lesser writers who contributed to *Pearson's, Strand, Windsor Magazine* and other periodicals. Doyle had established the pattern to which they usually conformed. This included an eccentric detective, nonchalant criminology, colorful adventures, and a naïvely weird pseudoscience: drugs with incredible properties, astonishing biological monsters, electrical machines, and, of course, highly romantic villains. It would be tempting to say that Freeman's work put the quietus to Indian idols who knifed gentlemen who pushed the wrong buttons, or beautiful mistress-minds of crime with disintegration devices, or memory-erasing drugs, but this may be claiming too much. Others were heading in the same direction. In England E. C. Bentley was trying to write a detective story of human relationships, in America M. D. Post was using the quirks of criminal law as the basis for stories, while Baroness Orczy was applying even more cerebral techniques to the solution of the mystery story, by abolishing everything except the explanation-denouement. The climate was generally trending away from romanticism. Let us simply say that Freeman was a major force in the evolution of the detective story, certainly today the most permanent and readable of his period.

ii

The life history, the personality and the interests of Richard Austin Freeman emerge in many ways in his fiction. Born the son of a London tailor, he knew the poverty of the slums, and he also knew the problems and rewards of the small craftsman. After training as a pharmacist, he graduated from Middlesex Hospital in London as a surgeon, with ear-nose-and-throat as a specialty. Without the funds to establish himself in practice, he worked for a time at the hospital, held various temporary situations, and then joined the Colonial Service on the Gold Coast of Africa. He was apparently highly competent, and his future seemed promising; but he contracted black water fever and was invalided home to England. Perpetual ill health dogged him for the remainder of his life, and writing, together with part-time practice and a brief episode in the Ambulance Corps in World War I, served as his livelihood. Shy, retiring, modest, gentle, he was considered a remarkable man by all who knew him. This charm, of course, emerges in his work, and is probably the main reason that his stories are still read.

Freeman's interests were many. He had a serious interest in medical jurisprudence, as can be determined from his stories, and taught for a time at Middlesex. Scientific knowledge of all sorts intrigued him, particularly biological. Among his other interests were eugenics—he was long reviewer for the *Eugenics Review;* workshop practice—one portion of his house was always a combination lab and workshop, where Freeman played his own Polton; arts—he was a very competent watercolorist. As his obituarist in the *Eugenics Review* stated: "We need not look far for the original of those qualities, above all the learning, scientific integrity and urbanity, which, for most of us, make Thorndyke the most appealing of all the successors of Dupin and Sherlock Holmes."

Dominating all Freeman's work is the gigantic personality of Dr. John Evelyn Thorndyke, barrister-at-law of the Inner Temple, Professor of Medical Jurisprudence at St. Margaret's Hospital, and scientific detective preeminent. As Freeman wrote of Thorndyke's origins,

Dr. Thorndyke was not based on any person, real or fictitious. He was deliberately invented. In a professional sense he may have been suggested to me by Dr. Alfred Swayne Taylor . . . but his personality was designed in accordance with certain principles and what I believed to be the probabilities as to what such a man would be like. As mental and bodily characters are usually in harmony, a fine physique tending to be associated with fine mind, I made him tall, strong, active and keen-sighted. As he was a man of acute intellect and sound judgment I decided to keep him free from eccentricities . . . and to endow him with the dignity of presence, appearance and manner appropriate to his high professional and social standing. Especially I decided to keep him perfectly sane and normal.

Dr. John Thorndyke was first born in a long short story or nouvelle entitled "31 New Inn,"[1] which later was expanded into the familiar novel *The Mystery of 31 New Inn*. But although he was created around 1905, Thorndyke did not appear in print until 1907, and then in a different story, *The Red Thumb Mark*. This novel was so cast as to provide an official "coming out" for Thorndyke. After this, Thorndyke occupied approximately three quarters of Freeman's writing, with a total of 21 novels and 42 short stories, two of which are doublets for the novels. In general the earlier novels are better known in America than the later.

The Stoneware Monkey (1938), together with the novel which immediately followed it, *Mr. Polton Explains* (1940), marks an Indian summer in Freeman's work. Written when Freeman was 75 years old, it came as a welcome surprise after several faltering stories of the thirties. It is a fine performance both as a mystery novel and as a satire on modern art, the glib humor with which Freeman mimics art critics being certain to delight even readers who disagree with him about modern art. The photograph used as a frontispiece represents Freeman's own idea of the monkey.

The Penrose Mystery (1936) is an oddity in detective fiction. We have heard of *romans à clef* that have toppled ministries, novels that have caused lawsuits or assaults, but *The Penrose Mystery* may be the only novel that has sponsored an archeological dig. The reader, toward the end of the book, will learn about Julliberrie's Grave, a large neolithic mound near Windmill Hill in England. As Norman Donaldson reveals in his fascinating and informative *In Search of Dr. Thorndyke*,[2] Freeman's account of a fictional excavation led immediately to a real excavation, undertaken by the very friend whom Freeman had written about in the novel.

These two novels demonstrate the ultimate answer to the survival value of R. Austin Freeman's best work. They illustrate his serene craftmanship; the subtlety of his thought, unbeset with the academism of many of his contemporaries; his marvelous sense of color in matters criminological; the gusto with which he develops his own technical apparatus; the touches of dry humor around his criminal

---

[1] This nouvelle, long lost, has recently been rediscovered, and has been reprinted in the collection *The Best Dr. Thorndyke Detective Stories*, Dover Publications, Inc., 1973.

[2] *In Search of Dr. Thorndyke. The Story of R. Austin Freeman's Great Scientific Investigator and His Creator*. Norman Donaldson. Bowling Green University Popular Press, Bowling Green, Ohio, 1971.

low-lives; the delightful evocation of Edwardian England; the personality of the inexhaustible Thorndyke; and above all the charm that fills his writing. Despite his occasional quirks, in this quality of charm he is unique in detective fiction, and for this he is likely to be a favorite as long as great detective stories are cherished.

E. F. BLEILER

P.E.I., 1971

Contents

The Stoneware Monkey, as sculpted by the author, Dr. Freeman.

The Stoneware Monkey

BOOK ONE

NARRATED BY JAMES OLDFIELD, M.D.

CHAPTER I

HUE AND CRY

The profession of medicine has a good many drawbacks in the way of interrupted meals, disturbed nights and long and strenuous working hours. But it has its compensations, for a doctor's life is seldom a dull life. Compared, for instance, with that of a civil servant or a bank official, it abounds in variety of experience and surroundings, to say nothing of the intrinsic interest of the work in its professional aspects. And then it may happen at any moment that the medical practitioner's duties may lead him into the very heart of a drama or a tragedy or bring him into intimate contact with crime.

Not that the incident which I am about to describe was, in the first place, directly connected with my professional duties. The initial experience might have befallen anyone. But it was my medical status that enlarged and completed that experience.

It was about nine o'clock on a warm September night that I was cycling at an easy pace along a by-road towards the town, or village, of Newingstead, in which I was temporarily domiciled as the *locum-tenens* of a certain Dr. Wilson. I had been out on an emergency call to a small village about three miles distant and had taken my bicycle instead of the car for the sake of the exercise; and having ridden out at the speed that the occasion seemed to demand, was now making a leisurely return, enjoying the peaceful quiet of the by-way and even finding the darkness restful with a good headlight to show the way and a rear light to secure me from collisions from behind.

At a turn of the lane, a few twinkling lights seen dimly through spaces in the hedgerow told me that I was nearing my destination. A little reluctant to exchange the quiet of the countryside for the light and bustle of the town, I dismounted, and, leaning my bicycle against a gate, brought out my pipe and was just dipping into my pocket for my tobacco pouch when I heard what sounded to me like the call of a police whistle.

I let go the pouch and put away my pipe as I strained my ears to listen. The sound had come from no great distance but I had not been able exactly to locate it. The cart track from the gate, I knew, skirted a small wood, from which a footpath joined it, and the sound had seemed to come from that direction. But the wood was invisible in the darkness, though I could judge its position by a group of ricks, the nearest of which loomed vaguely out of the murk.

I had switched off the lamps of my machine and was just considering the expediency of walking up the cart track to explore, when the unmistakable shriek of a police whistle rang out, considerably nearer than the last and much shorter, and was succeeded by the sound of voices—apparently angry voices—accompanied by obscure noises as of bodies bursting through the undergrowth of the wood, from the direction of which the sounds now clearly proceeded. On this I climbed over the gate and started up the cart track at a quick pace, treading as silently as I could and keeping a bright lookout. The track led through the groups of ricks, the great shapes of which loomed up one after another, looking strangely gigantic in the obscurity, and near the last of them I passed a farm wagon and was disposed to examine it with my flashlight, but then judged it to be more prudent not to show a light. So I pushed on with the flashlight in my hand, peering intently into the darkness and listening for any further sounds.

But there were none. The silence of the countryside—now no longer restful, but awesome and sinister— was deepened rather than broken by the faint sounds that belonged to it; the half-audible "skreek" of a bat, the faint murmur of leaves and, far away, the fantastic cry of an owl.

Presently I was able to make out the wood as a vague shape of deeper darkness and then I came on the little footpath that meandered away towards it. Deciding that this was the right direction, I turned on to it and followed it—not without difficulty, for it was but a narrow track through the grass—until I found myself entering the black shadows of the wood. Here I paused for a moment to listen while I peered into the impenetrable darkness ahead. But no sounds came to my ear save the hushed whisper of the trees. Whatever movement there had been was now stilled, and as I resumed my advance toward the wood I began to ask myself uneasily what this strange and sudden stillness might portend. But I had not gone more than a score of paces and was just entering the wood when the question was answered. Quite suddenly, almost at my feet, I saw the prostrate figure of a man.

Instantly I switched on my flashlight and as its beam fell on him it told the substance of the tragic story in a single flash. He was the constable whose whistle I had heard—it was still hanging loose at the end of its chain. He was bareheaded and at the first glance I thought he was dead; but when I knelt down by his side I saw that he was still breathing, and I now noticed a small trickle of blood issuing from an invisible wound above his ear. Very carefully I sought the wound by a light touch of my finger and immediately became aware of a soft area of the scalp, which further cautious and delicate palpation showed to be a depression of the skull.

I felt his pulse—a typical brain-compression pulse—and examined his eyes, but there was no doubt as to his condition. The dent in the skull was compressing his brain and probably the compression was being increased from moment to moment by internal bleeding. The question was, what was to be done? I could do nothing for him here, but yet I could hardly leave him to go in search of help. It was a horrible dilemma; whatever could be done for him would need to be done quickly, and the sands of his life were running out while I knelt helplessly at his side.

Suddenly I bethought me of his whistle. The sound of it had brought me to the spot and it must surely bring others. Picking it up, I put it to my lips and blew a loud and prolonged blast, and, after a few moments' pause, another and yet another. The harsh, strident screech, breaking in on the deathly stillness of the wood and setting the sleeping birds astir, seemed to strike my overstrung nerves a palpable blow. It was positive pain to me to raise that hideous din, but there was nothing else to do. I must keep it up until it should be heard and should attract someone to this remote and solitary place.

It took effect sooner than I had expected, for I was in the act of raising the whistle once more to my lips when I heard sounds from within the wood as of someone trampling through the undergrowth. I threw the beam of my flashlight in that direction but took the precaution to stand up until I should have seen who and what the newcomer might be. Almost immediately there appeared a light from the wood which flashed out and then disappeared as if a lantern were being carried among tree trunks. Then it became continuous and was evidently turned full on me as the newcomer ran out of the wood and advanced towards me. For a few moments I was quite dazzled by the glare of his light, but as he eame nearer, mine lighted him up and I then saw that he was a police constable. Apparently he had just observed the figure lying at my feet, for he suddenly quickened his pace and arrived so much out of breath that, for a moment or two, he was unable to speak, but stood with the light of his lantern cast on his unconscious comrade, breathing hard and staring down at him with amazement and horror.

"God save us!" he muttered at length. "What the devil has been happening? Who blew that whistle?"

"I did," I replied, upon which he nodded, and then, once more throwing his light on me, and casting a searching glance at me, demanded:

"And who are you, and how do you come to be here?"

I explained the position very briefly and added that it was urgently necessary that the injured man should be got to the hospital as quickly as possible.

"He isn't dead, then?" said he. "And you say you are a doctor? Can't you do anything for him?"

"Not here," I answered. "He has got a deep depressed fracture of the skull. If anything can be done, it will have to be done at the hospital; and he will have to be moved very gently. We shall want an ambulance. Could you go and fetch one? My bicycle is down by the gate."

He considered for a few moments. Apparently he was in somewhat of a dilemma, for he replied:

"I oughtn't to go away from here with that devil probably lurking in the wood. And you oughtn't to leave this poor chap. But there was another man coming along close behind me. He should be here any minute if he hasn't lost his way. Perhaps I'd better go back a bit and look for him."

He threw the beam from his lantern into the opening of the wood and was just starting to retrace his steps when there sounded faintly from that direction the voice of someone apparently hailing us.

"Is that you, Mr. Kempster?" the constable roared.

Apparently it was, though I could not make out the words of the reply, for a minute or so later a man emerged from the wood and approached us at a quick walk. But Mr. Kempster, like the constable, was a good deal the worse for his exertions, and, for a time, was able only to stand panting, with his hand to his side, while he gazed in consternation at the prostrate form on the ground.

"Can you ride a bicycle, Mr. Kempster?" the constable asked.

Mr. Kempster managed to gasp out that he could, though he wasn't much of a rider.

"Well," said the constable, "we want an ambulance to take this poor fellow to the hospital. Could you take the doctor's bicycle and run along to the police station and just tell them what has happened?"

"Where is the bicycle?" asked Kempster.

"It is leaning against the gate at the bottom of the cart track," I replied, adding, "You can have my flashlight to find your way and I will see you down the path to the place where it joins the track."

He agreed, not unwillingly, I thought, having no great liking for the neighbourhood, so I handed him my flashlight and conducted him along the path to its junction with the cart track, when I returned to the place where the constable was kneeling by his comrade, examining him by the light of his lantern.

"I can't make this out," said he as I came up. "He wasn't taken unawares. There seems to have been a considerable scrap. His truncheon's gone. The fellow must have managed to snatch it out of his hand, but I can't imagine how that can have happened. It would take a pretty hefty customer to get a constable's truncheon out of his fist, especially as that's just what he'd be on his guard against."

"He seems to have been a powerful ruffian," said I, "judging by the character of the injury. He must have struck a tremendous blow. The skull is stove in like an egg-shell."

"Blighter!" muttered the constable. Then, after a pause, he asked: "Do you think he is going to die, Doctor?"

"I am afraid his chances are not very good," I replied, "and the longer we have to wait for that ambulance, the worse they will be."

"Well," he rejoined, "if Mr. Kempster hustles along, we shan't have very long to wait. They won't waste any time at the station."

He stood up and swept the beam of his lantern around, first towards the wood and then in the direction of the ricks. Suddenly he uttered an indignant snort and exclaimed, angrily:

"Well, I'm damned! Here's Mr. Kempster coming back." He kept the light of his lantern on the approaching figure, and as it came within range he roared out: "What's the matter, sir? We thought you'd be half way there."

Mr. Kempster hurried up, breathing hard and looking decidedly resentful of the constable's tone.

"There is no bicycle there," he said, sulkily. "Somebody must have made off with it. I searched all about there but there was not a sign of it."

The constable cursed as a well trained constable ought not to curse.

"But that's put the lid on it," he concluded. "This murderous devil must have seen you come up, Doctor, and as soon as you were out of sight, he must have just got on your machine and cleared out. I suppose you had a headlight."

"I had both head and rear light," I replied, "but I switched them both off before I started up the cart track. But, of course, if he was anywhere near—hiding behind one of those ricks, for instance—he would have seen my lights when I came up to the gate."

"Yes," the constable agreed, gloomily, "it was a bit of luck for him. And now he's got clean away; got away for good and all unless he has left some sort of traces."

Mr. Kempster uttered a groan. "If he has slipped through your fingers," he exclaimed, indignantly, "there's about ten thousand pounds' worth of my property gone with him. Do you realize that?"

"I do, now you've told me," replied the constable, adding unsympathetically, "and it's bad luck for you; but still, you know, you are better off than my poor mate here who was trying to get it back for you. But we mustn't stop here talking. If the man has gone, there is no use in my staying here. I'll just run back the way I came and report at the station. You may as well wait here with the doctor until I come back with the ambulance."

But Mr Kempster had had enough of the adventure.

"There is no use in my waiting here," said he, handing me my flashlight. "I'll walk back through the wood with you and then get along home and see exactly what that scoundrel has taken."

The constable made no secret of his disapproval of this course, but he did not actually put it into words. With a brief farewell to me, he turned the light of his lantern on the entrance to the wood and set off at a pace that kept his companion at a brisk trot. And as the light faded among the trees and the sound of their footsteps died away in the distance, I found myself once more alone with my patient, encompassed by the darkness and wrapped in a silence

which was broken only by an occasional soft moan from the unconscious man.

It seemed to me that hours elapsed after the departure of the
constable; hours of weary expectation and anxiety. I possessed
myself of my patient's lantern and by its light examined him from
time to time. Naturally, there was no improvement; indeed, each time
that I felt his pulse it was with a faint surprise to find it still beating.
I knew that, actually, his condition must be getting worse with every
minute that passed, and it became more and more doubtful whether
he would reach the hospital alive.

Then my thoughts strayed towards my bicycle and the unknown
robber. We had taken it for granted that the latter had escaped on
the machine, and in all probability he had. Yet it was possible that
the cycle might have been stolen by some tramp or casual wayfarer
and that the robber might be still lurking in the neighbourhood.
However, that possibility did not disturb me, since he could have
no object in attacking me. I was more concerned about the loss of
my bicycle.

From the robber, my reflections drifted to the robbed. Who and
what was Mr. Kempster? And what sort of property was it that the
thief had made off with? There are not many things worth ten
thousand pounds which can be carried away in the pocket. Probably
the booty consisted of something in the nature of jewelry. But I was
not much interested. The value of property, and especially of such
trivial property as jewelry, counts for little compared with that of a
human life. My momentarily wandering attention quickly came back
to the man lying motionless at my feet, whose life hung so unsteadily
in the balance.

At last my seemingly interminable vigil came to an end. From
the road below came the distinctive clang of an ambulance bell, and
lights winked over the unseen hedgerow. Then the glare from a pair
of powerful headlamps came across the field, throwing up the ricks
in sharp silhouette, and telling me that the ambulance was passing
in through the gate. I watched the lights growing brighter from
moment to moment; saw them vanish behind the ricks and presently
emerge as the vehicle advanced up the cart track and at length
turned on to the footpath.

It drew up eventually within a few paces of the spot where the
injured man was lying, and immediately there descended from it a
number of men, including a police inspector and the constable who

had gone with Kempster. The former greeted me civilly, and, looking down on his subordinate with deep concern, asked me a few
questions while a couple of uniformed men brought out a stretcher
and set it down by the patient. I helped them to lift him on
to the stretcher and to convey the latter to its place in the
ambulance. Then I got in, myself, and, while the vehicle was being
turned round, the inspector came to take a last look at the
patient.

"I am not coming back with you, Doctor," said he. "I have got
a squad of men with some powerful lights to search the wood."

"But," said I, "the man has almost certainly gone off on my
bicycle."

"I know," said he. "But we are not looking for him. It's this poor
fellow's truncheon that I want. If the thief managed to snatch it
away from him, there are pretty certain to be finger-prints on it. At
any rate, I hope so, for it's our only chance of identifying the man."

With this, as the ambulance was now ready to start, he turned
away; and as we moved off towards the cart track, I saw him, with
the constable and three plain-clothes men advancing towards the
wood which, by the combined effects of all their lights, was illu-
minated almost to the brightness of daylight.

Once out on the road, the smoothly-running ambulance made
short work of the distance to the hospital. But yet the journey had
not been short enough. For when the stretcher had been borne into
the casualty room and placed on the table, the first anxious glance
showed that the feebly-flickering light had gone out. In vain the
visiting surgeon—who had been summoned by telephone—felt
the pulse and listened to the heart. Poor Constable Murray
—such, I learned, was his name—had taken his last turn of
duty.

"A bad business," said the surgeon, putting away his stethoscope
and passing his fingers lightly over the depression in the dead man's
skull. "But I doubt whether we could have done much for him even
if he had come in alive. It was a devil of a blow. The man was a
fool to hit so hard, for now he'll have to face a charge of wilful
murder—that is, if they catch him. I hope they will."

"I hope so, too," said I, "but I doubt whether they will. He seems
to have found my bicycle and gone off on it, and I gather that
nobody saw him near enough to recognize him."

"H'm," grunted the surgeon, "that's unfortunate; and bad luck for you, too, though I expect you will get your cycle back. Meanwhile, can I give you a lift in my car?"

I accepted the offer gladly, and, after a last look at the dead constable, we went out together to return to our respective homes.

CHAPTER 2

THE INQUIRY

It was on the fourth day after my adventure that I received the summons to attend the inquest—which had been kept back to enable the police to collect such evidence as was available—and in due course presented myself at the little Town Hall in which the inquiry was to be held. The preliminaries had already been disposed of when I arrived, but I was in time to hear the coroner's opening address to the jury. It was quite short, and amounted to little more than the announcement of his intention to take the evidence in its chronological order; a very sensible proceeding, as it seemed to me, whereby the history of the tragedy would evolve naturally from the depositions of the witnesses. Of these, the first was Mr. Arthur Kempster, who, by the coroner's direction, began with a narrative of the events known to him.

"I am a diamond merchant, having business premises in Hatton Garden and a private residence at The Hawthorns, Newingstead. On Friday, the 16th of September, I returned from a trip to Holland and came direct from Harwich to The Hawthorns. At Amsterdam I purchased a parcel of diamonds and I had them in a paper packet in my inside waistcoat pocket when I arrived home, which I did just about dinner time. After dinner, I went to my study to examine the diamonds and to check their weight on the special scales which I keep for that purpose. When I had finished weighing them and had looked them over, one by one, I put away the scales and looked about for the lens which I use to examine stones as to their cutting. But I couldn't find the lens. Then I had a faint recollection of having used it in the dining room, which adjoins the study, and I went to that room to see if I might have left it there. And I had. I found it after a very short search and went back with it to the study. But when I went to the table on which I had put the diamonds, to my amazement I found that they had vanished. As nobody could possibly have come into the study by the door, I looked at the window; and then I saw that it was open, whereas it had been shut when I went to the dining room.

"I immediately rushed out through the dining room to the front door, and as I came out of it I saw a man walking quickly down the drive. He was nearly at the end of it when I ran out, and, as soon as he heard me, he darted round the corner and disappeared. I ran down the drive as fast as I could go, and, when I came out into the road, I could see him some distance ahead, running furiously in the direction of the country. I followed him as fast as I could, but I could see that he was gaining on me. Then, as I came to a side turning—Bascombe Avenue—I saw a policeman approaching along it and quite near. So I hailed him and gave the alarm; and when he ran up, I told him, very briefly, what had happened; and, as the thief was still in sight, he ran off in pursuit. I followed as well as I could, but I was already out of breath and couldn't nearly keep up with him. But I saw the thief make off along the country road and get over a gate nearly opposite Clay Wood; and the policeman, who seemed to be gaining on the fugitive, also got over the gate, and I lost sight of them both.

"It seemed to me that it was useless to try to follow them, so I turned back towards the town to see if I could get any further assistance. Then, on the main road, I met Police Constable Webb and told him what had happened, and we started off together to the place where the thief had disappeared. We got over the gate, crossed a field, and entered the wood. But there we rather lost ourselves as we had missed the path. We heard a police whistle sounding from the wood while we were crossing the field; and we heard another shorter one just after we had entered. But we couldn't make out clearly the direction the sounds had come from, and we still couldn't find the path.

"Then, after a considerable time, we heard three long blasts of a whistle and at the same moment we saw a glimmer of light; so we ran towards the light—at least the constable did, for I was too blown to run any farther—and at last I found the path and came out of the wood and saw Dr. Oldfield standing by the deceased, who was lying on the ground. Constable Webb suggested that I should take Dr. Oldfield's bicycle and ride to the police station and the doctor gave me his flashlight to light me down the cart track to the gate where he had left the bicycle. But when I got to the gate, there was no sign of any bicycle, so I returned and reported to the con-stable, who then decided to go, himself, to the station, and we went back together through the wood. When we got back to the field he ran on ahead and I went back to my house."

"When you went to the dining room," said the coroner, "how long were you absent from the study?"

"About two minutes, I should say. Certainly not more than three."

"You say that the study window was closed when you went out of the room. Was it fastened?"

"No. It was open at the top. I opened it when I came in after dinner as it was a warm night and the room seemed rather close."

"Was the blind down?"

"There is no blind; only a pair of heavy curtains. They were drawn when I came into the room, but I had to pull them apart to open the window and I may not have drawn them close afterwards; in fact, I don't think I did."

"Do you think that anyone passing outside could have seen into the room?"

"Yes. The study is on the ground floor—perhaps a couple of feet above the level of the ground—and the window sill would be about the height of a man's shoulder, so that a man standing out-side could easily look into the room."

"Does the window face the drive?"

"No. It looks on the alley that leads to the back premises."

"You, apparently, did not hear the sound of the window sash being raised?"

"No, but I shouldn't, in the dining room. The sash slides up easily and I have all the sash pulleys of my windows kept oiled to prevent them from squeaking."

"Were the diamonds in an accessible position?"

"Yes, quite. They were lying, all together, on a square of black velvet on the table."

"Were they of any considerable value?"

"They were, indeed. The whole parcel would be worth about ten thousand pounds. There were fifteen of them, and they were all very exceptional stones."

"Would you be able to recognize them if they could be traced?"

"I could easily identify the complete parcel, and I think I could identify the individual stones. I weighed each one separately and the whole group together, and I made certain notes about them of which I have given a copy to the police."

"Was anything taken besides the diamonds?"

"Nothing, not even the paper. The thief must have just grabbed up the stones and put them loose in his pocket."

This completed Mr. Kempster's evidence. Some of the jury would have liked more detailed particulars of the diamonds, but the coroner reminded them gently that the inquiry was concerned, not with the robbery but with the death of Constable Alfred Murray. As there were no other questions, the depositions were read and signed and the witness was released.

Following the chronological sequence, I succeeded Mr. Kempster, and, like him, opened my evidence with a narrative statement. But I need not repeat this, or the examination that amplified it, as I have already told the story of my connection with the case. Nor need I record Constable Webb's evidence, which was mainly a repetition of Kempster's. When the constable had retired, the name of Dr. James Tansley was called and the surgeon whom I had met at the hospital came forward.

"You have made an examination of the body of deceased," said the coroner when the preliminary questions had been answered. "Will you tell us what conditions you found?"

"On external examination," the witness replied, "I found a deep depression in the skull two and a quarter inches in diameter starting from a point an inch and a half above the left ear, and a contused wound an inch and three quarters in length. The wound and the depressed fracture of the skull both appeared to have been produced by a heavy blow from some blunt instrument. There was no sign of more than one blow. On removing the cap of the skull I found that the inner table—that is, the hard inner layer of the skull—had been shattered and portions of it driven into the substance of the brain, causing severe lacerations. It had also injured one or two arteries and completely divided one, with the result that extensive bleeding had occurred between the skull and the brain, and this would have produced great pressure on the surface of the brain."

"What would you say was the cause of death?"

"The immediate cause of death was laceration and compression of the brain, but, of course, the ultimate cause was the blow on the head which produced those injuries."

"It is a mere formality, I suppose, to ask whether the injury could have been self-inflicted?"

"Yes. It is quite impossible that the blow could have been struck by deceased himself."

This was the substance of the doctor's evidence. When it was concluded and the witness had been released, the name of Inspector Charles Roberts was called, and that officer took his place by the table. Like the preceding witnesses, he began, at the coroner's invitation, with a general statement.

"On receiving Constable Webb's report, as the Chief Constable was absent, I ordered the sergeant to get out the ambulance and I collected a search party to go with it. When we arrived at the spot where the deceased was lying, I saw him transferred to the ambulance under the doctor's supervision, and when it had gone, I took my party into the wood. Each member of the party was provided with a powerful flashlight, so that we had a good light to work by.

"We saw no sign of anyone hiding in the wood, but near the path we found deceased's helmet. It was uninjured and had probably been knocked off by a branch of a tree. We searched especially for deceased's truncheon and eventually found it quite near to the place where he had been lying. I picked it up by the wrist strap at the end of the handle and carried it in that way until we reached the station, when I examined it carefully and could see that there were several finger-prints on it. I did not attempt to develop the prints, but hung up the truncheon by its strap in a cupboard, which I locked. On the following morning I delivered the key of the cupboard to the Chief Constable when I made my report."

"Did you find any traces of the fugitive?"

"No. We went down to the gate and found marks there on the earth where the bicycle had stood; and we could see where it had been wheeled off on to the road. But we were unable to make out any visible tracks on the road itself."

"Has the bicycle been traced since then?"

"Yes. Two days after the robbery it was found hidden in a cart shed near the London Road, about three miles from Clay Wood, towards London. I went over it carefully with developing powder to see if there were any finger-prints on it, but, although there were plenty of finger-marks, they were only smears and quite unidentifiable."

This was the sum of the inspector's evidence; and as there were no questions, the officer was released and was succeeded by Chief Constable Herbert Parker, who took up and continued the inspector's account of the dead constable's truncheon.

"The key of the cupboard at the police station was delivered to me by Inspector Roberts as he has deposed. I unlocked the cupboard and took out the truncheon, which I examined in a good light with the aid of a magnifying lens. I could see that there were, on the barrel of the truncheon, several finger-prints; and by their position and grouping, I judged that they had been made by the thief when he snatched the truncheon out of deceased's hand. They were quite distinct on the polished surface, but not sufficiently so to photograph without development; and I did not attempt to develop them because I thought that, having regard to their importance, it would be better to hand the truncheon intact to the experts at Scotland Yard. Accordingly, I packed the truncheon in such a way that the marked surfaces should be protected from any contact and took it up to the finger-print department at Scotland Yard, where I delivered it to the Chief Inspector, who examined it and developed the finger-prints with a suitable powder.

"It was then seen that there were four decipherable prints, evidently those of a left hand; one was a thumb-print and was perfectly clear, and the others, of the first three fingers, though less perfect, were quite recognizable. As soon as they had been developed, they were photographed; and when the photographs were ready, they were handed to the expert searchers who took them to the place where the collections are kept and went through the files with them. The result of the search was to make it certain that no such finger-prints were in any of the files; neither in those of the main collection nor in those containing single finger-prints."

"And what does that amount to?"

"It amounts to this: that, since these finger-prints are not in the principal files—those containing the complete sets taken by prison officers—it is certain that this man has never been convicted; and since they are not in the single finger-print files, there is no evidence that he has ever been connected with any crime. In short—so far as the finger-prints are concerned—this man is not known to the police."

"That is very unfortunate," said the coroner. "It would seem as if there were practically no chance of ever bringing the crime home to him."

"I wouldn't say that," the Chief Constable replied. "His finger-prints are now in the files at Scotland Yard, so that if ever he should get into trouble of any kind and have his finger-prints taken, he will certainly be identified and brought to trial. And then there is a very fair chance that the diamonds may be traced and the identity of the thief disclosed."

"Well, I hope it may be so," said the coroner. "But for the purposes of this inquiry, the important fact is that the identity of the man who killed deceased is at present unknown. Is there anything more that you have to tell us?"

"There is one other point," the officer replied. "When we came to examine the truncheon after it had been photographed, we found on its end distinct traces of blood and two hairs. The hairs have been preserved with the truncheon, and I have sent up to Scotland Yard several hairs and a sample of blood from the body of deceased."

"That may be useful as verification," said the coroner, "though there can be no doubt as to how deceased met his death. But as a final question, have you, by the light of your experience of crime, formed any ideas as to how this affair happened and what sort of person the criminal is likely to have been?"

"As to the criminal, my impression—which is shared by my fellow officers—is that he was not a regular hand. The whole affair is suggestive of the amateur. The man has no criminal record, he was obviously unarmed, and there was no occasion for any skill or experience. It looks as if some casual stranger, probably a tramp, had strayed into the premises and was prowling round the house when he came to a lighted window, and looking in between the curtains, saw Mr. Kempster weighing the diamonds and inspecting them on the black velvet. Then Mr. Kempster went out of the room, and there was the chance of a lifetime for a sneak thief. The man simply slid up the window, climbed in, grabbed up the diamonds, dropped out of the window and made off. Anyone could have done it. That is the unsatisfactory aspect of the case from the police point of view. On the other hand, if he is an amateur who doesn't know the ropes, he will probably get into difficulties when he tries to dispose of the diamonds."

The coroner agreed to this probability but was not greatly interested. And as he had now got all the available evidence relevant to the subject of the inquiry, he dismissed the Chief Constable and proceeded, briefly and concisely, to sum up.

"There is little," he began, "that I need say to you, members of the jury. You have heard the evidence, and the evidence tells the whole sad story. I do not suppose that you will have any doubt that the gallant officer whose tragic and untimely death is the subject of this inquiry, was killed by the runaway thief. But I have to point out to you that if that is your decision, you are legally bound to find a verdict of wilful murder against that unknown man. The law is quite clear on the subject. If any person, while engaged in committing a felony, and in furtherance of such felony, kills, or directly causes the death of any other person, he is guilty of wilful murder, whether he did or did not intend to kill that person.

"Now, there is no evidence that this fugitive desired or intended to kill the constable. But he dealt him a blow which might have killed him and which, in fact, did kill him; and the fugitive was at the time engaged in committing a felony. Therefore, he is guilty of wilful murder. That is all, I think, that I need say."

The jury had apparently already made up their minds on the subject, for after but the briefest whispered consultation with them, the foreman announced that they had agreed on their verdict.

"We find," he continued as the coroner took up his pen, "that deceased was murdered in Clay Wood by the unknown man who entered Mr. Kempster's house to commit a robbery."

The coroner nodded. "Yes," he said, "I am in entire agreement with you and I shall record a verdict of wilful murder against that unknown man; and I am sure you will concur with me in expressing our deepest sympathy with the family of this gallant officer whose life was sacrificed in the performance of a dangerous duty."

Thus, gloomily enough, ended the adventure that had brought me for the first time into intimate contact with serious crime. At least, it appeared to me that the adventure was at an end and that I had heard the last of the tragedy and of the sinister, shadowy figure that must have passed so near to me on the margin of the wood. It was a natural belief, since I had played but a super's part in the drama and seemed to be concerned with it no more, and since my connection with Newingstead and its inhabitants would cease when my principal, Dr. Wilson, should return from his holiday.

But it was, nevertheless, a mistaken belief, as will appear at a later stage of this narrative.

CHAPTER 3

PETER GANNET

A problem that has occasionally exercised my mind is that of the deterioration of London streets. Why do they always deteriorate and never improve? The change seems to be governed by some mysterious law. Constantly we meet with streets, once fashionable but now squalid, whose spacious houses have fallen from the estate of mansions, tenanted by the rich and great, to that of mere tenements giving shelter to all grades of the poverty-stricken, from the shabby genteel to the definitely submerged; streets where the vanished coaches have given place to the coster's barrow and the van of the yelling coal vendor. But never, in my experience, does one encounter a street that has undergone a change in the reverse direction; that has evolved from obscurity to fashion, from the shabby to the modish.

The reflection is suggested to me by the neighbourhood in which I had recently taken up my abode, on the expiration of my engagement at Newingstead. Not that Osnaburgh Street, Marylebone, could fairly be described as squalid. On the contrary, it is a highly respectable street. Nevertheless, its tall, flat-faced houses with their spacious rooms and dignified doorways are evidently survivors from a more opulent past, and the whole neighbourhood shows traces of the curious subsidence that I have referred to.

The occasion of my coming to Osnaburgh Street was the purchase by me of a "death vacancy"; very properly so described, for there was no doubt of the decease of my predecessor, and the fact of the vacancy became clearly established as I sat, day after day, the undisturbed and solitary occupant of the consulting room, incredulously turning over the pages of the old ledgers and wondering whether the names inscribed therein might perchance appertain to mythical persons, or whether those patients could, with one accord, have followed the late incumbent to his destination in Heaven or Gehenna.

Yet there were occasional calls or messages, at first from casual strangers or newcomers to the district; but presently, by introduction and recommendation, the vacancy grew into a visible "nucleus," which, expanding by slow degrees, seemed to promise an actual practice in the not too far distant future. The hours of solitary meditation in the consulting room began more frequently to be shortened by welcome interruptions, and my brisk, business-like walks through the streets to have some purpose other than mere geographical exploration.

Principally my little practice grew, as I have said, by recommendation. My patients seemed to like me and mentioned the fact to their friends; and thus it was that I made the acquaintance of Peter Gannet. I remember the occasion very clearly, though it seemed so insignificant at the time. It was a gloomy December morning, some three months after my departure from Newingstead, when I set forth on my "round" (of one patient), taking a short cut to Jacob Street, Hampstead Road, through the by-streets behind Cumberland Market and contrasting the drab little thoroughfares with the pleasant lanes around Newingstead. Jacob Street was another instance of the "law of decay" which I have mentioned. Now at the undeniably shabby genteel stage, it had formerly been the chosen resort of famous and distinguished artists. But its glory was not utterly departed; for, as several of the houses had commodious studios attached to them, the population still included a leavening of artists, though of a more humble and unpretentious type. Mr. Jenkins, the husband of my patient, was a monumental mason, and from the bedroom window I could see him in the small yard below, chipping away at a rather florid marble headstone.

The introduction came when I had finished my leisurely visit and was about to depart.

"Before you go, Doctor," said Mrs. Jenkins, "I must give you a message from my neighbour, Mrs. Gannet. She sent her maid in this morning to say that her husband is not very well and that she would be glad if you would just drop in and have a look at him. She knows that you are attending me and they've got no doctor of their own. It's next door but one; Number 12."

I thanked her for the introduction, and, having wished her good morning, let myself out of the house and proceeded to Number 12, approaching it slowly to take a preliminary glance at the premises. The result of the inspection was satisfactory as an index to the quality of my new patient, for the house was in better repair than most of its neighbours and the bright brass knocker and door-knob and the whitened door-step suggested a household rather above the general Jacob Street level. At the side of the house was a wide, two-leaved gate with a wicket, at which I glanced inquisitively. It seemed to be the entrance to a yard or factory, adapted to the passage of trucks or vans, but it clearly belonged to the house, for a bell-pull on the jamb of the gate had underneath it a small brass plate bearing the inscription, "P. Gannet."

In response to my knock, the door was opened by a lanky girl of about eighteeen with long legs, a short skirt, and something on her head which resembled a pudding cloth. When I had revealed my identity, she conducted me along a tiled hall to a door, which she opened, and having announced me by name, washed her hands of me and retired down the kitchen stairs.

The occupant of the room, a woman of about thirty-five, rose as I entered and laid down some needlework on a side table.

"Am I addressing Mrs. Gannet?" I asked.

"Yes," she replied. "I am Mrs. Gannet. I suppose Mrs. Jenkins gave you my message?"

"Yes. She tells me—which I am sorry to hear—that your husband is not very well."

"He is not at all well," said she, "though I don't think it is anything that matters very much, you know."

"I expect it matters to him," I suggested.

"I suppose it does," she agreed. "At any rate, he seems rather sorry for himself. He is sitting up in his bedroom at present. Shall I show you the way? I think he is rather anxious to see you."

I held the door open for her, and when she passed through, I followed her up the stairs, rapidly sorting out my first impressions. Mrs. Gannet was a rather tall, slender woman with light brown hair and slightly chilly blue eyes. She was decidedly good-looking but yet I did not find her prepossessing. Comely as her face undoubtedly was, it was not—at least to me—a pleasant face. There was a tinge of petulance in its expression, a faint suggestion of unamiability. And I did not like the tone in which she had referred to her husband.

Her introduction of me was as laconic as that of her maid. She opened the bedroom door and standing at the threshold, announced: "Here's the doctor." Then, as I entered, she shut me in and departed.

"Well, Doctor," said the patient, "I'm glad to see you. Pull up a chair to the fire and take off your overcoat."

I drew a chair up to the fire gladly enough, but I did not adopt the other suggestion; for already I had learned by experience that the doctor who takes off his overcoat is lost. Forthwith he becomes a visitor and his difficulties in making his escape are multiplied indefinitely.

"So you are not feeling very well?" said I, by way of opening the proceedings.

"I'm feeling devilish ill," he replied. "I don't suppose it's anything serious, but it's deuced unpleasant. Little Mary in trouble, you know."

I didn't know, not having heard the expression before, and I looked at him inquiringly, and probably rather vacantly.

"Little Mary," he repeated. "Tummy. Bellyache, to put it bluntly."

"Ha!" said I, with sudden comprehension. "You are suffering from abdominal pain. Is it bad?"

"Is it ever good?" he demanded, with a sour grin.

"It certainly is never pleasant," I admitted. "But is the pain severe?"

"Sometimes," he replied. "It seems to come and go—Whoo!"

A change of facial expression indicated that, just now, it had come. Accordingly, I suspended the conversation until conditions should be more favourable, and, meanwhile, inspected my patient with sympathetic interest. He was not as good-looking as his wife, and his appearance was not improved by a rather deep scar which cut across his right eyebrow, but he made a better impression than she; a strongly-built man, though not large, so far as I could judge, seeing him sitting huddled in his easy chair, of a medium complexion and decidedly lean. He wore his hair rather long and had a well-shaped moustache and a Vandyke beard. Indeed, his appearance in general was distinctly Vandykish, with his brown velveteen jacket, his open, deep-pointed collar, and the loose bow with drooping ends which served as a necktie. I also noted that his eyes looked red and irritable like those of a long-sighted person who is in need of spectacles.

"Phoo!" he exclaimed after a spell of silence. "That was a bit of a twister, but it's better now. Going to have a lucid interval, I suppose."

Thereupon I resumed the conversation, which, however, I need

not report in detail. I had plenty of time and could afford to encour-
age him to enlarge on his symptoms, the possible causes of his illness,
and his usual habits and mode of life. And as he talked, I looked
about me, bearing in mind the advice of my teacher, Dr. Thorndyke,
to observe and take note of a patient's surroundings as a possible
guide to his personality. In particular I inspected the mantelpiece
which confronted me and considered the objects on it in their
possible bearings on my patient's habits and life history.

They were rather curious objects; examples of pottery of a singularly uncouth and barbaric type which I set down as the gleanings
gathered in the course of travel in distant lands among primitive
and aboriginal peoples. There were several bowls and jars, massive,
rude and unshapely, of a coarse material like primitive stoneware,
and presiding over the whole collection, a crudely modeled effigy of
similar material, apparently the artless representation of some forest
deity, or, perhaps a portrait of an aboriginal man. The childish
crudity of execution carried my thoughts to Darkest Africa or the
Ethnographical galleries of the British Museum, or to those sham
primitive sculptures which have recently appeared on some of the
public buildings in London. I looked again at Mr. Gannet and
wondered whether his present trouble might be the aftermath of some
tropical illness contracted in the forests or jungles where he had
collected these strange and not very attractive curios.

Fortunately, however, I did not put my thoughts into words, but
in pursuance of another of Dr. Thorndyke's precepts to "let the
patient do most of the talking," listened attentively while Mr.
Gannet poured out the tale of his troubles. For, presently, he
remarked, after a pause:

"And it isn't only the discomfort. It's such a confounded hin-
drance. I want to get on with my work."

"By the way, what its your work?" I asked.

"I am a potter," he replied.

"A potter!" I repeated. "I didn't know that there were any
pottery works in London—except, of course, Doultons."

"I am not attached to any pottery works," said he. "I am an artist
potter, an individual worker. The pieces that I make are what is
usually called studio pottery. Those are some of my works on the
mantelpiece."

In the vulgar phrase, you could have knocked me down with a
feather. For the moment I was bereft of speech and could only sit

like a fool, gazing round-eyed and agape at these amazing products of the potter's art, while Gannet observed me gravely, and, I thought, with slight disfavour.

"Possibly," he remarked, "you find them a little over-simplified."

It was not the expression that I should have used, but I grasped at it eagerly.

"I think I had that feeling at the first glance," I replied; "that and the—er—the impression that perhaps—ha—in the matter of precision and—er—symmetry—that is, to an entirely inexpert eye —er—"

"Exactly!" he interrupted. "Precision and symmetry are what the inexpert eye looks for. But they are not what the artist seeks. Mechanical accuracy he can leave to the ungifted toiler who tends a machine."

"I suppose that is so," I agreed. "And the—" I was about to say "image" but hastily corrected the word to "statuette"—"that is your work, too?"

"The figurine," he corrected; "yes, that is my work. I was rather pleased with it when I had it finished. And apparently I was justified, for it was extremely well received. The art critics were quite enthusiastic, and I sold two replicas of it for fifty guineas each."

"That was very satisfactory," said I. "It is a good thing to have material reward as well as glory. Did you give it any descriptive title?"

"No," he replied. "I am not like those anecdote painters who must have a title for their pictures. I just called it 'Figurine of a monkey.' "

"Of a—oh, yes. Of a monkey. Exactly!"

I stood up, the better to examine it and then discovered that its posterior aspect bore something like a coil of garden hose, evidently representing a tail. So it obviously was a monkey and not a woodland god. The tail established the diagnosis; even as, in those sculptures that I have mentioned, the absence of a tail demonstrates their human character.

"And I suppose," said I, "you always sign your works?"

"Certainly," he replied. "Each piece bears my signature and a serial number; and, of course, the number of copies of a single piece is rigidly limited. You will see the signature on the base."

With infinite care and tenderness, I lifted the precious figurine and inverted it to examine the base, which I found to be covered with a thick layer of opaque white glaze, rather out of character with the rough grey body but excellent for displaying the signature. The latter was in thin blue lines as if executed with a pen and consisted of something resembling a bird, supported by the letters, "P.G." and underneath, "Op. 571A."

"The goose is, I suppose," said I, "your sign manual or personal mark—it is a goose, isn't it?"

"No," he replied, a little testily. "It's a gannet."

"Of course it is," I agreed, hastily. "How dull of me not to recognize your rebus, though a gannet is not unlike a goose."

He admitted this, and watched me narrowly as I replaced the masterpiece on the little square of cloth which protected it from contact with the marble shelf. Then it occurred to me that perhaps I had stayed long enough, and as I buttoned my overcoat, I reverted to professional matters with a few parting remarks.

"Well, Mr. Gannet, you needn't be uneasy about yourself. I shall send you some medicine which I think will soon put you right. But if you have much pain, you had better try some hot fomentations or a hot water bottle—a rubber one, of course; and you would probably be more comfortable lying down."

"It's more comfortable sitting by the fire," he objected; and as it appeared that he was the best judge of his own comfort, I said no more, but having shaken hands, took my departure.

As I was descending the stairs, I met a man coming up; a big man who wore a monocle and was carrying a glass jug. He stopped for a moment when he came abreast, and explained:

"I am just taking the invalid some barley water. I suppose that is all right? He asked for it."

"Certainly," I replied. "A most suitable drink for a sick person."

"I'll tell him so," said he, and with this we went our respective ways.

When I reached the hall, I found the dining room door open, and as Mrs. Gannet was visible within, I entered to make my report and give a few directions, to which she listened attentively though with no great appearance of concern. But she promised to see that the patient should take his medicine regularly, and to keep him supplied with hot water bottles. "though," she added, "I don't expect that he will use them. He is not a very tractable invalid."

"Well, Mrs. Gannet," said I, pulling on my gloves, "we must be patient. Pain is apt to make people irritable. I shall hope to find him better tomorrow. Good morning!"

At intervals during the day, my thoughts reverted to my new patient, but not, I fear, in the way that they should have done. For it was not his abdomen—which was my proper concern—that occupied my attention but his queer pottery and above all, the unspeakable monkey. My reflections oscillated between frank incredulity and an admission of the possibility that these pseudo-barbaric works might possess some subtle quality that I had failed to detect. Yet I was not without some qualifications for forming a judgment, for mine was a distinctly artistic family. Both my parents could draw, and my maternal uncle was a figure painter of some position who, in addition to his pictures, executed small, unpretentious sculptures in terra-cotta and bronze; and I had managed, when I was a student, to spare an evening a week to attend a life class. So I, at least, could draw, and knew what the human figure was like; and when I compared my uncle's graceful, delicately-finished little statuettes with Gannet's uncouth effigy, it seemed beyond belief that this latter could have any artistic quality whatever.

Yet it doesn't do to be too cocksure. It is always possible that one may be mistaken. But yet, again, it doesn't do to be too humble and credulous; for the simple, credulous man is the natural prey of the quack and the impostor. And the quack and the impostor flourish in our midst. The post-war twentieth century seems to be the golden age of "bunk."

So my reflections went around and around and brought me to no positive conclusion; and meanwhile, poor Peter Gannet's abdomen received less attention than it deserved. I assumed that a dose or two of bismuth and soda, with that fine old medicament, once so over-rated and now rather under-valued—*Compound Tincture of Carda-moms*—would relieve the colicky pains and set the patient on the road to recovery; and having dispatched the mixture, I dismissed the medical aspects of the case from my mind.

But the infallible mixture failed to produce the expected effect, for when I called on the following morning, the patient's condition was unchanged. Which was disappointing (especially to him) but not disturbing. There was no suspicion of anything serious; no fever and no physical signs suggestive of appendicitis or any other grave condition. I was not anxious about him, nor was he anxious about himself, though slightly outspoken on the subject of the infallible mixture, which I promised to replace by something more effectual, repeating my recommendations as to hot water bottles or fomentations.

The new treatment, however, proved no better than the old. At my third visit I found my patient in bed, still complaining of pain and in a state of deep depression. But even now, though the man looked definitely ill, neither exhaustive questioning nor physical examination threw any light either on the cause or the exact nature of his condition. Obviously, he was suffering from severe gastro-intestinal catarrh. But why he was suffering from it, and why no treatment gave him any relief, were mysteries on which I pondered anxiously as I walked home from Jacob Street, greatly out of conceit with myself and inclined to commiserate the man who had the misfortune to be my patient.

CHAPTER 4

DR. THORNDYKE TAKES A HAND

It was on the sixth day of my attendance on Mr. Gannet that my vague but increasing anxiety suddenly became acute. As I sat down by the bedside and looked at the drawn, haggard, red-eyed face that confronted me over the bedclothes, I was seized by something approaching panic. And not without reason. For the man was obviously ill—very ill—and was getting worse from day to day; and I had to admit—and did admit to myself—that I was completely in the dark as to what was really the matter with him. My diagnosis of gastro-enteritis was, in effect, no diagnosis at all. It was little more than a statement of the symptoms; and the utter failure of the ordinary empirical treatment convinced me that there was some essential element in the case which had completely eluded me.

It was highly disturbing. A young, newly established practitioner cannot afford to make a hash of a case at the very outset of his career, as I clearly realized, though to do myself justice, I must say that this was not the consideration that was uppermost in my mind. What really troubled me was the feeling that I had failed in my duty towards my patient and in ordinary professional competence. My heart was wrung by the obvious suffering of the quiet, uncomplaining man who looked to me so pathetically for help and relief—and looked in vain. And then there was the further, profoundly disquieting consideration that the man was now very seriously ill and that if he did not improve, his condition would presently become actually dangerous.

"Well, Mr. Gannet," I said, "we don't seem to be making much progress. I am afraid you will have to remain in bed for the present."

"There's no question about that, Doctor," said he, "because I can't get out, at least I can't stand properly if I do. My legs seem to have gone on strike and there is something queer about my feet;

sort of pins and needles, and a dead kind of feeling, as if they had got a coat of varnish over them."

"But," I exclaimed, concealing as well as I could my consternation at this fresh complication, "you haven't mentioned this to me before."

"I hadn't noticed until yesterday," he replied, "though I have been having cramps in my calves for some days. But the fact is that the pain in my gizzard occupies my attention pretty completely. It may have been coming on before I noticed it. What do you suppose it is?"

To this question I gave no direct answer. For I was not supposing at all. To me the new symptoms conveyed nothing more than fresh and convincing evidence that I was completely out of my depth. Nevertheless, I made a careful examination which established the the fact that there was an appreciable loss of sensibility in the feet and some abnormal conditions of the nerves of the legs. Why there should be I had not the foggiest idea, nor did I make any great effort to unravel the mystery; for these new developments brought to a definite decision a half-formed intention that I had been harbouring for the last day or two.

I would seek the advice of some more experienced practitioner. That was necessary as a matter of common honesty, to say nothing of humanity. But I had hesitated to suggest a second opinion since that would not only have involved the frank admission that I was graveled—an impolitic proceeding in the case of a young doctor— but it would have put the expense of the consultant's fee on the patient; whereas I felt that, since the need for the consultation arose from my own incompetence, the expense should fall upon me.

"What do you think, Doctor, of my going into a nursing home?" he asked, as I resumed my seat by the bed.

I rather caught at the suggestion, for it seemed to make my plan easier to carry out.

"There is something to be said for a nursing home," I replied. "You would be able to have more constant and skilled attention."

"That is what I was thinking," said he; "and I shouldn't be such a damned nuisance to my wife."

"Yes," I agreed, "there's something in that. I will think about your idea and make a few inquiries; and I will look in again later in the day and let you know the result."

With this I rose, and having shaken his hand, took my departure, closing the door audibly and descending the stairs with a slightly heavy tread to give notice of my approach to the hall. When I arrived there, however, I found no sign of Mrs. Gannet and the dining room door was shut; and glancing towards the hat-rack on which my hat was awaiting me, I noted another hat upon an adjoining peg and surmised that it possibly accounted for the lady's non-appearance. I had seen that hat before. It was a somewhat dandified velour hat which I recognized as appertaining to a certain Mr. Boles—the man whom I had met on the stairs at my first visit and had seen once or twice since—a big, swaggering, rather good-looking young man with a noisy, bullying manner and a tendency to undue familiarity. I had disliked him at sight. I resented his familiarity, I suspected his monocle of a merely ornamental function, and I viewed with faint disapproval his relations with Mrs. Gannet— though, to be sure, they were some sort of cousins, as I had understood from Gannet, and he obviously knew all about their friendship.

So it was no affair of mine. But still, the presence of that hat gave me pause. It is awkward to break in on a tête-à-tête. However, my difficulty was solved by Boles himself, who opened the dining room door a short distance, thrust out his head, and surveyed me through his monocle—or perhaps with the less-obstructed eye.

"Thought I heard you sneaking down, Doc," said he. "How's the sufferer? Aren't you coming in to give us the news?"

I should have liked to pull his nose. But a doctor must learn early to control his temper—especially in the case of a man of Boles's size. As he held the door open, I walked in and made my bow to Mrs. Gannet, who returned my greeting without putting down her needlework. Then I delivered my report, briefly and rather vaguely, and opened the subject of the nursing home. Instantly, Boles began to raise objections.

"Why on earth should he go to a nursing home?" he demanded. "He is comfortable enough here. And think of the expense."

"It was his own suggestion," said I, "and I don't think it a bad one."

"No," said Mrs. Gannet. "Not at all. He would get better attention there than I can give him."

There followed something like a wrangle between the two, to which I listened impassively, inwardly assessing their respective motives. Obviously the lady favoured the prospect of getting the invalid off her hands, while as to Boles, his opposition was due to mere contrariety; to an instinctive impulse to object to anything that I might propose.

Of course, the lady had her way—and I had intended to have mine in any case. So, when the argument had petered out, I took my leave with a promise to return some time later to report progress.

As I turned away from the house, I rapidly considered the position. I had no further visits to make, so for the present, my time was my own; and as my immediate purpose was to seek the counsel of some more experienced colleague, and as my hospital was the most likely place in which to obtain such counsel, I steered a course for the nearest bus route by which I could travel to its neighbourhood. There, having boarded the appropriate omnibus, I was presently delivered at the end of the quiet street in which St. Margaret's Hospital is situated.

It seemed but a few months since I had reluctantly shaken from my feet the dust of that admirable institution and its pleasant, friendly medical school, and now, as I turned into the familiar street, I looked about me with a certain wistfulness as I recalled the years of interesting study and companionship that I had spent here as I slowly evolved from a raw freshman to a fully qualified practitioner. And as, approaching the hospital, I observed a tall figure emerge from the gate and advance towards me, the sight brought back to me one of the most engrossing aspects of my life as a student. For the tall man was Dr. John Thorndyke, a lecturer on Medical Jurisprudence, perhaps the most brilliant and the most popular member of the teaching staff.

As we approached, Dr. Thorndyke greeted me with a genial smile and held out his hand.

"I think," said he, "this is the first time we have met since you fluttered out of the nest."

"We used to call it the incubator," I remarked.

"I think 'nest' sounds more dignified," he rejoined. "There is something rather embryonic about an incubator. And how do you like general practice?"

"Oh, well enough," I replied. "Of course, it isn't as thrilling as hospital practice—though mine happens, at the moment, to be a bit more full of thrills than I care for."

"That sounds as if you were having some unpleasant experiences."

"I am," said I. "The fact is that I am up a tree. That is why I am here. I am going to the hospital to see if one of the older hands can give me some sort of tip."

"Very wise of you, Oldfield," Thorndyke commented. "Would it seem impertinent if I were to ask what sort of tree it is that you are marooned in?"

"Not at all, sir," I replied, warmly. "It is very kind of you to ask. My difficulty is that I have got a rather serious case, and I am fairly graveled in the matter of diagnosis. It seems to be a pretty acute case of gastro-enteritis, but why the fellow should have got it and why none of my treatment should make any impression on it, I can't imagine at all."

Dr. Thorndyke's kindly interest in an old pupil seemed to sharpen into one more definitely professional.

"The term 'gastro-enteritis,' " said he, "covers a good many different conditions. Perhaps a detailed description of the symptoms would be a better basis for discussion."

Thus encouraged, I plunged eagerly into a minute description of poor Gannet's symptoms—the abdominal pain, the obstinate and distressing nausea and physical and mental depression—with some account of my futile efforts to relieve them; to all of which Dr. Thorndyke listened with profound attention. When I had finished, he reflected for a few moments and then asked:

"And that is all, is it? Nothing but the abdominal trouble? No neuritic symptoms, for instance?"

"Yes, by Jove, there are!" I exclaimed. "I forgot to mention them. He has severe cramps in his calves and there is quite distinct numbness of the feet with loss of power in the legs; in fact, he is hardly able to stand, at least so he tells me."

Dr. Thorndyke nodded, and after a short pause, asked:

"And as to the eyes—anything unusual about them?"

"Well," I replied, "they are rather red and watery, but he put that down to reading in a bad light; and then he seems to have a slight cold in his head."

"You haven't said anything about the secretions," Dr. Thorndyke remarked. "I suppose you made all the routine tests?"

"Oh yes," I replied, "most carefully. But there was nothing in the least abnormal; no albumen, no sugar, nothing out of the ordinary."

"I take it," said Thorndyke, "that it did not occur to you to try Marsh's test?"

"Marsh's test!" I repeated, gazing at him in dismay. "Good Lord, no! The idea never entered my thick head. And you think it may actually be a case of arsenic poisoning?"

"It is certainly a possibility," he replied. "The complex of symptoms that you have described is entirely consistent with arsenic poisoning, and it doesn't appear to me to be consistent with anything else."

I was thunderstruck. But yet no sooner was the suggestion made than its obviousness seemed to stare me in the face.

"Of course!" I exclaimed. "It is almost a typical case. And to think that I never spotted it, after attending all your lectures, too! I am a fool. I am not fit to hold a diploma."

"Nonsense, Oldfield," said Thorndyke, "you are not exceptional. The general practitioner nearly always misses a case of poisoning. Quite naturally. His daily experience is concerned with disease, and as the effects of a poison simulate disease, he is almost inevitably misled. He has, by habit, acquired an unconscious bias towards what we may call normal illness; whereas an outsider, like myself, coming to the case with an open mind, or even a bias towards the abnormal, is on the lookout for suspicious symptoms. But we mustn't rush to conclusions. The first thing is to establish the presence or absence of arsenic. That would be a good deal easier if we had him in hospital, but I suppose there would be some difficulty—"

"There would be no difficulty at all, sir," said I. "He has asked me to arrange for him to go to a nursing home."

"Has he?" said Thorndyke. "That almost seems a little significant; I mean that there is a slight suggestion of some suspicions on his own part. But what would you like to do? Will you make the test yourself, and carry on, or would you like me to come along with you and have a look at the patient?"

"It would be an enormous relief to me if you would see him, sir," I replied, "and it is awfully good of you to—"

"Not at all," said Thorndyke. "The question has to be settled, and settled without delay. In a poisoning case, the time factor may be vital. And if we should bring in a true bill, he should be got out of that house at once. But you understand, Oldfield, that I come as your friend. My visit has no financial implications."

I was disposed to protest, but he refused to discuss the matter, pointing out that no second opinion had been asked for by the patient. "But," he added, "we may want some reagents. I had better run back to the hospital and get my research case, which I had left to be called for, and see that it contains all that we are likely to need."

He turned and retraced his steps to the hospital where he entered the gateway, leaving me to saunter up and down the forecourt. In a few minutes he came out, carrying what looked like a small suitcase covered with green Willesden canvas; as there happened to to be a disengaged taxi at the main entrance, where it had just set down a passenger, Thorndyke chartered it forthwith. When I had given the driver the necessary directions, I followed my senior into the interior of the vehicle and slammed the door.

During the journey Dr. Thorndyke put a few discreet questions respecting the Gannet household, to which I returned correspondingly discreet answers. Indeed, I knew very little about the three persons— or four, including Boles—of whom it consisted and I did not think it proper to eke out my slender knowledge with surmises. Accordingly I kept strictly to the facts actually known to me, leaving him to make his own inferences.

"Do you know who prepares Gannet's food?" he asked.

"To the best of my belief," I replied, "Mrs. Gannet does all the cooking. The maid is only a girl. But I am pretty sure that Mrs. Gannet prepares the invalid's food; in fact, she told me that she did. There isn't much of it, as you may imagine."

"What is Gannet's business or profession?"

"I understand that he is a potter; an artist potter. He seems to specialize in some sort of stoneware. There are one or two pieces of his in the bedroom."

"And where does he work?"

"He has a studio at the back of the house; quite a big place, I believe, though I haven't seen it. But it seems to be bigger than he needs, as he lets Boles occupy part of it. I don't quite know what Boles does, but I fancy it is something in the goldsmithing and enameling line."

Here, as the taxi turned from Euston Road into Hampstead Road, Thorndyke glanced out of the window and asked:

"Did I hear you mention Jacob Street to the driver?"

"Yes, that is where Gannet lives. Rather a seedy-looking street. You don't know it, I suppose?"

"It happens that I do," he replied. "There are several studios in it, relics of the days when it was a more fashionable neighbourhood. I knew the occupant of one of the studios. But here we are, I think, at our destination."

As the taxi drew up at the house, we got out and he paid the cabman while I knocked at the door and rang the bell. Almost immediately the door was opened by Mrs. Gannet herself, who looked at me with some surprise and with still more at my companion. I hastened to anticipate questions by a tactful explanation.

"I've had a bit of luck, Mrs. Gannet. I met Dr. Thorndyke, one of my teachers at the hospital, and when I mentioned to him that I had a case which was not progressing very satisfactorily, he very kindly offered to come and see the patient and give me the benefit of his great experience."

"I hope we shall all benefit from Dr. Thorndyke's kindness," said Mrs. Gannet, with a smile and a bow to Thorndyke, "and most of all my poor husband. He has been a model of patience, but it has been a weary and painful business for him. You know the way up to his room."

While we were speaking, the dining room door opened softly and Boles's head appeared in the space, adorned with the inevitable eye-glass through which he inspected Thorndyke critically and was not, himself, entirely unobserved by the latter. But the mutual inspection was brief, for I immediately led the way up the stairs and was closely followed by my senior.

As we entered the sickroom after a perfunctory knock at the door, the patient raised himself in bed and looked at us in evident surprise. But he asked no question, merely turning to me interrogatively; whereupon I proceeded at once concisely to explain the situation

"It is very good of Dr. Thorndyke," said Gannet, "and I am most grateful and pleased to see him, for I don't seem to be making much progress. In fact, I seem to be getting worse."

"You certainly don't look very flourishing," said Thorndyke, "and I see that you haven't taken your arrowroot, or whatever it is."

"No," said Gannet, "I tried to take some, but I couldn't keep it down. Even the barley water doesn't seem to agree with me, though I am parched with thirst. Mr. Boles gave me a glassful when he brought it up with the arrowroot but I've been uncomfortable ever since. Yet you'd think that there couldn't be much harm in barley water."

While the patient was speaking, Thorndyke looked at him thoughtfully as if appraising his general appearance, particularly observing the drawn, anxious face and the red and watery eyes. Then he deposited his research case on the table, and remarking that the latter was rather in the way, carried it, with my assistance, away from the bedside over to the window, and in place of it drew up a couple of chairs. Having fetched a writing pad from the research case, he sat down, and without preamble, began a detailed interrogation with reference to the symptoms and course of the illness, writing down the answers in shorthand and noting all the dates. The examination elicited the statement that there had been fluctuations in the severity of the condition, a slight improvement being followed by a sudden relapse. It also transpired that the relapses, on each occasion, had occurred shortly after taking food or a considerable drink. "It seems," Gannet concluded, dismally, "as if starvation was the only possible way of avoiding pain."

I had heard all this before, but it was only now, when the significant facts were assembled by Thorndyke's skilful interrogation, that I could realize their unmistakable meaning. Thus set out, they furnished a typical picture of arsenic poisoning. And so with the brief but thorough physical examination. The objective signs might have been taken from a text-book case.

"Well, Doctor," said Gannet, as Thorndyke stood up and looked down at him gravely, "what do you think of me?"

"I think," replied Thorndyke, "that you are very seriously ill and that you require the kind of treatment and attention that you cannot possibly get here. You ought to be in a hospital or a nursing home, and you ought to be removed there without delay."

"I rather suspected that myself," said Gannet; "in fact, the doctor was considering some such arrangement. I'm quite willing."

"Then," said Thorndyke, "if you agree, I can give you a private ward or a cubicle at St. Margaret's Hospital; and as the matter is urgent, I propose that we take you there at once. Could you bear the journey in a cab?"

"Oh, yes," replied Gannet, with something almost like eagerness, "if there is a chance of some relief at the end of it."

"I think we shall soon be able to make you more comfortable," said Thorndyke. "But you had better just look him over, Oldfield, to make sure that he is fit to travel."

As I got out my stethoscope to listen to the patient's heart, Thorndyke walked over to the table, apparently to put away his writing pad. But that was not his only purpose. For as I stooped over the patient with the stethoscope at my ears, I could see him (though the patient could not) carefully transferring some arrowroot from the bowl to a wide-mouthed jar. When he had filled it and put in the rubber stopper, he filled another jar from the jug of barley water and then quietly closed the research case.

Now I understood why he had moved the table away from the bed to a position in which it was out of the range of the patient's vision. Of course, the specimens of food and drink could not have been taken in Gannet's presence without an explanation, which we were not in the position to give; for although neither of us had much doubt on the subject, still, the actual presence of arsenic had yet to be proved.

"Well, Oldfield," said Thorndyke, "do you think he is strong enough to make the journey?"

"Quite," I replied, "if he can put up with the discomfort of traveling in a taxi."

As to this, Gannet was quite confident, being evidently keen on the change of residence.

"Then," said Thorndyke, "perhaps you will run down and explain matters to Mrs. Gannet; and it would be just as well to send out for a cab at once. I suppose Madame is not likely to raise objections?"

"No," I replied. "She has already agreed to his going to a nursing home; and if she finds our methods rather abrupt, I must make her understand that the case is urgent."

The interview, however, went quite smoothly so far as the lady was concerned, though Boles was disposed to be obstructive.

"Do you mean that you are going to cart him off to the hospital now?" he demanded.

"That is what Dr. Thorndyke proposes," I replied.

"But why?" he protested. "You say that there is no question of an operation. Then why is he being bustled off in this way?"

"I think," said I, "if you will excuse me, I had better see about that cab," and I made a move towards the hall, whereupon Mrs. Gannet intervened, a little impatiently.

"Now, don't waste time, Fred. Run along and get a taxi while I go up with the doctor and make Peter ready for the journey,"

On this, Boles rather sulkily swaggered out into the hall, and without a word, snatched down the velour hat, jammed it on his head and departed on his quest, slamming the street door after him. As the door closed, Mrs. Gannet turned towards the staircase and began to ascend and I followed, passing her on the landing to open the bedroom door.

When we entered the room, we found Thorndyke standing

opposite the mantelpiece, apparently inspecting the stoneware image; but he turned, and bowing to the lady, suavely apologized for our rather hurried proceedings.

"There is no need to send any clothes with him," said he, "as he will have to remain in bed for the present. A warm dressing-gown and one or two blankets or rugs will do for the journey."

"Yes," she replied. "Rugs, I think, will be more presentable than blankets." Then turning to her husband, she asked: "Is there anything that you will want to take with you, Peter?"

"Nothing but my attaché case," he replied. "That contains all that I am likely to want, excepting the book that I am reading. You might put that in, too. It is on the small table."

When this had been done, Mrs. Gannet proceeded to make the few preparations that were necessary while Thorndyke resumed his study of the pottery on the mantelpiece. The patient was assisted to rise and sit on the edge of the bed while he was inducted into a thick dressing gown, warm woollen socks and a pair of bedroom slippers.

"I think we are all ready, now," said Mrs. Gannet. Then, as there seemed to be a pause in the proceedings, she took the opportunity to address a question to Thorndyke.

"Have you come to any conclusion," she asked, "as to what it is exactly that my husband is suffering from?"

"I think," Thorndyke replied, "that we shall be able to be more definite when we have had him under observation for a day or two."

The lady looked a little unsatisfied with this answer—which certainly was rather evasive—as, indeed, the patient also seemed to note. But here the conversation was interrupted, providentially, by the arrival of Boles to announce that the cab was waiting.

"And now, old chap," said he, "the question is, how are we going to get you down to it?"

That problem, however, presented no difficulty, for when the patient had been wrapped in the rugs, Thorndyke and I carried him, by the approved ambulance method, down the stairs and deposited him in the taxi, while Boles and Mrs. Gannet brought up the rear of the procession, the latter carrying the invaluable attaché case. A more formidable problem was that of finding room in the taxi for two additional large men; but we managed to squeeze in, and amidst valedictory hand wavings from the two figures on the doorstep, the cab started on its journey.

It seemed that Thorndyke must have given some instructions at the hospital for our arrival appeared to be not unexpected. A wheeled chair was quickly procured and in this the patient was trundled, under Thorndyke's direction, through a maze of corridors to the little private ward on the ground floor which had been allotted to him. Here we found a nurse putting the finishing touches to its appointments, and presently the sister from the adjacent ward came to superintend the establishment of the new patient. We stayed only long enough to see Gannet comfortably settled in bed, and then took leave of him; and in the corridor outside we parted after a few words of explanation.

"I am just going across to the chemical laboratories," said Thorndyke, "to hand Professor Woodfield a couple of samples for analysis. I shall manage to see Gannet tomorrow morning, and I suppose you will look in on him from time to time."

"Yes," I replied. "If I may, I will call and see him tomorrow."

"But of course you may," said he. "He is still your patient. If there is anything to report—from Woodfield, I mean—I will leave a note for you with Sister. And now I must be off."

We shook hands and went our respective ways; and as I looked back at the tall figure striding away down the corridor, research case in hand, I speculated on the report that Professor Woodfield would furnish on a sample of arrowroot and another of barley water.

CHAPTER 5

A TRUE BILL

Impelled by my anxiety to clear up the obscurities of the Gannet case, I dispatched the only important visit on my list as early on the following morning as I decently could and then hurried off to the hospital in the hope that I might be in time to catch Thorndyke before he left. It turned out that I had timed my visit fortunately, for as I passed in at the main entrance, I saw his name on the attendance board and learned from the hall porter that he had gone across to the school. Thither, accordingly, I directed my steps, but as I was crossing the garden, I met him coming from the direction of the laboratories and turned to walk back with him.

"Any news yet?" I asked.

"Yes," he replied. "I have just seen Woodfield and had his report. Of the two samples of food that I gave him for analysis, one— some of the arrowroot that you saw—contained no arsenic. The other—a specimen of the barley water—contained three-quarters of a grain of arsenic in the five fluid ounces of my sample. So, assuming that the jug held twenty fluid ounces, it would have contained about three grains of arsenic—that is, of arsenious acid."

"My word!" I exclaimed. "Why, that is a fatal dose, isn't it?"

"It is a possibly fatal dose," he replied. "A two grain dose has been known to cause death, but the effects of arsenic are very erratic. Still, we may fairly well say that if he had drunk the whole jugful, the chances are that it would have killed him."

I shuddered to think of the narrow escape that he—and I—had had. Only just in time had we—or rather Thorndyke—got him away from that house.

"Well," I said, "the detection of arsenic in the barley water settles any doubts that we might have had. It establishes the fact of arsenic poisoning."

"Not quite," Thorndyke dissented. "But we have established the fact by clinical tests. Woodfield and the House Physician have ascertained the presence of arsenic in the patient's body. The quantity was quite small; smaller than I should have expected, judging by the symptoms. But arsenic is eliminated pretty quickly; so we may infer that some days have elapsed since the last considerable dose was taken."

"Yes," said I, "and you were just in time to save him from the next considerable dose, which would probably have been the last. By the way, what are our responsibilities in this affair? I mean, ought we to communicate with the police?"

"No," he replied, very decidedly. "We have neither the duty nor the right to meddle in a case such as this, where the patient is a responsible adult in full control of his actions and his surroundings. Our duty is to inform him of the facts which are known to us and to leave him to take such measures as he may think fit."

That, in effect, is what we did when we had made the ordinary inquiries as to the patient's condition—which, by the way, was markedly improved.

"Yes," Gannet said, cheerfully, "I am worlds better; and it isn't from the effects of the medicine, because I haven't had any. I seem to be recovering of my own accord. Queer, isn't it? Or perhaps it isn't. Have you two gentlemen come to any conclusion as to what is really the matter with me?"

"Yes," Thorndyke replied in a matter-of-fact tone. "We have ascertained that your illness was due to arsenic poisoning."

Gannet sat up in bed and stared from one to the other of us with dropped jaw and an expression of the utmost astonishment and horror.

"Arsenic poisoning!" he repeated, incredulously. "I can't believe it. Are you sure that there isn't some mistake? It seems impossible."

"It usually does," Thorndyke replied, drily. "But there is no mistake. It is just a matter of chemical analysis, which can be sworn to and proved, if necessary, in a court of law. Arsenic has been recovered from your own body and also from a sample of barley water that I brought away for analysis."

"Oh!" said Gannet, "so it was in the barley water. I suppose you didn't examine the arrowroot?"

"I brought away a sample of it," replied Thorndyke, "and it was examined, but there was no arsenic in it."

"Ha!" said Gannet. "So it was the barley water. I thought there was something wrong with that stuff. But arsenic! This is a regular facer! What do you think I ought to do about it, Doctor?"

"It is difficult for us to advise you, Mr. Gannet," Thorndyke replied. "We know no more than that you have been taking poisonous doses of arsenic. As to the circumstances in which you came to take that poison, you know more than we do. If any person knowingly administered that poison to you, he, or she, committed a very serious crime; and if you know who that person is, it would be proper for you to inform the police."

"But I don't," said Gannet. "There are only three persons who could have given me the arsenic, and I can't suspect any one of them. There is the servant maid. She wouldn't have given it to me. If she had wanted to poison anybody, it would have been her mistress. They don't get on very well, whereas the girl and I are on quite amiable terms. Then there is my wife. Well, of course, she is outside the picture altogether. And then there is Mr. Boles. He often brought up my food and drink, so he had the opportunity; but I couldn't entertain the idea of his having tried to poison me. I would as soon suspect the doctor—who had a better opportunity than any of them." He paused to grin at me, and then summed up the position. "So, you see, there is nobody whom I could suspect, and perhaps there isn't any poisoner at all. Isn't it possible that the stuff might have got into my food by accident?"

"I wouldn't say that it is actually impossible," Thorndyke replied, "but the improbability is so great that it is hardly worth considering."

"Well," said Gannet, "I don't feel like confiding in the police and possibly stirring up trouble for an innocent party."

"In that," said Thorndyke, "I think you are right. If you know of no reason for suspecting anybody, you have nothing to tell the police. But I must impress on you, Mr. Gannet, the realities of your position. It is practically certain that some person has tried to poison you, and you will have to be very thoroughly on your guard against any further attempts."

"But what can I do?" Gannet protested. "You agree that it is of no use to go to the police and raise a scandal. But what else is there?"

"The first precaution that you should take," replied Thorndyke, "would be to tell your wife all that you know, and advise her to pass on the information to Mr. Boles—unless you prefer to tell him, yourself—and to anyone else whom she thinks fit to inform. The fact that the poisoning has been detected will be a strong deterrent

against any further attempts, and Mrs. Gannet will be on the alert to
see that there are no opportunities. Then you will be wise to take
no food or drink in your own house which is not shared by someone else; and, perhaps, as an extra precaution, it might be as well
to exchange your present maid for another."

"Yes," Gannet agreed, with a grin, "there will be no difficulty
about that when my wife hears about the arsenic. She'll send the
girl packing at an hour's notice."

"Then," said Thorndyke, "I think we have said all that there is
to say. I am glad to see you looking so much better, and if you
continue to improve at the same rate, we shall be able to send you
out in a few days to get back to your pottery."

With this, he took leave of the patient, and I went out with him in
case he should have anything further to say to me; but it was not
until we had passed out at the main entrance and the porter had
duly noted his departure, that he broke the silence. Then, as we
crossed the court-yard, he asked:

"What did you make of Gannet's statement as to the possible
suspects?"

"Not very much," I replied; "but I rather had the feeling that
he was holding something back."

"He didn't hold it back very far," Thorndyke commented, with
a smile. "I gathered that he viewed Mr. Boles with profound suspicion
and that he was not unwilling that we should share that suspicion.
By the way, are you keeping notes of this case?"

I had to admit that I had nothing beyond the entries in the Day
Book.

"That won't do," said he. "You may not have heard the last of
this case. If there should, in the future, be any further developments,
you ought not to be dependent on your memory alone. I advise you
to write out now, while the facts are fresh, a detailed account of the
case, with all the dates and full particulars of the persons who were
in any way connected with the affair. I will send you a certified copy
of Woodfield's analysis, and I should be interested to see your
memoranda of the case to compare with my own notes."

"I don't suppose you will learn much from mine," said I.

"They will be bad notes if I don't," said he. "But the point is that
if anything should hereafter happen to Gannet—anything, I mean,
involving an inquest or a criminal charge—you and I would be
called, or would volunteer, as witnesses, and our evidence ought to

agree. Hence the desirability of comparing notes now when we can discuss any disagreements."

Our conversation had brought us to the cross roads; and here, as our ways led in opposite directions, we halted for a few final words and then parted, Thorndyke pursuing his journey on foot and I waiting at the bus stop for my omnibus.

During Gannet's stay in the hospital, I paid him one or two visits, noting his steady improvement and copying into my notebook the entries on his case sheet. But his recovery was quite uneventful, and after a few days, I struck him off my visiting list, deciding to await his return home to wind up the case.

But in the interval I became aware that he had, at least in one particular, acted on Thorndyke's advice. The fact was conveyed to me by Mrs. Gannet, who appeared one evening, in a very disturbed state, in my consulting room. I guessed at once what her mission was, but there was not much need for guessing as she came to the point at once.

"I have been to see Peter this afternoon," said she, "and he has given me a most terrible shock. He told me—quite seriously—that his illness was really not an illness at all, but that his condition was due to poison. He says that somebody had been putting arsenic into his food, and he quotes you and Dr. Thorndyke as his authorities for this statement. Is he off his head or did you really tell him this story?"

"It is perfectly true, Mrs. Gannet," I replied.

"But it can't be," she protested. "It is perfectly monstrous. There is nobody who could have had either the means or the motive. I prepared all his food with my own hands and I took it up to him myself. The maid never came near it—though I have sent her away all the same—and even if she had had the opportunity, she had no reason for trying to poison Peter. She was really quite a decent girl and she and he were on perfectly good terms. But the whole thing is impossible—fantastic. Dr. Thorndyke must have made some extraordinary mistake."

"I assure you, Mrs. Gannet," said I, "that no mistake has been made. It is just a matter of chemical analysis. Arsenic is nasty stuff, but it has one virtue; it can be identified easily and with certainty. When Dr. Thorndyke saw your husband, he at once suspected arsenic poisoning, so he took away with him two samples of the food—one of arrowroot and one of barley water—for analysis.

They were examined by an eminent analyst and he found in the barley water quite a considerable quantity of arsenic—the whole jugful would have contained enough to cause death. You see, there is no doubt. There was the arsenic in the barley water. It was extracted and weighed, and the exact amount is known; and the arsenic itself has been kept and can be produced in evidence if necessary."

Mrs. Gannet was deeply impressed—indeed, for the moment, she appeared quite overwhelmed, for she stood speechless, gazing at me in the utmost consternation. At length she asked, almost in a whisper:

"And the arrowroot? I took that up to him, myself."

"There was no arsenic in the arrowroot," I replied; and it seemed to me that she was a little relieved by my answer, though she still looked scared and bewildered. I could judge what was passing in her mind, for I realized that she remembered—as I did—who had carried the barley water up to the sickroom. But whatever she thought, she said nothing, and the interview presently came to an end after a few questions as to her husband's prospects of complete recovery and an urgent request that I should come and see him when he returned from the hospital.

That visit, however, proved unnecessary, for the first intimation that I received of Gannet's discharge from the hospital was furnished by his bodily presence in my waiting room. I had opened the communicating door in response to the "ting" of the bell ("Please ring and enter") and behold! there he was with velveteen jacket and Vandyke beard, all complete. I looked at him with the momentary surprise that doctors and nurses often experience on seeing a patient for the first time in his ordinary habiliments and surroundings; contrasting this big, upstanding, energetic-looking man with the miserable, shrunken wretch who used to peer at me so pitifully from under the bedclothes.

"Come to report, sir," said he, with a mock naval salute, "and to let you see what a fine job you and your colleagues have made of me."   •

I shook hands with him and ushered him through into the consulting room, still pleasantly surprised at the completeness of his recovery.

"You didn't expect to see me looking so well," said he.

"No," I admitted. "I was afraid you would feel the effects for some time."

"So was I," said he, "and in a sense I do. I am still aware that I have got a stomach; but apart from that dyspeptic feeling, I am as well as I ever was. I am eternally grateful to you and Dr. Thorndyke. You caught me on the hop—just in time. Another few days and I suspect it would have been a case of *Hic jacet*. But what a rum affair it was. I can make nothing of it. Can you? Apparently, it couldn't have been an accident."

"No," I replied. "If the whole household had been poisoned, we might have suspected an accident, but the continued poisoning of one person could hardly have been accidental. We are forced to the conclusion that the poison was administered knowingly and intentionally by some person."

"I suppose we are," he agreed. "But what person? It's a regular corker. There are only three, and two of them are impossible. As to Boles, it is a fact that he brought up that jug of barley water and he poured out half a tumblerful and gave it me to drink. And he has brought me up barley water on several other occasions. But I really can't suspect Boles. It seems ridiculous."

"It is not for me to suggest any suspicions," said I. "But the facts that you mention are rather striking. Are there any other facts? What about your relations with Boles? There is nothing, I suppose, to suggest a motive?"

"Not a motive for poisoning me," he replied. "It is a fact that Boles and I are not as good friends as we used to be. We don't hit it off very well nowadays, though we remain, in a sort of way, partners. But I suspect that Boles would have cut it and gone off some time ago if it had not been for my wife. She and he have always been the best of friends—they are distant cousins of some kind—and I think they are quite attached to each other. So Boles goes on working in my studio for the sake of keeping in touch with her. At least, that is how I size things up."

It seemed to me that this was rather like an affirmative answer to my question, and perhaps it appeared so to him. But it was a somewhat delicate matter and neither of us pursued it any farther. Instead, I changed the subject and asked:

"What do you propose to do about it?"

"I don't propose to do anything," he replied. "What could I do? Of course, I shall keep my weather eyelid lifting, but I don't suppose anything further will happen now that you and Dr. Thorndyke have let the cat so thoroughly out of the bag. I shall just go on working in my studio in the same old way, and I shall make no difference whatever in my relations with Boles. No reason why I should as I really don't suspect him."

"Your studio is somewhere at the back of the house, isn't it?" I asked.

"At the side," he replied, "across the yard. Come along one day and see it," he added, cordially, "and I will unfold the whole art and mystery of making pottery. Come whenever you like and as soon as you can. I think you will find the show interesting."

As he issued this invitation (which I accepted gladly) he rose and picked up his hat; and we walked out together to the street door and said farewell on the door-step.

CHAPTER 6

SHADOWS IN THE STUDIO

Peter Gannet's invitation to me to visit his studio and see him at work was to develop consequences that I could not then have fore-seen; nor shall I hint at them now, since it is the purpose of this narrative to trace the course of events in the order in which they occurred. I merely mention the consequences to excuse the apparent triviality of this part of my story.

At my first visit I was admitted by Mrs. Gannet, to whom I explained that this was a friendly call and not a professional visit. Nevertheless, I loitered awhile to hear her account of her husband and to give a few words of advice. Then she conducted me along the hall to a side door which opened on a paved yard, in which the only salient object was a large galvanized dust-bin. Crossing this yard, we came to a door which was furnished with a large, grotesque, bronze knocker and bore in dingy white lettering the word "Studio." Mrs. Gannet executed a characteristic rat-tat on the knocker, and without waiting for an answer, opened the door and invited me to enter; I did, and found myself in a dark space, the front of which was formed by a heavy black curtain. As Mrs. Gannet had shut the door behind me, I was plunged in complete obscurity, but groping at the curtain, I presently drew its end aside and then stepped out into the light of the studio.

"Excuse my not getting up," said Gannet, who was seated at a large bench, "and also not shaking hands. Reasons obvious," and in explanation he held up a hand that was plastered with moist clay. "I am glad to see you, Doctor," he continued, adding, "Get that stool from Boles's bench and set it alongside mine."

I fetched the stool and placed it beside his at the bench, and having seated myself, proceeded to make my observations. And very inter-esting observations they were, for everything that met my eye—the place itself and everything in it—was an occasion of surprise. The whole establishment was on an unexpected scale. The studio, a great barn of a place, evidently, by its immense north window, designed and built as such, would have accommodated a sculptor specializing in colossal statues. The kiln looked big enough for a small factory; and the various accessories—a smaller kiln, a muffle furnace, a couple of grinding mills, a large iron mortar with a heavy pestle, and some other appliances—seemed out of proportion to what I supposed to be the actual output.

But the most surprising object was the artist, himself, considered in connection with his present occupation. Dressed correctly for the part in an elegant gown or smock of blue linen, and wearing a black velvet skull cap, "The Master" was, as I have said, seated at the bench, working at the beginnings of a rather large bowl. I watched him for a while in silent astonishment, for the method of work used by this "Master Craftsman" was that which I had been accustomed to associate with the Kindergarten. It was true that the latter had simply adopted, as suitable for children, the methods of ancient and primitive people, but these seemed hardly appropriate to a professional potter. However, such as the method was, he seemed to be quite at home with it and to work neatly and skilfully; and I was interested to note how little he appeared to be incommoded by a stiff joint in the middle finger of the right hand. Perhaps I might as well briefly describe the process.

On the large bench before him was a stout, square board, like a cook's pastry board, and on this was a plaster "bat," or slab, the upper surface of which had a dome-like projection (now hidden) to impart the necessary hollow to the bottom of the bowl. This latter (I am now speaking from subsequent experience) was made by coiling a roll, or cord, of clay into a circular disc, somewhat like a Catharine-wheel, and then rubbing the coils together with the finger to produce a flat plate. When the bottom was finished and cut true, the sides of the bowl were built up in the same way. At the side of the pastry board was an earthenware pan in which was a quantity of the clay cord, looking rather like a coil of gas tubing, and from this the artist picked out a length, laid it on top of the completed part of the side, and, having carried it round the circumference, pinched it off and then pressed it down lightly, and rubbed and stroked it with his finger and a wooden modeling tool until it was completely united to the part below.

"Why do you pinch it off?" I inquired. "Why not coil it up continuously?"

"Because," he explained, "if you built a bowl by just coiling the clay cord round and round without a break, it would be higher one side than the other. So I pinch it off when I have completed a circle; and you notice that I begin the next tier in a different place, so that the joins don't come over each other. If they did, there would be a mark right up the side of the bowl."

"Yes," I agreed, "I see that, though it hadn't occurred to me. But do you always work in this way?"

"With the clay coils?" said he. "No. This is the quick method and the least trouble. But for more important pieces, to which I seek to impart the more personal and emotional qualities and at the same time to express the highest degree of plasticity, I dispense with the coil and work, as a sculptor does, with simple pellets of clay."

"But," said I, "what about the wheel? I see you have one, and it looks quite a high-class machine. Don't you throw any of your work on it?"

He looked at me solemnly, almost reproachfully, as he replied:

"Never. The machine I leave to the machinist; to the mass-producer and the factory. I don't work for Woolworth's or the crockery shops. I am not concerned with speed of production or quantity of output or mechanical regularity of form. Those things appertain to trade. I, in my humble way, am an artist; and though my work is but simple pottery, I strive to infuse into it qualities that are spiritual, to make it express my own soul and personality. The clay is to me, as it was to other and greater masters of the medium—such as Della Robbia and Donatello—the instrument of emotional utterance."

To this I had nothing to say. It would not have been polite to give expression to my views, which were that his claims seemed to be extravagantly disproportionate to his achievements. But I was profoundly puzzled, and became more so as I watched him; for it appeared to me that what he was doing was not beyond my own powers, at least with a little practice, and I found myself half-unconsciously balancing the three obvious possibilities but unable to reach a conclusion.

Could it be that Gannet was a mere impostor, a pretender to artistic gifts that were purely fictitious? Or was he, like those mentally unbalanced "modernists" who honestly believe their crude and childish daubings to be great masterpieces, simply suffering from a delusion? Or was it possible that his uncouth, barbaric bowls and jars did really possess some subtle aesthetic qualities that I had failed to perceive merely from a lack of the necessary special sensibility? Modesty compelled me to admit the latter possibility. There are plenty of people to whom the beauties of nature or art convey nothing, and it might be that I was one of them.

My speculations were presently cut short by a thundering flourish on the knocker, at which Gannet started with a muttered curse. Then the door burst open and Mr. Frederick Boles swaggered into the studio, humming a tune.

"I wish you wouldn't make that damned row when you come in, Boles," Gannet exclaimed, irritably.

He cast an angry glance at his partner, or tenant, to which the latter responded with a provocative grin.

"Sorry, dear boy," said he. "I'm always forgetting the delicate state of your nerves. And here's the doctor. How de do, Doc? Hope you find your patient pretty well. Hm? None the worse for all that arsenic that they tell me you put into his medicine? Ha ha!"

He bestowed on me an impudent stare through his eyeglass, removed the latter to execute a solemn wink, and then replaced it; after which, as I received his attentions quite impassively (though I should have liked to kick him), he turned away and swaggered across to the part of the studio which appeared to be his own domain, followed by a glance of deep dislike from Gannet which fairly expressed my own sentiments.

Mr. Boles was not a prepossessing person. Nevertheless, I watched his proceedings with some interest, being a little curious as to the kind of industry that he carried on; and presently, smothering my distaste—for I was determined not to quarrel with him—I strolled across to observe him at close quarters. He was seated on a rough, box-like stool, similar to the one which I had borrowed, at an ordinary jeweler's bench fitted with a gas blowpipe and a tin tray in place of the usual sheep-skin. At the moment he was engaged in cutting with an engraving tool a number of shallow pits in a flattened gold object which might have been a sketchy model of a plaice or turbot. I watched him for some time, a little mystified as to the result aimed at, for the little pits seemed, themselves, to have no determinate shape nor could I make out any plan in their arrangement. At length I ventured on a cautious inquiry.

"Those little hollows, I suppose, form the pattern on this—er—object?"

"Don't call it an object, Doc," he protested. "It's a pendant, or it will be when it is finished; and those hollows will form the pattern—or more properly, the surface enrichment—when they are filled with enamel."

"Oh, they are to be filled with enamel," said I, "and the spots of enamel will make the pattern. But I don't quite see what the pattern represents."

"Represents!" he repeated, indignantly, fixing his monocle (which he did not use while working) to emphasize the reproachful stare that he turned on me. "It doesn't represent anything. I'm not a photographer. The enamel spots will just form a symphony of harmonious, gem-like colour with a golden accompaniment. You don't want representation on a jewel. That can be left to the poster artist. What I aim at is harmony—rhythm—the concords of abstract colour. Do you follow me?"

"I think I do," said I. It was an outrageous untruth, for his explanation sounded like mere meaningless jargon. "But," I added, "probably I shall understand better when I have seen the finished work."

"I can show you a finished piece of the same kind now," said he; and laying down his work and the scorer, he went to the small cupboard in which he kept his materials and produced from it a small brooch which he placed in my hand and requested me to consider as "a study in polychromatic harmony."

It was certainly a cheerful and pleasant-looking object but strangely devoid of workmanship (though I noticed, on turning it over, that the pin and catch seemed to be quite competently finished); a simple elliptical tablet of gold covered with irregular-shaped spots of many-coloured enamel distributed over the surface in apparently accidental groups. The effect was as if drops of wax from a number of coloured candles had fallen on it.

"You see," said Boles, "how each of these spots of colour harmonizes and contrasts with all the others and reinforces them?"

"Yes, I see that," I replied, "but I don't see why you should not have grouped the spots into some sort of pattern."

Boles shook his head. "No," said he, "that would never do. The intrusion of form would have destroyed the natural rhythm of contrasting colour. The two things must be kept separate. Gannet is concerned with abstract form mainly uncomplicated with colour. My concern is with abstract colour liberated from form."

I made shift to appear as if this explanation conveyed some meaning to me and returned the brooch with a few appreciative comments. But I was completely fogged; so much so that I presently took the opportunity to steal away in order that I might turn matters over in my mind.

It was quite a curious problem. What was it that was really going on in that studio? There was a singular air of unreality about the industries that were carried on there. Gannet, with his archaic pottery, had been difficult enough to accept as a genuine artist; but Boles was even more incredible. And different as the two men were in all other respects, they were strangely alike in their special activities. Both talked what sounded like inflated, pretentious nonsense. Both assumed the airs of artists and virtuosi. And yet each of them appeared to be occupied with work which—to my eye—showed no sign of anything more than the simplest technical skill, and nothing that I could recognize as artistic ability.

Yet I had to admit that the deficiency might be in my own powers of perception. The curious phase of art known as "modernism" made me aware of widespread taste for pictures and sculpture of a pseudo-barbaric or primitive type; and the comments of the art critics on some of these works were not so very unlike the stuff that I had heard from Boles and Gannet. So perhaps these queer productions were actually what they professed to be and I was just a Philistine who couldn't recognize a work of art when I saw it.

But there was one practical question that rather puzzled me. What became of these wares? Admittedly, neither of these men worked for the retail shops. Then how did they dispose of their works, and who bought them? Both men were provided with means and appliances on a quite considerable scale and it was to be presumed that their output corresponded to the means of production; moreover, both were apparently obtaining a livelihood by their respective industries. Somewhere there must be a demand for primitive pottery and barbaric jewelry. But where was it? I decided—though it was none of my business—to make a few cautious inquiries.

Another matter, of more legitimate interest to me, was that of the relations of these two men. Ostensibly they were friends, comrades, fellow-workers, and in a sense, partners. But real friends they certainly were not. That had been frankly admitted by Gannet; and even if it had not been, his dislike of Boles was manifest and hardly dissembled. And, of course, it was natural enough if he suspected Boles of having tried to poison him, to say nothing of the rather doubtful relations of that gentleman with Mrs. Gannet. Indeed, I could not understand why, if he harboured this suspicion—of which Thorndyke seemed to entertain no doubt—he should have allowed the association to continue.

But if Gannet's sentiments towards Boles were unmistakable, the converse was by no means true. Boles's manners were not agreeable. They were coarse and vulgar—excepting when he was talking "highbrow"—and inclined to be rude. But though he was a bounder he was not consciously uncivil, and—so far as I could at present judge— he showed no signs of unfriendliness towards Gannet. The dislike appeared to be all on the one side.

Yet there must have been something more than met the eye. For if it was the fact—and I felt convinced that it was—that Boles had made a deliberate, cold-blooded attempt to poison Gannet, that attempt implied a motive which, to put it mildly, could not have been a benevolent one.

These various problems combined to make the studio a focus of profound interest to me, and as my practice at this period was productive principally of leisure, I spent a good deal of my time there; more, indeed, than I should have if Gannet had not made it so plain that my visits were acceptable. Sometimes I wondered whether it was my society that he enjoyed, or whether it might have been that my frequenting the studio gave him some sort of feeling of security. It might easily have been so, for, whenever I found him alone, I took the opportunity to satisfy myself that all was well with him. At any rate, he seemed always glad to see me, and for my part, I found the various activities of the two workers interesting to watch, quite independently of the curious problems arising out of their very odd relations.

By degrees my status changed from that of a mere spectator to something like that of a co-worker. There were many odd jobs to be done requiring no special skill and in these I was able to "lend a hand." For instance, there was the preparation of the "grog"— why so-called I never learned, for it was a most unconvivial material, being simply a powder made by pounding the fragments of spoiled or defective earthenware or broken saggars and used to temper the clay to prevent it from cracking in the fire. The broken pots or saggars were pounded in a great iron mortar until they were reduced to small fragments, when the latter were transferred to the grog mill and ground to powder. Then the powder was passed through a series of sieves, each marked with the number of meshes to the inch, and the different grades of powder—coarse, medium and fine— stored in their appropriate bins.

Then there was the plaster work. Both men used plaster, and I was very glad to learn the technique of mixing, pouring and trimming. Occasionally, Gannet would make a plaster mould of a successful bowl or jar (much to my surprise, for it seemed totally opposed to his professed principles) and "squeeze" one or two replicas; a process in which I assisted until I became quite proficient. I helped Boles to fire his queer-looking enamel plaques and to cast his uncouth gold ornaments and took over some of the pickling and polishing operations. And then, finally, there was the kiln, which interested me most of all. It was a coal-fired kiln and required a great deal of attention both before and during the firing. The preparation of the kiln Gannet attended to, himself, but I stood by and watched his methods; observed the way in which he stacked the pieces, bedded in ground flint or bone-ash—he mostly used bone-ash—in the "saggars" (fire-clay cases or covers to protect the pieces from the flames) and at length closed the opening of the kiln with slabs of fire-clay.

But when the actual firing began, we were all kept busy. Even Boles left his work to help in feeding the fires, raking out the ashes and clearing the hearths, leaving Gannet free to control the draught and modify the fire to the required intensity. I was never able to observe the entire process from start to finish, for even at this time my practice called for some attention; but I was present on one occasion at the opening of the kiln—forty-eight hours after the lighting of the fires—and noted the care with which Gannet tested the temperature of the pieces before bringing them out into the cool air.

One day when I was watching him as he built up a wide-mouthed jar from a rough drawing—an extraordinarily rough drawing, very unskilfully executed, as I thought—which lay on the bench beside him, he made a new suggestion.

Why shouldn't you try your hand at a bit of pottery, Doctor?" said he. "Just a simple piece. The actual building isn't difficult and you've seen how I do it. Get some of the stoneware body out of the bin and see what sort of job you can make of it."

I was not very enthusiastic about built pottery, for recently I had purchased a little treatise on the potter's art and had been particularly thrilled by the directions for "throwing on" the wheel. I mentioned the fact to Gannet, but he gave me no encouragement. For some reason he seemed to have an invincible prejudice against the potter's wheel.

"It's all right for commercial purposes," said he, "for speed and quantity. But there's no soul in the mechanical stuff. Building is the artist's method; the skilled hand translating thought directly into form."

I did not contest the matter. With a regretful glance at the wheel, standing idle in its corner, I fetched a supply of the mixed clay from the bin and proceeded to roll it into cords on the board that was kept for the purpose. But it occurred to me as an odd circumstance that, hating the wheel as he appeared to, he should have provided himself with one.

"I didn't buy the thing," he explained, when I propounded the question. "I took over this studio as a going concern from the executors of the previous tenant. He was a more or less commercial potter and his outfit suited his work. It doesn't suit mine. I don't want the wheel or that big mixing mill and I would sooner have had a smaller, gas-fired kiln. But the place was in going order and I got it dirt cheap with the outfit included, so I took it as it was and made the best of it."

My first attempt, a simple bowl, was no great success, being distinctly unsymmetrical and lopsided. But Gannet seemed to think quite well of it—apparently for these very qualities—and even offered to fire it. However, it did not satisfy me, and eventually I crumpled it up and returned it to the clay-bin, whence, after re-moistening, it emerged to be rolled out into fresh coils of cord. For I was now definitely embarked on the industry. The work had proved more interesting than I had expected, and as usually happens in the case of any art, the interest increased as the difficulties began to be understood and technical skill developed and grew.

"That's right, Doctor," said Gannet. "Keep it up and go on trying; and remember that the studio is yours whenever you like to use it, whether I am here or not." (As a matter of fact, he frequently was not, for both he and Boles took a good many days off, and rather oddly, I thought, their absences often coincided.) "And you needn't trouble to come in through the house. There is a spare key of the wicket which you may as well have. I'll give it to you now."

He took a couple of keys from his pocket and handed me one, whereby I became, in a sense, a joint tenant of the studio. It was an insignificant circumstance, and yet, as so often happens, it developed unforeseen consequences, one of which was a little adventure for the triviality of which I offer no apology since it, in its turn, had further consequences not entirely irrelevant to this history.

It happened that on the very first occasion on which I made use of the key, I found the studio vacant, and the condition of the benches suggested that both my fellow tenants were taking a day off. On the bench that I used was a half-finished pot, covered with damp cloths. I removed these and fetched a fresh supply of moist clay from the bin with the intention of going on with the work, when the wheel happened to catch my eye; instantly I was assailed by a great temptation. Here was an ideal opportunity to satisfy my ambition; to try my prentice hand with this delightful toy, which, to me, embodied the real romance of the potter's art.

I went over to the wheel and looked at it hungrily. I gave it a tentative spin and tried working the treadle, and finding it rather stiff, fetched Boles's oil can and applied a drop of oil to the pivots. Then I drew up a stool and took a few minutes' practice with the treadle until I was able to keep up a steady rotation. It seemed quite easy to me, as I was accustomed to riding a bicycle, and I was so far encouraged that I decided to try my skill as a thrower. Placing a basin of water beside the wheel, I brought the supply of clay from the bench, and working it into the form of a large dumpling, slapped it down on the damped hardwood disc, and having wetted my hands, started the rotation with a vigorous spin.

The start was not a perfect success, as I failed to centre the clay ball correctly and put on too much speed, with the result that the clay flew off and hit me in the stomach. However, I collected it from my lap, replaced it on the wheel-head, and made a fresh start with more care and caution. It was not so easy as it had appeared. Attending to the clay, I was apt to forget the treadle, and then the wheel stopped; and when I concentrated on the treadle, strange things happened to the clay. Still, by degrees, I got the "hang" of the process, recalling the instructions in my handbook and trying to practice the methods therein prescribed.

It was a fascinating game. There was something almost magical in the behaviour of the revolving clay. It seemed, almost of its own accord, to assume the most unexpected shapes. A light pressure of the wet hands and it rose into the form of a column, a cylinder or a cone. A gentle touch from above turned it miraculously into a ball; and a little pressure of the thumbs on the middle of the ball hollowed it out and transformed it into a bowl. It was wonderful and most delightful. And all the transformations had the charm of unexpectedness. The shapes that came were not designed by me; they simply came of themselves, and an inadvertent touch instantly changed them into something different and equally surprising.

For more than an hour I continued, with ecstatic pleasure and growing facility, to play this incomparable game. By that time, however, signs of bodily fatigue began to make themselves felt, for it was a pretty strenuous occupation, and it occurred to me that I had better get something done. I had just made a shallow bowl (or, rather, it had made itself), and as I took it gently between my hands, it rose, narrowed itself, and assumed the form of a squat jar with slightly in-turned mouth. I looked at it with pleased surprise. It was really quite an elegant shape and it seemed a pity to spoil it by any further manipulation. I decided to let well alone and treat it as a finished piece.

When I took my foot off the treadle and let the wheel run down, some new features came into view. The jar at rest was rather different from the jar spinning. Its surface was scored all over with spiral traces of "the potter's thumb," which stamped it glaringly as a thrown piece. This would not quite answer my purpose, which was to practice a playful fraud on Peter Gannet by foisting the jar on him as a built piece. The telltale spirals would have to be eliminated and other deceptive markings substituted.

Accordingly, I attacked it cautiously with a modeling tool and a piece of damp sponge, stroking it lightly in vertical lines and keeping an eye on one of Gannet's own jars, until all traces of the wheel had been obliterated and the jar might fairly have passed for a hand-built piece. Of course, a glance at the inside, which I did not dare to touch, would have discovered the fraud, but I took the chance that the interior would not be examined.

The next problem was the decoration. Gannet's usual method— following the tradition of primitive and barbaric ornament—was either to impress an encircling cord into the soft clay or to execute simple thumb-nail patterns. He did not actually use his thumb-nail for this purpose. A bone mustard-spoon produced the same effect and was more convenient. Accordingly I adopted the mustard-spoon, with which I carried a sort of rude guilloche round the jar, varied by symmetrically placed dents, made with the end of my clinical thermometer. Finally, becoming ambitious for something more distinctive, I produced my latch-key, and, having made a few experiments on a piece of waste clay, found it quite admirable as a unit of pattern, especially if combined with the thermometer. A circle of key impressions radiating from a central thermometer dent produced a simple but interesting rosette which could be further developed by a circle of dents between the key-marks. It was really quite effective, and I was so pleased with it that I proceeded to enrich my masterpiece with four such rosettes, placing them as symmetrically as I could (not that the symmetry would matter to Gannet) on the bulging sides below the thumb-nail ornaments.

When I had finished the decoration and tidied it up with the modeling tool I stood back and looked at my work, not only with satisfaction but with some surprise. For, rough and crude as it was, it appeared to my possibly indulgent eye quite a pleasant little pot; and comparing it with the row of Gannet's works which were drying on the shelf, I asked myself once again what could be the alleged subtle qualities imparted by the hand of the master?

Having made a vacancy on the shelf by moving one of Gannet's pieces from the middle to the end, I embarked on the perilous task of detaching my jar from the wheel-head. The instrument that I employed was a thin wire with a wooden handle at each end, which we used for cutting slices of clay; a dangerous tool, for a false stroke would have cut the bottom off my jar. But Providence, which—sometimes—watches over the activities of the tyro, guided my hand, and at last the wire emerged safely, leaving the jar free of the surface to which it had been stuck. With infinite care and tenderness—for it was still quite soft—I lifted it with both hands and carried it across to the shelf, where I deposited it safely in the vacant space. Then I cleaned up the wheel, obliterating all traces of my unlawful proceedings, threw my half-finished built piece back into the clay-bin, and departed, chuckling over the surprise that awaited Gannet when he should come to inspect the pieces that were drying on the shelf.

As events turned out, my very mild joke fell quite flat, so far as I was concerned, for I missed the dénouement. A sudden outbreak of measles at a local school kept me so busy that my visits to the studio had to be suspended for a time, and when at last I was able to make an afternoon call, the circumstances were such as to occupy my attention in a more serious and less agreeable manner. As this episode was later to develop a special significance, I shall venture to describe it in some detail.

On this occasion, I did not let myself in, as usual, by the wicket, for at the end of Jacob Street I overtook Mrs. Gannet and we walked together to the house, which I entered with her. It seemed that she had some question to ask her husband, and when I had opened the side door, she came out to walk with me across the yard to the studio. Suddenly, as we drew near to the latter, I became aware of a singular uproar within; a clattering and banging, as if the furniture were being thrust about and stools overturned, mingled with the sound of obviously angry voices. Mrs. Gannet stopped abruptly and clutched my arm.

"Oh, dear, she exclaimed, "there are those two men quarreling again. It is dreadful. I do wish Mr. Boles would move to another workshop. If they can't agree, why don't they separate?"

"They don't hit it off very well, then?" I suggested, listening attentively and conscious of a somewhat unfortunate expression—for they seemed to be hitting it off rather too well.

"No," she replied, "especially since—you know. Peter thinks Mr. Boles gave him the stuff, which is ridiculous, and Mr. Boles— I think I won't go in now," and with this she turned about and retreated to the house, leaving me standing near the studio door, doubtful whether I had better enter boldly or follow the lady's discreet example and leave the two men to settle their business.

It was very embarrassing. If I went in, I could not pretend to be unaware of the disturbance. On the other hand, I did not like to retreat when my intervention might be desirable. Thus I stood hesitating between considerations of delicacy and expediency until a furious shout in Boles's voice settled the question.

"You're asking for it, you know!" he roared; whereupon, flinging delicacy to the winds, I rapped on the door with my knuckles and entered.

I had opened the door deliberately and rather noisily and I now stood for a few moments in the dark lobby behind the curtain while I closed it after me in the same deliberate manner to give time for any necessary adjustments. Sounds of quick movement from within suggested that these were being made, and when I drew aside the curtain and stepped in, the two men were on opposite sides of the studio. Gannet was in the act of buttoning a very crumpled collar and Boles was standing by his bench, on which lay a raising hammer that had a suspicious appearance of having been hastily put down there. Both men were obviously agitated: Boles, purple-faced, wild-eyed and furiously angry; Gannet, breathless, pale and venomous.

I greeted them in a matter-of-fact tone as if I had noticed nothing unusual, and went on to excuse and explain the suspension of my visits. But it was a poor pretense, for there were the overturned stools and there was Boles, scowling savagely and still trembling visibly, and there was that formidable-looking hammer the appearance of which suggested that I had entered only just in time.

Gannet was the first to recover himself, though even Boles managed to growl out a sulky greeting, and when I had picked up a fallen stool and seated myself on it, I made shift to keep up some sort of conversation and to try to bring matters back to a normal footing. I glanced at the shelf, but it was empty. Apparently the pieces that I had left drying on it had been fired and disposed of. What had happened to my jar, I could not guess and did not very much care. Obviously, the existing circumstances did not lend themselves to any playful interchanges between Gannet and me, nor did they seem to lend themselves to anything else; and I should have made an excuse to steal away but for my unwillingness to leave the two men together in their present moods.

I did not, however, stay very long; no longer, in fact, than seemed desirable. Presently, Boles, after some restless and apparently aimless rummaging in his cupboard, shut it, locked its door, and with a sulky farewell to me, took his departure; and as I had no wish to discuss the quarrel and Gannet seemed to be in a not very sociable mood, I took an early opportunity to bring my visit to an end.

It had been a highly disagreeable episode, and it had a permanent effect on me. Thenceforward, the studio ceased to attract me. Its pleasant, friendly atmosphere seemed to have evaporated. I continued to look in from time to time, but rather to keep an eye on Gannet, than to interest myself in the works of the two artists. Like Mrs. Gannet, I wondered why these two men, hating each other as they obviously did, should perversely continue their association. At any rate, the place was spoiled for me by the atmosphere of hatred and strife that seemed to pervade it, and even if the abundance of my leisure had continued—which it did not—I should still have been but an occasional visitor.

CHAPTER 7

MRS. GANNET BRINGS STRANGE TIDINGS

The wisdom of our ancestors has enriched us with the precept that the locking of the stable door fails in its purpose of security if it is postponed until after the horse has been stolen. Nevertheless (since it is so much easier to be wise after the event than before) this futile form of post-caution continues to be prevalent; of which truth my own proceedings furnished an illustrative instance. For having allowed my patient to be poisoned with arsenic under my very nose, and that, too, in the crudest and most blatant fashion, I now proceeded to devote my leisure to an intense study of Medical Jurisprudence and Toxicology.

Mine, however, was not a truly representative case. The actual horse had indeed been stolen, but still the stable contained a whole stud of potential horses. I might, and probably should, never encounter another case of poisoning in the practice of a life-time. On the other hand, I might meet with one tomorrow; or if not a poisoning case, perhaps some other form of crime which lay within the province of the medical jurist. There seemed to be plenty of them, judging by the lurid accounts of the authorities whose works I devoured, and I began almost to hope that my labours in their study would not be entirely wasted.

It was natural that my constant preoccupation with the detection and demonstration of crime should react more or less on my habitual state of mind. And it did. Gradually I acquired a definitely Scotland Yardish outlook and went about my practice—not neglectful, I trust, of the ordinary maladies of my patients—with the idea of criminal possibilities, if not consciously present, yet lurking on the very top surface of the subconscious. Little did my innocent patients or their equally innocent attendants suspect the toxicological balance in which symptoms and ministrations alike were being weighed; and little did the worthy Peter Gannet guess that, even while he was demonstrating the mysteries of stoneware, my perverted mind was canvassing the potentialities of the various glazes that he used for indirect and secret poisoning.

I mention these mental reactions to my late experience and my recent profound study of legal medicine in explanation of subsequent events. And I make no apology. The state of mind may seem odd, but yet it was very natural. I had been caught napping once and I didn't intend to be caught again; and that involved these elaborate precautions against possibilities whose probability was almost negligible

It happened on a certain evening that in the intervals of my evening consultations, my thoughts turned to my friend, Peter Gannet. It was now some weeks since I had seen him, my practice having of late made a temporary spurt and left me little leisure. I had also been acting as *locum tenens* for the Police Surgeon, who was on leave; this further diminished my leisure and possibly accentuated the state of mind that I have described. Nevertheless, I was a little disposed to reproach myself, for, solitary man as he was, he had made it clear that he was always pleased to see me. Indeed, it had seemed to me that I was the only friend that he had for certainly Boles could not be regarded in that light; and if the quarrel between them had given me a distaste for the studio, that very occurrence did, in fact, emphasize those obligations of friendship which had led me at first visit to the studio.

I had then felt that it was my duty to keep an eye on him, since some person had certainly tried to poison him. That person had some reason for desiring his death and had no scruple about seeking to compass it; and as the motive, presumably, still existed, there was no denying that, calmly as he had taken the position, Peter Gannet stood definitely in peril of a further and more successful attempt—to say nothing of the chance of his being knocked on the head with a raising hammer in the course of one of his little disagreements with Boles. I ought not to have left him so long without at least a brief visit of inspection.

Thus reflecting, I decided to walk round to the studio as soon as the consultations were finished and satisfy myself that all was well; and as the time ran on and no further patients appeared, my eye turned impatiently to the clock, the hands of which were creeping towards eight, when I should be free to go. There were now only three minutes to run and the clock had just given the preliminary hiccup by which clocks announce their intention to strike, when I heard the door of the adjoining waiting room open and close, informing me that a last minute patient had arrived.

It was very provoking; but after all it was what I was there for. So dismissing Gannet from my mind, I rose, opened the communicating door and looked into the waiting room.

The visitor was Mrs. Gannet and at the first glance at her my heart sank. For her troubled, almost terrified, expression told me that something was seriously amiss; and my imagination began instantly to frame lurid surmises.

"What is the matter, Mrs. Gannet?" I asked, as I ushered her through into the consulting room. "You look very troubled."

"I am very troubled," she replied. "A most extraordinary and alarming thing has happened. My husband has disappeared."

"Disappeared!" I repeated in astonishment. "Since when?"

"That I can't tell you," she answered. "I have been away from home for about a fortnight, and when I came back I found the house empty. I didn't think much of it at the time, as I had said, when I wrote to him, that I was not certain as to what time I should get home, and I simply thought that he had gone out. But then I found my letter in the letter box, which seemed very strange, as it must have been lying there two days. So I went up and had another look at his bedroom, but everything was in order there. His bed had not been slept in—it was quite tidily made—and his toilet things and hair brushes were in their usual place. Then I looked over his wardrobe, but none of his clothes seemed to be missing excepting the suit that he usually wears. And then I went down to the hall to see if he had taken his stick or his umbrella, but he hadn't taken either. They were both there; and what was more remarkable, both his hats were on their pegs."

"Do you mean to say," I exclaimed, "that there was no hat missing at all?"

"No. He has only two hats, and they were both there. So it seems as if he must have gone away without a hat."

"That is very extraordinary," said I. "But surely your maid knows how long he has been absent."

"There isn't any maid," she replied. "Our last girl, Mabel, was under notice and she left a week before I went away; and, as there was no time to get a fresh maid, Peter and I agreed to put it off until I came back. He said that he could look after himself quite well and get his meals out if necessary. There are several good restaurants near.

"Well, I waited all yesterday in hopes of his return and I sat up until nearly one in the morning, but he never came home, and there has been no sign of him today."

"You looked in at the studio, I suppose?" said I.

"No, I didn't," she replied almost in a whisper. "That is why I have come to you. I couldn't summon up courage to go there."

"Why not?" I asked.

"I was afraid," she answered in the same low, agitated tone, "that there might be something—something there that—well, I don't quite know what I thought, but you know—"

"Yes, I understand," said I, rising—for the clock had struck and I was free. "But that studio ought to be entered at once. Your husband may have had some sudden attack or seizure and be lying there helpless."

I went out into the hall and wrote down on the slate the address where I was to be found if any emergency should arise. Then Mrs. Gannet and I set forth together, taking the short cuts through the back streets, with which I was now becoming quite familiar. We walked along at a quick pace, exchanging hardly a word, and as we went, I cogitated on the strange and disquieting news that she had brought. There was no denying that things had a decidedly sinister aspect. That Gannet should have gone away from home hatless and unprovided with any of his ordinary kit, and leaving no note or message, was inconceivable. Something must have happened to him. But what? My own expectation was that I should find his dead body in the studio, and that was evidently Mrs. Gannet's, too, as was suggested by her terror at the idea of seeking him there. But that terror seemed to me a little unnatural. Why was she so afraid to go into the studio, even with the expectation of finding her husband dead? Could it be that she had some knowledge or suspicion that she had not disclosed? It seemed not unlikely. Even if she had not been a party to the poisoning, she must have known, or at least strongly suspected who the poisoner was; and it was most probable that she had been able to guess at the motive of the crime. But she would then realize, as I did, that the motive remained and might induce another crime.

When we reached the house, I tried the wicket in the studio gate, but it was locked, and the key which Gannet had given me was not in my pocket. Meanwhile, Mrs. Gannet had opened the street door with her latch-key and we entered the house together.

"Are you coming into the studio with me?" I asked, as we went through the hall to the side door that opened on the yard.

"No," she replied. "I will come with you to the door and wait outside until you have seen whether he is there or not."

Accordingly, we walked together across the yard, and when we came to the studio door, I tried it. But it was locked; and an inspection by means of my flashlight showed that it had been locked from the inside and that the key was in the lock.

"Now," said I, "what are we to do? How are we going to get in?"

"There is a spare key," she replied. "Shall I go and get it?"

"But," I objected, "we couldn't get it into the lock. There is a key there already. And the wicket is locked, too. Have you got a spare key of that?"

She had, so we returned to the house, where she found the key and gave it to me. And as I took it from her trembling hand, I could see—though she made no comment—that the locked door with the key inside had given her a further shock. And certainly it was rather ominous. But if the wicket should prove also to be locked from the inside, all hope or doubt would be at an end. It was, therefore, with the most acute anxiety that I hurried out into the street, leaving her standing in the hall, and ran to the wicket. But to my relief, the key entered freely and turned in the lock and I opened the little gate and stepped through into the studio. Lighting myself across the floor with my flashlight I reached the switch and turned it on, flooding the place with light. A single glance around the studio showed that there was no one in it, alive or dead. Thereupon, I unlocked the yard door and threw it open, when I perceived Mrs. Gannet standing outside.

"Well, he isn't here," I reported, whereupon she came, almost on tiptoe, into the lobby and peered round the curtain.

"Oh dear!" she exclaimed, "what a relief! But still, where can he be? I can't help thinking that something must have happened to him."

As I could not pretend to disagree with her, I made no reply to this, but asked: "I suppose you have searched the house thoroughly?"

"I think so," she replied, "and I don't feel as if I could search any more. But if you would be so kind as to take a look round and make sure that I haven't overlooked anything—"

"Yes," said I, "I think that would be just as well. But what are you going to do tonight? You oughtn't to be in the house all alone."

"I couldn't be," she replied. "Last night was dreadful, but now my nerves are all on edge. I couldn't endure another night. I shall go to my friend, Miss Hughes—she lives in Mornington Crescent—and see if she will come and keep me company."

"It would be better if she would put you up for the night," said I.

"Yes, it would," she agreed. "Much better. I would rather not stay in this house tonight. As soon as you have made your inspection, I will run round and ask her."

"You needn't wait for me," said I. "Go round to her at once, as it is getting late. Give me the number of her house and I will call on my way home and tell you whether I have discovered any clue to the mystery."

She closed with this offer immediately, being, evidently, relieved to get away from the silent, desolate house. I walked back with her across the yard, and when I had escorted her to the street door and seen her start on her mission, I closed the door and went back into the house, not displeased to have the place to myself and the opportunity to pursue my investigations at my leisure and free from observation.

I made a very thorough examination, beginning with the attics at the very top of the house and working my way systematically downwards. On the upper floors there were several unoccupied rooms, some quite empty and others more or less filled with discarded furniture and miscellaneous lumber. All these I searched minutely, opening up every possible—and even impossible—hiding-place, and peering, with the aid of my pocket flashlight, into the dim and musty recesses of the shapeless closets in the corners of the roof or under the staircases. In the occupied bedrooms I knelt down to look under the beds, I opened the cupboards and wardrobes and prodded the clothes that hung from the pegs to make sure that they concealed no other hanging object. I even examined the chimneys with my lamp and explored their cavities with my walking-stick, gathering a little harvest of soot up my sleeves but achieving no other result and making no discoveries, excepting that, when I came to examine Gannet's bedroom, I noticed that the pots and pans and the effigy of the monkey had disappeared from the mantelpiece.

It was an eerie business and seemed to become more so (by a sort of autosuggestion) as I explored one room after another. By the time I had examined the great stone-paved kitchen and the rather malodorous scullery and searched the cavernous, slug-haunted cellars, even probing the mounds of coal with my stick, I had worked myself up into a state of the most horrid expectancy.

But still there was no sign of Peter Gannet. The natural conclusion seemed to be that he was not there. But this was a conclusion that my state of mind made me unable to accept. His wife's statement set forth that he had disappeared in his ordinary indoor apparel, in which it was hardly imaginable that he could have gone away from the house. But if he had not, then he must be somewhere on the premises. Thus I argued, with more conviction than logic, as I ascended the uncarpeted basement stairs, noting the surprisingly loud sound that my footsteps made as they broke in on the pervading silence.

As I passed into the hall, I paused at the hat-stand to verify Mrs. Gannet's statement. There were the two hats, sure enough; a shabby, broad-brimmed, soft felt which I knew well by sight, and a rather trim billycock which I had never seen him wear, but which bore his initials in the crown, as I ascertained by taking it down and inspecting it. And there was his stick, a rough oak crook, and his umbrella with a legible P. G. on the silver band. There was also another stick which I had never seen before and which struck me as being rather out of character with the Bohemian Gannet; a smart, polished cane with a gilt band and a gilt tip to the handle. I took it out of the stand, and as it seemed to me rather long, I lifted out the oak stick and compared the two, when I found that the cane was the longer by a full inch. There was nothing much in this, and as the band bore no initials, I was putting it back in the stand when my eye caught a minute monogram on the gilt tip. It was a confused device, as monograms usually are, but eventually I managed to resolve it into the two letters F. and B.

Then it was pretty certain that the stick belonged to Frederick Boles. From which it followed that Boles had been to the house recently. But there was nothing abnormal in this, since he worked pretty regularly in the studio and usually approached it through the house. But why had he left his stick? And why had Mrs. Gannet made no mention of it, or, indeed, of Boles himself? For if he had been working here, he must have known when Gannet was last seen, for unless he had a latch-key, he must have been admitted by Gannet, himself.

Turning this over in my mind, I decided, before leaving the house, to take another look at the studio. It had certainly been empty when I had looked in previously, and there were no large cupboards or other possible hiding places. Still there was the chance that a more thorough examination might throw some light on Gannet's activities and on the question as to the time of his disappearance. Accordingly, I passed out by the side door, and crossing the yard, opened the studio door, switched on the lights, drew aside the curtain and stepped in.

CHAPTER 8

DR. OLDFIELD MAKES SURPRISING DISCOVERIES

On entering the studio, I halted close by the curtain and stood awhile surveying the vast, desolate, forbidding interior with no definite idea in my mind. Obviously, there was no one there, dead or alive, nor any closed space large enough to form a hiding place. And yet as I stood there, the creepy feeling that had been growing on me as I had searched the house seemed to become even more intense. It may have been that the deathly silence and stillness of the place, which I had known only under the cheerful influence of work and companionship, cast a chill over me.

At any rate, there I stood, vaguely looking about me with a growing uncomfortable feeling that this great, bare room which had been the scene of Gannet's labours and the centre of his interests, had been in some way connected with his unaccountable disappearance.

Presently my vague, general survey gave place to a more detailed inspection. I began to observe the various objects in the studio and to note what they had to tell of Gannet's recent activities. There was the potter's wheel, carefully cleaned—though never used—according to his invariable orderly practice, and there was a row of "green," unfired jars drying on a shelf until they should be ready for the kiln. But when I looked at the kiln itself, I was struck by something quite unusual, having regard to Gannet's habitual tidiness. The fire-holes which led into the interior of the kiln were all choked with ash; and opposite to each was a large mound of the ash which had been raked out during the firing and left on the hearths. Now, this was singularly unlike Gannet's practice. Usually, as he raked out the ash, he shoveled it up into a bucket and carried it out to the ash-bin in the yard; and as soon as the fires were out, he cleared each of the fireplaces of the remaining ash, leaving them clean and ready for the next firing.

Here, then, was something definitely abnormal. But there was a further discrepancy. The size of the mounds made it clear that there had been a rather prolonged firing and a "high fire." But where were the fired pieces? The shelves on which the pots were usually stored after firing were all empty and there was not a sign of any pottery other than the unfired jars. The unavoidable conclusion was that the "batch" must be still in the kiln. But if this were so, then Gannet's disappearance must have coincided with the end of the firing. But that seemed entirely to exclude the idea of a voluntary disappearance. It was inconceivable that he should have gone away leaving the fires still burning and the kiln unopened.

However, there was no need to speculate. The question could be settled at once by opening the kiln if it was sufficiently cool to handle. Accordingly, I walked over to it and cautiously touched the outside brick casing, which I found to be little more than lukewarm, and then I boldly unlatched and pulled open the big iron, fire-clay lined door, bringing into view the loose fire-bricks which actually closed the opening. As these, too, were only moderately warm, I proceeded to lift them out, one by one, which I was able to do the more easily since they had been only roughly fitted together.

It was not really necessary for me to take them all out, for, as soon as the upper tier was removed, I was able to throw the beam of my flashlight into the interior. And when I did so, I discovered, to my astonishment, that the kiln was empty.

The mystery, then, remained. Indeed, it grew more profound. For not only was the problem as to what had become of the fired pottery still unsolved, but there was the remarkable fact that the kiln must have been opened while it was still quite hot; a thing that Gannet would never have done, since a draught of cold air on the hot pottery would probably result in a disaster. And when I took away the rest of the fire-bricks and the interior of the kiln was fully exposed to view, another anomaly presented itself. The floor of the kiln, which during the firing would be covered with burnt flint or bone-ash, was perfectly clean. It had been carefully and thoroughly swept out, and this while the kiln was hot and while the fire-holes remained choked with ash.

As to the missing pottery, there was one possibility, though an unlikely one. It might have been treated with glaze and put into the glost oven. But it had not, for when I opened the oven and looked in, I found it empty and showing no sign of recent use.

It was all very strange; and the strangeness of it did nothing to allay my suspicion that the studio held the secret of Gannet's disappearance. I prowled round with uneasy inquisitiveness, scrutinizing all the various objects in search of some hint or leading fact. I examined the grog mill and noted that something white had been recently ground in it, and apparently ground dry, to judge by the coating of fine powder on the floor around it. I looked into the big iron mortar and noted that some white material had been pounded in it. I examined the rows of cupels on the shelves by Boles's little muffle, noted that they were badly made and of unusually coarse material, and wondered when Boles had made them. I even looked into the muffle—finding nothing, of course—and observing that the floor of the studio seemed to have been washed recently, speculated on the possible reason for this very unusual proceeding.

But speculation got me no more forward. Obviously, there was something abnormal about the kiln. There had been a prolonged and intense fire, but of the fired ware there was not a trace. What conceivable explanation could there be of such an extraordinary conflict of facts? The possibility occurred to me that the whole batch might have been disposed of by a single transaction or sent to an exhibition. But a moment's reflection showed me that this would not do. There had not been time for the batch to be cooled, finished, glazed and refired, for the kiln was still quite warm inside.

The rough, box-like stool that Gannet had made to sit on at the bench was standing near the kiln. I slipped my hand through the lifting hole and drew the stool up to the open door in order more conveniently to examine the interior. But the examination yielded nothing. I threw the beam of light from my flashlight into every corner, but it simply confirmed my original observation. The kiln was empty, and no trace of its late contents remained beyond the few obscure white smears that the brush had left on the fire-clay floor.

I sat there for some minutes facing the open door and reflecting profoundly on this extraordinary problem. But I could make nothing of it, and at length, I started up to renew my explorations. For it had suddenly occurred to me that I had forgotten to examine the contents of the bins. But as I rose and turned round, I noticed a small white object on the floor which had evidently been covered by the stool before I had moved it. I stooped and picked it up, and at the first glance at it all my vague and formless suspicions seemed to run together into a horrible certainty.

The little object was the ungual phalanx, or terminal joint, of a finger—apparently a forefinger—burned to the snowy whiteness characteristic of incinerated bone. It was unmistakable. For if I lacked experience in some professional matters, at least my osteology was fresh; and as the instant recognition flashed on me, I stood as if rooted to the ground, staring at the little relic with a shuddering realization of all that it meant.

The mystery of the absent pottery was solved. There had never been any pottery. That long and fierce fire had burned to destroy the evidence of a hideous crime. And the other mysteries, too, were solved. Now I could guess what the white substance was that had been ground in the grog mill; how it came that the hastily-made cupels were of such abnormally coarse material; and why it had been necessary to wash the studio floor. All the anomalies now fell into a horrid agreement and each served to confirm and explain the others.

I laid the little fragile bone tenderly on the stool and proceeded to re-examine the place by the light of this new and dreadful fact. First I went to the shelves by Boles's muffle and looked over the cupels, taking them in my hand the better to examine them. Their nature was now quite obvious. Instead of the finely powdered bone-ash of which they were ordinarily composed, they had been made by cramming fragments of crushed, incinerated bone into the cupel press; and the cohesion of these was so slight that one of the cupels fell to pieces in my hand.

Laying the loose fragments on the shelf, I turned away to examine the bins, of which there was a row standing against the wall. I began with the clay-bins, containing the material for the various "bodies" —stoneware, earthenware and porcelain. But when I lifted the lids, I saw that they contained clay and could contain nothing else. The grog-bins were nearly empty and showed nothing abnormal, and the same was true of the plaster-bin, though I took the precaution of dipping my hand deeply into the plaster to make sure that there was nothing underneath. When I came to the bone-ash-bin I natur-ally surveyed it more critically; for here, with the aid of the mill, the residue of a cremated body could have been concealed beyond the possibility of recognition.

I lifted off the lid and looked in, but at the first glance perceived nothing unusual. The bin was three parts full, and its contents appeared to be the ordinary finely powdered ash. But I was not prepared to accept the surface appearances. Rolling my sleeve up above the elbow, I thrust my hand deep down into the ash, testing its consistency by working it between my fingers and thumb. The result was what the cupels had led me to expect. About eight inches from the surface, the feel of the fine, smooth powder gave place to a sensation as if I were grasping a mixture of gravel and sand with occasional fragments of appreciable size. Some of these I brought up to the surface, dropping them into my other hand and dipping down for further specimens until I had collected a handful, when I carried them over the cupel shelves and, having deposited them on a vacant space, picked out one or two of the larger fragments and carried them across to the modeling stand to examine them by the light of the big studio lamp.

Of course, there could be no doubt as to their nature. Even to the naked eye, the characteristic structure of bone was obvious, and rendered more so by the burning away of the soft tissues. But I confirmed the diagnosis with the aid of my pocket lens, and then, having replaced the fragments on the shelf, I put the lid back on the bin and began seriously to consider what I should do next. There was no need for further exploration. I had all the essential facts. I now knew what had happened to Peter Gannet, and any further elucidation lay outside my province and within that of those whose business it is to investigate crime.

Before leaving the studio, I looked about for some receptacle in which to pack the little finger bone; for I knew that it would crumble at a touch, and that, as it was the one piece of undeniable evidence, it must be preserved intact at all costs. Eventually I found a nearly empty match box, and, having tipped out the remaining matches and torn a strip from my handkerchief, I rolled the little relic in this, packed it tenderly in the match box and bestowed the latter in my breast pocket. Then I took up my stick and prepared to depart; but just as I was starting towards the door, it occurred to me that I might as well take a few of the small fragments from the bin to examine more thoroughly at my leisure. Not that I had any doubts as to their nature, but the microscope would put the matter beyond dispute. Accordingly, I collected a handful from the shelf, and having wrapped them in the remainder of my handkerchief, put the little parcel in my pocket and then made my way to the door, switched off the lights and went out, taking the door-key with me.

Coming out from the glare of the studio into the darkness, I had to light myself across the yard with my flashlight, and, as I flashed it about, its beam fell on the big rubbish-bin which stood in a corner waiting for the dustman. For a moment, I was disposed to stop and explore it; but then I reflected that it was not my concern to seek further details, and as it was getting late and I still had to report to Mrs. Gannet, I went on into the house, and passing through the hall, let myself out into the street.

The distance from Jacob Street to Mornington Crescent is quite short; all too short for the amount of thinking that I had to do on the way thither. For it was only when I had shut the door and set forth on my errand that the awkwardness of the coming interview began to dawn on me. What was I to say to Mrs. Gannet? As I asked myself the question, I saw that it involved two others. The first was, how much did she know? Had she any suspicion that her husband had been made away with? I did not for a moment believe that she had been privy to the gruesome events that the studio had witnessed, but her agitation, her horror at the idea of spending the night in the house, and above all, her strange fear of entering the studio, justified the suspicion that, even if she knew nothing of what had happened, she had made some highly pertinent surmises.

Then, how much did I know? I had assumed quite confidently that a body had been cremated in the kiln and that the body was that of Peter Gannet. And I believed that I could name the other party to that grim transaction. But here I recalled Dr. Thorndyke's oft-repeated warnings to his students never to confuse inference or belief with knowledge and never to go beyond the definitely ascertained facts. But I had done this already; and now when I revised my convictions by the light of this excellent precept, I realized that the actual facts that I had ascertained (though they justified my inferences) were enough only to call for a thorough investigation.

Then should I tell Mrs. Gannet simply what I had observed and leave her to draw her own conclusions? Considered, subject to my strong distrust of the lady, this course did not commend itself. In fact, it was a very difficult question, and I had come to no decision when I found myself standing on Miss Hughes's door-step, and in response to my knock, the door was opened by Mrs. Gannet herself.

Still temporizing in my own mind, I began by expressing the hope that Miss Hughes was able to accommodate her.

"Yes," she replied, as she ushered me into the drawing room, "I am glad to say that she can give me the spare bedroom. She has been most kind and sympathetic. And how have you got on? You have been a tremendous time. I expected you at least half an hour ago."

"The search took quite a long time," I explained, "for I went through the whole house from the attics to the cellars and examined every nook and corner."

"And I suppose you found nothing, after all?"

"Not a trace in any part of the house."

"It was very good of you to take so much trouble," said she. "I don't know how to thank you and you such a busy man, too. I suppose you didn't go into the studio again?"

"Yes," I replied. "I thought I would have another look at it, in rather more detail, and I did pick up some information there as to the approximate time when he disappeared, for I opened the big kiln and found it quite warm inside. I don't know how long it takes to cool. Do you?"

"Not very exactly," she answered, "but quite a long time, I believe, if it is kept shut up. At any rate, the fact that it was warm doesn't tell us much more than we know. It is all very mysterious, and I don't know what on earth to do next."

"What about Mr. Boles?" I suggested. "He must have been at the studio some time quite lately. Wouldn't it be as well to look him up and see if he can throw any light on the mystery?"

She shook her head, disconsolately. "I have," she said. "I went to his flat yesterday and again this morning, but I could get no answer to my knocking and ringing. And the caretaker man in the office says that he hasn't seen him for about a week, though he has been on the lookout for him on account of a parcel that the postman left. He has been up to the flat several times, but could get no answer. And there hasn't been any light in the windows at night. So he must be away from home."

"Did he know when you would be returning?"

"Yes," she replied. "And there is another strange thing. I wrote and told him what day I should be back and asked him to drop in and have tea with me. But he not only never came, but he didn't even answer my letter."

I reflected on this new turn of events, which seemed less mysterious to me than it appeared to her. Then I cautiously approached the inevitable proposal.

"Well, Mrs. Gannet," said I, "it is, as you say, all very mysterious.

But we can't just leave it at that. We have got to find out what has happened to your husband; and as we haven't the means of doing it ourselves, we must invoke the aid of those who have. We shall have to apply for help to the police."

As I made this proposal, I watched her attentively and was a little relieved to note that it appeared to cause her no alarm. But she was not enthusiastic.

"Do you think it is really necessary?" she asked. "If we call in the police, it will be in all the papers and there will be no end of fuss and scandal; and after all, he may come back tomorrow."

"I don't think there is any choice," I rejoined, firmly. "The police will have to be informed sooner or later, and they ought to be notified at once while the events are fresh and the traces more easy to follow. It would never do for us to seem to have tried to hush the affair up."

That last remark settled her. She agreed that perhaps the police had better be informed of the disappearance, and to my great satisfaction, she asked me to make the communication.

"I don't feel equal to it," said she, "and as you have acted as police surgeon and know the officers, it will be easier for you. Hadn't you better have the latch-key in case they want to look over the house?"

"But won't you want it yourself?" I asked.

"No," she replied. "Miss Hughes has invited me to stay with her for the present. Besides, I have a spare key and I brought it away with me; and of course, if Peter should come back, he has his own key."

With this she handed me the latch-key and when I had pocketed it I took my leave and set forth at a swinging pace for home, hoping that I should find no messages awaiting me and that a substantial meal would be ready for instant production. I was very well pleased with the way in which the interview had gone off and congratulated myself on having kept my own counsel. For now I need not appear in the investigation at all. The police would, of course, examine the studio, and the discoveries that they would make, on my prompting, could be credited to them.

When I let myself in, I cast an anxious glance at the message slate and breathed a benediction on the blank surface that it presented. And as a savoury aroma ascending from the basement told me that all was well there, too, I skipped off to the bathroom, there to wash and brush joyfully and reflect on the delight of being really hungry—under suitable conditions.

As I disposed of the excellent dinner—or supper—that my thoughtful housekeeper had provided, it was natural that I should ruminate on the astonishing events of the last few hours. And now that the excitement of the chase had passed off, I began to consider the significance of my discoveries. Those discoveries left me in no doubt (despite Thorndyke's caution) that my friend, Peter Gannet, had been made away with; and I owed it to our friendship, to say nothing of my duty as a good citizen, to do everything in my power to establish the identity of the murderer in order that he—or she— might be brought within the grasp of the law.

Now who could it be that had made away with my poor friend? I had not the faintest doubt as to, at least, the protagonist in that horrid drama. In the very moment of my realization that a crime had been committed, I had confidently identified the criminal. And my conviction remained unshaken. Nevertheless, I turned over the available evidence as it would have to be presented to a stranger and as I should have to present it to the police.

What could we say with certainty as to the personality of the murderer? In the first place, he was a person who had access to the studio. Then he knew how to prepare and fire the kiln. He understood the use and management of the grog mill and of the cupel press, and he knew which of the various bins was the bone-ash-bin. But, so far as I knew, there was only one person in the world to whom this description would apply—Frederick Boles.

Then, to approach the question from the other direction, were there any reasons for suspecting Boles? And the answer was that there were several reasons. Boles had certainly been at the house when Gannet was there alone, and had thus had the opportunity. He had now unaccountably disappeared, and his disappearance seemed to coincide with the date of the murder. He had already, to my certain knowledge, violently assaulted Gannet on at least one occasion. But far more to the point was the fact that he was under the deepest suspicion of having made a most determined attempt to kill Gannet by means of poison. Indeed, the word "suspicion" was an understatement. It was nearly a certainty. Even the cautious Thorndyke had made no secret of his views as to the identity of the poisoner.

It was at this stage of my reflections that I had what, I think,

Americans call a "hunch"—a brain wave, or inspiration. Boles had made at least one attempt to poison poor Gannet. We suspected more than one attempt, but of the one I had practically no doubt. Now one of the odd peculiarities of the criminal mind is its strong tendency to repetition. The coiner, on coming out of prison, promptly returns to the coining industry; the burglar, the forger, the pick-pocket, all tend to repeat their successes or even their failures. So, too, the poisoner, foiled at a first attempt, tries again, not only by the same methods, but nearly always makes use of the same poison.

Now Boles had been alone in the house with Gannet. He had thus had the opportunity, and it might be assumed that he had the means. Was it possible that he might have made yet another attempt and succeeded? It was true that the appearances rather suggested violence, and that this would be, from the murderer's point of view, preferable to the relatively slow method of poisoning. Nevertheless, a really massive dose of arsenic, if it could be administered, would be fairly rapid in its effects; and after all, in the assumed circumstances, the time factor would not be so very important.

But there was another consideration. Supposing Boles had managed to administer a big, lethal dose of arsenic, would any trace of the poison be detectible in the incinerated remains of the body? It seemed doubtful, though I had no experience by which to form an opinion. But it was certainly worth while to try; for if the result of the trial should be negative, no harm would have been done, whereas if the smallest trace of arsenic should be discoverable, demonstrable evidence of the highest importance would have been secured.

I have mentioned that, since the poisoning incident, I had taken various measures to provide against any similar case in the future, and among other precautions, I had furnished myself with a very complete apparatus for the detection of arsenic. It included the appliances for Marsh's test—not the simple and artless affair that is used for demonstration in chemistry classes, but a really up-to-date apparatus, capable of the greatest delicacy and precision. And as a further precaution, I had made several trial analyses with it to make sure that, should the occasion arise, I could rely on my competence to use it.

And now the occasion had arisen. It was not a very promising one, as the probability of a positive result seemed rather remote. But I entered into the investigation with an enthusiasm that accelerated considerably my disposal of the rest of my dinner, and as soon as I had swallowed the last mouthful, I rose and proceeded forthwith to the dispensary which served also as a laboratory. Here I produced from my pocket the match box containing the finger bone and the parcel of crushed fragments from the bin. The match box I opened and tenderly transferred the little bone to a corked glass tube with a plug of cotton wool above and below it, and put the tube away in a locked drawer. Then I opened the parcel of fragments and embarked on the investigation.

I began by examining one or two of the fragments with a low power of the microscope and thereby confirming beyond all doubt my assumption that they were incinerated bone; and having disposed of this essential preliminary, I fell to work on the chemical part of the investigation. With the details of these operations—which, to tell the truth, I found rather tedious and troublesome—I need not burden the reader. Roughly, and in bare outline, the procedure was as follows: First, I divided the heap of fragments into two parts, reserving one part for further treatment if necessary. The other part I dissolved in strong hydrochloric acid and distilled the mixture into a receiver containing a small quantity of distilled water; a slow and tedious business which tried my patience severely, and which was, after all, only a preliminary to the actual analysis. But at last, the fluid in the retort dwindled to a little half-dry residue, whereupon I removed the lamp and transferred my attention to the Marsh's apparatus. With this I made the usual preliminary trial to test the purity of the reagents and then set the lamp under the hard glass exit tube, watching it for several minutes after it had reached a bright red heat. As there was no sign of any darkening or deposit in the tube, I was satisfied that my chemicals were free from arsenic—as indeed I knew them to be from previous trials.

And now came the actual test. Detaching the receiver from the retort, I emptied its contents—the distilled fluid—into a well-washed measure glass and from this poured it slowly, almost drop by drop, into the thistle funnel of the flask in which the gas was generating. I had no expectation of any result—at least, so I persuaded myself. Nevertheless, as I poured in the "distillate" I watched the exit tube with almost tremulous eagerness. For it was my first real analysis; and after all the trouble that I had taken, a completely negative result would have seemed rather an anticlimax. Hence the yearning and half-expectant eye that turned ever towards the exit tube.

Nevertheless, the result, when it began to appear, fairly astonished me. It was beyond my wildest hopes. For even before I had finished pouring in the distillate, a dark ring appeared on the inside of the glass exit tube, just beyond the red hot portion, and grew from moment to moment in intensity and extent until a considerable area of the tube was covered with a typical "arsenic mirror." I sat down before the apparatus and watched it ecstatically, moved not only by the natural triumph of the tyro who has "brought it off" at the first trial, but by satisfaction at the thought that I had forged an instrument to put into the hands of avenging justice.

For now the cause of poor Gannet's death was established beyond cavil. My original surmise was proved to be correct. By some means, the murderer had contrived to administer a dose of arsenic so enormous as to produce an immediately fatal result. It must have been so. The quantity of the poison in the body must have been prodigious; for even after the considerable loss of arsenic in the kiln, there remained in the ashes a measurable amount, though how much I had not sufficient experience to judge.

I carried the analysis no farther. The customary procedure is to cut off the piece of tube containing the "mirror" of metallic arsenic and subject it to a further, confirmatory test. But this I considered unnecessary and, in fact, undesirable. Instead, I carefully detached the tube from the flask and, having wrapped it in several layers of paper, packed it in a cardboard postal tube and put it away with the finger bone in readiness for my interview with the police on the morrow.

CHAPTER 9

INSPECTOR BLANDY INVESTIGATES

On the following morning, as soon as I had disposed of the more urgent visits, I collected the proceeds of my investigations—the finger bone, the remainder of the bone fragments, and the glass tube with the arsenic mirror—and bustled off to the police station, all agog to spring my mine and set the machinery of the law in motion. My entry was acknowledged by the sergeant, who was perched at his desk, with an affable smile and the inquiry as to what he could do for me.

"I wanted rather particularly to see the Superintendent, if he could spare me a few minutes," I replied.

"I doubt whether he could," said the sergeant. "He's pretty busy just now. Couldn't I manage your business for you?"

"I think I had better see the Superintentendent," I answered. "The matter is one of some urgency and I don't know how far it might be considered confidential. I think I ought to make my communication to him, in the first place."

"Sounds mighty mysterious," said the sergeant, regarding me critically, "however, we'll see what he says. Go in, Dawson, and tell the Superintendent that Dr. Oldfield wants to speak to him and that he won't say what his business is."

On this, the constable proceeded to the door of the inner office, on which he knocked, and having been bidden in a loud, impatient voice to "come in," went in. After a brief delay, occupied probably by explanations, he reappeared, followed by the Superintendent, carrying in one hand a large note-book and in the other a pencil. His expression was not genial, but rather irritably interrogative, conveying the question, "Now, then. What about it?" And in effect, that was also conveyed by his rather short greeting.

"I should like to have a few words with you, Superintendent," I said, humbly.

"Well," he replied, "they will have to be very few. I am in the middle of a conference with an officer from Scotland Yard. What is the nature of your business?"

"I have come to inform you that I have reason to believe that a murder has been committed," I replied.

He brightened up considerably at this, but still he accepted the sensational statement with disappointing coolness.

"Do you mean that you think, or suspect, that a murder has been committed?" he asked in an obviously sceptical tone.

"It is more than that," I replied. "I am practically certain. I came to give you the facts that are known to me; and I have brought some things to show you which I think you will find pretty convincing."

He reflected for a moment; then, still a little irritably, he said:

"Very well. You had better come in and let us hear what you have to tell us."

With this, he indicated the open door, and when I had passed through, he followed me and closed it after us.

As I entered the office I was confronted by a gentleman who was seated at the table with a number of papers before him. A rather remarkable-looking gentleman, slightly bald, with a long, placid face and a still longer, and acutely pointed nose, and an expression in which concentrated benevolence beamed on an undeserving world. I don't know what his appearance suggested, but it certainly did *not* suggest a detective inspector of the Criminal Investigation Department. Yet that was his actual status, as appeared when the Superintendent introduced him to me—by the name of Blandy— adding:

"This is Dr. Oldfield who has come to give us some information about a case of suspected murder."

"How good of him!" exclaimed Inspector Blandy, rising to execute a deferential bow and beaming a benediction on me as he pressed my hand with affectionate warmth. "I am proud, sir, to make your acquaintance. I am always proud to make the acquaintance of members of your learned and invaluable profession."

The Superintendent smiled sourly and offered me a chair.

"I suppose, Inspector," said he, "we had better adjourn our other business and take the doctor's information?"

"Surely, surely," replied Blandy. "A capital crime must needs take precedence. And as the doctor's time is even more valuable than ours, we can rely on him to economize both."

Accordingly, the Superintendent, with a distinct return to the "what about it?" expression, directed me shortly to proceed, which I did; and bearing in mind the Inspector's polite hint, I plunged into the matter without preamble.

I need not record my statement in detail since it was but a repetition, suitably condensed, of the story that I have already told. I began with the disappearance of Peter Gannet, went on to my search of the house (to which the Superintendent listened with undissembled impatience) and then to my examination of the studio and my discoveries therein, producing the finger bone and the packet of fragments in corroboration. To the latter part of my statement both officers listened with evidently aroused interest, asking only such questions as were necessary to elucidate the narrative; as, for instance, how I came to know so much about the kiln and Gannet's method of work.

At the conclusion of this part of my statement, I paused while the two officers pored over the little bone in its glass container and the open package of white, coral-like fragments. Then I prepared to play my trump card. Taking off the paper wrapping from the cardboard case, I drew out from the latter the glass tube and laid it on the table.

The Superintendent glared at it suspiciously while the Inspector picked it up and regarded it with deep and benevolent interest.

"To my untutored eye," said he, "this dark ring seems to resemble an arsenic mirror."

"It is an arsenic mirror," said I.

"And what is its connection with these burnt remains?" the Superintendent demanded.

"That arsenic," I replied, impressively, "was extracted from a quantity of bone fragments similar to those that I have handed to you;" and with this, I proceeded to give them an account of my investigations with the Marsh's apparatus, to which the Superintendent listened with open incredulity.

"But," he demanded, when I had finished, "what on earth led you to test these ashes for arsenic? What suggested to you that there might be arsenic in them?"

Of course, I had expected this question, but yet, curiously enough, I was hardly ready for it. The secret of the poisoning had been communicated to Gannet, but otherwise I had, on Thorndyke's advice, kept my own counsel. But now this was impossible. There was nothing for it but to give the officers a full account of the poisoning affair, including the fact that the discovery had been made and confirmed by Dr. Thorndyke.

At the mention of my teacher's name, both men pricked up their ears, and the Superintendent commented:

"Then Dr. Thorndyke would be available as a witness."

"Yes," I replied, "I don't suppose he would have any objection to giving evidence on the matter."

"Objection be blowed!" snorted the Superintendent. "He wouldn't be asked. He could be subpoenaed as a common witness to the fact that this man, Gannet, was suffering from arsenic poisoning. However, before we begin to talk of evidence, we have got to be sure that there is something like a *prima facie* case. What do you think, Inspector?"

"I agree with you, Superintendent, as I always do," the Inspector replied. "We had better begin by checking the doctor's observations on the state of affairs in Gannet's studio. If we find the conditions to be as he has described them—which I have no doubt that we shall —and if we reach the same conclusions that he has reached, there will certainly be a case for investigation."

"Yes," the Superintendent agreed. "But our conclusions on the primary facts would have to be checked by suitable experts; and I suppose an independent analysis would be desirable. The doctor's evidence is good enough, but counsel likes to produce a specialist with a name and a reputation."

"Very true," said the Inspector. "But the analysis can wait. It is quite possible that the arsenic issue may never be raised. If we find clear evidence that a human body has been burned to ashes in that kiln, we shall have the very strongest presumptive evidence that a murder has been committed. The method used doesn't really concern us, and an attempt to prove that deceased was killed in some particular manner might only confuse and complicate the case."

"I was thinking," said the Superintendent, "of what the doctor has told us about the attempt to poison Gannet. The presence of arsenic in the bones might point to certain possible suspects, considered in connection with that previous attempt."

"Undoubtedly," agreed the Inspector, "if we could prove who administered that arsenic. But we can't. And if Gannet is dead, I don't see how we are going to, he being the only really competent witness. No, Superintendent. My feeling is that we shall be wise to ignore the arsenic, or at any rate keep it up our sleeves for the present.

But to come back to the immediate business, we want to see that studio, Doctor. How can it be managed without making a fuss?"

"Quite easily," I replied. "I have the keys, and I have Mrs. Gannet's permission to enter the house and to admit you, if you want to inspect the premises. I could hand you the keys if necessary, but I would much rather admit you myself."

"And very proper, too," said the Inspector. "Besides, we should want you to accompany us, as you know all about the studio and we don't. Now when could you manage the personally conducted exploration? The sooner the better, you know, as the matter is rather urgent."

"Well," I replied, "I have got several visits to make, and it is about time that I started to make them. It won't do for me to neglect my practice."

"Of course it won't," the Inspector agreed. "If duty calls you must away; and after all, a live patient is better than a dead potter. What time shall we say?"

"I think I shall be clear by four o'clock. Will that do?"

"It will do for me," replied the Inspector, glancing inquiringly at his brother officer; and as the latter agreed, it was arranged that they should call at my house at four o'clock and that we should proceed together to the studio.

As I rose to depart, my precious mirror tube—despised by Blandy but dear to me—caught my eye, and I proceeded unostentatiously to resume possession of it, remarking that I would take care of it in case it should ever be wanted. As neither officer made any objection, I returned it to its case; and the packet of bone ash having served its purpose, I closed it and slipped it into my pocket with the tube.

On leaving the police station, I glanced rapidly through the entries in my visiting list, and having planned out a convenient route, started on my round, endeavouring—none too successfully—to banish from my mind all thoughts of the Gannet mystery that I might better concentrate my attention on the clinical problems that my patients presented. But if I suffered some distraction from my proper business, there was compensation in the matter of speed, for I dispatched my round of visits in record time, and even after a leisurely lunch, found myself with half an hour to spare before my visitors were due to arrive. This half hour I spent with my hat on, pacing my consulting room in an agony of apprehension lest an inopportune professional call should hinder me from keeping my appointment. But fortunately no message came, and punctually at four o'clock Inspector Blandy was announced and conducted me to a large roomy car which was drawn up outside the house.

"The Superintendent couldn't come," Blandy explained, as he ushered me into the car. "But it doesn't matter. This is not a case for the local police. If there is anything in it, the C.I.D. will have to carry out the investigation."

"And what are you proposing to do now?" I asked.

"Just to check your report," he replied. "Personally, having seen you and noted your careful and exact methods, I accept it without any hesitation. But our people take nothing on hearsay if they can get observed facts, so I must be in a position to state those facts on my own knowledge and the evidence of my own eyesight; though as you and I know, my eyesight would have been of no use without yours."

I was beginning a modest disclaimer, suggesting that I was but an amateur investigator, but he would have none of it, exclaiming:

"My dear Doctor, you undervalue yourself. The whole discovery is your own. Consider now what would have happened if I had looked into the studio as you did. What should I have seen? Nothing, my dear sir, nothing. My mere bodily senses would have perceived the visible objects but their significance would never have dawned on me. Whereas you, bringing an expert eye to bear on them, instantly detected the signs of some abnormal happenings. By the way, I am assuming that I am going to have the benefit of your co-operation and advice on this occasion."

I replied that I should be very pleased to stay for a time and help him (being, in fact, on the very tip-toe of curiosity as to his proceedings), on which he thanked me warmly, and was still thanking me when the car drew up opposite the Gannets' front door. We both alighted, Blandy lifting out a large, canvas covered suit-case, which he set down on the pavement while he stood taking a general view of the premises.

"Does that gate belong to Gannet's house?" he asked, indicating the wide, double-leaved studio door.

"Yes," I replied. "It opens directly into the studio. Would you like to go in that way? I have the key of the wicket."

"Not this time," said he. "We had better go in through the house so that I may see the lie of the premises."

Accordingly, I let him in by the front door and conducted him through the hall, where he looked about him inquisitively, giving special attention to the hat-rack and stand. Then I opened the side door and escorted him out into the yard, where again he inspected the premises and especially the walls and houses which enclosed the space. Presently he espied the rubbish-bin, and walking over to it, lifted its lid and looked thoughtfully into its interior.

"Is this domestic refuse?" he inquired, "or does it belong to the studio?"

"I think it is a general dump," I replied, "but I know that Gannet used it for ashes and anything that the dustmen would take away."

"Then," said he, "we had better take it in with us and look over the contents before the dustman has his innings."

As I had by this time got the studio door unlocked, we took the bin by its two handles and carried it in. Then, at the Inspector's suggestion, I shut the door and locked it on the inside.

"Now, I suppose," said I, "you would like me to show you round the studio and explain the various appliances."

"Thank you, Doctor," he replied, "but I think we will postpone that, if it should be necessary after your singularly lucid description, and get on at once with the essential part of the inquiry."

"What is that?" I asked

"Our present purpose," he replied, beaming on me benevolently, "is to establish what the lawyers call the *corpus delicti*. To ascertain whether a crime has been committed, and if so, what sort of crime it is. We begin by finding out what those bone fragments really amount to. I have brought a small sieve with me, but probably there is a better one here; preferably a fairly fine one."

"There is a set of sieves for sifting grog and other powders," said I. "The coarser ones are of wire gauze and the finer of bolting cloth, so you can take your choice. The number of meshes to the linear inch is marked on the rims."

I took him across to the place where the sieves were stacked, and, when he had looked through the collection, he selected the finest of the wire sieves, which had twenty meshes to the inch. Then I found him a scoop, and when he had tipped the contents of one grog bin into another and placed the empty bin by the side of that containing the bone-ash, he spread out on the bench a sheet of white paper from his case, laid the sieve on the empty bin and fell to work.

For a time, the proceedings were quite uneventful, as the upper part of the bin was occupied by the finely-ground ash, and when a scoopful of this was thrown on to the sieve, it sank through at once. But presently, as the deeper layers were reached, larger fragments, recognizable as pieces of burnt bone, began to appear on the wire-gauze surface, and these, when he had tapped the sieve and shaken all the fine dust through, the Inspector carefully tipped out on to the sheet of paper. Soon, he had worked his way down completely past the deposit of fine powder, and now each scoopful consisted almost entirely of bone fragments; and as these lay on the gauze surface, Blandy bent over them, scrutinizing them with amiable intentness and shaking the sieve gently to spread them out more evenly.

"There can be no doubt," said he, as he ran his eye over a fresh scoopful thus spread out, "that these are fragments of bone; but it may be difficult to prove that they are human bones. I wish our unknown friend hadn't broken them up quite so small."

"You have the finger bone," I reminded him. "There's no doubt that that is human."

"Well," he agreed, "if you are prepared to swear positively that it is a human bone, that will establish a strong probability that the rest of the fragments are human. But we want proof if we can get it. In a capital case, the court isn't taking anything for granted."

Here he stooped closer over the sieve with his eyes riveted on one spot. Then very delicately with finger and thumb, he picked out a small object, and laying it on the palm of his other hand, held it out to me with a smile of concentrated benevolence. I took it from his palm, and placing it on my own, examined it closely, first with the naked eye and then with my pocket lens.

"And what is the diagnosis?" he asked, as I returned it to him.

"It is a portion of a porcelain tooth," I replied. "A front tooth, I should say, but it is such a small piece that it is impossible to be sure. But it is certainly part of a porcelain tooth."

"Ha!" said he, "there is the advantage of expert advice and co-operation. It is pronounced authoritatively to be certainly a porcelain tooth. But as the lower animals do not, to the best of my knowledge and belief, ever wear porcelain teeth, we have corroborative evidence that these remains are human. That is a great step forward. But how far does it carry us? Can you suggest any particular application of the fact?"

"I can," said I. "It is known to me that Peter Gannet had a

nearly complete upper dental plate. I saw it in a bowl when he was ill."

"Excellent!" the Inspector exclaimed. "Peter Gannet wore porcelain teeth, and here is part of a porcelain tooth. The evidence grows. But if he wore a dental plate, he must have had a dentist. I suppose you cannot give that dentist a name?"

"It happens that I can. He is a Mr. Hawley of Wigmore Street!"

"Really, now," exclaimed the Inspector, "you are positively spoiling me. You leave me nothing to do. I have only to ask for information and it is instantly supplied."

He laid the fragment of tooth tenderly on the corner of the sheet of paper and made an entry in his note-book of the dentist's address. Then, having tipped the contents of the sieve on to the paper, he brought up another scoopful of bone fragments and shook it out on the gauze surface.

I need not follow the proceedings in detail. Gradually we worked our way through the entire contents of the bone-ash-bin, finishing up by holding the bin itself upside down over the sieve and shaking out the last grains. The net result was a considerable heap of bone fragments on the sheet of paper and no less than four other pieces of porcelain. As to the former, they were for the most part, mere crumbs of incinerated bone with just a sprinkling of lumps large enough to have some recognizable character. But the fragments of porcelain were more informative, for close examination and a few tentative trials at fitting them together left little doubt that they were all parts of the same tooth.

"But we won't leave it at that," said Blandy, as he dropped them one by one into a glass tube that he produced from his case. "We've got a man at Headquarters who is an expert at mending up broken articles. He'll be able to cement these pieces together so that the joins will hardly be visible. Then I'll take the tooth along to Mr. Hawley and see what he has to say to it."

He slipped the tube into his pocket and then, having produced from his case a large linen bag, shoveled the bone fragments into it, tied up its mouth and stowed it away in the case.

"This stuff," he remarked, "will have to be produced at the inquest, if we can identify it definitely enough to make an inquest possible. But I shall go over it again, a teaspoonful at a time, to make sure that we haven't missed anything; and then it will be passed to the Home Office experts. If they decide that the remains are certainly human remains, we shall notify the coroner."

While he was speaking his eyes turned from one object to another, taking in all the various fittings of the studio, and finally his glance lighted on Boles's cupboard and there remained fixed.

"Do you happen to know what is in that cupboard?" he asked.

"I know that it belongs to Mr. Boles," I replied, "and I think he uses it to keep his materials in."

"What are his materials?" the Inspector asked.

"Principally gold and silver, especially gold. But he keeps some of his enamel material there and the copper plates for his plaques."

The Inspector walked over to the cupboard and examined the keyhole narrowly.

"It isn't much of a lock," he remarked, "for a repository of precious metals. Looks like a common ward lock that almost any key would open. I think you said that Mr. Boles is not available at the moment?"

"I understand from Mrs. Gannet that he has disappeared from his flat and that no one knows where he is,"

"Pity," said Blandy. "I hate the idea of opening that cupboard in his absence, but we ought to know what is in it. And, as I have a search warrant, it is my duty to search. H'm! I happen to have one or two keys in my case. Perhaps one of them might fit this very simple lock."

He opened his case and produced from it a bunch of keys, and very odd-looking keys they were; so much so that I ventured to inquire:

"Are those what are known as skeleton keys?"

He beamed on me with a slightly deprecating expression.

"The word 'skeleton,'" said he, "as applied to keys, has disagreeable associations. I would rather call these simplified keys; just ordinary ward keys without wards. You will see how they act."

He illustrated their function by trying them one after another on the keyhole. At the third trial the key entered the hole, whereupon he gave it a turn and the door came open.

"There, you see," said he. "We break nothing, and when we go away we leave the cupboard locked as we found it."

The opened door revealed one or two shelves on which were glass pots of the powdered enamels, an agate mortar and a few small tools. Below the shelves were several small but deep drawers. The

Inspector pulled out one of these and looked inquisitively into it as he weighed it critically in his hand.

"Queer-looking stuff, this, Doctor," said he, "and just feel the weight of it. All these lumps of gold in a practically unlocked cupboard. Are these the things that Mr. Boles makes?"

As he spoke he turned the drawer upside down on the paper that still covered the bench and pointed contemptuously to the heap of pendants, rings and brooches that dropped out of it.

"Did you ever see such stuff?" he exclaimed. "Jewelry, indeed! Why, it might have been made by a plumber's apprentice. And look at the quantity of metal in it. Look at that ring. There's enough gold in it to make a bracelet. This stuff reminds me of the jewelry that the savages produce, only it isn't nearly so well made. I wonder who buys it. Do you happen to know?"

"I have heard," I replied, "that Mr. Boles exhibits it at some of the private galleries, and I suppose some of it gets sold. It must, you know, or he wouldn't go on making it."

Inspector Blandy regarded me with a rather curious, cryptic smile, but he made no rejoinder. He simply shot "the stuff" back into the drawer, replaced the latter, and drew out the next.

The contents of this seemed to interest him profoundly for he looked into the drawer with an expression of amiable satisfaction and seemed to meditate on what he saw as if it conveyed some new idea to him. At length he tipped the contents out on to the paper and smilingly invited me to make any observations that occurred to me. I looked at the miscellaneous heap of rings, brooches, lockets and other trinkets and noted that they seemed to resemble the ordinary jewelry that one sees in shop windows excepting that the stones were missing.

"I don't think Mr. Boles made any of these," said I.

"I am quite sure he didn't," said Blandy, "but I think he took the stones out. But what do you make of this collection?"

"I should guess," I replied, "that it is old jewelry that he bought cheap to melt down for his own work."

"Yes," agreed Blandy, "he bought it to melt down and work up again. But he didn't buy it cheap if he bought from the trade. You can't buy gold cheap in the open market. Gold is gold, whether old or new. It has its standard price per ounce and you can't get it any cheaper; and you can always sell it at that price. I am speaking of the open market."

Once more he regarded me with that curious, inscrutable smile, and then, sweeping the jewelry back into its drawer, he passed on to the next.

This drawer contained raw material proper; little ingots of gold, buttons from cupels or crucibles, and a few pieces of thin gold plate. It did not appear to me to present any features of interest, but evidently Blandy thought otherwise, for he peered into the drawer with a queer, benevolent smile for quite a considerable time. And he did not tip out its contents on to the bench. Instead, he took a pair of narrow-nosed pliers from one of the shelves and with these he delicately picked out the pieces of gold plate, and having examined them on both sides, laid them carefully on the paper.

"You seem to be greatly interested in those bits of plate," I remarked.

"I am," he replied. "There are two points of interest in them. First there is the fact that they are pieces of gold plate such as are supplied to the trade by bullion dealers. That goes to show that he bought some of his gold from the dealers in the regular way. He didn't get it all second hand. The other point is this."

He picked up one of the pieces of plate with the pliers and exhibited it to me, and I then observed that its polished surface was marked with the impression of a slightly greasy finger.

"You mean that finger-print?" I suggested.

"Thumb-print," he corrected, "apparently a left thumb; and on the other side, the print of a forefinger. Both beautifully clear and distinct, as they usually are on polished metal."

"Yes," said I, "they are clear enough. But what about it? They are Mr. Boles's finger-prints. But this is Mr. Boles's cupboard. We knew that he had used it and that he had frequented this studio. I don't see that the finger-prints tell you anything that you didn't know."

The Inspector smiled at me, indulgently. "It is remarkable," said he, "how the scientific mind instantly seizes the essentials. But there is a little point that I think you have missed. We find that Mr. Boles is a purchaser of second-hand jewelry. Now, in the Finger-print Department we have records of quite a number of gentlemen who are purchasers of second-hand jewelry. Of course, it is quite incredible that Mr. Boles's finger-prints should be among them. But the scientific mind will realize that proof is better than belief. The Finger-print experts will be able to supply the proof."

The hint thus delicately expressed conveyed a new idea to me and caused me to look with rather different eyes on the contents of the next, and last drawer. These consisted of three small cardboard boxes, which, being opened, were found to contain unmounted stones. One was nearly half-filled with the less precious kinds; moonstones, turquoises, garnets, agates, carnelians and the like. The second held a smaller number of definitely precious stones such as rubies, sapphires and emeralds, while the third contained only diamonds, mostly quite small. The Inspector's comments expressed only the thought which had instantly occurred to me.

"These stones," said he, "must have been picked out of the second-hand stuff. I shouldn't think he ever buys any stones from the dealers, for only two of his pieces are set with gems, and those only with moonstone and carnelian. He doesn't seem to use stones often; too much trouble; easier to stick on a blob of enamel. So he must sell them. I wonder who buys them from him."

I could offer no suggestion on this point, and the Inspector did not pursue the subject. Apparently the examination was finished, for he began to pack up the various objects that we had found in the drawers, bestowing especial care on the pieces of gold plate.

"As Mr. Boles seems to have disappeared," said he, "I shall take these goods into my custody. They are too valuable to leave in an unoccupied studio. And I must take temporary possession of these premises, as we may have to make some further investigations. We haven't examined the dust-bin yet, and it is too late to do it now. In fact, it is time to go. And what about the key, Doctor? I shall seal these doors before I leave—the wicket on the inside and the yard door on the outside— and the place will have to be watched. I should take it as a favour if you would let me have the key so that I need not trouble Mrs. Gannet. You won't be using it yourself."

As I saw that he meant to have it, and as it was of no further use to me, I handed it to him, together with the spare key of the wicket, on which he thanked me profusely and made ready to depart.

"Before we go," said he, "I will just make a note of Mrs. Gannet's present address in case we have to communicate with her, and you may as well give me Mr. Boles's, too. We shall have to get into touch with him, if possible."

I gave him both addresses, rather reluctantly as to the former, for I suspected that Mrs. Gannet was going to suffer some shocks. But there was no help for it. The police would have to communicate with her if only to acquaint her with the fact of her husband's death. But I was sorry for her, little as I liked her and little as I approved of her relations with Boles.

When the Inspector had locked, bolted and sealed the wicket, he took up his case and we went into the yard, where he locked the door with the key that I had left in it, pocketed the latter and sealed the door. Then we went out to the car, and, when the driver had put away his book and his cigarette, we started homeward and arrived at my premises just in time for my evening consultations.

CHAPTER 10

INSPECTOR BLANDY IS INQUISITIVE

My forebodings concerning Mrs. Gannet were speedily and abundantly justified. On the morning of the third day after the search of the studio, an urgent note from Miss Hughes, delivered by hand, informed me that her guest had sustained a severe shock and was in a state of complete nervous prostration. She had expressed a wish to see me and Miss Hughes hoped that I would call as soon as possible.

As the interview promised to be a somewhat lengthy one, I decided to dispose of the other patients on my modest visiting list and leave myself ample time for a leisurely talk, apart from the professional consultation. As a result, it was well past noon when I rang the bell at the house in Mornington Crescent. The door was opened by Miss Hughes herself, from whom I received forthwith the first instalment of the news.

"She is in an awful state, poor thing," said Miss Hughes. "Naturally, she was a good deal upset by her husband's extraordinary disappearance. But yesterday a gentleman called to see her—a police officer he turned out to be, though you'd never have suspected it to look at him. I don't know what he told her—it seems that she was sworn to secrecy—but he stayed a long time, and when he had gone and I went into the sitting room, I found her lying on the sofa in a state of collapse. But I mustn't keep you here talking. I made her stay in bed until you'd seen her, so I will take you up to her room."

Miss Hughes had not overstated the case. I should hardly have recognized the haggard, white-faced woman in the bed as the sprightly lady whom I had known. As I looked at her pallid, frightened face, turned so appealingly to me, all my distaste of her—it was hardly dislike—melted away in natural compassion for her obvious misery.

"Have you heard of the awful thing that has happened, Doctor?" she whispered when Miss Hughes had gone, discreetly shutting the door after her. "I mean what the police found in the studio."

"Yes, I know about that," I replied, not a little relieved to find that my name had not been mentioned in connection with the discovery. "I suppose that the officer who called on you was Inspector Blandy?"

"Yes, that was the name, and I must say that he was most polite and sympathetic. He broke the horrible news as gently as he could and told me how sorry he was to be the bearer of such bad tidings; and he did seem to be genuinely sorry for me. I only wished he would have left it at that. But he didn't. He stayed ever so long telling me over and over again how sincerely he sympathized with me, and then asking questions; dozens of questions he asked until I got quite hysterical. I think he might have given me a day or two to recover a little before putting me through such a catechism."

"It does seem rather inconsiderate," said I, "but you must make allowances. The police have to act promptly and they naturally want to get at the facts as quickly as possible."

"Yes. That is the excuse he made for asking so many questions. But it was an awful ordeal. And although he was so polite and sympathetic, I couldn't help feeling that he suspected me of knowing more about the affair than I admitted. Of course he didn't say anything to that effect."

"I think that must have been your imagination," said I. "He couldn't have suspected you of any knowledge of the—er—the tragedy, seeing that you were away from home when it happened."

"Perhaps not," said she. "Still, he questioned me particularly about my movements while I was away and wanted all the dates, which, of course, I couldn't remember off-hand. And then he asked a lot of questions about Mr. Boles, particularly as to where he was on certain dates; and somehow he gave the impression that he knew a good deal about him."

"What sort of questions did he put about Mr. Boles?" I asked with some curiosity, recalling Blandy's cryptic reference to the finger-print files at Scotland Yard.

"It began with his asking me whether the two men, Peter and Fred, were usually on good terms. Well, as you know, Doctor, they were not. Then he asked me if they had always been on bad terms; and when I told him that they used to be quite good friends, he wanted to know exactly when the change in their relationship occurred and whether I could account for it in any way. I told him, quite truthfully, that I could not; and as to the time when they first fell out, I could only say that it was some time in the latter part of last year. Then he began to question me about Mr. Boles's movements; where he was on this and that date, and, of course, I couldn't remember, if I had ever known. But his last question about dates I was able to answer. He asked me to try to remember where Mr. Boles was on the 19th of last September. I thought about it a little and then I remembered, because Peter had gone to spend a long week-end with him and I had taken the opportunity to make a visit to Eastbourne. As I was at Eastbourne on the 19th of September, I knew that Peter and Mr. Boles must have been at Newingstead on that date."

"Newingstead!" I exclaimed, and then stopped short.

"Yes," said she, looking at me in surprise. "Do you know the place?"

"I know it slightly," I replied, drawing in my horns rather suddenly as the finger-print files came once more into my mind. "I happen to know a doctor who is in practice there."

"Well, Mr. Blandy seemed to be very much interested in Mr. Boles's visit to Newingstead and particularly with the fact that Peter was there with him on that day; and he pressed me to try to remember whether that date seemed to coincide with the change in their feelings to each other. It was an extraordinary question. I can't imagine what could have put the idea into his head. But when I came to think about it, I found that he was right, for I remember quite clearly that when I came back from Eastbourne I saw at once that there was something wrong. They weren't a bit the same. All the old friendliness seemed to have vanished and they were ready to quarrel on the slightest provocation. And they did quarrel dreadfully. I was terrified, for they were both strong men and both inclined to be violent."

"Did you ever get any inkling as to what it was that had set them against each other?"

"No. I suspected that something had happened when they were away together, but I could never find out what it was. I spoke to them both and asked them what was the matter, but I couldn't get anything out of either of them. They simply said that there was nothing the matter; that it was all my imagination. But I knew that it wasn't, and I was in a constant state of terror as to what might happen."

"So I suppose," said I, "that the—er—the murder has not come as a complete surprise?"

"Oh, don't call it a murder!" she protested. "It couldn't have been that. It must have been some sort of accident. When two strong and violent men start fighting, you never know how it will end. I am sure it must have been an accident—that is, supposing that it was Mr. Boles who killed Peter. We don't know that it was. It's only a guess."

I thought that it was a pretty safe guess but I did not say so. My immediate concern was with the future. For Mrs. Gannet was my patient and I chose to regard her as my friend. She had been subjected to an intolerable strain, and I suspected that there was worse to come. The question was, what was to be done about it?

"Did the Inspector suggest that he would require any further information from you?" I asked.

"Yes. He said that he would want me to come to his office at Scotland Yard one day pretty soon to make a statement and sign it. That will be an awful ordeal. It makes me sick with terror to think of it."

"I don't see why it should," said I. "You are not in any way responsible for what has happened,"

"You know that I am not," said she, "but the police don't; and I am absolutely terrified of Mr. Blandy. He is a most extraordinary man. He is so polite and sympathetic and yet so keen and searching and he asks such unexpected questions and seems to have such uncanny knowledge of our affairs. And as I told you, I am sure he suspects that I had something to do with what has happened."

"I suppose he didn't seem to know anything about that mysterious affair of the arsenic poisoning?" I suggested.

"No," she replied, "but I am certain that he will worm it out of me when he has me in his office; and then he will think that it was I who put the poison into poor Peter's food."

At this point she broke down and burst into tears, sobbing hysterically and mingling incoherent apologies with her sobs. I tried to comfort her as well as I could, assuring her—with perfect sincerity—of my deep sympathy. For I realized that her fears were by no means unfounded. She probably had more secrets than I knew; and once within the dreaded office in the presence of a committee of detective officers, taking down in writing every word that she uttered, she might easily commit herself to some highly incriminating statements.

"It is a great comfort to me, Doctor," said she, struggling to control her emotion, "to be able to tell you all my troubles. You are the only friend that I have; the only friend, I mean, that I can look to for advice and help."

It wrung my heart to think of this poor, lonely woman in her trouble and bereavement, encompassed by perils at which I could only guess, facing those perils, friendless, alone and unprotected save by me —and who was I that I could give her any effective support? As I met the look of appeal that she cast on me, so pathetic and so confiding, it was borne in on me that she needed some more efficient adviser and that the need was urgent and ought to be met without delay.

"I am very willing," said I, "to help you, but I am not very competent. The advice that you want is legal, not medical. You ought to have a lawyer to protect your interests and to advise you."

"I suppose I ought," she agreed, "but I don't know any lawyers; and I trust in you because you know all about my affairs and because you have been such a kind friend. But I will do whatever you advise. Perhaps you know a lawyer whom you could recommend."

"The only lawyer whom I know is Dr. Thorndyke," I replied.

"Is he a lawyer?" she exclaimed in surprise. "I thought he was a doctor."

"He is both," I explained, "and what is more to the point, he is a criminal lawyer who knows all the ropes. He will understand your difficulties and also those of the police. Would you like me to see him and ask him to advise us?"

"I should be most grateful if you would," she replied, earnestly. "And you may take it that I agree to any arrangements that you may make with him. But," she added, "you will remember that my means are rather small."

I brushed this proviso aside in view of Thorndyke's known indifference to merely financial considerations and the fact that my own means admitted of my giving material assistance if necessary. So it was agreed that I should seek Thorndyke's advice forthwith and that whatever he might advise should be done.

"That will be a great relief," said she. "I shall have somebody to think for me, and that will leave me free to think about all that has to be done. There will be quite a lot of things to attend to. I can't stay here for ever, though dear Miss Hughes protests that she loves having me. And then there are the things at the gallery. They will have to be removed when the exhibition closes. And there are some pieces on loan at another place—but there is no hurry about them."

"What exhibition are you referring to?" I asked.

"The show at the Lyntondale Gallery in Bond Street. It is a mixed exhibition and some of Peter's work is being shown and a few pieces of Mr. Boles's. Whatever is left unsold will have to be fetched away at once to make room for the next show."

"And the other exhibition?" I asked, partly from curiosity and partly to keep her attention diverted from her troubles.

"That is a sort of small museum and art gallery at Haxton. They show loan collections there for the purpose of educating the taste of the people, and Peter has lent them some of his pottery on two or three occasions. This time he sent only a small collection—half a dozen bowls and jars and the stoneware figure that used to be on his bedroom mantelpiece. I daresay you remember it."

"I remember it very well," said I. "It was a figure of a monkey."

"Yes, that was what he called it, though it didn't look to me very much like a monkey. But then I don't understand much about art. At any rate, he sent it, and as he set a good deal of value on it, I took it myself and delivered it to the director of the museum."

As we talked, principally on topics not directly connected with the tragedy, her agitation subsided by degrees until, by the time when my visit had to end, she had become quite calm and composed.

"Now don't forget," said I, as I shook her hand at parting, "that you have nothing further to fear from Inspector Blandy. You are going to have a legal adviser, and he won't let anybody put undue pressure on you."

Her gratitude was quite embarrassing, and as she showed signs of a slight recrudescence of emotion, I withdrew my hand (which she was pressing fervently) at the first opportunity and bustled out of the room.

On my way home, I considered my next move. Obviously, no time ought to be lost in making the necessary arrangements. But, although I had the afternoon free, Thorndyke probably had not. He was a busy man and it would be futile for me to make a casual call on the chance of finding him at home and disengaged. Accordingly, as soon as I had let myself in and ascertained that there were no further engagements, I rang him up on the telephone to inquire when I could have a few words with him. In reply, a voice, apparently appertaining to a person named Polton, informed me that the doctor was out; that he would be in at three-thirty and that he had an engagement elsewhere at four-fifteen. Thereupon I made an appointment to call at three-thirty, and having given my name, rang off, and proceeded without delay to dispatch my immediate business, including the dispensing of medicine, the writing up of the Day Book and the wash and brush up preliminary to lunch.

As I had no clear idea of the geography of the Temple, I took the precaution of arriving at the main gate well in advance of the appointed time; with the result that having easily located King's Bench Walk, I found myself opposite the handsome brick portico of Number 5A at the very moment when a particularly soft-toned bell ventured most politely to suggest that it was a quarter past three.

There was, therefore, no need to hurry. I whiled away a few minutes inspecting the portico and surveying the pleasant surroundings of the dignified old houses—doubtless still more pleasant before the fine, spacious square had become converted into a parking lot—then I entered and took my leisurely way up the stairs to the first floor landing, where I found myself confronted by a grim-looking, iron bound door, above which was painted the name "Dr. Thorndyke." I was about to press the electric bell at the side of the door when I perceived, descending the stairs from an upper floor, a gentleman who appeared to belong to the premises; a small gentleman of a sedate and even clerical aspect, but very lively and alert.

"Have I the honour, sir, of addressing Dr. Oldfield?" he inquired, suavely.

I replied that I was, in fact, Dr. Oldfield. "But," I added, "I think I am a little before my time."

Thereupon, like Touchstone, he "drew a dial from his poke," and regarding it thoughtfully (but by no means "with a lacklustre eye"), announced that it was now twenty-four minutes and fifteen seconds past three. While he was making his inspection I looked at the watch, which was a rather large silver timepiece with an audible and very deliberate tick, and as he was putting it away, I ventured to remark that it did not appear to be quite an ordinary watch.

"It is not, sir," he replied, hauling it out again and gazing at it fondly. "It is an eight-day pocket chronometer; a most admirable timepiece, sir, with the full chronometer movement and even a helical balance spring."

Here he opened the case and then, in some miraculous way, turned the whole thing inside out, exhibiting the large, heavy balance and an unusual-looking balance spring which I accepted as helical.

"You can't easily see the spring detent," said he, "but you can hear it; and you will notice that it beats half-seconds."

He held the watch up towards my ear and I was able to distinguish the peculiar sound of the escapement. But at this moment he also assumed a listening attitude; but he was not listening to the watch, for after a few moments of concentrated attention, he remarked, as he closed and put away the chronometer:

"You are not much too early, sir. I think I hear the doctor coming along Crown Office Row and Dr. Jervis with him."

I listened attentively and was just able to make out the faint sound of quick footsteps which seemed to be approaching; but I had not my small friend's diagnostic powers, which, however, were demonstrated when the footsteps passed in at the entry, ascended the stairs and materialized into bodily forms of Thorndyke and Jervis. Both men looked at me a little curiously but any questions were forestalled by my new acquaintance.

"Dr. Oldfield, sir, made an appointment by telephone to see you at half-past three. I told him of your engagement at four-fifteen."

"Thank you, Polton," said Thorndyke. "So now, Oldfield, as you know the position, let us go in and make the best use of the available half-hour; that is, if this is anything more than a friendly call."

"It is considerably more," said I, as Mr. Polton opened the two doors and ushered us into a large room. "I have come on quite urgent business, but I think we can dispatch it easily in half an hour."

Here, Mr. Polton, after an interrogative glance at Thorndyke, took himself off, closing after him both the inner and outer doors.

"Now, Oldfield," said Jervis, setting out three chairs in a triangle, "sit down and let the bulgine run."

Thereupon we all took our seats facing one another and I proceeded, without preamble, to give a highly-condensed account of the events connected with Gannet's disappearance with a less-condensed statement of Mrs. Gannet's position in relation to them. To this account Thorndyke listened with close attention, but quite impassively and without question or comment. Not so Jervis. He did, indeed, abstain from interruptions; but he followed my recital with devouring interest, and I had hardly finished when he burst out:

"But, my good Oldfield, this is a first-class murder mystery. It is a sin to boil it down into a mere abstract. I want details, and more details, and, in short—or rather, in long—the whole story."

"I am with you, Jervis," said Thorndyke. "We must get Oldfield to tell us the story in extenso. But not now. We have an immediate and rather urgent problem to solve; how to protect Mrs. Gannet."

"Does she need protecting?" demanded Jervis. "The English police are not in the habit of employing 'third degree' methods."

"True," Thorndyke agreed. "The English police have usually the desire and the intention to deal fairly with persons who have to be interrogated. But an over-zealous officer may easily be tempted to press his examination—in the interests of justice, as he thinks—beyond the limits of what is strictly admissible. We must remember that, under our system of police procedure in the matter of interrogation, the various restrictions tend to weight the dice rather against the police and in favour of the accused person."

"But Mrs. Gannet is not an accused person," I protested.

"No," Thorndyke agreed. "But she may become one, particularly if she should make any indiscreet admissions. That is what we have to guard against. We don't know what the views of the police are, but one notes that our rather foxy friend, Blandy, was not disposed to be over-scrupulous. To announce to a woman that her husband has been murdered and his body burned to ashes, and then, while she is still dazed by the shock, to subject her to a searching interrogation, does not impress one as a highly considerate proceeding. I think her fear of Blandy is justified. No further interrogation ought to take place excepting in the presence of her legal adviser."

"She isn't legally bound to submit to any interrogation until she is summoned as a witness," Jervis suggested.

"In practice, she is," said Thorndyke. "It would be highly improper for her to withhold from the police any assistance that she could give them. And it would be extremely impolitic, as it would suggest that she had something serious to conceal. But it would be perfectly proper for her to insist that her legal adviser should accompany her and be present at the interrogation. And that is what will have to be done. She will have to be legally represented. But by whom? Can you make any suggestion, Jervis? It is a solicitor's job."

"What about the costs?" asked Jervis. "Is the lady pretty well off?"

"We can waive that question," said I. "The costs will be met. I will make myself responsible for that."

"I see," said Jervis. "Your sympathy takes a practical form. Well, if you are going to back the bill, we must see that it doesn't get too obese. A swagger solicitor wouldn't do; besides, he would be too busy to attend in person. But we should want a good man. Preferably a young man with a rather small practice. Yes, I think I know the very man. What do you say, Thorndyke, to young Linnell? He was Marchmont's managing clerk, but he has gone into practice on his own account and he has distinct leanings towards criminal work."

"I remember him," said Thorndyke. "A very promising young man. Could you get into touch with him?"

"I will see him today before he leaves his office and I think there is no doubt that he will undertake the case gladly. At any rate, Oldfield, you can take it that the matter is in our hands and that the lady will be fully protected, even if I have to accompany her to Scotland Yard myself. But you must play your hand, too. You are her doctor, and it is for you to see that she is not subjected to any strain that she is not fit to bear. A suitable medical certificate will put the stopper even on Blandy."

As Jervis ceased speaking, the soft-voiced bell of the unseen clock, having gently chimed the quarters, now struck (if one may use so violent an expression) the hour of four. I rose from my chair, and, having thanked both my friends profusely for their help, held out my hand.

"One moment, Oldfield," said Thorndyke. "You have tantalized us with a bare précis of the astonishing story that you have to tell. But we want the unabridged edition. When are we to have it? We realize that you are rather tied to your practice. But perhaps we could look in on you when you have some time to spare, say, one evening after dinner. How would that do?"

"Why after dinner?" I demanded. "Why not come and dine with me and do the pow-wow after?"

"That would be very pleasant," said Thorndyke. "Don't you agree, Jervis?"

Jervis agreed emphatically; and as it appeared that both my friends were free that very evening, it was settled that we should meet again at Osnaburgh Street and discuss the Gannet case at length.

"And remember," said I, pausing in the doorway, "that consultation hours are usually more or less blank, so you can come as early as you like."

With this parting admonition, I shut the door after me and went on my way.

CHAPTER ▌▌

MR. BUNDERBY EXPOUNDS

As I emerged from the Temple gateway into Fleet Street I was confronted by a stationary omnibus, held up temporarily by a block in the traffic; and glancing at it casually, my eye caught, among the names on its rear board, those of Piccadilly and Bond Street. The latter instantly associated itself with the gallery of which Mrs. Gannet had spoken that morning, and the effect of the association was to cause me to jump on to the omnibus just as it started to move. I had nearly two hours to spare and in that time could easily inspect the exhibition of Gannet's work.

I was really quite curious about this show, for Gannet's productions had always been somewhat of a mystery to me. They were so amazingly crude and so deficient, as I thought, in any kind of ceramic quality. And yet I felt there must be something more in them than I had been able to discover. There must be some deficiency in my own powers of perception and appreciation; for it was a fact that they had not only been publicly exhibited but actually sold, and sold at quite impressive prices; and one felt that the people who paid those prices must surely know what they were about. At any rate, I should now see the pottery in its appropriate setting and perhaps hear some comments from those who were better able than I to form a judgment.

I had no difficulty in finding the Lyntondale Gallery for a flag bearing its name hung out boldly from a first floor window; and when I had paid my shilling entrance fee and a further shilling for a catalogue, I passed in through the turnstile and was straightway spirited aloft in an elevator.

On entering the principal room of the gallery I was aware of a knot of people—about a dozen—gathered before a large glass case and appearing to surround a stout, truculent-looking gentleman with a fine, rich complexion and a mop of white hair which stood

up like the crest of a cockatoo. But my attention was more particularly attracted by another gentleman, who stood apart from the knot
of visitors and appeared to be either the proprietor of the gallery or
an attendant. What drew my attention to him was an indefinite
something in his appearance that seemed familiar. I felt that I had
seen him somewhere before. But I could not place him; and while I
was trying to remember where I might have seen him, he caught
my eye and approached with a deferential smile.

"You have arrived quite opportunely, sir," said he. "Mr. Bunderby,
the eminent art critic, is just about to give us a little talk on the
subject of Peter Gannet's very remarkable pottery. It will be worth
your while to hear it. Mr. Bunderby's talks are always most illuminating."

I thanked him warmly for the information, for an illuminating
talk on this subject by a recognized authority was precisely what I
wanted to hear; and as the cockatoo gentleman—whom I diagnosed
as Mr. Bunderby—had just opened a show case and transferred one
of the pieces to a small revolving stand, like a modeler's turntable, I
joined the group that surrounded him and prepared to "lend him
my ears."

The piece that he had placed on the stand was one of Gannet's
roughest; an uncouth vessel, in appearance something between a
bird's nest and a flower pot. I noticed that the visitors stared at it
in obvious bewilderment and Mr. Bunderby watched their expressions
with a satisfied smile.

"Before speaking to you," said he, "of these remarkable works,
I must say just a few words about their creator. Peter Gannet is a
unique artist. Whereas the potters of the past have striven after
more and yet more sophistication, Gannet has perceived the great
truth that pottery should be simple and elemental, and with wonderful courage and insight, he has set himself to retrace the path along
which mankind has strayed, back to that fountainhead of culture,
the New Stone Age. He has cast aside the potter's wheel and all
other mechanical aids, and relies solely on that incomparable instrument, the skilled hand of the artist.

"So in these works, you must not look for mechanical accuracy
or surface finish. Gannet is, first and foremost, a great stylist, who
subordinates everything to the passionate pursuit of essential form.
So much for the man. And now we will turn to the pottery."

He paused a few moments and stood with half-closed eyes and

his head on one side, contemplating the bowl on the stand. Then he resumed his discourse.

"I begin," said he, "by showing you this noble and impressive work because it is typical of the great artist by whose genius it was created. It presents in a nutshell" (he might have said a coconut shell) "the aims, the ambitions and the inmost thoughts and emotions of its maker. Looking at it, we realize with respectful admiration the wonderful power of analysis, the sensibility—at once subtle and intense—that made its conception possible; and we can trace the deep thought, the profound research—the untiring search for the essentials of abstract form."

Here a lady, who spoke with a slight American intonation, ventured to remark that she didn't quite understand this piece. Mr. Bunderby fixed her with his truculent blue eye and replied, impressively:

"You don't understand it! But of course you don't. And you shouldn't try to. A great work of art is not to be understood. It is to be felt. Art is not concerned with intellectual expositions. Those it leaves to science. It is the medium of emotional transfer whereby the soul of the artist conveys to kindred spirits the reactions of his own sensibility to the problems of abstract form."

Here another Philistine intervened with the objection that he was not quite clear as to what was meant by "abstract form."

"No," said Mr. Bunderby, "I appreciate your difficulty. Mere verbal language is a clumsy medium for the expression of those elusive qualities that are to be felt rather than described. How shall I explain myself? Perhaps it is impossible. But I will try.

"The words 'abstract form,' then, evoke in me the conception of that essential, pervading, geometric sub-structure which persists when all the trivial and superficial accidents of mere visual appearances have been eliminated. In short, it is the fundamental rhythm which is the basic aesthetic factor underlying all our abstract conceptions of spatial limitation. Do I make myself clear?"

"Oh, perfectly, thank you," the Philistine replied, hastily, and forthwith retired deep into his shell and was heard no more.

I need not follow Mr. Bunderby's discourse in detail. The portion that I have quoted is a representative sample of the whole. As I listened to the sounding phrases with their constantly recurring references to "rhythm" and "essential abstract form," I was conscious of growing disappointment. All this nebulous verbiage conveyed nothing to me. I seemed merely to be listening to Peter Gannet at second hand (though probably it was the other way about; that I had, in the studio talks, been listening to Bunderby at second hand). At any rate, it told me nothing about the pottery; and so far from resolving my doubts and misgivings, left me only still more puzzled and bewildered.

But enlightenment was to come. It came, in fact, when the whole collection seemed to have been reviewed. There was an impressive pause while Mr. Bunderby passed his fingers through his crest, making it stand up another two inches, and glared at the empty stand.

"And now," said he, "as a final *bonne bouche,* I am going to show you another facet of Peter Gannet's genius. May we have the decorated jar, Mr. Kempster?"

As the name was uttered, my obscure recognition of the proprietor was instantly clarified. But close as his resemblance was to the diamond merchant of Newingstead, he was obviously not the same man. Indeed he could not have been. Nevertheless, I observed him with interest as he advanced with slow steps, treading delicately and holding the precious jar in both hands as if it had been the Holy Grail or a live bomb. At length he placed it, with infinite care and tenderness, on the stand; slowly withdrew his hands and stepped back a couple of paces, still gazing at it reverentially.

"There," said Bunderby, "look at *that!*"

They looked at it and so did I,—with bulging eyes and mouth agape. It was amazing—incredible. And yet it was impossible that I could be mistaken. Every detail of it was familiar, including the marks of my own latch-key and the little dents made by the clinical thermometer. Eagerly I awaited Bunderby's exposition; and when it came it surpassed even my expectations.

"I have reserved this, the gem of the collection, to the last because, though at first glance it is different from the others, it is typical. It affords the perfect and unmistakable expression of Peter Gannet's artistic personality. Even more than the other it testifies to the rigorous, single-minded search for essential form and abstract rhythm. It is the fine flower of hand-built pottery. And mark you, not only does its hand-built character leap to the eye (the expert eye, of course), but it is obvious that by no method but that of direct modeling by hand could it have been created.

"Then consider the ornament. Note this charming guilloche,

executed with the most masterly freedom with the thumb-nail—just the simple thumb-nail; a crude instrument, you may say; but no other could produce exactly this effect, as the ancient potters knew."

He ran his finger lovingly over the mustard-spoon impressions and continued:

"Then look at these lovely rosettes. They tell us that when the artist created them he had in his mind the idea of 'what o'clocks'—the dandelion head. Profoundly stylized as the form is, generalized from the representational plane to that of ultimate abstraction, we can still trace the thought."

As he paused, one of the spectators remarked that the rosettes seemed to have been executed with the end of a key.

"They do," Bunderby agreed, "and it is quite possible that they were. And why not? The genius asks for no special apparatus. He uses the simple means that lie to his hand. But that hand is the hand of a master which transmutes to gold the very clay that feels its touch.

"So it has done in this little masterpiece. It has produced what we feel to be a complete epitome of abstract three-dimensional form. And then the rhythm! The rhythm!"

He paused, having apparently exhausted his vocabulary (if such a thing were possible). Then suddenly he looked at his watch and started.

"Dear me!" he exclaimed. "How the time flies! I must be running away. I have four more galleries to inspect. Let me thank you for the courteous interest with which you have listened to my simple comments and express the hope that some of you may be able to secure an example of the work of a great and illustrious artist. I had intended to say a few words about Mr. Boles's exquisite neo-primitive jewelry but my glass has run out. I wish you all good afternoon."

He bowed to the assembly and to Mr. Kempster and bustled away, and I noticed that with his retirement all interest in the alleged masterpieces seemed to lapse. The visitors strayed away to other parts of the gallery and the majority soon strayed towards the door.

Meanwhile, Mr. Kempster took possession of the jar and carried it reverently back to its case. I followed him with my eyes and then with the rest of my person. For, like Mr. Tite Barnacle (or, rather, his visitor), I "wanted to know, you know." I had noticed a red wafer stuck to the jar, and this served as an introduction.

"So the masterpiece is sold," said I. "Fifteen guineas, according to the catalogue. It seems a long price for a small jar."

"It does," he admitted. "But it is a museum piece; hand-built and by an acknowledged master."

"It looks rather different from most of Gannet's work. I suppose there is no doubt that it is really from his hand?"

Mr. Kempster was shocked. "Good gracious, no!" he replied. "He drew up the catalogue himself. Besides—"

He picked up the jar quickly (no Holy Grail touch this time) and turned it up to exhibit the bottom.

"You see," said he, "the piece is signed and numbered. There is no question as to its being Gannet's work."

If the inference was erroneous, the fact was correct. On the bottom of the jar was Gannet's distinctive mark; a sketchy gannet, the letters "P. G." with the number, Op. 961. That disposed of the possibility which had occurred to me that the jar might have been put among Gannet's own works by mistake, possibly by Mrs. Gannet. The fraud had evidently been deliberate.

As he replaced the jar on its shelf, I ventured to indulge my curiosity on another point.

"I heard Mr. Bunderby mention your name. Do you happen to be related to Mr. Kempster of Newingstead?"

"My brother," he replied. "You noticed the likeness, I suppose. Do you know him?"

"Very slightly. But I was down there at the time of the robbery; in fact, I had to give evidence at the inquest on the unfortunate policeman. It was I who found him by the wood."

"Ah, then you will be Dr. Oldfield. I read the report of the inquest, and, of course, heard all about it from my brother. It was a disastrous affair. It appears that the diamonds were not covered by insurance and I am afraid that it looks like a total loss. The diamonds are hardly likely to be recovered now. They are probably dispersed, and it would be difficult to identify them singly."

"I was sorry," said I, "to miss Mr. Bunderby's observations on Mr. Boles's jewelry. It seems to me to need some explaining."

"Yes," he admitted, "it isn't to everybody's taste. My brother, for instance, won't have it at any price, though he knows Mr. Boles and rather likes him. And speaking of Newingstead, it happens that Mr. Boles is a native of that place."

"Indeed. Then I suppose that is how your brother came to know him?"

"I can't say, but I rather think not. Probably he made the acquaintance through business channels. I know that he has had some dealings—quite small transactions—with Mr. Boles."

"But surely," I exclaimed, "Mr. Boles doesn't ever use diamonds in his neolithic jewelry?"

"Neo-primitive," he corrected with a smile. "No, I should think he was a vendor rather than a buyer or he may have made exchanges. Like most jewelers, Mr. Boles picks up oddments of old or damaged jewelry, when he can get it cheap, to use as scrap. Any diamonds or faceted stones would be useless to him as he uses only simple stones, cabochon cut, and not many of those. But that is only a surmise based on remarks that Mr. Boles has let fall; I don't really know much about his affairs."

At this moment I happened to glance at a clock at the end of the gallery, and to my dismay saw that it stood at ten minutes to six. With a few words of apology and farewell, I rushed out of the gallery, clattered down the stairs and darted out into the street. Fortunately, an unoccupied taxi was drifting towards me and slowed down as I hailed it. In a moment I had given my address, scrambled in and slammed the door and was moving on at a pace that bid fair to get me home within a minute or two of six.

The short journey gave me little time for reflection. Yet in those few minutes I was able to consider the significance of my recent experiences sufficiently to be conscious of deep regret and disillusionment. Of the dead, one would wish not only to speak but to think nothing but good; and though Peter Gannet had been more an acquaintance than a friend, and one for whom I had entertained no special regard, I was troubled that I could no longer even pretend to think of him with respect. For the doubts that I had felt and tried to banish were doubts no longer. The bubble was pricked. Now I knew that his high pretensions were mere clap-trap, his "works of art" a rank imposture.

But even worse than this was the affair of "the decorated jar." To pass off as his own work a piece that had been made by another—though that other were but an incompetent beginner—was unspeakably shabby; to offer it for sale was sheer dishonesty. Not that I grudged the fifteen guineas, since they would benefit poor Mrs. Gannet, nor did I commiserate the "mug" who had paid that preposterous price. Probably, he deserved all he got—or lost. But it irked me to think that Gannet, whom I had assumed to be a gentleman, was no more than a common rogue.

As to Bunderby, obviously, he was an arrant quack. An ignoramus, too, if he really believed my jar to have been hand-built, for a glance at its interior would have shown the most blatant traces of the wheel. But at this point my meditations were interrupted by the stopping of the taxi opposite my house. I hopped out, paid the driver, fished out my latch-key and had it in the keyhole at the very moment when the first—and, as it turned out, also the last—of the evening's patients arrived on the door-step.

CHAPTER 12

A SYMPOSIUM

To the ordinary housewife, the casual invitation to dinner of two large, able-bodied men would seem an incredible proceeding. But such is the way of bachelors; and perhaps it is not, after all, a bad way. Still, as I immured the newly-arrived patient in the waiting room, it did dawn on me that my housekeeper, Mrs. Gilbert, ought to be notified of the expected guests. Not that I had any anxiety, for Mrs. Gilbert appeared to credit me with the appetite of a Gargantua (and, in fact, I had a pretty good "twist"), and she seemed to live in a state of chronic anxiety lest I should develop symptoms of impending starvation.

Having discharged my bombshell down the kitchen stairs, I proceeded to deal with the patient—fortunately, a "chronic" who required little more than a "repeat"—and having safely launched him, bottle in hand, from the door step, repaired to the little glory-hole, known as "the study," to make provision for my visitors. Of their habits I knew nothing; but it seemed to me that a decanter of whiskey, another of sherry, a siphon and a box of cigars would meet all probable exigencies; and I had just finished these preparations when my guests arrived.

As they entered the study, Jervis looked at the table on which the decanters were displayed and grinned.

"It's all right, Thorndyke," said he. "Oldfield has got the restoratives ready. You won't want your smelling salts. But he is evidently going to make our flesh creep properly."

"Don't take any notice of him, Oldfield," said Thorndyke. "Jervis is a perennial juvenile. But he takes quite an intelligent interest in this case, and we are both all agog to hear your story. Where shall I put my note-book? I want to take rather full notes."

As he spoke, he produced a rather large block of ruled paper and fixed a wistful eye on the table; whereupon, having, after a brief discussion, agreed to take the restoratives as read, we transferred the whole collection—decanters, siphon and cigar box—to the top of a cupboard and Thorndyke laid his block on the vacant table and drew up a chair.

"Now, Oldfield," said Jervis, when we had all taken our seats and filled our pipes, "fire away. Art is long but life is short. Thorndyke is beginning to show signs of senile decay already, and I'm not as young as I was."

"The question is," said I, "where shall I begin?"

"The optimum place to begin," replied Jervis, "is at the beginning."

"Yes, I know. But the beginning of the case was the incident of the arsenic poisoning, and you know all about that."

"Jervis doesn't," said Thorndyke, "and I only came in at the end. Tell us the whole story. Don't be afraid of repetition and don't try to condense."

Thus directed, I began with my first introduction to the Gannet household and traced the history of my attendance up to the point at which Thorndyke came into the case, breaking off at the cessation of my visits to the hospital.

"I take it," said Jervis, "that full notes and particulars of the material facts are available if they should be wanted."

"Yes," Thorndyke replied, "I have my own notes and a copy of Woodfield's, and I think Oldfield has kept a record."

"I have," said I, "and I had intended to send you a copy. I must write one out and send it to you."

"Don't do that," said Jervis. "Lend it to me and I will have a typewritten copy made. But get on with the story. What was the next phase?"

"The next phase was the return home of Peter Gannet. He called on me to report and informed me that, substantially, he was quite fit."

"Was he, by Jove?" exclaimed Jervis. "He had made a pretty rapid recovery, considering the symptoms. And how did he seem to like the idea of coming home? Seem at all nervous?"

"Not at all. His view was that, as the attempt had been spotted and we should be on our guard, they wouldn't risk another. And apparently he was right—up to a certain point. I don't know what precautions he took—if he took any. But nothing further happened until—but we shall come to that presently. I will carry the narrative straight on."

This I did, making a brief and sketchy reference to my visits to the studio and the activities of Gannet and Boles. But at this point Jervis pulled me up.

"A little vague and general, this, Oldfield. Better follow the events more closely and in full detail."

"But," I protested, "all this has really nothing to do with the case."

"Don't you let Thorndyke hear you say that, my child. He doesn't admit that there is such a thing as an irrelevant fact, ascertainable in advance as such. Detail, my friend, detail; and again I say detail."

I did not take him quite literally, but I acted as if I did. Going back to the beginning of the studio episode, I recounted it with the minutest and most tedious circumstantiality, straining my memory in sheer malice to recall any trivial and unmeaning incident that I could recover, and winding up with a prolix and exact description of my prentice efforts with the potter's wheel and the creation of the immortal jar. I thought I had exhausted their powers of attention, but to my surprise Thorndyke asked:

"And what did your masterpiece look like when you had finished it?"

"It was very thick and clumsy, but it was quite a pleasant shape. The wheel tends to produce pleasant shapes if you let it."

"Do you know what became of it?"

"Yes. Gannet fired it and passed it off as his own work. But I will tell you about that later. I only discovered the fraud this afternoon."

He nodded and made a note on a separate slip of paper and I then resumed my narrative; and as this was concerned with the discovery of the crime, I was genuinely careful not to omit any detail, no matter how unimportant it might appear to me. They both listened with concentrated attention, and Thorndyke apparently took my statement down verbatim in shorthand.

When I had finished with the gruesome discoveries in the studio, I paused and prepared to play my trump card, confident that, unlike Inspector Blandy, they would appreciate the brilliancy of my inspiration and its important bearing on the identity of the criminal. And I was not disappointed, at least as to the impression produced, for as I described how the "brain wave" had come to me, Thorndyke looked up from his note-book with an appearance of surprise and Jervis stared at me, open-mouthed.

"But, my dear Oldfield!" he exclaimed, "what in the name of Fortune gave you the idea of testing the ashes for arsenic?"

"Well, there had been one attempt," I replied, "and it was quite possible that there might have been another. That was what occurred to me."

"Yes, I understand," said he. "But surely you did not expect to get an arsenic reaction from incinerated bone?"

"I didn't, very much. It was just a chance shot; and I must admit that the result came quite as a surprise."

"The result!" he exclaimed. "What result?"

"I will show you," said I; and forthwith I produced from a locked drawer the precious glass tube with its unmistakable arsenic mirror.

Jervis took it from me and stared at it with a ludicrous expression of amazement, while Thorndyke regarded him with a quiet twinkle.

"But," the former exclaimed, when he had partially recovered from his astonishment, "the thing is impossible. I don't believe it!" Whereupon Thorndyke chuckled aloud.

"My learned friend," said he, "reminds me of that German professor who, meeting a man wheeling a tall cycle—a thing that he had never before seen the like of—demonstrated conclusively to the cyclist that it was imposible to ride the machine for the excellent reason that, if you didn't fall off to the right, you must inevitably fall off to the left."

"That's all very well," Jervis retorted, "but you don't mean to tell me that you accept this mirror at its face value?"

"It is certainly a little unexpected," Thorndyke replied, "but you will remember that Soderman and O'Connell state definitely that it has been possible to show the presence of arsenic in the ashes of cremated bodies."

"Yes. I remember noting their statement and finding myself unable to accept it. They cited no instances and they gave no particulars. A mere *ipse dixit* has no evidential weight. I am convinced that there is some fallacy in this case. What about your reagents, Oldfield? Is there a possibility that any of them might have been contaminated with arsenic?"

"No," I replied, "it is quite impossible. I tested them exhaustively. There was no sign of arsenic until I introduced the bone ash."

"By the way," Thorndyke asked, "did you use up all your material, or have you some left?"

"I used only half of it, so if you think it worth while to check the analysis, I can let you have the remainder."

"Excellent!" said Thorndyke. "A control experiment will settle the question whether the ashes do, or do not, contain arsenic. Meanwhile, since the mirror is an undeniable fact, we must provisionally adopt the affirmative view. I suppose you told the police about this?"

"Yes, I showed them the tube. Inspector Blandy spotted the arsenic mirror at a glance, but he took a most extraordinary attitude. He seemed to regard the arsenic as of no importance whatever; quite irrelevant, in fact. He would, apparently, like to suppress it altogether; which appears to me a monstrous absurdity."

"I think you are doing Blandy an injustice," said Thorndyke. "From a legal point of view, he is quite right. What the prosecution has to prove is, first, the fact that a murder has been committed; second, the identity of the person who has been murdered; and third, the identity of the person who committed the murder. Now the fact of murder is established by the condition of the remains and the circumstances in which they were found. The exact cause of death is, therefore, irrelevant. The arsenic has no bearing as proof of murder, because the murder is already proved. And it has no bearing on the other two questions."

"Surely," said I, "it indicates the identity of the murderer, in view of the previous attempt to poison Gannet."

"Not at all," he rejoined. "There was never any inquiry as to who administered that poison and there is no evidence. The court would not listen to mere surmises or suspicions. The poisoner is an unknown person, and at present the murderer is an unknown person. But you cannot establish the identity of an unknown quantity by proving that it is identical with another unknown quantity. No, Oldfield, Blandy is perfectly right. The arsenic would only be a nuisance and a complication to the prosecution. But it would be an absolute godsend to the defense."

"Why?" I demanded.

"Well," he replied, "you saw what Jervis's attitude was. That would be the attitude of the defense. The defending counsel would pass lightly over all the facts that had been proved and that he could not contest, and fasten on the one thing that could not be proved and that he could make a fair show of disproving. The element of doubt introduced by the arsenic might wreck the case for the prosecution and be the salvation of the accused. But we are wandering away from your story. Tell us what happened next."

I resumed my narrative, describing my visit to the police station and Blandy's investigations at the studio, dwelling expecially on the interest shown by the Inspector in Boles's works and materials. They appeared to arouse a similar interest on the part of my listeners, for Jervis commented:

"The plot seems to thicken. There is a distinct suggestion that the studio was the scene of activities other than pottery and the making of modernist jewelry. I wonder if those finger-prints will throw any light on the subject?"

"I rather suspect that they have," said I, "judging by the questions that Blandy put to Mrs. Gannet. He had got some information from somewhere."

"I don't want to interrupt the narrative," said Thorndyke, "but when we have finished with the studio, we might have Blandy's questions. They probably represent his views on the case, and as you say, they may enable us to judge whether he knows more about it than we do."

"There is only one more point about the studio," said I, "but it is a rather important one, as it seems to bear on the motive for the murder." And with this I gave a detailed account of the quarrel between Gannet and Boles, an incident that, in effect, brought my connection with the place and the men to an end.

"Yes," Thorndyke agreed, "that is important, for all the circumstances suggest that it was not a mere casual falling out but the manifestation of a deep-seated enmity."

"That was what I thought," said I, "and so, evidently, did Mrs. Gannet; and it was on this point that Blandy's questions were so particularly searching. First, he elicited the fact that the two men were formerly quite good friends and that the change had occurred quite recently. He inquired as to the cause of the change, but she was quite unable to account for it. Then he wanted to know when the change had occurred, but she was only able to say that it occurred some time in the latter part of last year. The next questions related to Boles's movements about that time, and naturally, she couldn't tell him very much. And then he asked a most remarkable question, which was, could she remember where Boles was on the 19th of last September? And it happened that she could. For at that time Gannet had gone to spend a week-end with Boles and she had taken the opportunity to spend a week-end at Eastbourne. And as she remembered clearly that she was at Eastbourne on the 19th of

September, it followed that on that date Boles and Gannet were staying together at a place called Newingstead."

At the mention of Newingstead, Thorndyke looked up quickly, but he made no remark, and I continued:

"This information seemed greatly to interest Inspector Blandy, especially the fact that the two men were at Newingstead together on that date; and he pressed Mrs. Gannet to try to remember whether the sudden change from friendship to enmity seemed to coincide with that date. The question naturally astonished her; but on reflection, she was able to recall that she first noticed the change when she returned from Eastbourne."

"There is evidently something significant," said Jervis, "about that date and that place, but I can't imagine what it can be."

"I think," said I, "that I can enlighten you to some extent, for it happens that I also was at Newingstead on the 19th of last September."

"The deuce you were!" exclaimed Jervis. "Then it seems that you did not begin your story at the beginning, after all."

"I take it," said Thorndyke, "that you are the Dr. Oldfield who gave evidence at the inquest on Constable Murray?"

"That is so. But how do you come to know about that inquest? I suppose you read about it in the papers? But it is odd that you should happen to remember it."

"It isn't, really," said Thorndyke. "The fact is that Mr. Kempster —the man who was robbed, you remember—consulted me about the case. He wanted me to trace the thief, and if possible, to trace the diamonds, too. Of course, I told him that I had no means of doing anything of the kind. It was purely a police case. But he insisted on leaving the matter in my hands and he provided me with a verbatim report of the inquest from the local paper. Don't you remember the case, Jervis? I know you read the report."

"Yes," replied Jervis. "I begin to have a hazy recollection of the case. I remember now that a constable was murdered in a wood; killed with his own truncheon, wasn't he?"

"Yes," I replied; "and some very distinct finger-prints were found on the truncheon—finger-prints from a left hand, with a particularly clear thumb-print."

"Ha!" said Jervis. "Yes, of course, I remember; and I think I begin to 'rumble' Mr. Blandy, as Miller would say. Did you see those finger-prints on the gold plate?"

"I just had a look at them, though I was not particularly interested. But they were extremely clear—they would be, on polished gold plate. There was a thumb on one side and a forefinger on the reverse."

"Do you know whether they were left or right?"

"I couldn't tell; but Blandy said they were from a left hand."

"I expect he was right," said Jervis. "I am not fond of Blandy, but he certainly does know his job. It looks as if there were going to be some startling developments in this case. What do you think, Thorndyke?"

"It depends," replied Thorndyke, "on what Blandy found at the studio. If the finger-prints on the gold plate were the same as those found on the truncheon, they can be assumed to be those of the man who murdered the constable; and as Blandy will have assumed —quite properly—that they were the finger-prints of Boles, we can understand his desire to ascertain where Boles was on the day of the murder, and his intense interest in learning from Mrs. Gannet that Boles was actually at Newingstead on that very day. Further, I think we can understand his disinclination to have any dealings with the arsenic."

"I don't quite see why," said I.

"It is partly a matter of legal procedure," he explained. "Boles cannot be charged with any crime until he is caught. But, if he is arrested, and his finger-prints are found to be the same as those on the truncheon, he will be charged with the murder of the constable. He may also be charged with the murder of Gannet. Thus when it comes to the trial, there will be two indictments. But, whereas— in the circumstances that we are assuming—the evidence against him in the matter of the murder at Newingstead appears to be conclusive and unanswerable, that relating to the murder of Gannet is much less convincing; in fact, there is hardly enough at present to support the charge.

"Hence it is practically certain that the first indictment would be the one to be proceeded with; and as this would almost certainly result in a conviction, the other would be of no interest. The police would not be willing to waste time and effort on preparing a difficult and inconclusive case which would never be brought to trial. That is how the matter presents itself to me."

"Yes," Jervis agreed, "that seems to be the position. But yet we can't dismiss the Gannet murder altogether. Boles is the principal suspect, but he hasn't the monopoly. He might have had an accomplice—an accessory, either before or after the fact. As I see the case, it seems to leave Mr. Boles fairly in the soup and Mrs. Gannet, so to speak, sitting on the edge of the tureen. But I may be wrong."

"I think you are," said I, with some warmth. "I don't believe that Mrs. Gannet has any guilty knowledge of the crime at all."

"I am inclined to agree with you, Oldfield," said Thorndyke. "But I think Jervis was referring to the views of the police, which may be different from ours."

At this moment the clock in the adjacent consulting room struck eight, and, before its reverberations had died away, the welcome sound of the gong was heard summoning us to dinner. I conducted my guests to the dining room, and a quick glance at the table as I entered assured me that Mrs. Gilbert had been equal to the occasion. And that conviction deepened as the meal proceeded and evidently communicated itself to my guests, for Jervis remarked, after an appreciative sniff at his claret glass:

"Oldfield seems to do himself pretty well for a struggling G.P."

"Yes," Thorndyke agreed. "I think we may congratulate him on his housekeeper."

"And his wine merchant," added Jervis. "I propose a vote of thanks to them both."

I bowed my acknowledgments and promised to convey the sentiments of the company to the proper quarters (which I did, subsequently, to our mutual satisfaction), and we then reverted to the activities proper to the occasion. Presently Jervis looked up at me as if a sudden thought had struck him.

"When you were describing Gannet's method of work, Oldfield, you didn't give us a very definite idea of the result. I gather that he posed as a special kind of artist potter. Did you consider that his productions justified that claim?"

"To tell the truth," I replied, "I didn't know what to think. To my eye his pottery looked like the sort of rough, crude stuff that is made by primitive people—but not so good—or the pottery that children turn out at the kindergartens. But you see I am not an expert. It seemed possible that it might have some subtle qualities which I was too ignorant to detect."

"A very natural state of mind for a modest man," said Thorndyke, "and a perfectly proper one; but a dangerous one, nevertheless. For it is just that self-distrust, that modest assumption that 'there must be something in it, after all,' that lets in the charlatan and the impostor. I saw some of Gannet's pottery in his bedroom, including that outrageous effigy, and I am afraid that I was less modest than you were, for I decided definitely that the man who made it was no potter."

"And you were absolutely right," said I. "The question has been settled conclusively, so far as I am concerned, this very day. I have just visited an exhibition of Gannet's works, and the bubble of his reputation was burst before my eyes. I will give you the particulars. It was quite a quaint experience."

With this I produced the catalogue from my pocket and having read to them Bunderby's introduction, I gave them a full description of the proceedings, including as much of Bunderby's discourse as I could remember, and finishing up with the amazing incident of the "decorated jar." They both listened with deep interest and with appreciative chuckles, and when I had concluded, Jervis remarked:

"Well, the jar incident fairly puts the lid on it. Obviously, the whole of the pottery business was what the financiers call a ramp. And I should say that Bunderby was in it up to the neck."

"That is not so certain," said Thorndyke. "He is either an ignoramus or a sheer impostor, and possibly both. It doesn't matter much, as he is apparently not our pigeon. But the affair of the jar—a mere beginner's experiment—is more interesting, for it concerns Gannet, who *is* our pigeon. As Jervis says, it explodes Gannet's pretensions as a skilled artist, and thus convicts him of deliberate imposture, but it also proves him guilty of an act, not only mean but quite definitely dishonest. For the jar might conceivably be sold."

"It is sold," said I, "for fifteen guineas."

"Which," Jervis pronounced, oracularly, "illustrates the proverbial lack of cohesion between a fool and his money. I wonder who the mug is."

"I didn't discover that; in fact, I didn't ask. But I picked up some other items of information. I had quite a long chat with Mr. Kempster, the proprietor of the gallery."

"Mr. Kempster?" Thorndyke repeated, with a note of interrogation.

"Yes, but not your Mr. Kempster. This man is the brother of your client and a good deal like him. That is how I came to speak to him."

"And what did you learn from Mr. Kempster?" Thorndyke asked.

"I learned, in the first place, that Boles is a Newingstead man; that he is acquainted with your Mr. Kempster, and that they have had certain business transactions."

"Of what kind?" asked Thorndyke.

"Either the sale or exchange of stones. It seems that Boles buys up oddments of old or damaged jewelry to melt down for his own work. If they contain any diamonds, he picks them out and passes them on to Kempster, either in exchange for the kind of stones that he uses, or else, I suppose, for cash. Apparently the transactions are on quite a small scale."

"Small or large," said Jervis, "it sounds a bit fishy. Wouldn't Blandy be interested?"

"I don't quite see why," said I. "Blandy is all out on the murder charge. It wouldn't help him if he could prove Boles to be a receiver, or even a thief."

"I think you are wrong there," said Thorndyke. "If you recall the circumstances of the diamond robbery, which led to the murder of the constable, you will see that what you have told us has a distinct bearing. It was assumed that the thief was a chance stranger who had strayed into the premises. But a man who was suspected of being either a receiver or a thief, who had had dealings with Kempster—possibly in that very house—and knew something of his habits, and who happened to be in Newingstead at the time of the robbery, would fit into the picture much better than a chance stranger. However, that case really turns on the finger-print. If the print on the truncheon is Boles's print, Boles will hang if he is caught; and if it is not, he is innocent both of the murder and of the robbery."

I did not pursue the topic any farther, and the conversation drifted into other channels. But suddenly it occurred to me that nothing had been said on the very subject that had occasioned the present meeting.

"By the way," said I, "you haven't told me what has been done about poor Mrs. Gannet. I hope you have been able to make some arrangements."

"We have," said Jervis. "You need have no further anxiety about her. I called on Linnell this afternoon and put the proposal to him, and he agreed, not only quite willingly but with enthusiasm, to undertake the case. He is keen on criminal practice, and for a solicitor he has an unusual knowledge of criminal law and procedure. So we can depend on him in both respects. He will see that Mrs.

Gannet's rights and interests are properly safeguarded, and on the other hand, he won't obstruct and antagonize the police."

"I am relieved to hear that," said I, "for I was most distressed to think of the terrible position that this poor lady finds herself in. I feel the deepest sympathy for her."

"Very properly," said Thorndyke, "as her medical adviser, and I think I am disposed to agree with your view of the case. But we must be cautious. We must not take sides. In the words of a certain ecclesiastic, 'we must keep a warm heart and a cool head.' You will remember that when the arsenic poisoning occurred, both you and I, having regard to Mrs. Gannet's relations with Boles, felt that she was a possible suspect, either as an accessory or a principal. That view was perfectly correct and I must remind you that nothing has changed since then. The general probabilities remain. I do not believe that she had any hand in this crime, but you and I may both be wrong. At any rate, the police will consider all the possibilities, and our business is to see that Mrs. Gannet gets absolutely fair treatment; and that we shall do."

"Thank you, sir," said I. "It is most kind of you to take so much interest, and so much trouble, in this case, seeing that you have no personal concern in it. Indeed, I don't quite know why you have interested yourselves in it in the way that you have done."

"That is easily explained," replied Thorndyke. "Jervis and I are medico-legal practitioners, and here is a most unusual crime of the greatest medico-legal interest. Such cases we naturally study for the sake of the knowledge and experience that may be gleaned from them. But there is another reason. It has repeatedly happened that when we have studied some unusual case from the outside for its mere professional interest, we have suddenly acquired a personal interest in it by being called on to act for one of the parties. Then we have had the great advantage of being able to take it up with full and considered knowledge of most of the facts."

"Then," I asked somewhat eagerly, "if you were asked to take up this case on behalf of Mrs. Gannet, would you be willing— assuming, of course, that the costs would be met?"

"The costs would not be an essential factor," he replied. "I think that if a charge should be brought against Mrs. Gannet, I would be willing to investigate the case—with an open mind and at her risk as to what I might discover—and if I were satisfied of her innocence, to undertake her defense."

"Only if you were satisfied of her innocence?"

"Yes. Reasonably satisfied when I had all the facts. Remember, Oldfield, that I am an investigator. I am not an advocate."

I found this slightly disappointing, but as no charge was probable, and as Thorndyke's view of the case was substantially similar to my own, I pursued the subject no farther. Shortly afterwards, we adjourned to the study and spent the remainder of the evening discussing Gannet's pottery and the various aspects of modernist art.

CHAPTER 13

THE INQUIRY

The results of Mr. Linnell's activities on Mrs. Gannet's behalf were slightly disappointing, though she undoubtedly derived great encouragement from the feeling that his advice and support were always available. But Inspector Blandy was quietly but doggedly persistent in his search for information. Characteristically, he welcomed Linnell with almost affectionate warmth. It was such a relief to him to know that this poor lady now had a really competent and experienced legal adviser to watch over her interests. He had formerly been so distressed at her friendless and solitary condition. Now he was quite happy about her, though he deplored the necessity of troubling her occasionally with tiresome questions.

Nevertheless, he returned to the charge again and again in spite of Linnell's protests that all available information had been given. There were two points on which he yearned for more exact knowledge. The first related to the movements of Mr. Boles; the second to her own movements during the time that she had been absent from home. As to the first, the last time she had seen Boles was about a week before she went away, and she then understood that he was proposing to take a short holiday to Burnham-on-Crouch. Whether, in fact, he did go to Burnham she could not say. She had never seen or heard from him since that day. As to his usual places of resort, he had an aunt at Newingstead with whom he used to stay from time to time as a paying guest. She knew of no other place which he was in the habit of visiting, and she had no idea whatever as to where he might be now.

As to her own movements, she had been staying at Westcliff-on-Sea with an old servant who had a house there and let lodgings to visitors. While there, she had usually walked along the sea front to Southend in the mornings and returned to tea or dinner. Sometimes she spent the whole day at Southend and went to a theatre or other entertainment, coming back at night by train. Naturally she could not give exact dates or say positively where she was at a certain time on a given day, though she tried to remember. And when the questions were repeated on subsequent occasions, the answers that she gave inevitably tended to vary.

From these repeated questionings, it was evident to Linnell (from whom, as well as from Mrs. Gannet, I had these particulars) that, in the intervals, Blandy had checked all these statements by exhaustive inquiries on the spot; and further, that he had been carefully studying the fast train service between Southend and London. Apparently he had discovered no discrepancy, but yet it seemed that he was not satisfied; that he still harboured a suspicion that Mrs. Gannet knew more about the affair than she had admitted and that she could, if she chose, give a useful hint as to where Boles was in hiding.

Such was the state of affairs when I received a summons to attend and give evidence at an inquest "on certain remains, believed to be human, found on the premises of No. 12 Jacob Street." The summons came rather as a surprise, and on receiving it I gave very careful consideration to the questions that I might be asked and the evidence that I should give. Should I, for instance, volunteer any statements as to the arsenic poisoning and my analysis of the bone-ash? As to the latter, I knew that Blandy would have liked me to suppress it, and my own enthusiasm on the subject had largely evaporated after witnessing Jervis's open incredulity. But I would be sworn to tell the whole truth, and as the analysis was a fact, it would have to be mentioned. However, as will be seen, the choice was not left to me; the far-sighted Blandy had anticipated my difficulty and provided the necessary counterblast.

On the morning of the inquest, I made a point of calling on Mrs. Gannet to satisfy myself that she was in a fit state to attend and to ascertain whether Linnell would be there to represent her. On both points I was reassured; for, though naturally a little nervous, she was quite composed and prepared to face courageously what must necessarily be a rather painful ordeal.

"I can never be grateful enough to you and Dr. Thorndyke," said she, "for sending Mr. Linnell to me. He is so kind and sympathetic and so wise. I should have been terrified of this inquest if I had had to go to it alone; but now that I know Mr. Linnell will be there to support me, I feel quite confident. For you know I really haven't anything that I need conceal."

"Of course you haven't," I replied, cheerfully, though with not very profound conviction, "and there is nothing at all for you to worry about. You can trust Mr. Linnell to keep Inspector Blandy in order."

With this I took my departure, greatly relieved to find her in so satisfactory a state, and proceeded to dispatch my visits so as to leave the afternoon clear. For my evidence would probably occupy a considerable time and I wanted, if possible, to hear the whole of the inquiry; I managed this so successfully that I was able to present myself only a few minutes late and before the business had actually commenced.

Looking round the room as I entered, I was surprised to find but a mere handful of spectators; not more than a dozen, and these occupied two benches at the back, while the witnesses were accommodated on a row of chairs in front of them. Before seating myself on the vacant chair at the end, I glanced along the row, which included Blandy, Thorndyke, Jervis, Mrs. Gannet, Linnell and one or two other persons who were unknown to me.

I had hardly taken my seat when the coroner opened the proceedings with a brief address to the jury.

"The general nature of this inquiry," said he, "has been made known to you in the course of your visit to the studio in Jacob Street. There are three questions to which we have to find answers. First, are these fragments of burnt bones the remains of a human being? Second, if they are, can we give a name and identity to that person? And third, how did that person come by his death? To these questions the obvious appearances and the known circumstances suggest certain answers; but we must disregard all preconceived opinions and consider the facts with an open mind. To do that, I think the best plan will be to trace, in the order of their occurrence, the events which seem to be connected with the subject of our inquiry. We will begin by taking the evidence of Dr. Oldfield."

Here I may say that I shall not follow the proceedings in detail since they dealt with matters with which the reader is already acquainted; and for such repetition as is unavoidable, I hereby offer a comprehensive apology.

When the preliminaries had been disposed of, the coroner opened his examination with the question:

"When, and in what circumstances, did you first meet Peter Gannet?"

"On the 16th of December, 1930," I replied. "I was summoned

to attend him professionally. He was then an entire stranger to me."

"What was the nature of his illness?"

"He was suffering from arsenic poisoning."

"Did you recognize the condition immediately?"

"No. The real nature of his illness was discovered by Dr. Thorndyke, whom I consulted."

Here, in answer to a number of questions, I described the circumstances of the illness up to the time when Peter Gannet called on me to report his recovery.

"Were you able to form any opinion as to whom administered the poison to Gannet?"

"No. I had no facts to go upon other than those that I have mentioned."

"You have referred to a Mr. Frederick Boles as being in attendance on Gannet. What was his position in the household?"

"He was a friend of the family and he worked with Gannet in the studio."

"What were his relations with Gannet? Were they genuinely friendly?"

"I thought so at the time, but afterwards I changed my opinion."

"What were the relations of Boles and Mrs. Gannet?"

"They were quite good friends."

"Should you say that their relations were merely friendly? Nothing more?"

"I never had any reason to suppose that they were anything more than friends. They seemed to be on the best of terms, but their mutual liking was known to Gannet and he used to refer to it without any sign of disapproval. He seemed to accept their friendship as quite natural and proper."

The questions now concerned themselves with what I may call the second stage; my relations with Gannet up to the time of the disappearance, including the quarrel in the studio which I had overheard. This evidently produced a deep impression and evoked a number of searching questions from the coroner and from one or two of the jury. Then came the disappearance itself, and as I told the story of my search of the house and my discoveries in the studio, the profound silence in the court and the intent looks of the jury testified to the eager interest of the listeners. When I had finished the account of my doings in the studio, the coroner (who I suspected had been primed by Blandy) asked:

"What about the sample of bone-ash that you took away with you? Did you make any further examination of it?"

"Yes. I examined it under the microscope and confirmed my belief that it was incinerated bone; and I also made a chemical test to ascertain whether it contained any arsenic."

"Had you any expectation that it would contain arsenic?"

"I thought it just possible that it might contain traces of arsenic. It was the previous poisoning incident that suggested the examination."

"Did you, in fact, find any arsenic?"

"Yes. To my surprise, I discovered a considerable quantity. I don't know how much, as I did not attempt to estimate it, but I could see that there was a comparatively large amount."

"And what conclusion did you reach from this fact?"

"I concluded that deceased, whoever he was, had died from the effects of a very large dose of arsenic."

"Is that still your opinion?"

"I am rather doubtful. There may have been some source of error which is not known to me, but the arsenic was certainly there. Really, its significance is a matter for an expert, which I am not."

This, substantially, brought my evidence to an end. I was followed by Sir Joseph Armadale, the eminent medico-legal authority, acting for the Home Office. As he took his place near the coroner, he produced and laid on the table a shallow, glass-topped box. In reply to the coroner's question, he deposed:

"I have examined a quantity of fragments of incinerated bone submitted to me by the Commissioner of Police. Most of them were too small to have any recognizable character, but some were large enough to identify as parts of particular bones. These I found, in every case, to be human bones."

"Would you say that all these fragments are the remains of a human being?"

"That, of course, is an inference, but it is a reasonable inference. All I can say is that every fragment that I was able to recognize as part of a particular bone was part of a human bone. It is reasonable to infer that the unrecognizable fragments were also human. I have picked out all the fragments that were identifiable and put them in this box, which I submit for your inspection."

Here the box was passed round and examined by the jury, and while the inspection was proceeding, the coroner addressed the witness.

"You have heard Dr. Oldfield's evidence as to the arsenic that he found in the ashes. Have you any comments to make on his discovery?"

"Yes. The matter was mentioned to me by Inspector Blandy and I accordingly made an analysis to check Dr. Oldfield's findings. He is perfectly correct. The ashes contain a considerable quantity of arsenic. From two ounces of the ash I recovered nearly a tenth of a grain."

"And do you agree that the presence of that arsenic is evidence that deceased died from arsenic poisoning?"

"No. I do not associate the arsenic with the body of deceased at all. The quantity is impossibly large. As a matter of fact, I do not believe that, if deceased had been poisoned even by a very large dose of arsenic, any trace of the poison would have been discoverable in the ashes. Arsenic is a volatile substance which changes into a vapour at a comparatively low temperature—about 300 degrees Fahrenheit. But these bones had been exposed for hours to a very high temperature—over 2000° Fahrenheit. I should say that the whole of the arsenic would have been driven off in vapour. At any rate, the quantity which was found in the ashes was quite impossible as a residue. The arsenic must have got into the ashes in some way after they had become ashes."

"Can you suggest any way in which it could have got into the ashes?"

"I can only make a guess. Inspector Blandy has informed me that he found a jar of arsenic in the studio among the materials for making glazes or enamels. So it appears that arsenic was one of the materials used, in which case it would have been possible for it to have got mixed with the ashes either in the grinding apparatus or in the bin. But that is only a speculative suggestion. There may be other possibilities."

"Yes," the coroner agreed. "But it doesn't matter much. The important point is that the arsenic was not derived from the body of deceased, and you are clear on that?"

"Perfectly clear," replied Sir Joseph; and that completed his evidence.

The next witness was Mr. Albert Hawley, who described himself as a dental surgeon and deposed that he had attended Mr. Peter Gannet professionally and had made for him a partial upper denture which included the four incisors. The coroner then handed to him a small stoppered tube which I could see contained a tooth, remark-ing:

"I think you have seen that before, but you had better examine it."

"Yes," the witness replied as he withdrew the stopper and shook the tooth out into the palm of his hand. "It was shown to me by Inspector Blandy. It is a porcelain tooth—a right upper lateral incisor—which has been broken into several fragments and very skilfully mended. It is of the type known as Du Trey's."

"Does it resemble any of the teeth in the denture which you made for Peter Gannet?"

"Yes. I used Du Trey's teeth in that denture, so this is exactly like the right upper lateral incisor in that denture."

"You can't say, I suppose, whether this tooth actually came from that denture?"

"No. The teeth are all alike when they come from the makers, and if I have to make any small alterations in adjusting the bite, no record is kept. But nothing seems to have been done to this tooth."

"If it were suggested to you that this tooth came from Gannet's denture, would you have any reason to doubt the correctness of that suggestion?"

"None whatever. It is exactly like a tooth in his denture and it may actually be that tooth. Only I cannot say positively that it is."

"Thank you," said the coroner. "That is all that we could expect of you, and I think we need not trouble you any further."

Mr. Hawley was succeeded by Inspector Blandy who gave his evidence with the ease and conciseness of the professional witness. His description of the researches in the studio and the discovery of the fragments of the tooth were listened to by the jury with the closest interest, though in the matter of sensation I had rather "stolen his thunder." But the turning out of Boles's cupboard was a new feature and several points of interest arose from it. The discovery, for instance, of a two-pound jar of arsenic, three-quarters full, was one of them.

"You had already learned of Dr. Oldfield's analysis?"

"Yes. He showed me the tube with the arsenic deposit in it, but I saw at once that there must be some mistake. It was too good to be true. There was too much arsenic for a cremated body."

"Did you gather what the arsenic was used for?"

"No. The cupboard contained a number of chemicals, apparently used for preparing enamels and fluxes, and I presumed that the arsenic was used for the same purpose."

The discovery of the finger-prints raised some other interesting questions, particularly as to their identity, concerning which the coroner asked:

"Can you say whose finger-prints those were?"

"Not positively. But there were quite a lot of them on various objects, on bottles and jars, and some on tool-handles, and they were all from the same person; and as the cupboard was Boles's cupboard and the tools and bottles were his, it is fair to assume that the finger-prints were his."

"Yes," the coroner agreed, "that seems a reasonable assumption. But I don't see the importance of it, unless the finger-prints are known to the police. Is it expedient to ask whether they are?"

"I don't want to go into particulars," said Blandy, "but I may say that these finger-prints are known to the police and that their owner is wanted for a very serious crime against the person; a crime involving extreme violence. That is their only bearing on this case. If they are Boles's finger-prints, then Boles is known to be a violent criminal; and there seems to be evidence in this case that a violent crime has been committed."

"Have you had an opportunity of interviewing Mr. Boles?" the coroner asked.

The Inspector smiled, grimly. "No," he replied. "Mr. Boles disappeared just about the time when the body was burned, and so far, he has managed to keep out of sight. Apparently he doesn't desire an interview."

That was the substance of the Inspector's evidence, and, as he was disposed to be evasive and reticent, the coroner discreetly refrained from pressing him. Accordingly, when the depositions had been read and signed, he was allowed to retire to his seat and the name of Letitia Gannet was called. As she advanced to the table, where a chair was placed for her, I watched her with some uneasiness; for though I felt sure that she knew nothing that she had not already disclosed, the atmosphere of the court was not favourable. It was easy to see that the jury regarded her with some suspicion, and that Blandy's habitually benevolent expression but thinly disguised a watchful attention which was not entirely friendly.

As I had expected, the coroner began with an attempt to get more light on the incident of the arsenic poisoning, and Mrs. Gannet recounted the history of the affair in so far as it was known to her.

"Of what persons did your household consist at that time?" the coroner asked.

"Of my husband, myself and one maid. Perhaps I should include Mr. Boles as he worked in the studio with my husband and usually took his meals with us and was at the house a good deal."

"Who prepared your husband's food?"

"I did while he was ill. The maid did most of the other cooking."

"And the barley water? Who prepared that?"

"Usually I did; but sometimes Mr. Boles made it."

"And who took the food and drink to your husband's room?"

"I usually took it up to him myself, but sometimes I sent the maid up with it and occasionally Mr. Boles took it up."

"Is the maid still with you?"

"No. As soon as I heard from my husband that there had been arsenic in his food, I sent the girl away with a month's wages in lieu of notice."

"Why did you do that? Did you suspect her of having put the arsenic in the food?"

"No, not in the least, but I thought it best to be on the safe side."

"Did you form any opinion as to who might have put it in?"

"No, there was nobody whom I could suspect. At first I thought that there must have been some mistake, but when Dr. Oldfield explained to me that no mistake was possible, I supposed that the arsenic must have got in by accident; and I think so still."

The next questions were concerned with the relations existing between Gannet and Boles and the time and circumstances of the break-up of their friendship.

"As to the cause of this sudden change from friendship to enmity—did you ever learn from either of the men what the trouble was?"

"Neither of them would admit that there was any trouble, though I saw that there must be. But I could never guess what it was."

"Did it ever occur to you that your husband might be jealous on account of your intimacy with Mr. Boles?"

"Never, and I am sure he was not. Mr. Boles and I were relatives—second cousins—and had known each other since we were children. We were always the best of friends, but there was never anything between us that could have occasioned jealousy on my husband's part, and he knew it. He never made the least objection to our friendship."

"You spoke of Mr. Boles as working with your husband in the studio. What, precisely, does that mean? Was Mr. Boles a potter?"

"No. He sometimes helped my husband, particularly in firing the kiln; but his own work, for the last year or two, was the making of certain kinds of jewelry and enamels."

"You say 'for the last year or two'—what was his previous occupation?"

"He was originally a dental mechanic; but when my husband took the studio, as it contained a jeweler's and enameler's plant, Mr. Boles came there and began to make jewelry."

Here I caught the eye of Inspector Blandy, and a certain fluttering of the eyelid recalled his observations on Mr. Boles's "neo-primitive" jewelry. But a dental mechanic is not quite the same as a plumber's apprentice.

The inquiry now proceeded to the circumstances of Peter Gannet's disappearance and the dates of the various events.

"Can you remember exactly when you last saw Mr. Boles?"

"I think it was on Tuesday, the 21st of April; about a week before I went away. He came to the studio and had lunch with us, and then he told us that he was going to spend a week or ten days at Burnham in Essex. I never saw or heard from him after that."

"You say that you went away. Can we have particulars as to when and where you went?"

"I left home on the 29th of April to stay for a fortnight at Westcliff-on-Sea with an old servant, Mrs. Hardy, who has a house there and lets rooms to visitors in the season. I returned home on Thursday, the 14th of May."

"Between those two dates, were you continuously at Westcliff, or did you go to any other places?"

To this she replied in the same terms that she had used in her answers to Blandy, which I have already recorded. Here again I suspected that the coroner had received some help from the Inspector for he inquired minutely into the witness's doings from day to day while she was staying at Westcliff.

"In effect," said he, "you slept at Westcliff, but you frequently spent whole days elsewhere. During that fortnight, did you ever come to London?"

"No."

"If you had wished to spend a day in London, could you have done so without your landlady being aware of it?"

"I suppose so. There is a very good train service. But I never did."

"And what about Burnham? That is not so very far from Westcliff. Did you ever go there during your stay?"

"No. I never went farther than Southend."

"During that fortnight, did you ever write to your husband?"

"Yes, twice. The first letter was sent a day or two after my arrival at Westcliff and he replied to it a couple of days later. The second letter I wrote a few days before my return, telling him when he might expect me home. I received no answer to that, and when I got home I found it in the letter box."

"Can you give us the exact dates of those letters? You see that they are important as they give, approximately, the time of the disappearance. Can you remember the date of your husband's reply to your first letter? Or perhaps you have the letter itself."

"I have not. It was only a short note, and when I had read it I tore it up. My first letter was written and posted, I am nearly sure, on Monday, the 4th of May. I think his reply reached me by the first post on Friday, the 8th, so it would have been sent off on Thursday, the 7th. My second letter, I remember quite clearly, was written and posted on Sunday, the 10th of May, so it would have been delivered at our house early on Monday, the 11th."

"That is the one that you found in the letter box. Is it still in existence?"

"No. Unfortunately, I destroyed it. I took it from the letter box and opened it to make sure that it was my letter, and then, when I had glanced at it, I threw it on the fire that I had just lit. But I am quite sure about the date."

"It is a pity you destroyed the letter," said the coroner, "but no doubt your memory as to the date is reliable. Now we come to the incidents connected with the disappearance. Just give us an account of all that happened from the time when you arrived home."

In reply to this, Mrs. Gannet told the story of her alarming discovery in much the same words as she had used in telling it to me, but in greater detail, including her visit to me and our joint examination of the premises. Her statement was amplified by various questions from the coroner, but her answers to them conveyed nothing new to me with one or two exceptions. For instance, the coroner asked:

"You looked at the hall stand and noticed that your husband's hats and stick were there. Did you notice another walking-stick?"

"I saw that there was another stick in the stand."

"Did you recognize it as belonging to any particular person?"

"No, I had never seen it before."

"Did you form any opinion as to whose stick it was?"

"I felt sure that it did not belong to my husband. It was not the kind of stick that he would have used; and as there was only one other person who was likely to be the owner—Mr. Boles—I assumed that it was his."

"Did you take it out and examine it?"

"No, I was not interested in it. I was trying to find out what had become of my husband."

"But you assumed that it was Mr. Boles's stick. Did it not occur to you as rather strange that he should have left his stick in your stand?"

"No. I suppose that he had gone out of the studio by the wicket and had forgotten about his stick. He was sometimes inclined to be forgetful. But I really did not think much about it."

"Was that stick in the stand when you went away from home?"

"No. I am sure it was not."

"You have mentioned that you called at Mr. Boles's flat. Why did you do that?"

"For two reasons. I had written to him telling him when I should be home and asking him to come and have tea with us. As he had not answered my letter and did not come to the house, I thought that something unusual must have happened. But especially I wanted to find out whether he knew anything about my husband."

"When you found that he was not at his flat, did you suppose that he was still at Burnham?"

"No, because I learned that he had returned about a week previously at night and had slept at the flat and had the next day gone away again."

"Did you know, or could you guess, where he had gone?"

"No, I had not the least idea."

"Have you any idea as to where he may be at this moment?"

"Not the slightest."

"Do you know of any places to which he is in the habit of going?"

"The only place I know of is his aunt's house at Newingstead. But I understand from Inspector Blandy that inquiries have been made there and that his aunt has not seen or heard of him for some months. I know of no other place where he might be."

"When you were describing your search of the premises, you said that you did not look in the studio. Why did you not? Was it not the most likely place in which he might be?"

"Yes, it was. But I was afraid to go in. Since my husband and Mr. Boles had been on bad terms, they had quarreled dreadfully. And they were both rather violent men. On one occasion—which Dr. Oldfield has mentioned—I heard them actually fighting in the studio, and I think it had happened on other occasions. So, when I could find no trace of my husband in the house, I began to fear that something might have happened in the studio. That was why I was afraid to go there."

"In short, you were afraid that you might find your husband's dead body in the studio. Isn't that what you mean?"

"Yes, I think that was in my mind. I suspected that something awful had happened."

"Was it only a suspicion? Or did you know that there had been some trouble?"

"I knew nothing whatever about any trouble. I did not even know whether the two men had met since I went away. And it was hardly a suspicion; only, remembering what had happened in the past, the possibility occurred to me."

When the coroner had written down this answer, he sat for a few moments looking reflectively at the witness. Apparently, he could think of nothing further to ask her, for, presently, turning to the jury, he said:

"I think the witness has told us all that she knows about this affair, but possibly some members of the jury might wish to ask a further question."

There was a short pause, during which the members of the jury gazed solemnly at the witness. At length one enterprising juryman essayed a question.

"Could we ask Mrs. Gannet if she knows, or has any idea, who murdered her husband?"

"I don't believe," the coroner replied with a faint smile, "that we could ask that question, even if it were a proper one to put to a witness, because we have not yet decided that anyone murdered Peter Gannet, or even that he is dead. Those are precisely the questions that you will have to answer when you come to consider your verdict."

He paused and still regarded the jury inquiringly, but none of them made any sign; then, after waiting for yet a few more moments, he read the depositions, took the signature, released the witness, and pronounced the name of her successor, Dr. Thorndyke; who came forward and took the place which she vacated. Having been sworn, he deposed, in answer to the coroner's question:

"I attended Peter Gannet in consultation with Dr. Oldfield last January. I formed the opinion that he was suffering from arsenic poisoning."

"Had you any doubt on the subject?"

"No. His symptoms were the ordinary symptoms of poisoning by arsenic, and, when I had him in the hospital under observation, it was demonstrated chemically that there was arsenic in his body. The chemical tests were made by Professor Woodfield and by me."

He then went on to confirm the account which I had given, including the analysis of the arrowroot and the barley water. When he had finished his statement, the coroner asked, tentatively:

"I suppose you were not able to form an opinion as to how, or by whom, the poison was administered, or whether the poisoning might have been accidental?"

"No. I had no first-hand knowledge of the persons or the circumstances. As to accidental poisoning, I would not say that it was impossible, but I should consider it too improbable to be seriously entertained. The poisoning affected only one person in the house, and when the patient returned home after the discovery it did not recur. Those facts are entirely opposed to the idea of accidental poisoning."

"What do you say about the arsenic that Dr. Oldfield found in the ashes?"

"I agree with Sir Joseph Armadale that there must have been some contamination of the ashes. I do not associate the arsenic with the body of the person who was burned—assuming the ashes to be those of a burned human body."

"On that matter," said the coroner, "perhaps you will give us your opinion on the fragments which Sir Joseph Armadale has shown us."

He handed the box to Thorndyke, who took it and examined the contents with an appearance of the deepest interest, assisting his eyesight with his pocket lens. When he had—apparently—inspected each separate fragment, he handed the box back to the coroner, who asked, as he replaced it on the table:

"Well, what do say about those fragments?"

"I have no doubt," replied Thorndyke, "that they are all fragments of human bones."

"Would it be possible to identify deceased from these fragments?"

"I should say that it would be quite impossible."

"Do you agrce that the ashes as a whole may be assumed to be the remains of a burned human body?"

"That is an obviously reasonable assumption, though it is not susceptible of proof. It is the assumption that I should make in the absence of any reasons to the contrary."

That concluded Thorndyke's evidence, and when he retired, his place was taken by Professor Woodfield. But I need not record the Professor's evidence since it merely repeated and confirmed that of Thorndyke and Sir Joseph. With the reading and signing of his depositions the body of evidence was completed and when he had returned to his seat, the coroner proceeded to his summing up.

"In opening this inquiry," he began, "I said that there were three questions to which we had to find answers. First, are these ashes the remains of a human being? Second, if they are, can we identify that human being as any known person? And third, if we can so identify him, can we decide how he came by his death?

"Let us take these questions in their order. As to the first, it is definitely answered for us by the medical evidence. Sir Joseph Armadale and Dr. Thorndyke, both authorities of the highest eminence, have told us that all the fragments which are large enough to have any recognizable characters are undoubtedly portions of human bones; and they agree—as, indeed, common sense suggests— that the unrecognizable remainder of the ashes must also be presumed to be fragments of human bones. Thus our first question is answered in the affirmative. The bone ashes found in the studio are the remains of a human being.

"The next question presents much more difficulty. As you have heard from Dr. Thorndyke, the fragments are too small to furnish any clue to the identity of deceased. Our efforts to discover who this person was must be guided by evidence of another kind. We have to consider the persons, the places and the special circumstances known to us.

"As to the place, these remains were found in the studio

occupied by Peter Gannet; and we learn that Peter Gannet has disappeared under most mysterious circumstances. I need not repeat the evidence in detail, but the fact that when he disappeared he was wearing only his indoor clothing, seems to preclude the possibility of his having gone away from his home in any ordinary manner. Now the connection between a man who has mysteriously disappeared, and unrecognizable human remains found on his premises after his disappearance, appears strongly suggestive and invites the inquiry, What is the nature of the connection? To answer this, we must ask two further questions: When did the man disappear and when did the remains make their appearance?

"Let us take the first question. We learn from Mrs. Gannet's evidence that she received a letter from her husband on the 8th of May. That letter, we may presume, was written on the 7th. Then she wrote and posted a letter to him on the 10th of May, and we may assume that it was delivered on the 11th. Most unfortunately, she destroyed that letter, so we can not be absolutely certain about the date on which it was delivered, but we can feel little doubt that it was delivered in the ordinary way on the 11th of May. If that is so, we can say with reasonable confidence that Peter Gannet was undoubtedly alive on the 7th of May; but inasmuch as Mrs. Gannet found her letter in the letter box, we must conclude that at the date of its delivery, Peter Gannet had already disappeared. That is to say that his disappearance occurred at some time between the 7th and the 11th of May.

"Now let us approach the problem from another direction. You have seen the kiln. It is a massive structure of brick and fire-clay with enormously thick walls. During the burning of the body, we know from the condition of the bones that its interior must have been kept for several hours at a temperature which has been stated in evidence as well over 2000° Fahrenheit; that is to say, at a bright red heat. When Dr. Oldfield examined it, the interior was just perceptibly warm. Now I don't know how long a great mass of brick and fire-clay such as this would take to cool down to that extent. Allowing for the fact that it had been opened to extract the ashes, as it had then been reclosed, its condition was undoubtedly favourable to slow cooling. We can confidently put down the time taken by the cooling which had occurred at several days; probably somewhere about a week. Now Dr. Oldfield's inspection was made on the evening of the 15th. A week before that was the 8th. But we have seen that the disappearance occurred between the 7th and the 11th of May; and the temperature of the kiln shows that the burning of the body must have occurred at some time before the 11th and almost certainly after the 7th. It thus appears that the disappearance of Peter Gannet and the destruction of the body both occurred between those two dates. The obvious suggestion is that the body which was burned was the body of Peter Gannet.

"Is there any evidence to support that conclusion? There is not very much. The most striking is the discovery among the ashes of a porcelain tooth. You have heard Mr. Hawley's evidence. He identifies that tooth as one of a very distinctive kind, and he tells us that it is identically and indistinguishably similar to a tooth on the denture which he supplied to Peter Gannet. He will not swear that it is the same tooth; only that is is the exact facsimile of that tooth. So you have to consider what are the probabilities that the body of some unknown person should have been burned in Peter Gannet's kiln and that that person should have worn a denture containing a right upper lateral incisor of the type known as Du Trey's, in all respects identical with that in Peter Gannet's denture; and how such probabilities compare with the alternative probability that the tooth came from Peter Gannet's own denture.

"There is one other item of evidence It is circumstantial evidence and you must consider it for what it seems to be worth. You have heard from Dr. Oldfield and Dr. Thorndyke that some months ago Peter Gannet suffered from arsenic poisoning. Both witnesses agree that the suggestion of accidental poisoning cannot be entertained. It is therefore practically certain that some person or persons administered this poison to Gannet with the intention of causing his death. That intention was frustrated by the alertness of the doctors. The victim survived and recovered.

"But let us see how those facts bear on this inquiry. Some unknown person or persons desired the death of Peter Gannet and sought, by means of poison, to compass it. The attempted murder failed; but we have no reason to suppose that the motive ceased to exist. It it did not, then Peter Gannet went about in constant peril. There was some person who desired his death and who was prepared, given the opportunity, to take appropriate means to kill him.

"Apply these facts to the present case. We see that there was some person who wished Gannet to die and who was prepared to realize that wish by murdering him. We find in Gannet's studio the remains of a person who may be assumed to have been murdered. Gannet has unaccountably disappeared, and the date of his disappearance coincides with that of the appearance of these remains in his studio. Finally, among these remains, we find a tooth of a rather unusual kind which is in every respect identical with one known to have been worn by Peter Gannet. Those are the facts known to us, and I think you will agree with me that they yield only one conclusion; that the remains found in Peter Gannet's studio were the remains of Peter Gannet, himself.

"If you agree with that conclusion, we have answered two of the three questions to which we had to find answers. We now turn to the third: How, and by what means, did deceased come by his death? It appears almost an idle question, for the body of deceased was burned to ashes in a kiln. By no conceivable accident could this have happened, and deceased could not have got into the kiln by himself. The body must have been put in by some other person and deliberately destroyed by fire. But such destruction of a body furnishes the strongest presumptive evidence that the person who destroyed the body had murdered the dead person. We can have no reasonable doubt that deceased was murdered.

"That is as far as we are bound to go. It is not our function to fix the guilt of this crime on any particular person. Nevertheless, we are bound to take notice of any evidence that is before us which seems to point to a particular person as the probable perpetrator of the crime. And there is, in fact, a good deal of such evidence. I am not referring to the arsenic poisoning. We must ignore that, since we have no certain knowledge as to who the poisoner was. But there are several important points of evidence bearing on the probable identity of the person who murdered Peter Gannet. Let us consider them.

"In the first place, there is the personality of the murderer. What do we know about him? Well, we know that he must have been a person who had access to the studio, and he must have had some acquaintance with its arrangements; knew where the various appliances were to be found, which of the bins was the bone-ash-bin, and so on. Then he must have known how to prepare and fire the kiln and where the fuel was kept; and he must have understood the use and management of the appliances that he employed—the grinding-mills and the cupel press, for instance.

"Do we know of any person to whom this description applies?

Yes, we know of one such person, and only one—Frederick Boles. He had free access to the studio, for it was also his own workshop and he had the key. He was familiar with all its arrangements, and some of the appliances, such as the cupel press, were his own. He knew all about the kiln, for we have it in evidence that he was accustomed to helping Gannet light and stoke it when pottery was being fired. He agrees completely with the description, in these respects, which we know must have applied to the murderer; and, I repeat, we know of no other person to whom it would apply.

"Thus there is a *prima facie* probability that the murderer was Frederick Boles. But that probability is conditioned by possibility. Could Boles have been present in the studio when the murder was committed? Our information is that he had been staying at Burnham. But he came home one night and passed that night at his flat and then went away again. What night was it that he spent at the flat? Now, Mrs. Gannet came home on the 14th of May, and she called at Boles's flat on the following day, the 15th. There she learned that he had come to the flat about a week previously, spent the night there and gone away the next day. Apparently, then, it would have been the night of the 8th that he spent at the flat; or it might have been the 7th or the 9th. But Gannet's death occurred between the 7th or the 11th. Consequently, Boles would appear to have been in London at the time when the murder was committed.

"But is there any evidence that he was actually on these premises at this time? There is. A walking-stick was found by Dr. Oldfield in the hall-stand on the night of the 15th. You have seen that stick and I pass it round again. On the silver mount of the handle you can see the initials 'F. B.'—Boles's initials. Mrs. Gannet had no doubt that it belonged to Boles, and indeed there is no one else to whom it could belong. But she has told us that it was not in the hall-stand when she went away. Then it must have been deposited there since. But there is only one day on which it could have been deposited; the day after Boles's arrival at the flat. We thus have clear evidence that Boles was actually on the premises on the 8th, the 9th, or the 10th, that is to say, his presence on these premises seems to coincide in time with the murder of Peter Gannet; and we further note the significant fact that at the time when Boles came to the house, Gannet—if still alive—was there all alone.

"Thus the circumstantial evidence all points to Boles as the probable murderer and we know of no other person against whom any suspicion could rest. Add to this the further fact that the two men—Boles and the deceased—are known to have been on terms of bitter enmity and actually, on at least one occasion, to have engaged in violent conflict; and that evidence receives substantial confirmation

"I think I need say no more than this. You have heard the evidence and I have offered you these suggestions as to its bearing. They are only suggestions. It is you who have to decide on your verdict; and I think you will have little difficulty in answering the three questions that I mentioned in opening this inquiry."

The coroner was right up to a certain point. The jury had apparently agreed on their verdict before he had finished speaking, but found some difficulty in putting it into words. Eventually, however, after one or two trials on paper, the foreman announced that he and his fellow jurors had reached a conclusion; which was that the ashes found in the studio were the remains of the body of Peter Gannet, and that the said Peter Gannet had been murdered by Frederick Boles at some time between the 7th and the 11th of May.

"Yes," said the coroner, "that is the only verdict possible on the evidence before us. I shall record a verdict of wilful murder against Frederick Boles." He paused, and glancing at Inspector Blandy, asked the latter: "Is there any object in my issuing a warrant?"

"No, sir," Blandy replied. "A warrant has already been issued for the arrest of Boles on another charge."

"Then," said the coroner, "that brings these proceedings to an end, and I can only hope that the perpetrator of this crime may shortly be arrested and brought to trial."

On this, the court rose. The reporters hurried away, intent on gorgeous publicity; the spectators drifted out into the street; and the four experts (including myself for this occasion only), after a brief chat with the coroner and the Inspector, departed also and went their respective ways. And here it is proper for me to make my bow to the reader and retire from the post of narrator. Not that the story is ended, but that the pen now passes into another, and I hope more capable, hand. My function has been to trace the antecedents and describe the intimate circumstances of this extraordinary crime, and this I have done to the best of my humble ability. The rest of the story is concerned with the elucidation, and the centre of interest is now transferred from the rather drab neighbourhood of Cumberland Market to the historic precinct of the Inner Temple.

BOOK TWO

NARRATED BY CHRISTOPHER JERVIS, M.D.

CHAPTER 14

DR. JERVIS IS PUZZLED

The stage which the train of events herein recorded had reached when the office of narrator passed to me from the hands of my friend Oldfield, found me in a state of some mental confusion. It seemed that Thorndyke was contemplating some kind of investigation. But why? The Gannet case was no concern of ours. No client had engaged us to examine it, and a mere academic interest in it would not justify a great expenditure of valuable time and effort.

But further, what was there to investigate? In a medico-legal sense there appeared to be nothing. All the facts were known, and though they were lurid enough, they were of little scientific interest. Gannet's death presented no problem, since it was a bald and obvious case of murder; and if his mode of life seemed to be shrouded in mystery, that was not our affair, nor, indeed, that of anybody else, now that he was dead.

But it was precisely this apparently irrelevant matter that seemed to engage Thorndyke's attention. The ostensible business of the studio had, almost certainly, covered some other activities, doubtful if not actually unlawful, and Thorndyke seemed to be set on ascertaining what they were; whereas, to me, that question appeared to be exclusively the concern of the police in their efforts to locate the elusive Boles.

I had the first inkling of Thorndyke's odd methods of approach to this problem on the day after our memorable dinner at Osnaburgh Street. On our way home, he had proposed that we should look in at the gallery where Gannet's pottery was on view, and I had agreed readily, being quite curious as to what these remarkable works were really like. So it happened naturally enough that when, on the following day, we entered the temple of the Fine arts, my attention was at first entirely occupied with the exhibits.

I will not attempt to describe those astonishing works for I feel that my limited vocabulary would be unequal to the task. There are some things that must be seen to be believed, and Gannet's pottery was one of them. Outspoken as Oldfield had been in his description of them, I found myself totally unprepared for the outrageous reality. But I need not dwell on them. Merely remarking that they looked to me like the throw-outs from some very juvenile handiwork class, I will dismiss them—as I did, in fact—and proceed to the apparent purpose of our visit.

Perhaps the word "apparent" is inappropriate, for in truth, the purpose of our visit was not apparent to me at all. I can only record this incomprehensible course of events, leaving their inner meaning to emerge at a later stage of this history. By the time that I had recovered from the initial shock and convinced myself that I was not the subject of an optical illusion, Thorndyke had already introduced himself to the gallery proprietor, Mr. Kempster, and seemed to be discussing the exhibits in terms of the most extraordinary irrelevance.

"Having regard," he was saying, as I joined them, "to the density of the material and the thickness of the sides, I should think that these pieces must be rather inconveniently ponderous."

"They are heavy," Mr. Kempster admitted, "but you see they are collector's pieces. They are not intended for use. You wouldn't want, for instance, to hand this one across the dinner table."

He picked up a large and massive bowl and offered it to Thorndyke, who took it and weighed it in his two hands with an expression of ridiculous earnestness.

"Yes," he said, as he returned it to Mr. Kempster, "it is extremely ponderous for its size. What should you say it weighs? I should guess it at nearly eight pounds."

He looked solemnly at the obviously puzzled Kempster, who tried it again and agreed to Thorndyke's estimate. "But," he added, "there's no need to guess. If you are interested in the matter, we can try it. There is a pair of parcel scales in my office. Would you like to see what it really does weigh?"

'If you would be so kind," Thorndyke replied; whereupon Kempster picked up the bowl and we followed him in procession to the office, as if we were about to perform some sacrificial rite, where the uncouth pot was placed on the scale and found to be half an ounce short of eight pounds.

"Yes," said Thorndyke, "it is abnormally heavy even for its size. That weight suggests an unusually dense material."

He gazed reflectively at the bowl, and then, producing a spring tape from his pocket, proceeded carefully to measure the principal dimensions of the piece while Mr. Kempster looked on like a man in a dream. But not only did Thorndyke take the measurements. He made a note of them in his note-book together with one of the weight.

"You appear," said Mr. Kempster, as Thorndyke pocketed his note-book, "to be greatly interested in poor Mr. Gannet's work."

"I am," Thorndyke replied. "but not from the connoisseur's point of view. As I mentioned to you, I am trying, on Mrs. Gannet's behalf, to elucidate the very obscure circumstances of her husband's death."

"I shouldn't have supposed," said Kempster, "that the weight of his pottery would have had much bearing on that. But of course you know more about evidence than I do; and you know—which I don't—what obscurities you want to clear up."

"Thank you," said Thorndyke. "If you will adopt that principle, it will be extremely helpful."

Mr. Kempster bowed. "You may take it, Doctor," said he, "that, as a friend of poor Gannet's, though not a very intimate one, I shall be glad to be of assistance to you. Is there anything more that you want to know about this work?"

"There are several matters," Thorndyke replied; "in fact, I want to know all that I can about his pottery, including its disposal and its economic aspects. To begin with, was there much of it sold? Enough, I mean, to yield a living to the artist?"

"There was more sold than you might have expected, and the pieces realized good prices; ten to twenty guineas each. But I never supposed that Gannet made a living by his work. I assumed that he had some independent means."

"The next question," said Thorndyke, "is what became of the pieces that were sold? Did they go to museums or to private collectors?"

"Of the pieces sold from this gallery—and I think that this was his principal market—one or two were bought by provincial museums, but all the rest were taken by private collectors."

"And what sort of people were those collectors?"

"That," said Kempster, with a deprecating smile, "is a rather delicate question. The things were offered for sale in my gallery and the purchasers were, in a sense, my clients."

"Quite so," said Thorndyke. "It was not really a fair question; and not very necessary as I have seen the pottery. I suppose you don't keep any records of the sales or the buyers?"

"Certainly I do," replied Kempster. "I keep a Day Book and a ledger. The ledger contains a complete record of the sales of each of the exhibitors. Would you like to see Mr. Gannet's account?"

"I am ashamed to give you so much trouble," Thorndyke replied, "but if you would be so very kind—"

"It's no trouble at all," said Kempster, stepping across to a tall cupboard and throwing open the doors. From the row of books therein revealed, he took out a portly volume and laid it on the desk, turning over the leaves until he found the page that he was seeking.

"Here," he said, "is a record of all of Mr. Gannet's works that have been sold from this gallery. Perhaps you may get some information from it."

I glanced down the page while Thorndyke was examining it and was a little surprised at the completeness of the record. Under the general heading, "Peter Gannet Esq." was a list of the articles sold, with a brief description of each, and in separate columns, the date, the price and the name and address of each purchaser.

"I notice," said Thorndyke, "that Mr. Francis Broomhill of Stafford Square has made purchases on three occasions. Probably he is a collector of modernist work?"

"He is," replied Kempster, "and a special admirer of Mr. Gannet. You will observe that he bought one of the two copies of the figurine in stoneware of a monkey. The other copy, as you see, went to America."

"Did Mr. Gannet ever execute any other figurines?" Thorndyke asked.

"No," Kempster replied. "To my surprise, he never pursued that form of art, though it was a striking success. Mr. Bunderby, the eminent art critic, was enthusiastic about it, and as you see, the only copies offered realized fifty guineas each. But perhaps if he had lived he might have given his admirers some further examples."

"You speak of copies," said Thorndyke, "so I presume that they were admittedly replicas, probably squeezed in a mould or possibly slip-casts? It was not pretended that they were original modelings?"

"No, they couldn't have been. A small pottery figure must be made in a mould, either squeezed or cast, to get it hollow. Of course it would be modeled in the solid in the first place and the mould made from the solid model."

"There was a third specimen of this figurine," said Thorndyke, "I saw it in Gannet's bedroom. Would that also be a squeeze, or do you suppose it might be the original? It was certainly stoneware."

"Then it must have been squeezed from a mould," replied Kempster. "It couldn't have been fired solid; it would have cracked all to pieces. The only alternative would have been to excavate the solid original; which would have been extremely difficult and quite unnecessary, as he certainly had a mould."

"From your recollection of the figurines, should you say that they were as thick and ponderous as the bowls and jars?"

"I can't say, positively," replied Kempster, "but they could hardly have been. A figure is more likely to crack in the fire than an open bowl or jar, but the thinner it is, in reason, the safer it is from fire cracks. And it is just as easy to make a squeeze thin as thick."

This virtually brought our business with Mr. Kempster to an end. We walked out into the gallery with him, when Thorndyke had copied out a few particulars from the ledger, but our conversation, apart from a brief discussion of Boles's jewelry exhibits, obviously had no connection with the purpose of our visit—whatever that might be. Eventually, having shaken his hand warmly and thanked him for his very courteous and helpful treatment of us, we took our departure, leaving him, I suspect, as much puzzled by our proceedings as I was myself.

"I suppose, Thorndyke," said I, as we walked away down Bond Street, "you realize that you have enveloped me in a fog of quite phenomenal density?"

"I can understand," he replied, "that you find my approach to the problem somewhat indirect."

"The problem!" I exclaimed. "What problem? I don't see that there is any problem. We know that Gannet was murdered and we can fairly assume that he was murdered by Boles. But whether he was or not is no concern of ours. That is Blandy's problem; and in any case, I can't imagine that the weight and density of Gannet's pottery has any bearing on it, unless you are suggesting that Boles biffed deceased on the head with one of his own pots."

Thorndyke smiled indulgently as he replied:

"No, Jervis. I am not considering Gannet's pots as possible lethal weapons, but the potter's art has its bearing on our problem, and even the question of weight may be not entirely irrelevant."

"But what problem are you alluding to?" I persisted.

"The problem that is in my mind," he replied, "is suggested by the very remarkable story that Oldfield related to us last night. You listened to that story very attentively and no doubt you remember the substance of it. Now, recalling that story as a whole and considering it as an account of a series of related events, doesn't it seem to you to suggest some very curious and interesting questions?"

"The only question that it suggested to me was how the devil that arsenic got into the bone-ash. I could make nothing of that."

"Very well," he rejoined, "then try to make something of it. The arsenic was certainly there. We agree that it could not have come from the body. Then it must have got into the ash after the firing. But how? There is one problem. Take it as a starting point and consider what explanations are possible; and further, consider what would be the implications of each of your explanations."

"But," I exclaimed, "I can't think of any explanation. The thing is incomprehensible. Besides, what business is it of ours? We are not engaged in the case."

"Don't lose sight of Blandy," said he. "He hasn't shot his bolt yet. If he can lay hands on Boles, he will give us no trouble, but if he fails in that, he may think it worth while to give some attention to Mrs. Gannet. I don't know whether he suspects her of actual complicity in the murder, but it is obvious that he does suspect her of knowing and concealing the whereabouts of Boles. Consequently, if he can get no information from her by persuasion, he might consider the possibility of charging her as an accessory either before or after the fact."

"But," I objected, "the choice wouldn't lie with him. You are surely not suggesting that either the police or the Public Prosecutor would entertain the idea of bringing a charge for the purpose of extorting information—virtually as a measure of intimidation?"

"Certainly not," he replied, "unless Blandy could make out a *prima facie* case. But it is possible that he knows more than we do about the relations of Boles and Mrs. Gannet. At any rate, the position is that I have made a conditional promise to Oldfield that if any proceedings should be taken against her I will undertake the defense. It is not likely that any proceedings will be taken, but still it is necessary for me to know as much as I can learn about the circumstances connected with the murder. Hence these inquiries."

"Which seem to me to lead nowhere. However, as Kempster remarked, you know—which I do not—what obscurities you are trying to elucidate. Do you know whether there is going to be an inquest?"

"I understand," he replied, "that an inquest is to be held in the course of a few days and I expect to be summoned to give evidence concerning the arsenic poisoning. But I should attend in any case, and I recommend you to come with me. When we have heard what the various witnesses, including Blandy, have to tell, we shall have a fairly complete knowledge of the facts, and we may be able to judge whether the Inspector is keeping anything up his sleeve."

As the reader will have learned from Oldfield's narrative—which this account overlaps by a few days—I adopted Thorndyke's advice and attended the inquest. But though I gained thereby a knowledge of all the facts of the case, I was no nearer to any understanding of the purpose that Thorndyke had in view in his study of Gannet's pottery; nor did I find myself entirely in sympathy with his interest in Mrs. Gannet. I realized that she was in a difficult and trying position, but I was less convinced than he appeared to be of her complete innocence of any complicity in the murder or the very suspicious poisoning affair that had preceded it.

But his interest in her was quite remarkable. It went so far as actually to induce him to attend the funeral of her husband and even to persuade me to accept the invitation and accompany him. Not that I needed much persuasion, for the unique opportunity of witnessing a funeral at which there was no coffin and no corpse— where "our dear departed brother" might almost have been produced in a paper bag—was not to be missed.

But it hardly came up to my expectations, for it appeared that the ashes had been deposited in the urn before the proceedings began, and the funeral service took its normal course, with the terra-cotta casket in place of the coffin. But I found a certain grim humour in the circumstance that the remains of Peter Gannet should be enshrined in a pottery vessel of obviously commercial origin which in all its properties—in its exact symmetry and mechanical regularity— was the perfect antithesis of his own masterpieces.

CHAPTER 15

A MODERNIST COLLECTOR

My experiences at Mr. Kempster's gallery were only a foretaste of what Thorndyke could do in the way of mystification, for I need not say that the most profound cogitation on Oldfield's story and on the facts which had transpired at the inquest had failed completely to enlighten me. I was still unable to perceive that there was any real problem to solve, or that, if there were, the physical properties of Gannet's pottery could possibly be a factor in its solution.

But obviously I was wrong. For Thorndyke was no wild goose hunter or discoverer of mare's nests. If he believed that there was a problem to investigate, I could safely assume that there was such a problem; and if he believed that Gannet's pottery held a clue to it, I could assume—and did assume—that he was right. Accordingly, I waited, patiently and hopefully, for some further developments which might dissipate the fog in which my mind was enshrouded.

The further developments were not long in appearing. On the third day after the funeral, Thorndyke announced to me that he had made, by letter, an appointment, which included me, with Mr. Francis Broomhill of Stafford Square, for a visit of inspection of his famous collection of works of modernist art. I gathered, subsequently, by the way in which we were received, that Thorndyke's letter must have been somewhat misleading, in tone if not in matter. But any little mental reservations as to our views on contemporary art were, I suppose, admissible in the circumstances.

Of course I accepted gleefully for I was on the tiptoe of curiosity as to Thorndyke's object in making the appointment. Moreover, the collection included Gannet's one essay in the art of sculpture; which, if it matched his pottery, ought certainly to be worth seeing. Accordingly, we set forth together in the early afternoon and made our way to the exclusive and aristocratic region in which Mr. Broomhill had his abode.

The whole visit was a series of surprises. In the first place, the door was opened by a footman, a type of organism that I supposed to be virtually extinct. Then, no sooner had we entered the grand old Georgian house than we seemed to become enveloped in an atmosphere of unreality suggestive of Alice in Wonderland or of a nightmare visit to a lunatic asylum. The effect began in the entrance hall, which was hung with strange, polychromatic picture frames enclosing objects which obviously were not pictures but appeared to be panels or canvases on which some very extravagant painter had cleaned his palette. Standing about the spacious floor were pedestals supporting lumps of stone or metal, some—to my eye—completely shapeless, while others had faint hints of obscure anthropoidal character such as one might associate with the discarded failures from the workshop of some Easter Island sculptor. I glanced at them in bewilderment as the footman, having taken possession of our hats and sticks, solemnly conducted us along the great hall to a fine pedimented doorway, and opening a noble, many-paneled, mahogany door, ushered us into the presence.

Mr. Francis Broomhill impressed me favourably at the first glance; a tall, frail-looking man of about forty with a slight stoop and the forward poise of the head that one associates with near sight. He wore a pair of deep concave spectacles mounted in massive tortoise-shell frames; looking at those spectacles with a professional eye, I decided that without them his eyesight would have been negligible. But though the pale blue eyes, seen through those powerful lenses, appeared ridiculously small, they were kindly eyes that conveyed a friendly greeting, and the quiet, pleasant voice confirmed the impression.

"It is exceedingly kind of you," said Thorndyke, when we had shaken hands, "to give us this opportunity of seeing your treasures."

"But not at all," was the reply. "It is I who am the beneficiary. The things are here to be looked at and it is a delight to me to show them to appreciative connoisseurs. I don't often get the chance; for even in this golden age of artistic progress, there still lingers a hankering for the merely representational and anecdotal aspects of art."

As he was speaking, I glanced round the room and especially at the pictures which covered the walls, and as I looked at them they seemed faintly to recall an experience of my early professional life when, for a few weeks, I had acted as *locum-tenens* for the superintendent of a small lunatic asylum (or "mental hospital" as we say nowadays). The figures in them—when recognizable as such—all seemed to have a certain queer psychopathic quality as if they were looking out at me from a padded cell.

After a short conversation, during which I maintained a cautious reticence and Thorndyke was skilfully elusive, we proceeded on a tour of inspection round the room under the guidance of Mr. Broomhill, who enlightened us with comment and exposition, somewhat in the Bunderby manner. There was a quite considerable collection of pictures, all by modern artists—mostly foreign, I was glad to note—and all singularly alike. The same curious psychopathic quality pervaded them all, and the same odd absence of the traditional characteristics of pictures. The drawing—when there was any—was childish, the painting was barbarously crude, and there was a total lack of any sort of mental content or subject matter.

"Now," said our host, halting before one of these masterpieces, "here is a work that I am rather fond of though it is a departure from the artist's usual manner. He is not often as realistic as this."

I glanced at the gold label beneath it and read: "Nude. Israel Popoff"; and nude it certainly was—apparently representing a naked human being with limbs like very badly made sausages. I did not find it painfully realistic. But the next picture—by the same artist—fairly "got me guessing," for it appeared to consist of nothing more than a disorderly mass of streaks of paint of various rather violent colours. I waited for explanatory comments as Mr. Broomhill stood before it, regarding it fondly.

"This," said he, "I regard as a truly representative example of the Master; a perfect piece of abstract painting. Don't you agree with me?" he added, turning to me, beaming with enthusiasm.

The suddenness of the question disconcerted me. What the deuce did he mean by "abstract painting"? I hadn't the foggiest idea. You might as well—it seemed to me—talk about "abstract amputation at the hip-joint." But I had got to say something, and I did.

"Yes," I burbled incoherently, gazing at him in consternation. "Certainly—in fact, undoubtedly—a most remarkable and—er—" (I was going to say "cheerful" but mercifully saw the red light in time) "most interesting demonstration of colour contrast. But I am afraid I am not perfectly clear as to what the picture represents."

"Represents!" he repeated in a tone of pained surprise. "It doesn't represent anything. Why should it? It is a picture. But a picture is an independent entity. It doesn't need to imitate something else."

"No, of course not," I spluttered mendaciously. "But still, one has been accustomed to find in pictures representations of natural objects—"

"But why?" he interrupted. "If you want the natural objects, you can go and look at them; and if you want them represented, you can have them photographed. So why allow them to intrude into pictures?"

I looked despairingly at Thorndyke but got no help from that quarter. He was listening impassively; but from long experience of him, I knew that behind the stony calm of his exterior his inside was shaking with laughter. So I murmured a vague assent, adding that it was difficult to escape from the conventional ideas that one had held from early youth; and so we moved on to the next "abstraction." But warned by this terrific experience, I maintained thereafter a discreet silence tempered by carefully prepared ambiguities, and thus managed to complete our tour of the room without further disaster.

"And now," said our host as we turned away from the last of the pictures, "you would like to see the sculptures and pottery. You mentioned in your letter that you were especially interested in poor Mr. Gannet's work. Well, you shall see it in appropriate surroundings, as he would have liked to see it."

He conducted us across the hall to another fine door which he threw open to admit us to the sculpture gallery. Looking around me as we entered, I was glad that I had seen the pictures first; for now I was prepared for the worst and could keep my emotions under control.

I shall not attempt to describe that chamber of horrors. My first impression was that of a sort of infernal Mrs. Jarley's; and the place was pervaded by the same madhouse atmosphere as I had noticed in the other room. But it was more unpleasant, for debased sculpture can be much more horrible than debased painting; and in the entire collection there was not a single work that could be called normal. The exhibits ranged from almost formless objects, having only that faint suggestion of a human head or figure that one sometimes notices in queer-shaped potatoes or flint nodules, to recognizable busts or torsos; but in these the faces were hideous and bestial and the limbs and trunks misshapen and characterized by a horrible obesity suggestive of dropsy or myxœdema. There was a little pottery, all crude and coarse, but Gannet's pieces were easily the worst.

"This, I think," said our host, "is what you specially wanted to see."

He indicated a grotesque statuette labeled "Figurine of a Monkey: Peter Gannet," and I looked at it curiously. If I had met it anywhere else it would have given me quite a severe shock; but here, in this collection of monstrosities, it looked almost like the work of a sane barbarian.

"There was some question," Mr. Broomhill continued, "that you wanted to settle, was there not?"

"Yes," Thorndyke replied, "in fact, there are two. The first is that of priority. Gannet executed three versions of this figurine. One has gone to America, one is on loan at a London Museum, and this is the third. The question is, which was made first?"

"There ought not to be any difficulty about that," said our host. "Gannet used to sign and number all his pieces and the serial number should give the order of priority at a glance."

He lifted the image carefully, and having inverted it and looked at its base, handed it to Thorndyke.

"You see," said he, "that the number is 571B. Then there must have been a 571A and a 571C. But clearly, this must have been the second one made, and if you can examine the one at the museum, you can settle the order of the series. If that is 571A, then the American copy must be 571C, or vice versa. What is the other question?"

"That relates to the nature of the first one made. Is it the original model or is it a pressing from a mould? This one appears to be a squeeze. If you look inside, you can see traces of the thumb impressions, so it can't be a cast."

He returned it to Mr. Broomhill who peered into the opening of the base and then, having verified Thorndyke's observation, passed it to me. I was not deeply interested, but I examined the base carefully and looked into the dark interior as well as I could. The flat surface of the base was smooth but unglazed and on it was inscribed in blue around the central opening "Op. 571B P. G." with a rudely drawn figure of a bird, which might have been a goose but which I knew was meant for a gannet, interposed between the number and the initials. Inside, on the uneven surface, I could make out a number of impressions of a thumb—apparently a right thumb. Having made these observations, I handed the effigy back to Mr. Broomhill who replaced it on its stand, and resumed the conversation.

"I should imagine that all of the three versions were pressings, but that is only an opinion. What is your view?"

"There are three possibilities, and bearing in mind Gannet's personality, I don't know which of them is the most probable. The original figure was certainly modeled in the solid. Then Opus 571A may either be that model, fired in the solid, or that model excavated and fired, or a squeeze from the mould."

"It would hardly have been possible to fire it in the solid," said Mr. Broomhill.

"That was Mr. Kempster's view, but I am not so sure. After all, some pottery articles are fired solid. Bricks, for instance."

"Yes, but a few fire cracks in a brick don't matter. I think he would have had to excavate it, at least. But why should he have taken that trouble when he had actually made a mould?"

"I can imagine no reason at all," replied Thorndyke, "unless he wished to keep the original. The one now at the museum was his own property and I don't think it had ever been offered for sale."

"If the question is of any importance," said our host—who was obviously of opinion that it was not—"it could perhaps be settled by inspection of the piece at the museum, which was probably the first one made. Don't you think so?"

"It might," Thorndyke replied, "or it might not. The most satisfactory way would be to compare the respective weights of the two pieces. An excavated figurine would be heavier than a pressing, and, of course, a solid one would be much heavier."

"Yes," Mr. Broomhill agreed with a slightly puzzled air, "that is true. So I take it that you would like to know the exact weight of this piece. Well, there is no difficulty about that."

He walked over to the fireplace and pressed the bell-push at its side. In a few moments the door opened and the footman entered the room.

"Can you tell me, Hooper," Mr. Broomhill asked, "if there is a pair of scales that we could have to weigh this statuette?"

"Certainly, sir," was the reply. "There is a pair in Mr. Laws's pantry. Shall I bring them up, sir?"

"If you would, Hooper—with the weights, of course. And you might see that the pan is quite clean."

Apparently the pan was quite clean, for in a couple of minutes Hooper reappeared carrying a very spick and span pair of scales with a complete set of weights. When the scales had been placed on the table with the weights beside them, Mr. Broomhill took up the effigy with infinite care and lowered it gently on to the scale pan. Then, with the same care to avoid jars or shocks, he put on the weights, building up a little pile until the pan rose, when he made the final adjustment with a half-ounce weight.

"Three pounds, three and a half ounces," said he. "Rather a lot for a small figure."

"Yes," Thorndyke agreed, "but Gannet used a dense material and was pretty liberal with it. I weighed some of his pottery at Kempster's gallery and found it surprisingly heavy."

He entered the weight of the effigy in his note-book, and, when the masterpiece had been replaced on its stand and the scales borne away to their abiding place, we resumed our tour of the room. Presently Hooper returned, bearing a large silver tray loaded with the materials for afternoon tea, which he placed on a small circular table.

"You needn't wait, Hooper," said our host. "We will help ourselves when we are ready." As the footman retired, we turned to the last of the exhibits—a life-sized figure of a woman, naked, contorted and obese, whose brutal face and bloated limbs seemed to shout for thyroid extract—and having expatiated on its noble rendering of abstract form and its freedom from the sickly prettiness of "mere imitative sculpture," our host dismissed the masterpieces and placed chairs for us by the table.

"Which museum is it," he asked, as we sipped the excellent China tea, "that is showing Mr. Gannet's work?"

"It is a small museum at Hoxton," Thorndyke replied, "known as 'The People's Museum of Modern Art.' "

"Ah!" said Broomhill, "I know it; in fact, I occasionally lend some of my treasures for exhibition there. It is an excellent institution. It gives the poor people of that uncultured region an opportunity of becoming acquainted with the glories of modern art; the only chance they have."

"There is the Geffrye Museum close by," I reminded him.

"Yes," he agreed, "but that is concerned with the obsolete furniture and art of the bad old times. It contains nothing of this sort," he added, indicating his collection with a wave of the hand. Which was certainly true. Mercifully, it does not.

"And I hope," he continued, "that you will be able to settle your question when you examine the figurine there. It doesn't seem to me to matter very much, but you are a better judge of that than I am."

When we had taken leave of our kind and courteous host and set forth on our homeward way, we walked for a time in silence, each occupied with his own thoughts. As to Thorndyke's ultimate purpose in this queer transaction, I could not make the vaguest guess and I gave it no consideration. But the experience, itself, had been an odd one with a peculiar interest of its own. Presently I opened the subject with a question.

"Could you make anything of this stuff of Broomhill's or of his attitude to it?"

Thorndyke shook his head. "No," he replied. "It is a mystery to me. Evidently Broomhill gets a positive pleasure from these things, and that pleasure seems to be directly proportionate to their badness; to the absence in them of all the ordinary qualities—fine workmanship, truth to nature, intellectual interest and beauty—which have hitherto been considered to be the essentials of works of art. It seems to be a cult, a fashion, associated with a certain state of mind; but what that state of mind is, I cannot imagine. Obviously it has no connection with what has always been known as art, unless it is a negative connection. You noticed that Broomhill was utterly contemptuous of the great work of the past, and that, I think, is the usual modernist attitude But what can be the state of mind of a man who is completely insensitive to the works of the accomplished masters of the older schools, and full of enthusiasm for clumsy imitations of the works of savages or ungifted children, I cannot begin to understand."

"No," said I, "that is precisely my position," and with this the subject dropped.

CHAPTER 16

AT THE MUSEUM

"It is curious to reflect," Thorndyke remarked, as we took our way eastward along Old Street, "that this, which is commonly accounted one of the meanest and most squalid regions of the town, should be, in a sense, the last outpost of a disappearing culture."

"To what culture are your referring?" I asked.

"To that of the industrial arts," he replied, "of which we may say that it is substantially the foundation of all artistic culture. Nearly everywhere else those arts are dead or dying, killed by machinery and mass production, but here we find little groups of surviving craftsmen who still keep the lamp burning. To our right in Curtain Road and various small streets adjoining, are skilled cabinet makers, making chairs and other furniture in the obsolete tradition of what Broomhill would call the bad old times of Chippendale and his contemporaries; near by in Bunhill Row the last of the makers of fine picture frames have their workshops, and farther ahead in Bethnal Green and Spitalfields a remnant of the ancient colony of silk weavers is working with the hand-loom as was done in the eighteenth century."

"Yes," I agreed, "it seems rather an anomaly; and our present mission seems to rub in the discrepancy. I wonder what inspired the founders of The People's Museum of Modern Art to dump it down in this neighbourhood and almost in sight of the Geffrye Museum?"

Thorndyke chuckled softly. "The two museums," said he, "are queer neighbours; the one treasuring the best work of the past and the other advertising the worst work of the present. But perhaps we shan't find it as bad as we expect."

I don't know what Thorndyke expected, but it was bad enough for me. We located it without difficulty by means of a painted board inscribed with its name and description set over what looked like a reconstructed shop front, to which had been added a pair of massive folding doors. But those doors were closed and presumably locked, for a large card affixed to the panel with drawing pins bore the announcement, "Closed temporarily. Re-open 11:15."

Thorndyke looked at his watch. "We have a quarter of an hour to wait," said he, "but we need not wait here. We may as well take a stroll and inspect the neighbourhood. It is not beautiful, but it has a character of its own which is worth examining."

Accordingly, we set forth on a tour of exploration through the narrow streets where Thorndyke expounded the various objects of interest in illustration of his previous observations. In one street we found a row of cabinet makers' shops, through the windows of which we could see the half-finished carcases of wardrobes and sideboards and "period" chairs, seatless and unpolished; and I noticed that the names above the shops were mostly Jewish and many of them foreign. Then, towards Shoreditch, we observed a timber yard with a noble plank of Spanish mahogany at the entrance, and noted that the stock inside seemed to consist mainly of hardwoods suitable for making furniture. But there was no time to make a detailed examination for the clock of a neighbouring church now struck the quarter and sent us hurrying back to the temple of modernism, where we found that the card had vanished and the doors stood wide open, revealing a lobby and an inner door.

As we opened the latter and entered the gallery we were met by an elderly, tired-looking man who regarded us expectantly.

"Are you Mr. Sancroft?" Thorndyke asked.

"Ah!" said our friend, "then I was right. You will be Dr. Thorndyke. I hope I haven't kept you waiting."

"Only a matter of minutes," Thorndyke replied, in his suavest manner, "and we spent those quite agreeably."

"I am so very sorry," said Sancroft, with evidently genuine concern, "but it was unavoidable. I had to go out, and as I am all alone here, I had to lock up the place while I was away. It is very awkward having no one to leave in charge."

"It must be," Thorndyke agreed, sympathetically. "Do you mean that you have no assistant of any kind, not even a doorkeeper?"

"No one at all," replied Sancroft. "You see, the society which runs this museum has no funds but the members' contributions. There's only just enough to keep the place going, without paying any salaries. I am a voluntary worker, but I have my living to earn.

Mostly I can do my work in the curator's room—I am a law writer—
but there are times when I have to go out on business, and then—
well, you saw what happened this morning."

Thorndyke listened to this tale of woe, not only with patience
but with a concern that rather surprised me.

"But," said he, "can't you get some of your friends to give you
at least a little help? Even a few hours a day would solve your
difficulties."

Mr. Sancroft shook his head wearily. "No," he replied, "it is a
dull job, minding a small gallery, especially as so few visitors come
to it, and I have found nobody who is willing to take it on. I
suppose," he added, with a sad smile, "you don't happen to know
of any enthusiast in modern art who would make the sacrifice in the
interests of popular enlightenment and culture?"

"At the moment," said Thorndyke, "I can think of nobody but
Mr. Broomhill, and I don't suppose he could spare the time. Still,
I will bear your difficulties in mind, and if I should think of any
person who might be willing to help, I will try my powers of persuasion on him."

I must confess that this reply rather astonished me. Thorndyke
was a kindly man, but he was a busy man and hardly in a position
to enter into Mr. Sancroft's difficulties. And with him a promise
was a promise, not a mere pleasant form of words; a fact which I
think Sancroft hardly realized for his expression of thanks seemed
to imply gratitude for a benevolent intention rather than any
expectation of actual performance.

"It is very kind of you to wish to help me," said he. "And now,
as to your own business. I understand that you want to make some
sort of inspection of the works of Mr. Gannet. Does that involve
taking them out of the case?"

"If that is permissible," Thorndyke replied. "I wanted, among
other matters, to feel the weight of them."

"There is no objection to your taking them out," said Sancroft,
"for a definite purpose. I will unlock the case and put the things in
your custody for the time being. And then I will ask you to excuse
me. I have a lease to engross, and I want to get on with it as quickly
as I can."

With this he led us to the glass case in which Gannet's atrocities
were exposed to view, and having unlocked it, made us a little bow
and retired into his lair.

"That lease," Thorndyke remarked, "is a stroke of luck for us. Now we can discuss the matter freely."

He reached into the case and lifting out the effigy, began to examine it in the closest detail, especially as to the upturned base.

"The questions, as I understand them," said I, "are, first, priority, and second, method of work; whether it was fired solid, or excavated, or squeezed in a mould. The priority seems to be settled by the signature. This is 571A. Then it must have been the first piece made."

"Yes," Thorndyke agreed, "I think we may accept that. What do you say as to the method?"

"That, also, seems to be settled by the character of the base. It is a solid base without any opening, which appears to me to prove that the figure was fired solid."

"A reasonable inference," said Thorndyke, "from the particular fact. But if you look at the sides, you will notice on each a linear mark which suggests that a seam or join had been scraped off. You probably observed similar marks on Broomhill's copy, which were evidently the remains of the seam from the mould. But the question of solidity will be best determined by the weight. Let us try that."

He produced from his pocket a portable spring balance and a piece of string. In the latter he made two "running bowlines," and, hitching them over the figure near its middle, hooked the "bight" of the string on to the balance. As he held up the latter, I read off from the index, "Three pounds, nine and a half ounces. If I remember rightly, Broomhill's image weighed three pounds, three and a half ounces, so this one is six ounces heavier. That seems to support the view that this figure was fired in the solid."

"I don't think it does, Jervis," said he. "Broomhill's copy was undoubtedly a pressing with a considerable cavity and not very thick walls. I should say that the solid figure would be at least twice the weight of the pressing."

A moment's reflection showed me that he was right. Six ounces obviously could not account for the difference between a hollow and a solid figure.

"Then," said I, "it must have been excavated. That would probably just account for the difference in weight."

"Yes," Thorndyke agreed, but a little doubtfully, "so far as the weight is concerned, that is quite sound. But there are these marks, which certainly look like the traces of a seam which has been scraped down. What do you say to them?"

"I should say that they are traces of the excavating process. It would be necessary to cut the figure in halves in order to hollow out the interior. I say that these marks are the traces of the join where the two halves were put together."

"The objection to that," said he, "is that the figure would not have been cut in halves. When a clay work, such as a terra-cotta bust, is hollowed out, the usual practice is to cut off the back in as thin a slice as possible, excavate the main mass of the bust, and when it is as hollow as is safe, to stick the back on with slip and work over the joins until they are invisible. And that is the obvious and reasonable way in which to do it. But these marks are in the middle, just where the seams would be in a pressing, and in the same position as those in Broomhill's copy. So that, in spite of the extra weight, I am disposed to think that this figure is really a pressing, like Broomhill's. And that is, on other grounds, the obvious probability. A mould was certainly made, and it must have been made from the solid figure. But it would have been much more troublesome to excavate the solid model than to make a squeeze from the mould."

As he spoke, he tapped the figure lightly with his knuckle as it hung from the balance, but the dull sound that he elicited gave no information either way, beyond proving—which we knew already from the weight—that the walls of the shell were thick and clumsy. Then he took off the string, and having offered the image to me for further examination (which I declined), he put it back in the case. Then we went into the curator's room to let Mr. Sancroft know that we had finished our inspection, and to thank him for having given us the facilities for making it.

"Well," said he, laying aside his pen, "I suppose that now you know all about Peter Gannet's works, which is more than I do. They are rather over the heads of most of our visitors, and mine, too."

"They are not very popular, then," Thorndyke ventured.

"I wouldn't say that," Sancroft replied with a faint smile. "The monkey figure seems to afford a good deal of amusement. But that is not quite what we are out for. Our society seeks to instruct and elevate, not to give a comic entertainment. I shan't be sorry when the owner of that figure fetches it away."

"The owner?" Thorndyke repeated. "You mean Mrs. Gannet?"

"No," replied Sancroft, "it doesn't belong to her. Gannet sold it, but as the purchaser was making a trip to America he got permission to lend it to us until such time as the owner should return and claim it. I am expecting him at any time now; and as I said, I shall be glad when he does come, for the thing is making the gallery a laughing stock among the regular visitors. They are not advanced enough for the really extreme modernist sculpture."

"And suppose the owner never does turn up?" Thorndyke asked.

"Then I suppose we should hand it back to Mrs. Gannet. But I don't anticipate any difficulty of that sort. The purchaser—a Mr. Newman, I think—gave fifty pounds for it, so he is not likely to forget to call for it."

"No, indeed," Thorndyke agreed. "It is an enormous price. Did Gannet himself tell you what he sold it for?"

"Not Gannet. I never met him. It was Mrs. Gannet who told me when she brought it with the pottery."

"I suppose," said Thorndyke, "that the owner, when he comes to claim his property, will produce some evidence of his identity? You would hardly hand over a valuable piece such as this seems to be, to anyone who might come and demand it, unless you happen to know him by sight?"

"I don't," replied Sancroft. "I've never seen the man. But the question of identity is provided for. Mrs. Gannet left a couple of letters with me from her husband which will make the transaction quite safe. Would you like to see them? I know you are interested in Mrs. Gannet's affairs."

Without waiting for a reply, he unlocked and pulled out a drawer in the writing table, and having turned over a number of papers, took out two letters pinned together.

"Here they are," said he, handing them to Thorndyke, who spread them out so that we could both read them. The contents of the first one were as follows:

> "12, Jacob Street.
> "April 13th, 1931.

"DEAR MR. SANCROFT,

"In addition to the collection of pottery for exhibition on loan, I am sending you a stoneware figurine of a monkey. This is no longer my property as I have sold it to a Mr. James Newman. But as he is making a business trip to the United States, he has given me permission to deposit it on loan with you until he returns to England; this he expects to do in about three months' time. He will then call on you and present the letter of introduction of which I attach a copy; and you will then deliver the figurine to him and take a receipt from him which I will ask you kindly to send on to me.

"Yours sincerely,

"PETER GANNET."

The second letter was the copy referred to, and read thus:

"DEAR MR. SANCROFT,

"The bearer of this, Mr. James Newman, is the owner of the figurine of a monkey which I deposited on loan with you. Will you kindly deliver it to him, if he wants to have possession of it, or take his instructions as to its disposal? If he wishes to take it away with him, please secure a receipt for it before handing it over to him.

"Yours sincerely,

"PETER GANNET."

"You see," said Sancroft, as Thorndyke returned the letters, "he wrote on the 13th of April, so, as this is the 7th of July, he may turn up at any moment; as he will bring the letter of introduction with him, I shall be quite safe in delivering the figure to him, and the sooner the better. I am tired of seeing the people standing in front of that case and sniggering."

"You must be," said Thorndyke. "However, I hope Mr. Newman will come soon and relieve you of the occasion of sniggers. And I must thank you once more for the valuable help that you have given us; and you may take it that I shall not forget my promise to try to find you a deputy so that you can have a little more freedom."

With this, and a cordial handshake, we took our leave; once more I was surprised and even a little puzzled by Thorndyke's promise to seek a deputy for Mr. Sancroft. I could understand his sympathy with that overworked curator; but really, Mr. Sancroft's troubles were no affair of ours. Indeed, so abnormal did Thorndyke's attitude appear that I began to ask myself whether it was possible that some motive other than sympathy might lie behind it. No one, it is true, could be more ready than Thorndyke to do a little act of kindness if the chance came his way, but on the other hand, experience had taught me that no one's motives could be more difficult to assess than Thorndyke's. For there was always this difficulty— that one never knew what was at the back of his mind.

CHAPTER 17

MR. SNUPER

When we arrived at our chambers we were met on the landing by Polton, who had apparently observed our approach from an upper window, and who communicated to us the fact that Mr. Linnell was waiting to see us.

"He has been here more than half an hour, so perhaps you will invite him to stay to lunch. I've laid a place for him, and lunch is ready now in the breakfast room."

"Thank you, Polton," said Thorndyke, "we will see what his arrangements are," and as Polton retired up the stairs, he opened the oak door with his latch-key and we entered the room. There we found Linnell pacing the floor with a distinctly unrestful air.

"I am afraid I have come at an inconvenient time, sir," he began, apologetically, but Thorndyke interrupted:

"Not at all. You have come in the very nick of time; for lunch is just ready, and as Polton has laid a place for you, he will insist on your joining us."

Linnell's rather careworn face brightened up at the invitation, which he accepted gratefully, and we adjourned forthwith to the small room on the laboratory floor which we had recently, for labour-saving reasons, adopted as the place in which meals were served. As we took our places at the table, Thorndyke cast a critical glance at our friend and remarked:

"You are not looking happy, Linnell. Nothing amiss, I hope?"

"There is nothing actually amiss, sir," Linnell replied, "but I am not at all happy about the way things are going. It's that confounded fellow, Blandy. He won't let matters rest. He is still convinced that Mrs. Gannet knows, or could guess, where Boles is hiding; whereas, I am perfectly sure that she has no more idea where he is than I have. But he won't leave it at that. He thinks that he is being bamboozled and he is getting vicious—politely vicious, you know—and I am afraid he means mischief."

"What sort of mischief?" I asked.

"Well, he keeps letting out obscure hints of a prosecution."

"But," said I, "the decision for or against a prosecution doesn't rest with him. He is just a detective inspector."

"I know," said Linnell. "That's what he keeps rubbing in. For his part, he would be entirely opposed to subjecting this unfortunate lady to the peril and indignity of criminal proceedings—you know his oily way of speaking—but what can he do? He is only a police officer. It is his superiors and the Public Prosecutor who will decide. And then he goes on, in a highly confidential, friend-of-the-family sort of way, to point out the various unfortunate (and, as he thinks, misleading) little circumstances that might influence the judgment of persons unacquainted with the lady. And after all, he remarked to me in confidence, he found himself compelled to admit that if his superiors should decide (against his advice) to prosecute, they would be able, at least, to make out a *prima facie* case."

"I doubt whether they could," said I, "unless Blandy knows more than we know after attending the inquest."   •

"That is just the point," said Thorndyke. "Does he? Has he got anything up his sleeve? I don't think he can have; for if he had knowledge of any material facts, he would have to communicate them to his superiors. And as those superiors have not taken any action so far, we may assume that no such facts have been communicated. I suppose Blandy's agitations are connected with Boles?"

"Yes," Linnell replied. "He keeps explaining to me, and to Mrs. Gannet, how the whole trouble would disappear if only we could get into touch with Boles. I don't see how it would, but I do think that if Blandy could lay his hands on Boles, his interest in Mrs. Gannet would cease. All this fuss is to bring pressure on her to make some sort of statement."

"Yes," said Thorndyke, "that seems to be the position. It is not very creditable, and very unlike the ordinary practice of the police. But there is this to remember: Blandy's interest in Boles, and that of the police in general, is not connected with the murder in the studio, but with the murder of the constable at Newingstead. Blandy's idea is, I suspect—assuming that he seriously entertains a prosecution —that if Mrs. Gannet were brought to trial, she would have to be put into the witness box and then some useful information might be extracted from her in cross-examination. He is not likely to have made any such suggestions to his superiors, but seeing how anxious the police naturally are to find the murderer of the constable, they might be ready to give a sympathetic consideration to Blandy's view, if he could make out a really plausible case. And that is the question. What sort of case could he make out? Have you any ideas on that subject, Linnell? I take it that he would suggest charging Mrs. Gannet as an accessory after the fact."

"Yes, he has made that clear to both of us. If the Public Prosecutor decided to take action, the charge would be that she, knowing that a felony had been committed, subsequently sheltered or relieved the felon in such a way as to enable him to evade justice. Of course, it is the only charge that would be possible."

"So it would seem," said I. "But what facts has he got to support it? He can't prove that she knows where Boles is hiding."

"No," Linnell agreed, "at least, I suppose he can't. But there is that rather unfortunate circumstance that, when her husband was missing, she was—as she has admitted—afraid to enter the studio to see if he was there. Blandy fears that her behaviour might be interpreted as proving that she had some knowledge of what had happened."

"There isn't much in that," said I. "What are the other points?"

"Well, Blandy professes to think that the relations between Boles and Mrs. Gannet would tend to support the charge. No one suggests that their relations were in any way improper, but they were admittedly on affectionate terms."

"There is still less in that," said I. "The suggestion of a possible motive for doing a certain act is no evidence that the act was done. If Blandy has nothing better than what you have mentioned, he would never persuade a magistrate to commit her for trial. What do you say, Thorndyke?"

"It certainly looks as if Blandy held a remarkably weak hand," he replied. "Of course, we have to take all the facts together; but even so, assuming that he has nothing unknown to us in reserve, I don't see how he could make out a *prima facie* case."

"He has also," said Linnell, "dropped some obscure hints about that affair of the arsenic poisoning."

"That," said Thorndyke, "is pure bluff. He would not be allowed to mention it, and he knows he wouldn't. He said so explicitly, to Oldfield. It looks as if the threat of a prosecution were being made to exert pressure on Mrs. Gannet to make some revelation. Still, it is possible that he may manage to work up a case sufficiently plausible to induce the authorities to launch proceedings. Blandy is a remarkably ingenious and resourceful man, and none too scrupulous. He is a man whom one has to take seriously."

"And suppose he does manage to get a prosecution started," said Linnell, "what do you advise me to do?"

"Well, Linnell," Thorndyke replied, "you know the ordinary routine. We are agreed that the lady is innocent and you will act accordingly. As to bail, we will settle the details of that later, but we can manage any amount that may be required."

"Do you think that she might be admitted to bail?"

"But why not?" said Thorndyke. "She will be charged only as an accessory after the fact. That is not a very grave crime. The maximum penalty is only two years' imprisonment, and in practice, the sentences are usually quite lenient. You will certainly ask for bail, and I don't see any grounds on which the police could oppose it.

"And now as to the general conduct of the case, I advise you very strongly to play for time. Delay the proceedings as much as you can. Find excuses to ask for remands, and in all possible ways keep the pot boiling as slowly as you can contrive. The longer the date of the final hearing can be postponed, the better will be the chance of finding a conclusive answer to the charge. I will tell you why, following Blandy's excellent example by taking you into my confidence.

"I have been examining this case in considerable detail, partly in Mrs. Gannet's interests and partly for other reasons; and I have a clear and consistent theory of the crime, both as to its motive and approximate procedure. But at present it is only a theory. I can prove nothing. The one crucial fact which will tell me whether my theory is right or wrong is still lacking. I cannot test the truth of it until certain things have happened. I hope that they may happen quite soon, but still, I have to wait on events. If those events turn out as I expect, I shall know that my construction of the crime has been correct; and then I shall be able to show that Mrs. Gannet could not possibly have been an accessory to it. But I can give no date because I cannot control the course of events."

Linnell was visibly impressed, and so was I—though less visibly. I was still in the same state of bewilderment as to Thorndyke's proceedings. I still failed to understand why he was busying himself in a case which did not seem to concern him—apart from his sympathy with Mrs. Gannet. Nor could I yet see that there was anything to discover beyond what we already knew.

Of course I had realized all along that I must have missed some essential point in the case, and now this was confirmed. Thorndyke had a consistent theory of the crime, which, indeed, might be right or wrong. But long experience with Thorndyke told me that it was pretty certainly right, though what sort of theory it might be I was totally unable to imagine. I could only, like Thorndyke, wait on events.

The rest of the conversation concerned itself with the question of bail. Oldfield we knew could be depended on for one surety, and by a little manoeuvring, it was arranged that Thorndyke should finance the other without appearing in the transaction. Eventually Linnell took his departure in greatly improved spirits, cheered by Thorndyke's encouragement and all the better for a good lunch and one or two glasses of sound claret.

Thorndyke's "confidence," if it mystified rather than enlightened me, had at least the good effect of arousing my interest in Mrs. Gannet and her affairs. From time to time during the next few days I turned them over in my mind, though with little result beyond the beneficial mental exercise. But in another direction I had better luck, for I did make an actual discovery. It came about in this way.

A few days after Linnell's visit, I had occasion to go to the London Hospital to confer with one of the surgeons concerning a patient in whom I was interested. When I had finished my business there and came out into the Whitechapel Road, the appearance of the neighbourhood recalled our expedition to the People's Museum, and I suddenly realized that I was within a few minutes' walk of that shrine of the fine arts. Now I had occasionaily speculated on Thorndyke's object in making that visit of inspection and on his reasons for interesting himself in Sancroft's difficulties. Was it pure benevolence or was there something behind it? And there was the further question, had his benevolent intentions taken effect? The probability was that they had. He had given Sancroft a very definite promise, and it was quite unlike him to leave a promise unfulfilled.

These questions recurred to me as I turned westward along the Whitechapel Road, and I decided that at least some of them should be answered forthwith. I could now ascertain whether any deputy for Mr. Sancroft had been found, and if so, who that deputy might be. Accordingly, I turned up Commercial Street and presently struck the junction of Norton Folegate and Shoreditch; and, traversing the length of the latter, came into Kingsland Road and so to the People's Museum.

One of my questions was answered as soon as I entered. There was no sign of Mr. Sancroft, but the priceless collection was being watched over by a gentleman of studious aspect who was seated in an armchair—a representative specimen of Curtain Road Chippendale —reading a book with the aid of a pair of horn-framed spectacles. So engrossed was he with his studies that he appeared to be unaware of my entrance, though, as I was the only visitor, I must have been a rather conspicuous object and worthy of some slight notice.

Taking advantage of his preoccupation, I observed him narrowly; and though I could not place him or give him a name, I had the distinct impression that I had seen him before. Continuing a strategic advance in his direction under cover of the glass cases, and still observing him as unobtrusively as I could, I had a growing sense of familiarity until, coming within a few yards of him, I suddenly realized who he was.

"Why," I exclaimed, "it is Mr. Snuper!"

He lowered his book and smiled, blandly. "Mr. Snuper it is," he admitted. "And why not? You seem surprised."

"So I am," I replied. "What on earth are you doing here?"

"To tell the truth," said he, "I am doing very little. You see me here, taking my ease and spending my very acceptable leisure profitably in reading books that I usually have not time to read."

I glanced at the book which he was holding and was not a little surprised to discover that it was Bell's *British Stalk-eyed Crustacea*. Observing my astonishment, he explained, apologetically:

"I am a collector of British crustacea in a small way, a very small way. The beginnings were made during a seaside holiday, and now I occasionally secure small additions from the fishmongers' shops."

"I shouldn't have thought," said I, "that the fishmongers' shops would have yielded many rare specimens."

"No," he agreed, "you wouldn't. But it is surprising how many curious and interesting forms of life you may discover among the heaps of shell-fish on a fishmonger's slab; especially the mussels and winkles. Only the day before yesterday, I obtained a nearly perfect specimen of *Stenorhynchus phalangium* from a winkle stall in the Mile End Road."

Now this was very interesting. I have often noticed how the discovery of some unlikely hobby throws most unexpected light on a man's character and personality. And so it was now. The enthusiastic pursuit of this comparatively erudite study presented a feature of Mr. Snuper's rather elusive personality that was quite new to me, and somewhat surprising. But I had not come here to study Mr. Snuper, and it suddenly occurred to me that that very discreet gentleman might be making this conversation expressly to divert my attention from other topics. Accordingly, I returned to my business with a direct question.

"But how do you come to be here?"

"It was Dr. Thorndyke's idea," he replied. "You see there was nothing doing in my line at the moment, and Mr. Sancroft was badly in need of someone who could look after the place while he went about his business, so the doctor suggested that I might as well spend my leisure here as at home, and do a kindness to Mr. Sancroft at the same time."

This answer left me nothing to say. The general question that I had asked was all that was admissible. I could not pursue the matter further, for that would have been a discourtesy to Thorndyke, to say nothing of the certainty that the discreet Snuper would keep his own counsel if there were any counsel to keep. So I brought the conversation gracefully to an end with a few irrelevant observations, and having wished my friend good day, went forth and set a course for Shoreditch Station.

But if it was not admissible for me to question Snuper, I was at liberty to turn the matter over in my mind. But that process had the effect rather of raising questions than of disposing of them. Snuper's account of his presence at the gallery was perfectly reasonable and plausible. Thorndyke had no use for him at the moment and Sancroft had. That seemed quite simple. But was it the whole explanation? I had my doubts, and they were based principally on what I knew of Mr. Snuper.

Now Mr. Snuper was a very remarkable man. Originally he had been a private inquiry agent whom Thorndyke had employed occasionally to carry out certain observation duties which could not be discharged by either of us. But Snuper had proved so valuable— so dependable, so discreet, and so quick in the uptake—that Thorndyke had taken him on as a regular member of our staff. For apart from his other good qualities, he had a most extraordinary gift of inconspicuousness. Not only was he at all times exactly the kind of person whom you would pass in the street without a second glance, but in some mysterious way he was able to keep his visible personality in a state of constant change. Whenever you met him, you found him a little different from the man whom you had met before, with the natural result that you were constantly failing to recognize him. That was my experience, as it had been on this very occasion. I never discovered how he did it. He seemed to use no actual disguise (though I believe that he was a master of the art of make-up), but he appeared to be able, in some subtle way, to manage to look like a different person.

But whatever his methods may have been, the results made him invaluable to Thorndyke, for he could keep up a continuous observation on persons or places with practically no risk of being recognized.

Reflecting on these facts—on Mr. Snuper's remarkable personality, his peculiar gifts and the purposes to which they were commonly applied—I asked myself once more, could there be anything behind his presence at the People's Museum of Modern Art? And—so far as I was concerned—answer there was none. My discovery had simply landed me with one more problem to which I could find no solution.

CHAPTER 18

MR. NEWMAN

The premonitory rumblings which had so disturbed Linnell continued for some days, warning him to make all necessary preparations for the defense; and in spite of the scepticism which we all felt as to the practicability of a prosecution, the tension increased from day to day.

And then the bombshell exploded. The alarming fact was communicated to us in a hurried note from Linnell which informed us that a summons had been served on Mrs. Gannet that very morning, citing her to appear at the Police Court on the third day after that on which it was issued to answer to the charge of having, as an accessory after the fact of the murder of Peter Gannet, harboured, sheltered, or otherwise aided the accused person to evade justice.

Thorndyke appeared to be as surprised as I was, and a good deal more concerned. He read Linnell's note with a grave face and reflected on it with what seemed to me to be uncalled for anxiety.

"I can't imagine," said I, "what sort of evidence Blandy could produce. He can't know where Boles is, or he would have arrested him. And if he doesn't, he couldn't have discovered any evidence of any communications between Boles and Mrs. Gannet."

"No," Thorndyke agreed, "that seems quite clear. There can have been no intercepted letters from her, for the obvious reason that such letters would have had to be addressed in such a way as to reach him and thus reveal his whereabouts. And yet one feels that the police would not have taken action unless Blandy had produced enough facts to enable them to make out a *prima facie* case. Blandy might have been ready to gamble on his powers of persuasion, but the responsible authorities would not risk having the case dismissed by the magistrate. It is very mysterious. On my theory of the crime, it is practically certain that Mrs. Gannet could not have been an accessory either before or after the fact."

These observations gave me some clue to Thorndyke's anxiety; for they conveyed to me that Blandy's case, if he really had one, would not fit Thorndyke's theory. I put the suggestion to him in so many words, and he agreed frankly.

"The trouble is," said he, "that my scheme of the crime is purely hypothetical. It is based on a train of deductive reasoning from the facts which are known to us all. I am in possession of no knowledge other than that which is possessed equally by Blandy and by you. The reasoning by which I reached my conclusions seems to me perfectly sound. But I may have fallen into some fallacy, or it may be that there are some material facts which are not known to me, but which are known to Blandy. One of us is mistaken. Naturally, I hope that the mistake is Blandy's; but it may be mine. However, we shall see when the prosecution opens the case."

"I assume," said I, "that you will attend at the hearing."

"Undoubtedly," he replied. "We must be there to hear what Blandy has to say, if he gives evidence, and what sort of case the prosecution proposes to make out; and then we have to give Linnell any help that he may require. I suppose you will lend us the support of your presence?"

"Of course I shall come," I replied. "I am as curious as you are to hear what the prosecution has to say. I shall make a very special point of being there."

But that visit to the Police court was never to take place, for on that very night the "events" on which Thorndyke had been waiting began to loom up on our horizon. They were ushered in by the appearance at our chambers of a young man of Jewish aspect and secretive bearing who, having been interviewed by Polton, had demanded personal audience of Thorndyke and had refused to indicate his name or business to any other person. Accordingly, he was introduced to us by Polton, who, having conducted him into the presence, stood by and kept him under observation until he was satisfied that the visitor had no unlawful or improper designs; then he retired and shut the door.

As the door closed, the stranger produced from an inner pocket a small packet wrapped in newspaper which he proceeded to open; and, having extracted from it a letter in a sealed envelope, silently handed the letter to Thorndyke; who broke the seal and read through the evidently short note which it contained.

"If you will wait a few minutes," said he, placing a chair for the messenger, "I will give you a note to take with you. Are you going straight back?"

"Yes," was the reply. "He's waiting for me."

Thereupon Thorndyke sat down at the writing table, and having written a short letter, put it in an envelope, which he sealed with wax and handed to the messenger, together with a ten shilling note.

"That," said he, "is the fee for services rendered so far. There will be another at the end of the return journey. I have mentioned the matter in my letter."

The messenger received the note with an appreciative grin and a few words of thanks, and having disposed of it in some secret receptacle, wrapped the letter in the newspaper which had enclosed the other, stowed it away in an inner pocket and took his departure.

"That," said Thorndyke, when he had gone, "was a communication from Snuper, who is deputizing for Sancroft at the People's Museum. He tells me that the owner of Gannet's masterpiece is going to call tomorrow morning and take possession of his property."

"Is that any concern of ours?" I asked.

"It is a concern of mine," he replied. "I am anxious not to lose sight of that monkey. There are several things about it which interest me, and if it is to be taken away from the museum, I want to learn, if I can, where it is going, in case I might wish at some future time to make a further examination of it. So I propose to go to the museum tomorrow morning and try to find out from Mr. Newman where he keeps his collection and how the monkey is to be disposed of. It is possible, for instance, that he may be a dealer, in which case there would be the danger of the monkey's disappearing to some unknown destination."

"I shouldn't think that he is a dealer," said I. "He would never get his money back. Probably he is a sort of Broomhill, but, of course, he may live in the provinces or even abroad. At what time do you propose to turn up at the museum?"

"The place opens at nine o'clock in the morning and Snuper expects Mr. Newman to arrive at about that time. I have told him that I shall be there at half-past eight."

Now on the face of it, the transaction did not promise any very thrilling experiences, but there was something a little anomalous about the whole affair. Thorndyke's interest in that outrageous monkey was quite incomprehensible to me, and I had the feeling that there was something more in this expedition than was conveyed in the mere statement of Thorndyke's intentions and objects. Accordingly, I threw out a tentative suggestion.

"If I should propose to make one of the party, would my presence be helpful or otherwise?"

"My dear fellow," he replied, "your presence is always helpful. I had, in fact, intended to ask you to accompany me. Up to the present you have not seemed to appreciate the importance of the monkey in this remarkable case; but it is possible that you may gather some fresh ideas on the subject tomorrow morning. So come by all means. And now I must go and make the necessary preparations, and you had better do the same. We shall start from here not later than a quarter to eight."

With this he went up to the laboratory floor, whence, presently, I heard the distant tinkle of the telephone bell. Apparently he was making some kind of appointment, for shortly afterwards his footsteps were audible on the stairs descending to the entry, and I saw him no more until he came in to smoke a final pipe before going to bed.

On the following morning, Polton, having aroused me by precautionary and (as I thought, premature) thumpings on my door, served a ridiculously early breakfast and then took his stand on the door-step to keep a lookout for the taxi which had been chartered overnight. Evidently he had been duly impressed with the importance of the occasion, as apparently had the taxi man, for he arrived at half-past seven and his advent was triumphantly reported by Polton just as I was pouring out my second cup of tea. But after all there was not so very much time to spare, for in Fleet Street, Cornhill and Bishopsgate, all the wheeled vehicles in London seemed to have been assembled to do us honour and retard our progress; it was a quarter past eight when we alighted opposite the Geffrye Museum, and having dismissed the taxi, began to walk at a leisurely pace northward along the Kingsland Road.

When we were a short distance from our destination, I observed a man walking towards us, and at a second glance, I actually recognized Mr. Snuper. As soon as he saw us, he turned about and walked back to the People's Museum, where he unlocked the door and entered. On our arrival we found the door ajar and Mr. Snuper lurking just inside, ready to close the door as soon as we had passed in.

"Well, Snuper," said Thorndyke, as we emerged from the lobby into the main room, "everything seems to have gone according to plan so far. You didn't give any particulars in your letter. How did you manage the adjournment?"

"It didn't require much management, sir," Snuper replied. "The affair came off by itself quite naturally. Mr. Sancroft didn't come to the museum yesterday. He had to go out of town on business and, of course, as I was here, there was no reason why he shouldn't go. So I was here all alone when Mr. Newman came just before closing time. He told me what he had come for and showed me the letter of introduction and the receipt which he had written out and signed. But I explained to him that I was not the curator and had no authority to allow any of the exhibits to be taken away from the museum. Besides, the case was locked and Mr. Sancroft had the key of the safe in which the other keys were kept, so I could not get the figure out even if I had been authorized to part with it.

"He was very disappointed and inclined to be huffy, but it couldn't be helped, and after all, he had only to wait a few hours. I told him that Mr. Sancroft would be here today and would arrive in time to open the museum as usual, so I expect Newman will turn up pretty punctually about nine o'clock. Possibly, he will be waiting outside when Mr. Sancroft comes to let himself in."

This forecast, however, was falsified a few minutes later, for Mr. Sancroft arrived before his time and locked the door when he had entered. Naturally, he knew nothing of what had been happening in his absence and was somewhat surprised to find Thorndyke and me in the museum. But whatever explanations were called for must have been given by Snuper, who followed Sancroft into the curator's room and shut the door behind him; and, judging by the length of the interview, I assumed that Sancroft was being put in possession of such facts as it was necessary for him to know.

While this conference was proceeding, Thorndyke reconnoitered the galleries in what seemed to me a very odd way. He appeared to be searching for some place whence he could observe the entrance and the main gallery without being himself visible. Having tried one or two of the higher cases, and apparently finding them unsuitable, owing to his exceptional stature, he turned his attention to the small room which opened from the main gallery and was devoted entirely to water colours. The entrance of this room was exactly opposite the case which contained the "Figurine of a Monkey," and it also faced the main doorway. But it seemed to have a further attraction for Thorndyke; for, on the wall nearly opposite to the entrance, hung a large water colour painting, the glass of which, taken at the proper angle, reflected the whole of the principal room, the main doorway, and the case in which the monkey was exhibited. I tried it when Thorndyke had finished his experiments, and found that, not only did it reflect a perfectly clear image, owing to the very dark colouring of the picture, but that the observer looking into it was quite invisible from the main gallery, or indeed, to anyone who did not actually enter the small room.

This was an interesting discovery, in its way. But the most interesting part of it was Thorndyke's motive in seeking this secret point of observation. Once more I decided that things were not quite what they had seemed. As I had understood the programme, Thorndyke was going to introduce himself to Mr. Newman and try to ascertain the destination and future whereabouts of the monkey. But with this purpose, Thorndyke's present proceedings seemed to have no connection.

However, there was not much time for speculation on my part, for, at this point Mr. Snuper emerged from the curator's room and, walking up the gallery, unlocked the front door and threw it open; and, as he returned, accompanied by a man who had slipped in as the door opened, I realized that the proceedings, whatever they might be, had begun.

"Keep out of sight for the present," Thorndyke directed me in a whisper; and, forthwith, I flattened myself against the wall and fixed an eager gaze on the picture as well as I could without obstructing Thorndyke's view. In the reflection I could see Snuper and his companion advance until they were within a few yards of the place where we were lurking, and then I heard Snuper say:

"If you will give me the letter and the receipt, I will take them in to Mr. Sancroft and get the key of the case, unless he wishes to hand the figure to you himself."

With this, he retired into the curator's room and shut the door; and as he disappeared, the stranger—presumably Mr. Newman—who, I could now see, carried a largish hand-bag, advanced to the case which contained the monkey and stood peering into it with his back to us, and so near that I could have put out my hand and touched him. As he stood thus, Thorndyke put his head round the jamb of the doorway to examine him by direct vision, and after a few moments' inspection, stepped out, moving quite silently on the solid parquet floor, and took up a position close behind him. Whereupon I, following his example, came out into the middle of the doorway and stood behind Thorndyke to see what was going to happen next.

For a few moments nothing happened; but just then I became aware of two men lurking in the lobby of the main entrance, half hidden by the inner door and quite hidden from Newman by the case at which he was standing. Suddenly Newman seemed to become conscious of the presence of someone behind him, for he turned sharply and faced Thorndyke. Then I knew that something critical was going to happen, and I realized, too, that Thorndyke had got his "one crucial fact." For as the stranger's eyes met Thorndyke's, he gave one wild stare of horror and amazement and his face blanched to a deathly pallor. But he uttered no word; and after that one ghastly stare, turned about and appeared to resume his contemplation of the figurine.

Then three things happened in quick succession: First, Thorndyke took off his hat; then the door of the curator's room opened and Snuper and Sancroft emerged; and then the two men whom I had noticed came out of the lobby and walked quickly up to the place where Newman and Thorndyke were standing. I looked at them curiously as they approached, and recognized them both. One was Detective Sergeant Wills of the C.I.D. The other was no less a person than Detective Inspector Blandy.

By this time Newman seemed, to some extent, to have recovered his self-possession, whereas Blandy, on the contrary, looked nervous and embarrassed. The former, ignoring the police officers, addressed himself to Sancroft, demanding the speedy conclusion of his business. But here Blandy intervened, with little confidence but more than his usual politeness.

"I must ask you to pardon me, sir," he began, "for interrupting your business, but there are one or two questions that I want you to be so kind as to answer."

Newman looked at him in evident alarm but replied gruffly:

"I have no time to answer questions. Besides, you are a stranger to me, and I don't think I have any concern in your affairs."

"I am a police officer," Blandy explained, "and I—"

"Then I am sure I haven't," snapped Newman.

"I wanted to ask you a few questions in connection with a most unfortunate affair that happened at Newingstead last September," Blandy continued persuasively; but Newman cut him short with the brusque rejoinder:

"Newingstead? I never heard of the place, and of course I know nothing about it."

Blandy looked at him with a baffled expression and then turned an appealing face to Thorndyke.

"Can you give us something definite, sir?" he asked.

"I thought I had," Thorndyke replied. "At any rate, I now accuse this man, Newman, as he calls himself, of having murdered Constable Murray at Newingstead on the 19th of last September. That justifies you in making the arrest; and then—well, you know what to do."

But still Blandy seemed undecided. The man's evident terror and the glare of venomous hatred that he cast on Thorndyke, proved nothing. Accordingly, the Inspector, apparently puzzled and unconvinced, sought to temporize.

"If you would allow me, Mr. Newman," said he, "to take an impression of your left thumb, any mistake that may have been made could be set right in a moment. Now what do you say?"

"I say that I will see you damned first," Newman replied fiercely, edging away from the Inspector and thereby impinging on the massive form of Sergeant Wills, which occupied the only avenue of escape.

"You've got a definite charge, you know, Inspector," Thorndyke reminded him in a warning tone, still narrowly watching the accused man; and something significant in the way the words were spoken helped Blandy to make up his mind.

"Well, then, Mr. Newman," said he, "if you won't give us any assistance, it's your own look-out. I arrest you on the charge of having murdered Police Constable Murray at Newingstead on the 19th of last September and I caution you that—"

The rest of the caution faded out, for Newman made a sudden movement and was in an instant clasped in the arms of Sergeant Wills, who had skilfully seized the prisoner's wrists from behind and held them immovably pressed against his chest. Almost at the same moment, Blandy sprang forward and grasped the prisoner's ears in order to secure his head and defeat his attempts to bite the sergeant's hands. But Newman was evidently a powerful ruffian, and his struggles were so violent that the two officers had the greatest difficulty in holding him, even when Snuper and I tried to control his arms. In the narrow interval between two glass cases, we all swayed to and fro, gyrating slowly and making uncomfortable contacts with sharp corners. Presently Blandy turned his streaming face towards Thorndyke and gasped:

"Could you manage the print, Doctor? You can see I can't let go. The kit is in my right hand coat pocket."

"I have brought the necessary things, myself," said Thorndyke, producing from his pocket a small metal box. "It is understood," he added, as he opened the box, "that I am acting on your instructions."

Without waiting for a reply, he took out of the box a tiny roller which had been fixed by its handle in a clip, and having run it along the inside of the lid, which formed an inking-plate, he approached the squirming prisoner; waiting his opportunity, he suddenly seized the left thumb, and holding it steady, ran the little roller over its bulb. Then he produced a small pad of smooth paper, and again watching for a moment when the thumb was fixed immovably, quickly pressed the pad on the inked surface. The resulting print was not a very perfect impression, but it showed the pattern clearly enough for practical purposes.

"Have you got the photograph with you?" he asked.

"Yes," replied Blandy, "but I can't—could you take hold of his head for a moment?"

Thorndyke laid the pad on the top of the nearest case and then, following Blandy's instructions, grasped the prisoner's head so as to relieve the Inspector; Blandy then stepped back, and having taken up the pad, thrust his hand into his pocket and brought out a photograph mounted on a card. For a few moments he stood, eagerly glancing from the pad to the photograph and evidently comparing them point by point.

"Is it the right print?" Thorndyke asked.

Blandy did not answer immediately but continued his scrutiny with evidently growing excitement. At length he looked up, and forgetting his usual bland smile, replied, almost in a shout:

"Yes, by God! It's the man himself."

And then came the catastrophe.

Whether it was that the sergeant's attention was for the moment distracted by the absorbing interest of Blandy's proceedings, or that Newman had been watching his opportunity, I cannot say, but, after a brief cessation of his struggles, as if he had become exhausted, he made a sudden violent effort and twisted himself out of his captors' grasp, darting instantly into the passage between two cases. Thither the sergeant followed, but the prisoner, with incredible quickness and dexterity, delivered a smashing blow on the chest which sent the officer staggering backwards; the next moment, the prisoner was standing in the narrow space with an automatic pistol covering his pursuers.

I will do Blandy the justice (which I am glad to do, as I never liked the man) to say that he faced the deadly danger without a sign of fear or a moment's hesitation. How he escaped with his life I have never understood, for he dashed straight at the prisoner, looking into the very muzzle of the pistol. But by some miracle the bullet passed him by, and before another shot could be fired, he had grabbed the man's wrist and got some sort of control of the weapon. Then the sergeant and Snuper and I came to his assistance, and the old struggle began again, but with the material difference that each and all of us had to keep a wary eye on the barrel of the pistol.

Of the crowded and chaotic events of the next minute I have but the obscurest recollection. There comes back to me a vague idea of violent, strenuous effort; a succession of pistol shots with a sort of infernal obbligato accompaniment of shattering glass; the struggles of the sergeant to reach a back pocket without losing his hold on the prisoner; and the manoeuvres of Mr. Sancroft, at first ducking at every shot and finally retreating hurriedly—almost on all fours— into his sanctum. Nor when the end came, am I at all clear as to the exact manner of its happening. I know only that the firing ceased, and that almost as the last shot was fired, the writhing, struggling body became suddenly still and began limply to sag towards the floor; and that I then noticed in the man's right temple a small hole from which issued a little trickle of blood.

Blandy rose, and looking down gloomily at the prostrate body, cursed softly under his breath.

"What infernal luck!" he exclaimed. "I suppose he is dead?"

"I am afraid there is no doubt of that," I replied, as the last faint twitchings died away.

"Infernal luck," he repeated, "to have him slip through our fingers just as we had made sure of him."

"It was the making sure of him that did it," growled the sergeant. "I mean the finger-prints. We ought to have waited for them until we had got the darbies on."

"I know," said Blandy. "But you see I wasn't sure that we had got the right man. He didn't seem to me to answer to the description at all."

"The description of whom?" asked Thorndyke.

"Of Frederick Boles," replied Blandy. "This is Boles, isn't it?"

"No," replied Thorndyke. "This is Peter Gannet."

Blandy was thunderstruck. "But," he exclaimed, incredulously, "it can't be. We identified Gannet's remains quite conclusively."

"Yes," Thorndyke agreed, blandly, "that is what you were intended to do. The remains were actually those of Boles—with certain additions."

Blandy smiled sourly. "Well," said he, "this is a knockout. To think that we have been barking up the wrong tree all the time. But you might have given us the tip a bit sooner, Doctor."

"My dear Blandy," Thorndyke protested, "I told you all that I knew as soon as I knew it."

"You didn't tell us who this man Newman was."

"But, my dear Inspector," Thorndyke replied, "I didn't know myself. When I came here today, I suspected that Mr. Newman was Peter Gannet. But I didn't know until I had seen the man and recognized him and seen that he recognized me. I told you last night that it was merely a case of suspicion."

"Well, well," said Blandy, "it's no use crying over spilt milk. Is there a telephone in the office? If there is, you had better ring up the Police Station, Sergeant, and tell them to send an ambulance along as quickly as they can."

The tinkle of the telephone bell answered Blandy's question, and while the message was being sent and answered, Thorndyke and I proceeded to lay out the body, in view of the probability of premature *rigor mortis*. Then we adjourned to the curator's room, where Blandy showed a tendency to revert to the topic of the might-have-been. But our stay there was short, for the ambulance arrived in an almost incredibly short time; and when the body had been carried out by the stretcher bearers and the outer door shut, the Inspector and the Sergeant made ready to depart.

"There are some other particulars, Doctor," said Blandy, "that we shall want you to give us, if you will; but now I must get back to the Yard and report what has happened. They won't be over-pleased, but at least we have cleared up a rather mysterious case."

With this, he and the Sergeant went forth to their car, being let out by Mr. Sancroft, who, having affixed a notice to the main door, shut it and locked it. Then he came back to the room and gazed round ruefully at the wreck of the People's Museum of Modern Art.

"The Lord knows," said he, "who is going to pay for all this damage. Seven glass cases smashed and the nose knocked off Israel Popoff's Madonna. It has been a shocking business; and there is that damned image—if you will excuse me—which has been the cause of all the trouble, still standing in one of the few undamaged cases. But I will soon have it out of there; only the question is, what on earth is to be done with it? The beastly thing seems to be nobody's property now."

"It is the property of Mrs. Gannet," said Thorndyke. "I think it would be best if I were to take custody of it and hand it over to her. I will give you a receipt for it."

"You need not trouble about a receipt," said Sancroft, hauling out his keys and joyfully unlocking the case. "I accept you as Mrs. Gannet's representative and I am only too delighted to get the thing out of the museum. Shall I make it up into a parcel?"

"There is no need," replied Thorndyke, picking up Gannet's bag from the floor, on which it had been dropped when the struggle began. "This will hold it, and there is probably some packing inside."

He opened the bag, and finding it lined with a thick woollen scarf, took the figure from the open case, carefully deposited it in the folds of the scarf and shut the bag.

That seemed to conclude our business, and after a few more words with the still agitated Sancroft and a brief farewell to Mr. Snuper, we accompanied the former to the door, whence we were let out into the street.

CHAPTER 19

THE MONKEY REVEALS HIS SECRET

By lovers of paradox we are assured that it is the unexpected that always happens. But this is, to put it mildly, an exaggeration. Even the expected happens sometimes. It did, for instance, on the present occasion, for when we passed into the entry of our chambers on our return from the museum, and began to ascend the stairs, I expected that Thorndyke would pass by the door of our sitting room and go straight up to the laboratory floor. And that is precisely what he did. He made directly for the larger workshop, and having greeted Polton as we entered, laid Gannet's bag on the bench.

"We need not disturb you, Polton," said he, noting that our assistant was busily polishing the pallets of a dead beat escapement appertaining to a "regulator" that he was constructing. But Polton had already fixed an inquisitive eye on the bag, and, coupling its presence with our mysterious expedition, had evidently sniffed something more exciting than clockwork.

"You are not disturbing me, sir," said he, laying the pallets on the table of the polishing lathe and bearing down with a purposeful air on the bag. "The clock is a spare time job. Can I give you any assistance?"

Thorndyke smiled appreciatively, and opening the bag, carefully took out the figure and stood it up on the bench.

"There, Polton," said he, "what do you think of that for a work of art?"

"My word!" exclaimed Polton, regarding the figure with profound disfavour, "but he is an ugly fellow. Now what part of the world might he have come from? South Sea Islands he looks like."

Thorndyke lifted the image, and turning it up to exhibit the base, handed it to Polton, who examined it with fresh astonishment.

"Why," he exclaimed, "it seems to have been made by a civilized man! It's English lettering, though I don't recognize the mark."

"It was made by an Englishman," said Thorndyke. "But do you find anything abnormal about it apart from its ugliness?"

Polton looked long and earnestly at the base, turned the figure over and examined every part of it, finally tapping it with his knuckles and listening attentively to the sound elicited.

"I don't think it is solid," said he, "though it is mighty thick."

"It is not solid," said Thorndyke, "We have ascertained that."

"Then," said Polton, "I don't understand it. The body looks like ordinary stoneware. But it can't be if it's hollow. There is no opening in it anywhere. But it couldn't have been fired without a vent-hole of some kind. It would have blown to pieces."

"Yes," Thorndyke agreed. "That is the problem. But have another look at the base. What do you say to that white glazed slip on which the signature is written?"

Polton inspected it afresh, and finally stuck a watchmaker's eye-glass in his eye to assist in the examination.

"I don't know what to make of it," said he. "It looks a little like a tin glaze, but I don't think it is. I don't see how it could be. What do you think it is, sir?"

"I suspect that it is some kind of hard white cement—possibly Keene's—covered with a clear varnish."

Polton looked up at him, and his expressive countenance broke out into a characteristic crinkly smile.

"I think you have hit it, sir," said he; "and I think I begin to ogle, as Mr. Miller would say. What are we going to do about it?"

"The obvious thing," said Thorndyke, "is to make what surgeons would call an exploratory puncture; drill a small hole in it and see what the base is really made of and what its thickness is."

"Would a drill go into stoneware?" I asked.

"No," replied Thorndyke, "not an ordinary drill. But I do not think that there is any stoneware in the middle of the base. You remember Broomhill's specimen? There was a good-sized elliptical opening in the base, and I imagine that this figure was originally the same, but that the opening has been filled up. What we have to ascertain is what it has been filled with and how far the filling goes into the cavity."

"We had better do it with a hand-drill," said Polton, "and steady the image on the bench, as it wouldn't be safe to fix it in the vise. Then it will be convenient if we want to enlarge the hole."

He wrapped the "image" in one or two thick dusters and laid it on the bench, when I took charge of it and held it as firmly as I could to resist the pressure of the drill. Then, having fitted an eighth-inch Morse into the stock, he began operations, cautiously, and with only a light pressure; but I noticed that at first the hard drill-point seemed to make very little impression.

"What do you suppose the filling consists of, sir?" Polton asked, as he withdrew the drill to examine the shallow pit its point had made, "and how far do you suppose it goes in?"

"My idea is," replied Thorndyke—"but it is only a guess—that there is a comparatively thin layer of Keene's cement and then a plug of plaster, perhaps three or four inches thick. Beyond that, I should expect to come to the cavity. I hope I am right, for if it should turn out to be Keene's cement all the way, we shall have some trouble in making a hole large enough for our purpose."

"What is our purpose?" I asked. "To see if there is anything in the cavity, I presume."

"Yes," Thorndyke replied, "though it is practically certain that there is. Otherwise, there would have been no object in stopping up the opening."

Here Polton returned to the charge, now sensibly increasing the pressure. Still, for a while, the drill seemed to make little progress. Then quite suddenly, as if some obstruction had been removed, it began to enter freely and had soon penetrated as far as the chuck would allow it to go.

"You said, three or four inches, I think, sir?" Polton remarked, as he withdrew the drill and examined the white powder in the grooves.

"Yes," Thorndyke replied, "but possibly more. A six-inch drill would be best; and you might use a stouter one—say a quarter-inch —to avoid the risk of its bending."

Polton made the necessary change and resumed operations with the larger drill, which soon enlarged the opening and then began quickly to penetrate the softer plaster. When it had entered about four inches, even this slight resistance seemed to cease, for it ran in suddenly right up to the chuck.

"Four inches it is, sir," said Polton, with a triumphant crinkle, as he withdrew the drill and inspected the grooves. "How big an opening will you want?"

"An inch might do," replied Thorndyke, "but an inch and a half would be better. I think that is possible without encroaching on the stoneware body. But you will see."

On this, Polton produced a set of reamers and a brace, and beginning with one which would just enter the hole, turned the brace cautiously while I continued to steady the figure. Meanwhile, Thorndyke, having cut off a piece of stout copper wire about eight inches long, fixed it in the vise, and with an adjustable die, cut a screw thread about an inch long on one end.

"We may as well see what the conditions are," said he, "before we go any further."

He took the wire out of the vise, and as Polton withdrew the third reamer—which had enlarged the hole to about half an inch—he passed the wire into the hole and began gently to probe the bottom of the cavity. Then he pressed it in somewhat more firmly and gave it one or two turns, slowly drawing it out while he continued to turn. When it finally emerged, its end held a small knob of cotton wool from which a little twisted strand of the same material extended into the invisible interior. I watched its emergence with profound interest and a certain amount of self-contempt; for obviously he had expected to find the interior filled with cotton wool as was demonstrated by the making of the cotton wool holder. And yet I, who knew as much of the essential facts as he did, had never guessed, and even now had only a vague suspicion of what its presence suggested.

As the operations with the reamers progressed, it became evident that the larger opening was possible, for the material cut through was still only cement and plaster. When the full inch and a half had been reached, Thorndyke fixed his wire in the chuck of the hand-drill, and passing the former into the wide hole, pressed the screw end into the mass of cotton wool, and began to turn the handle, slowly withdrawing it as he turned. When the end of the wire appeared at the opening, it bore a ball of cotton wool from which a thick strand, twisted by the rapid rotation of the wire into a firm cord, extended to the mass inside; and as Thorndyke slowly stepped back, still turning the handle, the cord grew longer and longer until at last its end slipped out of the opening, showing that the whole of the cotton wool had been extracted.

"Now," said Thorndyke, "let us see what all that cotton wool enclosed."

He laid aside the drill, and carefully lifting the figure, held it upright over the bench, when there dropped out a small, white paper packet tied up with thread. Having cut the thread, he laid the packet on the bench and opened it, while Polton and I craned forward inquisitively. I suppose we both knew approximately what to expect, and I was better able to guess than Polton; but the reality was quite beyond my expectations, and as for Polton, he was, for the moment, struck dumb. Only for the moment, however, for recovering himself, he exclaimed impressively, with his eyes fixed on the packet:

"Never in all my life have I seen the like of this. Fifteen diamonds and every one of them a specimen stone. And look at the size of them! Why, that little lot must be worth a king's ransom!"

"I understand," said Thorndyke, "that they represent about ten thousand pounds. That will be their market price; and you can add to that three human lives—not as their value, which it is not, but as their cost."

"I take it," said I, "that you are assuming these to be Kempster's diamonds?"

"It is hardly a case of assuming," he replied. "The facts seem to admit of no other interpretation. This was an experiment to test the correctness of my theory of the crime. I expected to find in this figure fifteen large diamonds. Well, we have opened the figure and here are the fifteen large diamonds. This figure belonged to Peter Gannet, and whatever was in it was put in by him, as is shown by the sealing on the base which bears his signature. But Peter Gannet has been proved to be the murderer of the constable, and that murderer was undoubtedly the man who stole Kempster's diamonds; and these diamonds correspond in number and appearance with the diamonds which were stolen. However, we won't leave it at a mere matter of appearance. Kempster gave me full particulars of the diamonds, including the weight of each stone, and of course the total weight of the whole parcel. We need hardly take the weight of each stone separately, but if we weigh the whole fifteen together and we find that the total weight agrees with that given by Kempster, even my learned and sceptical friend will admit that the identity is proved sufficiently for our present purposes."

I ventured mildly to repudiate the alleged scepticism but agreed that the verification was worth while; and when Thorndyke had carefully closed the packet, we all adjourned to the chemical laboratory, where Polton slid up the glass front of the balance and went through the formality of testing the truth of the latter with empty cans.

"What weight shall I put on, sir?" he asked.

"Mr. Kempster put the total weight at 380.4 grains. Let us try that."

Polton selected the appropriate weights, and when they had been checked by Thorndyke, they were placed in the pan and the necessary "rider" put on the beam to make up the fraction. Then Polton solemnly closed the glass front and slowly depressed the lever; and as the balance rose, the index deviated barely a hair's breadth from the zero mark.

"I think that is near enough," said Thorndyke, "to justify us in deciding that these are the diamonds that were stolen from Kempster."

"Yes," I agreed; "at any rate, it is conclusive enough for me. What do you propose to do with them? Shall you hand them to Kempster?"

"No," he replied. "I don't think that would be quite in order. Stolen property should be delivered to the police, even if its ownership is known. I shall hand these diamonds to the Commissioner of Police, explain the circumstances, and take his receipt for them. Then I shall notify Kempster and leave him to collect them. He will have no difficulty in recovering them as the police have a complete description of the stones. And that will finish the business, so far as I am concerned. I have more than fulfilled my obligations to Kempster and I have proved that Mrs. Gannet could not possibly have been an accessory to the murder of her husband. Those were the ostensible objects of my investigation, apart from the intrinsic interest of the case, and now that they have both been achieved, it remains only to sing *Nunc Dimittis* and celebrate our success with a modest festivity of some kind."

"There is one other little matter that remains," said I. "Today's events have proved that your theory of the crime was correct, but they haven't shown how you arrived at that theory, and I have only the dimmest ideas on the subject. But perhaps the festivity will include a reasoned exposition of the evidence."

"I see nothing against that," he replied. "It would be quite interesting to me to retrace the course of the investigation; and if it would also interest you and Oldfield—who must certainly be one of the party—then we shall all be pleased."

He paused for a few moments, having, I think, detected a certain wistfulness in Polton's face, for he continued:

"A restaurant dinner would hardly meet the case, if a prolonged and necessarily confidential pow-wow is contemplated. What do you think, Polton?"

"I think, sir," Polton replied, promptly and with emphasis, "that you would be much more comfortable and more private in your own dining room, and you'd get a better dinner, too. If you will leave the arrangements to me, I will see that the entertainment does you credit."

I chuckled inwardly at Polton's eagerness. Not but that he would at any time have delighted in ministering, in our own chambers, to Thorndyke's comfort and that of his friends. But apart from these altruistic considerations, I felt sure that on this present occasion the "arrangements" would include some very effective ones for enabling him to enjoy the exposition.

"Very well, Polton," said Thorndyke. "I will leave the affair in your hands. You had better see Dr. Oldfield and find out what date will suit him, and then we will wind up the Gannet case with a flourish."

CHAPTER 20

THORNDYKE REVIEWS THE EVIDENCE

Our invitation to Oldfield came very opportunely, for he was just preparing for his holiday and had already got a *locum-tenens* installed. So when, on the appointed evening, he turned up in buoyant spirits, it was as a free man, immune from the haunting fear of an urgent call.

Polton's artful arrangements for unostentatious eavesdropping had come to naught, for Thorndyke and I had insisted on his laying a place for himself at the table and joining us as the colleague that he had actually become in late years, rather than the servant that he still proclaimed himself to be. For the gradual change of status from servant to friend had occurred quite smoothly and naturally. Polton was a man in whom perfect manners were inborn; and as for his intellect, well, I would gladly have swapped my brain for his.

"This is very pleasant," said Oldfield, as he took his seat and cast an appreciative glance round the table, "and it is most kind of you, sir, to have invited me to the celebration, especially when you consider what a fool I have been and what a mess I made of my part of the business."

"You didn't make a mess of it at all," said Thorndyke.

"Well, sir," Oldfield chuckled, "I made every mistake that was humanly possible, and no man can do more than that."

"You are doing yourself a great injustice, Oldfield," Thorndyke protested. "Apparently you don't realize that you were the actual discoverer of the crime."

Oldfield laid down his knife and fork to gaze at Thorndyke.

"I, the discoverer!" he exclaimed; and then, "Oh, you mean that I discovered the ashes. But any other fool could have done that. There they were, plainly in sight, and it just happened that I was the first person to go into the studio."

"I am not so sure even of that," said Thorndyke. "There was some truth in what Blandy said to you. It was the expert eye which saw at once that something strange had happened. Most persons, going into the studio, would have failed to observe anything abnormal. But that is not what I am referring to. I mean that it was you who made the discovery that exposed the real nature of the crime and led to the identification of the criminal."

Oldfield shook his head, incredulously, and looked at Thorndyke as if demanding further enlightenment.

"What I mean," the latter explained, "is that here we had a crime, carefully and subtly planned and prepared in detail with admirable foresight and imagination. There was only a single mistake, and but for you, that mistake would have passed unnoticed and the scheme would have worked according to plan. It very nearly did, as you know."

Oldfield still looked puzzled, as well he might; for he knew, as I did, that all his conclusions had been wrong; and I was as far as he was from understanding what Thorndyke meant.

"Perhaps," Oldfield suggested, "you will explain in a little more detail what my discovery was?"

"Not now," replied Thorndyke. "Presently, we are going to have a reasoned analysis of the case. You will see plainly enough then."

"I suppose I shall," Oldfield agreed, doubtfully, "but I should have said that the entire discovery was your own, sir. I know that it came as a thunder-bolt to me, and so I expect it did to Blandy. And he must have been pretty sick at losing his prisoner, after all."

"Yes," said I, "he was. And it *was* unfortunate. Gannet ought to have been brought to trial and hanged."

"I am not sorry that he wasn't, all the same," said Oldfield. "It would have been horrible for poor Mrs. Gannet."

"Yes," Thorndyke agreed, "a trial and a hanging would have ruined her life. I am inclined to feel that the suicide, or accident, was all for the best, especially as there are signs that very warm and sympathetic relations are growing up between her and our good friend Linnell. One likes to feel that the future holds out to her the promise of some compensation for all the trials and troubles that she has had to endure."

"Still," I persisted, "the fellow was a villain and ought to have been hanged."

"He wasn't the worst kind of villain," said Thorndyke. "The murder of the constable was, if not properly accidental, at least rather in the nature of 'chance medley.' There could have been no intention to kill. And as to Boles, he probably offered considerable provocation."

From this point the conversation tended to peter out, the company's jaws being otherwise engaged. What there was ranged over a variety of topics—including Polton's *magnum opus,* the regulator, now in a fair way of being completed—and kept us entertained until the last of the dishes had been dealt with and removed and the port and the dessert had been set on the table. Then, when Oldfield and I had filled our pipes (Polton did not smoke but took an occasional, furtive pinch of snuff), Thorndyke, in response to our insistent demands, put down his empty pipe and proceeded to the promised analysis.

"In order," he began, "to appreciate the subtlety and imagination with which this crime was planned, it is necessary to recall the whole sequence of events and to note how naturally and logically it evolved. It begins with a case of arsenic poisoning; a perfectly simple and ordinary case with all the familiar features. A man is poisoned by arsenic in his food. That food is prepared by his wife. The wife has a male friend to whom she is rather devoted, and she is not very devoted to her husband. Taken at its face value, there is no mystery at all. It appears to be just the old, old story.

"The poisoning is detected, the man recovers and returns home to resume his ordinary habits. But any observer, noting the facts, must feel that this is not the end. There will surely be a sequel. A murder has been attempted and has failed; but the will to murder has been proved, and it presumably still exists, awaiting a fresh opportunity. Anyone knowing what has happened, will naturally be on the lookout for some further attempt.

"Then, during his wife's absence at the seaside, the man disappears. She comes home and finds that he is missing. He has not gone away in any ordinary sense, for he has taken nothing with him, not even a hat. In her alarm she naturally seeks the advice of the doctor. But the doctor, recalling the poisoning incident, at once suspects a tragedy, and the more so since he knows of the violent enmity existing between the husband and the wife's friend. But he does not merely suspect a tragedy in the abstract. His suspicions take a definite shape. The idea of murder comes into his mind, and when it does it is associated naturally enough with the man who was suspected of having administered the poison. He is not, perhaps, fully conscious of his suspicions; but he is in such a state of mind that in the instant when the fact of the murder becomes evident, he confidently fills in the picture and identifies not only the victim but the murderer, too.

"Thus, you see how perfectly the stage had been set for the events that were to follow; how admirably the minds of all who knew the facts had been prepared to follow out a particular line of thought. There is the preliminary crime with Boles as the obvious suspect. There is the expectation that, since the motive remains, there will be a further attempt—by Boles. Then comes the expected sequel, and instantly, by the most natural and reasonable association, the *dramatis personae* of the first crime are transferred, in the same rôles, to the second crime. It is all quite plain and consistent. Taking things at their face value, it seemed obvious that the murdered man must be Peter Gannet and his murderer, Frederick Boles. I think that I should have been prepared to accept that view, myself, if there had been nothing to suggest a different conclusion.

"But it was just at this point that Oldfield made his valuable contribution to the evidence. Providence inspired him to take a sample of the bone-ash and test it for arsenic; and to his surprise, and still more to mine, he proved that the ash did contain arsenic. Moreover, the metal was present, not as a mere trace but in measurable quantities. And there could be no doubt about it. Oldfield's analysis was carried out skilfully and with every precaution against error, and I repeated the experiment with the remainder of the sample and confirmed his results.

"Now here was a definite anomaly, a something which did not seem to fit in with the rest of the facts; and I am astonished that neither Blandy nor the other investigators appreciated its possible importance. To me an anomalous fact—a fact which appears unconnected, or even discordant with the body of known facts—is precisely the one on which attention should be focused. And that is what I did in this present case. The arsenic was undeniably present in the ashes, and its presence had to be accounted for.

"How did it come to be there? Admittedly, it was not in the body before the burning. Then it must have found its way into the ashes after their removal from the kiln. But how? To me there appeared to be only two possible explanations, and I considered each, comparing it with the other in terms of probability.

"First, there was the suggestion made at the inquest that the ashes might have become contaminated with arsenic in the course of grinding or transference to the bin. That, perhaps, sounded plausible if it was only a verbal formula for disposing of a curious but irrelevant fact. But when one tried to imagine how such contamination could have occurred, no reasonable explanation was forthcoming. What possible source of contamination was there? Arsenic is not one of the potter's ordinary materials. It would not have been present in the bin, nor in the iron mortar nor in the grinding mills. It was a foreign substance, so far as the pottery studio was concerned, and the only arsenic known to exist in the place was that which was contained in a stoppered jar in Boles's cupboard.

"Moreover, it had not the character of a mere chance contamination. Not only was it present in a measurable quantity; it appeared to be fairly evenly distributed throughout the ashes, as was proved by the fact that the Home Office chemist obtained results substantially similar to Oldfield's and mine. After a critical examination of this explanation, I felt that it explained nothing, that it did not agree with the facts, and was itself inexplicable.

"Then, if one could not accept the contamination theory, what was the alternative? The only other explanation that could be suggested was that the arsenic had been intentionally mixed with the ashes. At the first glance this did not look very probable. But, if it was not the true explanation, it was at least intelligible. There was no impossibility; and in fact, the more I considered it, the less improbable did it appear.

"When this hypothesis was adopted provisionally, two further questions at once arose: if the arsenic was intentionally put into the ashes, who put it there and for what purpose? Taking the latter question first, a reasonable answer immediately suggested itself. The most obvious purpose would be that of establishing a connection between the present crime and the previous arsenic poisoning; and when I asked myself what could be the object of trying to establish such a connection, again a perfectly reasonable answer was forthcoming. In the poisoning crime, the victim was Peter Gannet, and the would-be murderer was almost certainly Frederick Boles. Then the introduction of the arsenic as a common factor linking together the two crimes would have the purpose of suggesting a repetition of the characters of victim and murderer. That is to say, the ultimate object of putting the arsenic into the ashes would be to create the conviction that the ashes were the remains of Peter Gannet, that he had been murdered by means of arsenic, and that the murderer was Frederick Boles.

"But who would wish to create this conviction? Remember that our picture contains only three figures: Gannet, his wife and Boles. If the arsenic had been planted, it must have been planted by one of those three. But by which of them? By Mrs. Gannet? Certainly not, seeing that she was under some suspicion of having been an accessory to the poisoning. And obviously Boles would not wish to create the belief that he was the murderer.

"Thus, of the three possible agents of this imposture, we had excluded two. There remained only Gannet. The suggestion was that he was dead and, therefore, could not have planted the arsenic. But could we accept that suggestion? The arsenic was (by the hypothesis) admittedly an imposture. But with the evidence of imposture, we could no longer take the appearances at their face value. The only direct evidence that the remains were those of Gannet was the tooth that was found in the ashes. It was, however, only a porcelain tooth and no more an integral part of Gannet's body than his shirt button or his collar stud. If the arsenic had been planted to produce a particular belief, it was conceivable that the tooth might have been planted for the very same purpose. It was in fact conceivable that the ashes were not those of Gannet and that consequently Gannet was not dead.

"But if Gannet had not been the victim of this murder, then he was almost certainly the murderer; and if Boles had not been the murderer, then he must almost certainly have been the victim. Both men had disappeared and the ashes were undoubtedly the remains of one of them. Suppose the remains to be those of Boles and the murderer to be Peter Gannet? How does that affect our question as to the planting of the arsenic?

"At a glance we can see that Gannet would have had the strongest reasons for creating the belief that the remains were those of his own body. So long as that belief prevailed, he was absolutely safe. The police would have written him off as dead and would be engaged in an endless and fruitless search for Boles. With only a trifling change in his appearance—such as the shaving off of his beard and moustache—he could go his way in perfect security. Nobody would be looking for him; nobody would even believe in his existence. He would have made the perfect escape.

"This result appeared to me very impressive. The presence of the arsenic was a fact. The hypothesis that it had been planted was the only intelligible explanation of that fact. The acceptance of that hypothesis was conditional on the discovery of some motive for planting it. Such a motive we had discovered, but the acceptance of that motive was conditional on the assumption that Peter Gannet was still alive.

"Was such an assumption unreasonable? Not at all. Gannet's death had rather been taken for granted. He had disappeared mysteriously, and certain unrecognizable human remains had been found on his premises. At once it had been assumed that the remains were his. The actual identification rested on a single porcelain tooth; but as that tooth was no part of his body and could, therefore, have been purposely planted in the ashes, the evidence that it afforded as to the identity of the remains was not conclusive. If any grounds existed for suspecting imposture, it had no evidential value at all. But apart from that tooth there was not, and never had been, any positive reasons for believing that those ashes were the remains of Peter Gannet.

"The completeness and consistency of the results thus arrived at, by reasoning from the hypothesis that the arsenic had been planted, impressed me profoundly. It really looked as if that hypothesis might be the true one and I decided to pursue the argument and see whither it led; and especially to examine one or two other slight anomalies that I had noticed.

"I began with the crime itself. The picture presented (and accepted by the police) was this: Boles had murdered Gannet and cremated his body in the kiln, after dismembering it, if necessary, to get it into the cavity. He had then pounded the incinerated bones and deposited the fragments in the bone-ash-bin. Then, after having done all this, he was suddenly overcome by panic and fled.

"But why had he fled? There was no reason whatever for him to flee. He was in no danger. He was alone in the studio and could lock himself in. There was no fear of interruption, since Mrs. Gannet was away at the seaside, and even if any chance visitor should have come, there was nothing visible to excite suspicion. He had done the difficult and dangerous part of the work and all that remained were the few finishing touches. If he had cleaned up the kiln and put it into its usual condition, the place would have looked quite normal, even to Oldfield; and as to the bone fragments, there was not only the grog-mill but also a powerful edge-runner mill in which they could have been ground to fine powder. If this powder had been put into the bone-ash-bin—the ordinary contents of which were powdered bone ash—every trace of the crime would have been destroyed. Then Boles could have gone about his work in the ordinary way or taken a holiday if he had pleased. There would have been nothing to suggest that any abnormal events had occurred in the studio or that Gannet was not still alive.

"Contrast this with the actual conditions that were found. The kiln had been left in a state that would instantly attract the attention of anyone who knew anything about the working of a pottery studio. The incinerated bones had been pounded into fragments, just too small to be recognizable as parts of any known person, but large enough to be recognized, not only as bones, but as human bones. After all the risk and labour of cremating the body and pounding the bones, there had still been left clear evidence that a man had been murdered.

"I think you will agree that the suggested behaviour of Boles is quite unaccountable; is entirely at variance with reasonable probabilities. On the other hand, if you consider critically the conditions that were found, they will convey to you, as they did to me, the impression of a carefully arranged tableau. Certain facts, such as the murder and the cremation, were to be made plain and obvious, and certain issues, such as the identities of victim and murderer, were to be confused. But furthermore, they conveyed to me a very interesting suggestion, which was that the tableau had been set for a particular spectator. Let us consider this suggestion.

"The crime was discovered by Oldfield, and it is possible that he was the only person who would have discovered it. His potter's eye, glancing at the kiln, noted its abnormal state and saw that something was wrong. Probably there was a good deal of truth, as well as politeness, in Blandy's remark that if he had come to the studio without his expert guide and adviser, though he would have seen the visible objects, he would have failed to interpret their meaning. But Oldfield had just the right knowledge. He knew all about the kiln, he knew the various bins and what was in them, and what the mills were for. So, too, with the little finger bone. Most persons would not have known what it was; but Oldfield, the anatomist, recognizes it at once as the ungual phalanx of a human index finger. He would seem to have been the pre-appointed discoverer.

"The suggestion is strengthened by what we know of the previous events; of Gannet's eagerness to cultivate the doctor's friendship, to induct him into all the mysteries of the studio and all the routine of the work that was carried on there. There is an appearance of Oldfield's being prepared to play the part of discoverer—a part that would naturally fall to him, since it was certain that when the blow fell, Mrs. Gannet would seek the help and advice of the doctor.

"The suggestion of preparation applies also to the arsenic in the ashes. If that arsenic was planted, the planting of it must have been a mere gamble, for it was most unlikely that anyone would think of testing the ashes for arsenic. But if there was any person in the world who would think of doing so, that person was most assuredly Oldfield. Any young doctor who has the misfortune to miss a case of arsenic poisoning is pretty certain thereafter to develop what the psychological jargonists would call 'an arsenic complex.' When any abnormal death occurs, he is sure to think first of arsenic.

"The whole group of appearances then suggested that Oldfield had been prepared to take a particular view and to form certain suspicions. But did not that suggestion carry us back still farther? What of the poisoning affair itself? If all the other appearances were false appearances, was it not possible that the poisoning was an imposture, too? When I came to consider that question, I recalled certain anomalies in the case which I had observed at the time. I did not attach great importance to them, since arsenic is a very erratic poison, but I noted them and I advised Oldfield to keep full notes of the case; and now that the question of imposture had arisen, it was necessary to reconsider them, and to review the whole case critically.

"We had to begin our review by reminding ourselves that practically the whole of our information was derived from the patient's statements. The phenomena were virtually all subjective. Excepting the redness of the eyes, which could easily have been produced artificially, there were no objective signs; for the appearance of the tongue was not characteristic. Of the subjective symptoms we were told; we did not observe them for ourselves. The abdominal pain was felt by the patient, not by us. So with the numbness, the loss of tactile sensibility, the tingling, the cramps and the inability to stand; we learned of their existence from the patient and we could not check his statements. We accepted those statements as there appeared to be no reason for doubting them; but it was quite possible for them all to have been false. To an intelligent malingerer who had carefully studied the symptoms of arsenic poisoning, there would have been little difficulty in making up a quite convincing set of symptoms."

"But," Oldfield objected, "there really was arsenic in the body. You were not forgetting that?"

"Not at all," replied Thorndyke. "That was the first of the anomalies. You will remember my remarking to you that the quantity of arsenic obtained by analysis of the secretions was less than I expected. Woodfield and I were both surprised at the smallness of the amount; which was, in fact, not much greater than might have been found in a patient who was taking arsenic medicinally. But it was not an extreme discrepancy, since arsenic is rapidly eliminated, though the symptoms persist, and we explained it by assuming that no considerable dose had been taken quite recently. Nevertheless, it was rather remarkable, as the severity of the symptoms would have led us to expect a considerable quantity of the poison.

"The next anomaly was the rapidity and completeness of Gannet's recovery. Usually, in severe cases, recovery is slow and is followed by a somewhat long period of ill-health. But Gannet began to recover almost immediately, and when he left the hospital he seemed to be quite well.

"The third anomaly—not a very striking one, perhaps—was his state of mind on leaving hospital. He went back home quite happily and confidently, though his would-be murderer was still there; and he would not entertain any sort of inquiry or any measures to ascertain that murderer's identity. He seemed to assume that the affair was finished and that there was nothing more to fear.

"Now, looking at the case as a whole with the idea of a possible imposture in our minds, what did it suggest? Was there not the possibility that all the symptoms were simulated? That Gannet took just enough arsenic to supply the means of chemical demonstration (a fairly full daily dose of Fowler's solution would do) and on the appropriate occasion, put a substantial quantity of arsenic into the barley water? In short, was it not possible that the poisoning affair was a deception from beginning to end?

"The answer to this question obviously was that it was quite possible, and the next question was as to its probability. But the answer to this also appeared to be affirmative; for on our hypothesis, the appearances in the studio were false appearances, deliberately produced to create a certain erroneous belief. But those appearances were strongly supported by the previous poisoning crime and obviously connected with it. The reasonable conclusion seemed to be that the poisoning affair was a deception calculated to create this same erroneous belief (that an attempt had been made to murder Gannet) and to lead on naturally to the second crime.

"Now let us pause for a moment to see where we stand. Our hypothesis started with the assumption that the arsenic had been put into the ashes for a definite purpose. But we found that the only person who could have had a motive for planting it was Peter Gannet. Thus we had to conclude that Gannet was the murderer and Boles the victim. We have examined this conclusion, point by point, and we have found that it agrees with all the known facts and that it yields a complete, consistent and reasonable scheme of the studio crime. Accordingly, we adopt that conclusion—provisionally, of course, for we are still in the region of hypothesis and have, as yet, actually proved nothing.

"But assuming that Gannet had committed this murder, it was evident that it must have been a very deliberate crime; long premeditated, carefully planned and carried out with extraordinary foresight and infinite patience. A crime of this kind implies a proportionate motive; a deep seated, permanent and intense motive. What could it have been? Was there anything known to us in Gannet's circumstances that might seem to account for his entertaining murder as a considered policy? Taking the usual motives for planned and premeditated murder, I asked myself whether any of them could apply to him. We may put them roughly into five categories: jealousy, revenge, cupidity, escape and fear. Was there any suggestion that Gannet might have been affected by any of them?

"As to jealousy, there was the undeniable fact that Mrs. Gannet's relations with Boles were unusual and perhaps indiscreet. But there was no evidence of any impropriety and no sign that the friendship was resented by Gannet. It did not appear to me that jealousy as a motive could be entertained.

"As to revenge, this is a common motive among Mediterranean peoples but very rare in the case of Englishmen. Boles and Gannet disliked each other to the point of open enmity. An unpremeditated murder might easily have occurred, but there was nothing in their mere mutual dislike to suggest a motive for a deliberately planned murder. So, too, with the motive of cupidity; there was nothing to show that either stood to gain any material benefit by the death of the other. But when I came to consider the last two motives— escape and fear—I saw that there was a positive suggestion which invited further examination; and the more it was examined, the more definite did it become."

"What, exactly, do you mean by escape?" I asked.

"I mean," he replied, "the desire to escape from some intolerable position. A man, for instance, whose life is being made unbearable by the conduct of an impossible wife, may contemplate getting rid of her, especially if he sees the opportunity of making a happy and desirable marriage; or who is haunted by a blackmailer who will never leave him to live in peace. In either case, murder offers the only means of escape, and the motive to adopt that means will tend to develop gradually. From a mere desirable possibility, it will grow into a definite intention; and then there will be careful consideration of practicable and safe methods of procedure. Now in the present case, as I have said, it appeared to me that such a motive might have existed; and when I considered the circumstances, that impression became strongly confirmed. The possible motive came into view in connection with certain facts which were disclosed by Inspector Blandy's activities, and which were communicated to me by Oldfield when he consulted me about Mrs. Gannet's difficulties.

"It appeared that Blandy, having finished with the bone fragments, proceeded to turn out Boles's cupboard. There he found fairly conclusive evidence that Boles was a common receiver, which was not our concern. But he also found a piece of gold plate on which were some very distinct finger-prints. They were the prints from a left hand, and there was a particularly fine and clear impression of a left thumb. Of this plate Blandy took possession with the expressed intention of taking it to the Finger-print Department at Scotland Yard to see if Boles happened to be a known criminal. Presumably, he did so, and we may judge of the result by what followed. Two days later he called on Mrs. Gannet and subjected her to a searching interrogation, asking a number of leading questions, among which were two of very remarkable significance. He wanted to know where Boles was on the 19th of last September, and when it was that his friendship with Gannet suddenly turned to enmity. Both these questions she was able to answer; and the questions and the answers were highly illuminating.

"First, as to the questions. The 19th of September was the date of the Newingstead murder; and the murdered constable's truncheon bore a very distinct print of a left thumb—evidently that of the murderer. At a glance, it appeared to me obvious that the thumb-print on the gold plate had been found to correspond with the thumb print on the truncheon and that Boles had been identified thereby as the murderer of the constable. That was the only possible explanation of Blandy's question. And this assumption was confirmed by the answer; by which it transpired that Boles was at Newingstead on that fatal day and that, incidentally, Gannet was with him, the two men, apparently, staying at the house of Boles's aunt.

"Blandy's other question and Mrs. Gannet's answer were also profoundly significant; for she recalled, clearly, that the sudden change in the relations of the two men was first observed by her when she met them after their return from Newingstead. They went there friends; they came back enemies. She knew of no reason for the change; but those were the facts.

"Here we may pause to fill in, as I did, the picture thus presented to us in outline. There are two men (whom we may conveniently call A and B) staying together at a house in Newingstead. On the 19th of September, one of them, A, goes forth alone. Between eight and nine in the evening he commits the robbery. At about nine o'clock he kills the constable. Then he finds Oldfield's bicycle and on it he pedals away some four miles along the London Road. Having thus got away from the scene of the crime, he dismounts and seeks a place in which to hide the bicycle. He finds a cart shed, and having concealed the bicycle in it, sets out to return to Newingstead. Obviously, he would not go back by the same route, with the chance of encountering the police, for he probably suspects that he has killed a man, and at any rate, he has the stolen diamonds on his person. He must necessarily make a detour so as to approach Newingstead from a different direction, and his progress would not be rapid, as he would probably try to avoid being seen. The cart shed was over four miles from Newingstead along the main road, and his detour would have added considerably to that distance. By the time that he arrived at his lodgings it would be getting late; at least eleven o'clock and probably later. Quite a late hour by village standards.

"The time of his arrival home would probably be noted by B. But there is something else he would note. A had been engaged in a violent encounter with the constable and could hardly fail to bear some traces of it on his person. The constable was by no means passive. He had drawn his truncheon and was using it when it was snatched away from him. We may safely assume that A's appearance, when he sneaked home and let himself into the house, must have been somewhat unusual.

"By the next morning the hue and cry was out. All the village knew of the robbery and the murder, and it would be inevitable that B should connect the crime with A's late homecoming and disordered condition. Not only did the times agree but the man robbed, Arthur Kempster, was known to them both, and known personally at least by one of them. Then came the inquest with full details of the crime and the vitally important fact that a clear finger-print, left by the murderer, was in the possession of the police. Both the men must have known what was proved at the inquest for a very full report of it was published in the local paper, as I know from having read a copy that Kempster gave me. Both men knew of the existence of the thumb-print; and one knew, and the other was convinced, that it was A's thumb-print.

"From these facts it was easy to infer what must have followed. For it appears that it was just at this time that the sudden change from mutual friendship to mutual enmity occurred. What did that change (considered in connection with the aforesaid facts) imply? To me it suggested the beginning of a course of blackmail. B was convinced that A was the robber and he demanded a share of the proceeds as the price of his silence. But A could not admit the robbery without also admitting the murder. Consequently, he denied all knowledge of either.

"Then began the familiar train of events that is characteristic of blackmail; that so commonly leads to its natural end in either suicide or murder. B felt sure that A had in his possession loot to the value of ten thousand pounds and he demanded, with menaces, his share of that loot; demands that A met with stubborn denials. And so it went on with recurring threats and recriminations and violent quarrels.

"But it could not go on forever. To A the conditions were becoming intolerable. A constant menace hung over him. He lived in the shadow of the gallows. A word from B could put the rope round his neck; a mere denunciation without need of proof. For there was the deadly thumb-print, and they both knew it. To A a simple accusation showed the way directly to the execution shed.

"Was there no escape? Obviously, mere payment was of no use. It never is of use in the case of blackmail. For the blackmailer may sell his silence but he retains his knowledge. If A had surrendered the whole of the loot to B he would still not have been safe. Still B would have held him in the hollow of his hand, ready to blackmail again when the occasion should arise. Clearly, there was no escape that way. As long as B remained alive, the life of A hung upon a thread.

"From this conclusion the corollary was obvious. If B's existence was incompatible with the safe and peaceful existence of A, then B must be eliminated. It was the only way of escape. And having come to this decision, A could give his attention, quietly and without hurry, to the question of ways and means; to the devising of a plan whereby B could be eliminated without leaving a trace, or, at any rate, a trace that would lead in the direction of A. And thus came into being the elaborate, ingeniously devised scheme which I had been examining and which looked, at that time, so much like a successful one.

"The next problem was to give a name to each of the two men. A and B represented Boles and Gannet; but which was which? Was Boles, for instance, A the murderer, or B the Blackmailer? By Blandy, Boles was confidently identified as the Newingstead murderer. But then Blandy accepted all the appearances at their face value. In his view Gannet was not in the picture. He was not a person: he was a mere basketful of ashes. The thumb-print had been found in Boles's cupboard on Boles's own material. Therefore it was Boles's thumb-print.

"But was this conclusion in accordance with ordinary probabilities? From Blandy's point of view it may have been, but from mine it certainly was not. So great was the improbability that it presented that, even if I had known nothing of the other facts, I should have approached it with profound scepticism. Consider the position: Here is a man whose thumb-print is filed at Scotland Yard. That print is capable of hanging him, and he knows it. Then is it conceivable that, if he were not an abject fool—which Boles was not —he would be dabbing that print on surfaces that anyone might see? Would he not studiously avoid making that print on anything? Would he not, when working alone, wear a glove on his left hand? And if by chance he should mark some object with that print, would he not be careful to wipe it off? Above all, if he were absconding as he was assumed to have absconded, would he leave a perfect specimen of that incriminating print in the very place which the police would be quite certain to search for the express purpose of discovering finger-prints? The thing was incredible. The very blatancy of it was enough to raise a suspicion of imposture.

"That, as I have said, is taking the thumb-print apart from any other facts or deductions. But now let us consider it in connection with what we have deduced. If we suggest that the thumb-print was Gannet's and that he had planted it where it was certain to be found by the police, at once we exchange a wild improbability for a very striking probability. For thus he would have contrived to kill an additional, very important, bird with the same stone. He has got rid of Boles, the blackmailer. But now he has also got rid of the Newingstead murderer. He has attached the incriminating thumb-print to the person of Boles, and as Boles has ceased to exist, the fraud can never be discovered. He has made himself absolutely safe; for the police have an exact description of Boles—who was at least three inches taller than Gannet and had brown eyes. So that even if, by some infinitely remote chance, Gannet should leave his thumb-print on some object and it should be found by the police, still he would be in no danger. They would assume as a certainty that it had been made by a tall, brown-eyed man, and they would search for that man—and never find him.

"Here, then, is a fresh agreement; and you notice that our deductions are mounting up, and that they conform to the great rule of circumstantial evidence; that all the facts shall point to the same conclusion. Our hypothesis is very largely confirmed, and we are justified in believing it to be the true one. That, at least, was my feeling at this stage. But still there remained another matter that had to be considered; an important matter, too, since it might admit of an actual experimental test. Accordingly I gave it my attention.

"I had concluded (provisionally) that Gannet was the Newingstead murderer. If he were, he had in his possession fifteen large diamonds of the aggregate value of about ten thousand pounds. How would he have disposed of those diamonds? He could not carry them on his person, for apart from their great value, they were highly incriminating. Merely putting them under lock and key would hardly be sufficient, for Boles was still frequenting the house and he probably knew all about the methods of opening drawers and cupboards. Something more secure would be needed; something in the nature of an actual hiding place. But he was planning to dispose of Boles and then to disappear; and naturally, when the time should come for him to disappear, he would want to take the diamonds with him. But still he might be unwilling to have them on his person. How was this difficulty to be met?

"Here, once more, enlightenment came from the invaluable Oldfield. In the course of his search of the deserted house he observed that the pottery which had been on the mantelpiece of Gannet's bedroom had disappeared. Now this was a rather remarkable circumstance. The disappearance of the pottery seemed to coincide with the disappearance of Gannet, and one naturally asked oneself whether there could be any connection between the two events, and if so, what the nature of that connection might be. The pottery consisted, as I remembered, of a number of bowls and jars and a particularly hideous stoneware figure. The pots seemed to be of no special interest. But the figure invited inquiry. A pottery figure is necessarily made hollow, for lightness and to allow of even shrinkage during the firing; and the cavity inside would furnish a possible hiding place, though not, perhaps, a very good one, if the figure were of the ordinary type.

"But this figure was not of the ordinary type. I ascertained the fact from Oldfield, who had examined it and who gave me an exact description of it. And a most astonishing description it was; for it seemed to involve a physical impossibility. The figure, he informed me, had a flat base covered with some sort of white enamel on which was the artist's signature. There was no opening in it, nor was there any opening either at the back or the top. That was according to his recollection, and he could hardly have been mistaken, for he had examined the figure all over and he was certain that there was no hole in it anywhere.

"Now, here was a most significant fact. What could be the explanation? There were only two possibilities, and one of them could be confidently rejected. Either the figure was solid or an opening in it had been filled up. But it could not be solid, for there must be some cavity in a pottery figure to allow for shrinkage without cracking. But if it was hollow, there must have been some opening in it originally. For a hollow figure in which there was no opening would be blown to pieces by the expansion of the imprisoned air during the firing. The only possible conclusion was that an opening originally existing had been filled up; and this conclusion was supported by the condition of the base. It is there that the opening is usually placed, as it is hidden when the figure is standing; and there it had apparently been in this case; for the white, glazed enamel looked all wrong, seeing that the figure itself was salt-glazed, and in any case, it was certainly an addition. Moreover, as it must have been added after the firing, it could hardly have been a ceramic enamel but was more probably some kind of hydraulic cement such as Keene's. But whatever the material may have been, the essential fact was that the opening had been filled up and concealed, and the open cavity converted into a sealed cavity.

"Here, then, was an absolutely perfect hiding place, which had the additional virtue of being portable. But if it contained the diamonds, as I had no doubt that it did, it was necessary to find out without delay what had become of it. For wherever the diamonds were, sooner or later Gannet would be found there. In short, it seemed that the stoneware monkey might supply the crucial fact which would tell us whether our hypothesis was true or false.

"There was no difficulty in tracing the monkey, for Oldfield had learned that it had been sent, with the other pottery, to a loan exhibition at a museum in Hoxton. But before going there to examine it and check Oldfield's description, I had to acquire a few preliminary data. From Mr. Kempster of the Bond Street gallery I obtained the name and address of the owner of a replica of the figure; and as the question of weight might arise, I took the opportunity to weigh and measure one of Gannet's bowls.

"The owner of the replica, a Mr. Broomhill, gave us every facility for examining it, even to weighing it. We found that it was hollow, and judging by the weight, that it had a considerable interior cavity. There was an oval opening in the base of about an inch and a half in the longer diameter, through which we could see the marks of a thumb, showing that the figure was a squeeze from a mould; and it was a little significant that all the impressions appeared to be those of a right thumb.

"Armed with these data, we went to the museum, where we were able to examine, handle and weigh Gannet's figure. It corresponded completely with Oldfield's description, for there was no opening in any part of it. The appearance of the base suggested that the original opening had been filled with Keene's cement and glazed with cellulose varnish. That the figure was hollow was proved by its weight, but this was about six ounces greater than that of Broomhill's replica; a difference that would represent, roughly, the weight of the diamonds, the packing and the cement stopping. Thus the observed facts were in complete agreement with the hypothesis that the diamonds had been concealed in the figure; and you will notice that they were inexplicable on any other supposition.

"We now went into the office and made a few inquiries, and the answers to these—quite freely and frankly given by the curator, Mr. Sancroft—disclosed a most remarkable and significant group of facts. It appeared that the figure had been sold a short time before it had been sent to the museum. The purchaser, Mr. James Newman, had then gone abroad but expected to return in about three months, when he proposed to call at the museum and claim his property. The arrangements to enable him to do so were very simple but very interesting. As Mr. Newman was not known personally to Mr. Sancroft (who also, by the way, had never met Peter Gannet), he would produce a letter of introduction and a written order to Mr. Sancroft to deliver the figurine to Newman, who would then give a receipt for it.

"These arrangements presented a rather striking peculiarity. They involved the very minimum of contacts. There was no correspondence by which an address would have had to be disclosed. Mr. Newman, a stranger to Sancroft, would appear in person, would present his order, receive his figurine and then disappear, leaving no clue as to whence he had come or whither he had gone. The appearances were entirely consistent with the possibility that Mr. Newman and Peter Gannet were one and the same person. And this I felt convinced was the fact.

"But if Newman was Gannet, what might we predict as to his personal appearance? He would almost certainly be clean shaven and there might be a certain amount of diguise. But the possibilities of disguise off the stage are very limited, and the essential personal characteristics remain. Stature cannot be appreciably disguised, and eye colour not at all. Gannet's height was about five feet eight and his eyes were of a pale grey. He had a scar across his left eyebrow and the middle finger of his right hand had an ankylosed joint. Neither the scar nor the stiff joint could be disguised, and it would be difficult to keep them out of sight.

"We learned from Sancroft that the three months had expired and that Mr. Newman might be expected at any moment. Evidently, then, whatever was to be done must be done at once. But what was to be done? The final test was the identity of Newman, and that test could be applied only by me. I had to contrive, if possible, to be present when Newman arrived, for no subsequent shadowing of him was practicable. Until he was identified as Gannet he could not be stopped or prevented from leaving the country.

"At first it looked almost like an impossible problem, but certain peculiar circumstances made it comparatively easy. I was able to install my man, Snuper, at the museum to hold the fort in my absence. I gave him the description of Gannet and certain instructions which I need not repeat in detail as it never became necessary to act on them. By good luck it happened that Newman arrived in the evening when Snuper was in charge alone. He had no authority to deliver up the figure so he made an appointment for the following morning. Then he sent me a message stating what had happened and that Mr. Newman seemed to answer my description; whereupon I got into communication with Blandy and advised him to come to the museum on the chance that Newman might be the man whom he wanted for the Newingstead affair.

"You know the rest. Jervis and I were at the museum when Newman arrived and Blandy was lurking in the entry. But, even then, the case was still only a train of hypothetical reasoning. Nothing had really been proved. Even when I stood behind Newman waiting for him to discover my presence, it was still possible that he might turn and reveal himself as a perfectly innocent stranger. Only at the very last moment, when he turned to face me and I recognized him as Gannet and saw that he recognized me, did I know that there had been no flaw in my reasoning. It was a dramatic moment, and a more unpleasant one I hope never to experience."

"It *was* rather horrible," I agreed. "The expression on the poor devil's face when he saw you, haunts me to this day. I was almost sorry for him."

"Yes," said Thorndyke, "it was a disagreeable duty. The pursuit had been full of interest, but the capture I would gladly have left to the police, if that had been possible. But it was not. Our mutual recognition was the crucial fact.

"And now, after all this logic chopping, perhaps a glass of wine would not come amiss. Let us pledge our colleague, Oldfield, who set our feet on the right track. And I may remark, Polton, that one fluid drachm is not a glass of wine within the meaning of the act."

The abstemious Polton crinkled guiltily and poured another thirty minims into the bottom of his glass. Then we solemnly pledged our friend, who received the tribute with a rather sheepish smile.

"It is very good of you, sir," said he, "to give me so much undeserved credit, and most kind of you all to drink my health. I realize my limitations, but it is a satisfaction to me to know that, if my wits are none of the most brilliant, I have at least been the occasion of wit in others."

There is little more to tell. The repentant Blandy, by way of making amends to his late victim (and possibly of casting a discreet veil over his own mistakes), so arranged matters with the coroner that the inquest on "a man who called himself James Newman" was conducted with the utmost tact and the minimum of publicity; whereby the future of Mrs. Gannet was left unclouded and the susceptibilities of our friend Linnell unoffended.

As to the monkey, it experienced various vicissitudes before it finally came to rest in appropriate surroundings. First, by Mrs. Gannet, it was presented to Thorndyke "as a memorial." But we agreed that it was too ugly even for a memorial, and I secretly took possession of it and conveyed it to Oldfield; who accepted it gleefully with a cryptic grin which I did not, at the time, understand. But I understood it later when he informed me—with a grin which was not at all cryptic—that he had presented it to Mr. Bunderby.

The
Penrose
Mystery

BOOK ONE

BEING THE NARRATIVE OF
ERNEST LOCKHART, BARRISTER-AT-LAW

CHAPTER I

A GOSSIPY CHAPTER IN WHICH COMING EVENTS CAST THEIR SHADOWS BEFORE THEM

I have been asked to make my contribution to the curious history of the disappearance of Mr. Daniel Penrose, and I accordingly do so; but not without reluctance and a feeling that my contribution is but a retailing of the smallest of small beer. For the truth is that of that strange disappearance I knew nothing at the time, and, even now, my knowledge is limited to what I have learned from those who were directly concerned in the investigation. Still, I am assured that the little that I have to tell will elucidate the accounts which the investigators will presently render of the affair, and I shall, therefore, with the above disclaimer, proceed with my somewhat trivial narrative.

Whenever my thoughts turn to that extraordinary case, there rises before me the picture of a certain antique shop in a by-street of Soho. And quite naturally; for it was in that shop that I first set eyes on Daniel Penrose, and it was in connection with that shop, directly or indirectly, that my not very intimate relations with Penrose existed.

It was a queer little shop; an antique shop in both senses. For not only were the goods that it contained one and all survivors from the past, but the shop was an antique in itself. Indeed, it was probably a more genuine museum piece than anything in its varied and venerable stock, with its small-paned window bulging in a double curve—as shop-fitters could make them in the eighteenth century—and glazed with the original crown glass, greenish in tone and faintly streaked, like an oyster-shell, with concentric lines. I dated the shop at the first half of the eighteenth century, basing my estimate on a pedimented stone tablet at the corner of the street; which set forth the name, "Nassau Street in Whetten's Buildings," and the date, 1734. It was a pleasant and friendly shop, though dingy; dignified and reticent, too, for the fascia above the window bore only, in dull gilt letters, the name of the proprietor, "D. Parrott."

For some time I remained under the belief that this superscription referred to some former incumbent of the premises whose name was retained for the sake of continuity, since the only persons whom I encountered in my early visits were Mrs. Pettigrew, who appeared to manage the business, and, more rarely, her daughter, Joan, a strikingly good-looking girl of about twenty; a very modern young lady, frank, friendly and self-possessed, quite well-informed on the subject of antiques though openly contemptuous of the whole genus.

Presently, however, I discovered that Parrott, so far from being a mere disembodied name, was a very real person. He was, in fact, the mainspring of the establishment, for he was not only the buyer —and an uncommonly good buyer—but he had quite a genius for converting mere dismembered carcasses into hale and hearty pieces of furniture. Somewhere in the regions behind the shop he had a workshop where, with the aid of an incredibly aged cabinet-maker named Tims, he carried out the necessary restorations. And they were real restorations, not fakes; honest repairs carried out for structural reasons and left open and undisguised. I came to have a great respect for Mr. Parrott.

My first visit was undoubtedly due to the ancient shop-front. But when I crossed the narrow street to examine it and discovered in the window a court cupboard and a couple of Jacobean chairs, I decided to avail myself of the courteous invitation, written on a card, to enter and inspect and indulge a mild passion for ancient furniture.

There were three persons in the shop; a comely woman of about fifty, who greeted me with a smile and a little bow, and thereafter took no further notice of me; a stout, jovial, rather foxy-looking gentleman who was inspecting a trayful of old silver; and a small clerical-looking gentleman who appeared to be disembowelling a bloated verge watch and prying into its interior through a watch-maker's eye-glass, which stuck miraculously in his eye, giving him somewhat the appearance of a one-eyed lobster.

"Now," said the stout gentleman, "that's quite an elegant little milk-jug, in my opinion. Don't you agree with me, Mrs. Pettigrew?"

I looked at him in some surprise. For the thing was not a milk-jug. It was a coffee-pot. However, Mrs. Pettigrew did not contest the description. She merely agreed that the shape was pleasant and graceful.

"I am glad, Mrs. Pettigrew," said the stout gentleman, regarding the coffee-pot with his head on one side, "that you regard the lactiferous receptacle with favour. I am encouraged and confirmed. The next question is that of the date of its birthday. I am reluctant to interrupt the erudite Mr. Polton in his studies of the internal anatomy of the Carolean warming-pan, but I have no skill in galactophorous genealogies. May I venture?"

He held out the coffee-pot engagingly towards the small gentleman, who thereupon laid the watch down tenderly, removed the eye-glass from his eye and smiled. And I found Mr. Polton's smile almost as astonishing as the other gentleman's vocabulary. It was the most amazingly wrinkly smile that I have ever seen, but yet singularly genial and pleasant. And here I may remark that this amiable little gentleman was for some time a profound mystery to me. I could make nothing of him. I could not place him socially or otherwise. By his appearance, he might—in different raiment—have been a dignitary of the Church. His deferential manner suggested some superlative kind of manservant, but his hands and his comprehensive and inexhaustible knowledge of the products of the ancient crafts hinted at the dealer or expert collector. It was only after I had known him some months that the mystery was resolved through the medium of a legal friend, as will be related in due course. To return to the present incident, Mr. Polton took the coffee-pot in his curiously prehensile hands, beamed on it approvingly, and, having stuck his eye-glass in his eye, examined the hall-mark and the maker's "touch."

"It was made," he reported, "in 1765 by a man named John Hammond, who had a shop in Water Lane, Fleet Street. And an excellent tradesman he must have been."

"There, now!" exclaimed the stout gentleman. "Just listen to that! It's my belief that Mr. Polton carries in his head a complete directory of all the artful craftsmen and crafty artists who ever made anything, with the dates of every piece they made. Don't you agree, Mrs. Pettigrew?"

"Yes, indeed!" she replied. "His knowledge is perfectly wonderful. Perhaps," she added, addressing Mr. Polton, "you can tell us something about that watch. It is said to have belonged to Prince Charlie, and, of course, that would add to its value if it were really the fact. What do you think, Mr. Polton?"

"Well, ma'am," was the cautious reply, "I see no reason why it should not have belonged to him, if he was not a very punctual gentleman. It was made in Edinburgh in 1735, and there is a crucifix engraved inside the outer case. I don't know what the significance of that may be."

"Neither do I," said the lady. "What do you think, Mr. Penrose?"

"I should say," replied the stout gentleman, "that the evidence is conclusive. Charles Edward, being a Scotchman, would have a Scottish watch; and being a papistical Romanist would naturally have a crucifix engraved in it. Q.E.D."

Mrs. Pettigrew smiled indulgently, and, as Mr. Penrose had indicated his adoption of the coffee-pot, she proceeded to swathe it in tissue-paper and make it up into a presentable parcel; and, meanwhile, I browsed round the premises and inspected those specimens of the stock which were more particularly within my province. But it was not a very peaceful inspection, for Mr. Penrose persisted in accompanying me and expounding and commenting upon the various pieces in terms which I found rather distracting. For Mr. Penrose, as the reader has probably observed, was a wag, and his waggery took the form of calling things by quaintly erroneous names and of using odd and facetious circumlocutions; which was all very well at first and was even mildly amusing, but it very soon became tiresome. A constant effort was necessary to arrive at what he really meant.

However, in the end, I lighted upon a bible-box of dark-brown oak, pleasantly carved and bearing the incised date, 1653, and, as the little chest rather took my fancy and the price marked on the attached ticket seemed less than its value, I closed with Mrs. Pettigrew, and, having paid for my purchase and given the address to which it was to be sent, took my departure. And, as I strolled at a leisurely pace in the direction of Wardour Street, I reflected idly on my late experience, and especially on the three rather unusual persons whose acquaintance I had just made. I am not in general a curious man, but I found in each of these three persons matter for speculation. There was Mrs. Pettigrew, for instance. Admirably as she played her part in the economy of the shop, she did not completely fit her surroundings. One is accustomed nowadays to finding women of a very superior class serving in shops. But not quite of Mrs. Pettigrew's type. She gave me the impression of being very definitely a lady; and I found myself speculating on the turn of the wheel of Fortune that had brought her there.

Then there was the enigmatical Mr. Polton with his strangely prehensile hands and his astonishing memory for hall-marks. And there was the facetious Penrose. And at this point, being then about halfway along Gerrard Street, the subject of my reflections overtook me and announced himself characteristically by expressing the hope that I was pleased with my bacon cupboard. I replied that I was quite pleased with my purchase and had thought it decidedly cheap.

"So did I," said he. "But our psittacoid friend has the wisdom to temper the breeze to the shorn collector."

"Our psittacoid friend?" I repeated.

"I refer to the tropic bird who presides over the museum of domestic archæology," he explained, and, as I still looked at him questioningly, he added, by way of elucidation: "The proprietor of the treasure-house of antiquities in which you discovered the repository of ancestral piety."

"Oh!" I exclaimed. "You mean Mr. Parrott."

"Certainly!" he replied. "Did I not say so?"

"Perhaps you did," I admitted, with a slightly sour laugh; at which he smiled his peculiar, foxy smile, looking at me out of the corners of his eyes, and evidently pleased at having "stumped" me. It was a pleasure that he must have enjoyed pretty often.

"I take it," he resumed, after a short pause, "that you, like myself, are a devotee of St. Margaret Pie?"

I considered this fresh puzzle and decided that the solution was "magpie"; and apparently I was right as he did not correct me.

"No," I replied, "there is nothing of the magpie about me. I don't accumulate old things for the sake of forming a collection. I buy old furniture and use it. One must have furniture of some kind, old or new, and I prefer the old. It was made by men who knew all about it and who enjoyed making it and took their time. It is much more companionable to live with than new machine-made stuff, turned out by the thousand by people who don't care a straw what it is like. But my object is quite utilitarian. I am no collector."

"Ah!" said he, "that isn't my case. I am a convinced disciple of the great John Daw, a snapper-up of unconsidered trifles, a hoarder of miscellaneous treasure. Nothing comes amiss to me, from a blue diamond to a Staffordshire dog."

"Have you no special fancy?" I asked.

"I have a special fancy for any relic of the past that I can lay hands on," he replied. "But perhaps, like the burglars, I have a particular leaning towards precious stones—those and the other kind of stones—the silicious variety—with which our impolite forefathers used to fracture one another's craniums."

"Your collection must take up a lot of space," I remarked.

"It does," said he. "That's the trouble. John Daw's nest has a tendency to overflow. And still they come. I'm always finding fresh treasures."

"By the way," said I, "where do you find the stuff?"

"Oh, call it not stuff," he protested, regarding me with a foxy smile. "I spoke of treasures. As to where I discover them; well, well, surely there is a mine for silver and a place for gold where they refine it; a place also—many places, mostly cottage parlours, that no bird of prey knoweth, neither hath the traveling dealer's eye seen them, where may be found ancestral Wrotham pots and Staffordshire figures, to say nothing of venerable tickers and crocks from far Cathay. These the wise collector makes a note of—and locks up the note."

I was half amused and half exasperated by his evasive verbiage and his unabashed, and quite unnecessary caution. A mighty secretive gentleman, this, I reflected; and proceeded to fire a return shot.

"In effect," said I, "you go rooting about in cottage parlours, snapping up rustic heirlooms, probably at a fraction of their value."

"Undoubtedly," he agreed, with a snigger. "That is the essence of the sport. I once, in a labourer's cottage, picked up a genuine 'Vicar and Moses' by Ralph Wood for five shillings. But that was a windfall."

"It wasn't much of a windfall for the owner," I remarked.

"He was quite satisfied," said Penrose, "and so was I. What more would you have? But windfalls are not frequent, and when they fail I fall back on the popinjay."

"The pop— Oh, you mean Mr. Parrott?"

"Exactly," said he. "Our friend Monsieur le Perroquet. Actually, I let him do most of the rooting about. He knows all the ropes, and, as we agreed, he doesn't demand payment through the proboscis."

"No," said I, "he doesn't appear to be grasping, to judge by the price of my own purchase; and I gather that you have got most of your stuff—I beg pardon; treasure—from him."

"Oh, I wouldn't say that," he replied. "Mere purchase from a dealer is a dull affair, though necessary. But one wants the sport as well, the pleasure of the chase, not to mention those of the pick and shovel."

"The pick and shovel!" I repeated. "That sounds as if you did a little in the resurrection line. You are not a tomb-robber, I trust?"

I was, of course, only jesting, but he took me up quite seriously.

"But why not? We may grant the impropriety of disturbing the repose of the freeholders in Finchley Cemetery. Besides, they have nothing but their bones, which, at present, are not collector's pieces. But our rude forefathers had a foolish—but, for us, convenient— habit of taking their goods and chattels to bed with them, so to speak. Now, a man's title to his goods, after his decease, does not extend to an indefinite period. When a deceased gentleman has enjoyed the possession of his chattels for a couple of thousand years or more, I think he ought to be satisfied. His title has lapsed by the effluxion of time; and my title, by right of discovery, has come into being. The expression 'tomb-robber' is not applicable to an archæological excavator. Don't you agree?"

I admitted that excavation for scientific purposes seemed to be a permissible proceeding, though I had secret doubts as to whether the expression was properly applicable to his activities. He did not impress me as a scientific investigator.

"But," I asked, "what sort of things do you turn up when you go a-digging?"

"All sorts of things," he replied. "Mostly preposterous stone substitutes for cutlery, decayed and fragmentary pots and pans, with an occasional—very occasional—torque or brooch and portions of the deceased proprietor. But I leave those. I don't collect proprietors."

"And I suppose," said I, "that when you find a gold or silver ornament you notify the coroner of the discovery of treasure trove?"

"That," he replied with his queer, foxy smile, "is indispensable. But you seem to be interested in my miscellaneous gleanings. I wonder if you would care to cast a supercilious eye on my little hoard. I don't often display my treasures because your regular collector is usually a man of one idea—indefinitely repeated—and he is disappointed to find that I am not. But you, like myself, are more eclectic in taste and I should have great pleasure in introducing you to Aladdin's Cave, if you would care to inspect its contents."

I was not, really, particularly interested, but yet I was faintly curious as to the nature of his "hoard." It sounded like a very queer collection, and might include some objects of real interest. Besides which, the man, himself, despite his exasperating verbosity and obscurities of speech, rather attracted me. Accordingly, I accepted his invitation, and, when we had exchanged visiting cards and arranged the day and hour of my visit, we separated; he shaping a course in a westerly direction and I bearing east, towards my chambers in Lincoln's Inn.

CHAPTER 2

ALADDIN'S CAVE

Mr. Penrose's residence or John Daw's Nest, as he would have called it, was situated in Queen Square, Bloomsbury, and, what is more, it was one of the few remaining original houses, dating back to the time when residents could look out of their windows through the open end of the square, across the meadows to the heights of Highgate. Appropriately to the house of a collector of antiquities, its door was garnished with a pair of link-extinguishers, as well as with a fine brass knocker and an old-fashioned bell-handle.

A flourish on the knocker, reinforced by a hearty tug at the bell-pull, resulted in the opening of the door and the appearance thereat of an elderly man of depressed and nephritic aspect, with puffy eyelids and a complexion like that of a suet pudding. He received the announcement of my identity with resignation, and, having admitted me, took my hat and stick and silently introduced me to a small room, the window of which commanded a view of the leaden statue of Her late Majesty, Queen Anne. At this window I had taken up a position from which I could contemplate that rather neglected example of an extinct art when the door opened briskly and Mr. Penrose entered.

"Ha!" said he, "I see you are admiring the mimic rendering of our proverbially deceased twenty-shilling Lady."

"I am afraid," said I, as we shook hands, "that your paraphrase fails in precision. You would have to pay thirty shillings to-day to buy a sovereign, if you could find one."

"There," he retorted, "is exemplified the pedantic accuracy of the legal mind. But I spoke in terms of the past. The aureous reality is now as dead as madame herself. But what think you of that master-piece of the plumber's art? I rather like it; and it is the genuine metal. I have tried it with my pocketknife. To tell you a little secret, I had thought of making an offer for it."

"Do you mean," I exclaimed, "that you want to buy it?"

"If it should come into the market," he replied. "Unfortunately it has not, up to the present."

"But what on earth could you do with a leaden statue?" I protested.

"Put it in my gallery," he replied, "if the floor would stand it."

"You can take it," said I, "that it would not. Why, the thing must weigh tons. Besides, it is much better in the place that it was made to occupy and which it does really adorn in its rather mouldy way."

"In short," said he, "you think me a bit of a vandal" (which was the literal truth). "Well, you needn't be alarmed. It is safe from my acquisitive instincts for the present."

He turned to a nondescript piece of furniture, half sideboard and half armoire, and, opening a door, took out a decanter and two glasses, which he placed on the table.

"Before we venture into Aladdin's Cave," said he, taking out the stopper of the decanter, "shall we fortify ourselves with a morsel of cake?"

He looked at me interrogatively as he picked up the decanter. Of course, there was no cake visible; but my growing skill in interpreting his verbal puzzles enabled me to diagnose the dark-brown wine as Madeira.

Without giving me time to refuse, he filled the two glasses, and, having handed me one, proceeded in a very deliberate and workmanlike fashion to empty the other.

"The vintages of the Fortunate Isles," said he, as he refilled his glass, "have always commended themselves to me, rivalled only in my affection by the product of the vines of Xeres" (he pronounced the name in the Spanish manner, "Hereth," as a slight additional precaution against being too readily understood), "preferably the elderly and fuscous variety."

I noted the fact—while he filled his third glass—as explaining the vinous aroma which I had noticed in Parrott's shop as apparently exhaling from his person. It turned out later to be not without significance. Madeira and old brown sherry by no means share the innocuousness of what Penrose would probably have called "the celestial herb."

When I had resolutely declined a refill, he reluctantly returned the decanter to its abiding-place and locked the door thereof.

"And now," said he, "we shall proceed to explore the secret recesses of the cavern."

He conducted me out into the fine, spacious hall, from which a noble staircase gave access to the upper floors. In one swift glance I noted that the appointments were not worthy of the architecture, for the furniture—of which there was a good deal too much—consisted of undeniable "dentist's oak," and there were one or two shabby-looking busts, the obvious plaster of which had been varnished by some optimist in the hope that they might thereby be mistaken for bronze. But I had little opportunity for detailed inspection, for my host threw open, with something of a flourish, an adjacent door and motioned to me to enter; which I did, and found myself in one of a pair of great, lofty communicating rooms, and forthwith began my tour of inspection.

I had expected to find Mr. Penrose's collection something of an oddity, but the reality far exceeded my expectations. It was an amazing hoard. Alike, in respect of matter and manner, it was astonishing and bewildering. Of the ordinary collector's fastidious selection, prim tidiness and orderly arrangement there was no trace. The things that jostled one another on the crowded shelves and tables were in every respect incongruous; for, on the one hand, rare and valuable pieces, such as the "Vicar and Moses" and a fine slip-ware tyg, stood cheek by jowl with common, worthless oddments, and, on the other, the objects themselves were devoid of any sort of kinship or relation. The "Vicar," for instance, was accompanied by a broken Roman pot, a few worthless fragments of Samian ware, a dried crab covered with acorn barnacles and half a dozen horse-brasses; while the tyg had as its immediate neighbour a Sheffield coffee-pot, a Tunbridge-ware wafer-box, a pewter candlestick and one or two flint implements.

The confusion and disorder that prevailed were perfectly astounding. These fine old rooms, with such splendid possibilities, suggested nothing more or less than the store of some curio dealer or the premises of an auctioneer on the day preceding a sale of miscellaneous property. I ventured tentatively to comment on the lack of arrangement.

"You have certainly got a very remarkable collection," said I, "but don't you think that its interest would be increased if you adopted some sort of classification? Here, for instance, is a wineglass, a Jacobite glass, apparently."

"Not apparently," he objected. "Actually. An undoubtedly genuine piece. An appropriate memorial, too. 'Charlie loved good ale and wine.' "

"So he did, as 'his nose doth show' in the portraits. But why put this glass next to that barbaric-looking pot? There is no relation whatever between the two things."

"There is the relation of unlikeness," he replied. "And don't disparage that rare and precious pot. It is extremely ancient. Prehistoric. Neolithic, I believe, is the correct word."

"But why not put all the prehistoric pots together instead of mixing them up with table-glass and Scandinavian carvings?"

"That would seem a dull arrangement," said he. "You would lose the effect of variety, the thrill of unexpectedness. How delightful, for instance, after considering this book of hours and this highly ornate sternutatorium"—he indicated a handsome tortoise-shell snuff-box —"to come upon these siliceous relics of the childhood of the race— also neolithic, I believe—the products of my own fossatory activities."

The "relics" referred to consisted of half a dozen rough flint nodules which looked as if they might have been gathered from a road-mender's heap. They may have been genuine flint implements, but they were certainly not neolithic. No one with the most elementary knowledge of stone implements could have supposed that they were. But my host's easy-going acceptance of them, and his indifference as to the actual facts, brought home to me a state of mind at which I wondered more and more as I examined this amazing collection.

For, in the first place, Mr. Penrose displayed the most complete and comprehensive ignorance of "antiques" of every kind. He knew no more of them than their names, and he frequently got those wrong. But not only was he ignorant. He was quite indifferent. He seemed to be totally devoid of interest in the individual things which he had accumulated; and the question that I asked myself was what earthly object he could have in making this enormous and miscellaneous collection. Apparently, he was possessed by an insatiable acquisitiveness, with no other motive behind it. Mere possession seemed to be the object of his desire; and with mere possession he appeared to be satisfied. Not without reason had he likened himself to "The Great John Daw."

My long tour of inspection came at last to an end. I had examined the collection very thoroughly, not only to please my host—though he was evidently gratified and flattered by the interest that I displayed in his "hoard"—but because it contained, mingled with a good deal of rubbish, many curious and beautiful objects that invited examination. The last piece that I inspected was an ancient gold brooch, richly decorated with gilt filigree work and set with garnets. I lifted it tenderly from the dusty scrap of paper (marked in pencil with the number 963) on which it rested and carried it to the window to look at it in a better light.

"This is a very fine piece of work, Mr. Penrose," I remarked.

"Ha!" said he, "the papistical fibula commends itself. I am glad you like it."

"A Roman fibula!" I exclaimed in surprise. "I should have taken it for a Saxon brooch."

"You may be right," he admitted; "in fact, I am inclined to think that you are. At any rate, it is one or the other."

"But," I protested, "surely you keep some sort of record. I see that the pieces are numbered. Haven't you a catalogue?"

"To be sure I have," he replied. "Excellent idea! We'll get out the Domesday book and see which of us is right."

He pulled out the drawer of a table and produced therefrom a manuscript book which he opened and began to turn over the leaves. Still holding the brooch, I stepped across to him and looked over his shoulder. And then I got a fresh surprise, though I ought to have been prepared for something unusual. For if the collection was eccentric, the catalogue was positively fantastic. It seemed to be (and probably was) expressly designed to be as completely unintelligible as possible. The brief entries, scribbled illegibly in pencil, were apparently worded in Mr. Penrose's peculiar, cryptic dialect, and, for the most part, I could make nothing of them. Running my eye down the pages, I deciphered with difficulty such entries as: "Up+. Mudlarks," "Sammy. Pot sand. Sinbad," "Funereal flowerpot, Julie-Polly," "Carver, Jul. Pop."

I stood gazing in speechless astonishment at this amazing record while Penrose slowly turned the leaves, glancing slyly at me from time to time, apparently to see how I took it. At length—at unnecessary length—Number 963 was found; but it was not very illuminating—to me—for it consisted only of the laconic statement, "Sweeney's resurrection." Apparently, however, it conveyed something to him, for he said, "Yes, you are right. I recollect now." But he did not enter into any particulars.

I laid the brooch down on its slip of paper and began to think of departing; and meanwhile he looked at me with a very odd expression; an expression of mingled anxiety and hesitation.

"I have to thank you, Mr. Penrose," said I, "for a very pleasant and profitable afternoon. It was very good of you to let me see all your treasures. I *have* seen them all, I suppose?"

He did not reply for a few moments, but continued to look at me in that queer, anxious, irresolute fashion. Suddenly, his hesitation gave way and he burst out in low, impressive tones, in a manner of the deepest secrecy:

"The fact is that you haven't. There is another little hoard, which I don't show to any one, but just gloat over in secret. I don't even mention its existence. But, somehow I feel tempted to make an exception in your case. What do you say? Would you like to have a peep at the contents of Bluebeard's chamber?"

"This sounds rather alarming," said I. "Were there not certain penalties for undue curiosity?"

"I hold you immune from those," he replied. "Only I stipulate that this private view shall be really a private view, to be spoken of to nobody. I can rely on you to keep my secret?"

I did not much like this. Like most lawyers, I am a cautious man, and cautious men do not care to be made the unprivileged repositories of other people's secrets. But I could hardly refuse; and when I had, rather reluctantly, given the required undertaking, he moved off towards a door in a corner of the room and I followed, wondering anxiously what he was going to show me and whether it would commit me to any unlawful knowledge.

The room into which he led me—and of which he closed and bolted the door—was a smallish apartment, at one end of which was a massive mahogany cupboard or armoire. When he had unlocked this and thrown open the doors, there was revealed the steel front of a large safe or small strong room. Apparently the safe-key was not in his bunch, for he returned the latter to his pocket and then, retiring a few paces, stood with his back to me while he dived into some secret recesses of his clothing. In a few moments he turned round, rather red from his exertions, and stepped up to the safe with the key in his hand, while I watched with growing curiosity.

The lock clicked softly, a turn of the handle withdrew the bolts and the ponderous door swung open, disclosing a range of shallow drawers which occupied the whole of the interior. My host, first withdrawing the key and slipping it into his waistcoat pocket, proceeded to pull out the top drawer and carry it to a table under the window. And then I breathed a sigh of relief. There was nothing incriminating, after all. The drawer was simply filled with jewellery, looking, indeed, like a tray from a jeweller's window. My host's secrecy was naturally and reasonably explained by the value of his treasures and their high portable and negotiable character.

I looked over the contents of the drawer with keen interest, for I am rather fond of gems, though I have no special knowledge of them. My host, too, showed a pleasure and enthusiasm in regard to the things, themselves, which contrasted strikingly with the indifference that he had displayed towards the general collection.

Yet, even here, there was no glimmer of connoisseurship. His manner suggested mere miserly gloating; and his ignorance of these beautiful baubles astonished me. It was suggested by the absence of any classification, by the way in which totally unrelated stones were jumbled together, and the suggestion was confirmed by his comments. For instance, in this first drawer were two cat's-eyes placed side by side; but they belonged to totally different categories. One, a dark yellowish-green stone with a bright band of bluish light, was a cymophane or true cat's-eye—a chrysoberyl. The other, a charming stone of the hue known as "honey yellow," was a quartz cat's-eye and should have been placed with the other quartz gems. I ventured to comment on the fact, referring to the cymophane as a chrysoberyl, but he interrupted me with the protest:

"Chrysoberyl! Violin-bows, my dear sir! Call not the optic of the fair Tabitha a chrysoberyl."

As he obviously knew—and cared—nothing of the actual characters of precious stones, I did not pursue the question, but continued my inspection of the really interesting and remarkable collection. The admiration that I expressed evidently gave him considerable pleasure and he also made admiring comments from time to time, though without much appearance of taste or discrimination. But his enthusiasm did really wake up when he brought forth the third drawer, which was devoted entirely to opals, and as these beautiful gems are special favourites of mine, we examined them with sympathetic pleasure.

It was a really magnificent collection, and what rather surprised me (considering the collector's comprehensive ignorance) was its genuinely representative character. There were specimens of every variety of the gem. Of the noble, or precious, opal a long range of examples was shown, of all the varied rainbow hues and of various sizes up to nearly an inch in diameter; some in plain mounts but most of them encircled with borders of rose diamonds or brilliants. There were harlequin opals, Mexican fire opals, glowing like blazing coals, black opals, a large series of the common, non-prismatic form, of various hues, and one or two examples of the dark, pitchy "root" or matrix streaked and speckled with points of prismatic colour.

But the gem of the collection, in interest if not in beauty, was a cameo, cut in a disc of precious opal embedded in its dark matrix. The oval slab of matrix, carrying the glowing cameo, was worked into a pendant with a broad border of small rose diamonds and coloured stones forming the design of a rose, a thistle and a central star, while, at the bottom, worked in tiny diamonds, was the word "Fiat"; which, with the engraved portrait of a middle-aged gentleman in a wig, gave a clue to the significance of the jewel.

As I pored over this curious memorial, Penrose watched me with a smile of evident gratification.

"My favourite child," he remarked, taking it out of its compartment and handing it to me, together with a magnifying glass. "Just look at the detail of the face."

I examined it through the lens and was greatly impressed by the perfection of the modelling on so minute a scale.

"Yes," I said, "it is quite a wonderful piece of work. One gets the impression that it might be a really good portrait. And now I know," I added, as I returned the jewel to him, "why you swore me to secrecy."

He paused with the trinket in his hand, looking at me with a distinctly startled expression.

"What do you mean?" he demanded.

"Well," I replied, "you must admit that it is a rather incriminating object to have in your possession."

He gazed at me uneasily, almost with an appearance of alarm, and rejoined:

"I don't understand you. How, incriminating?"

I chuckled with mischievous satisfaction. For an inveterate joker, he seemed decidedly "slow in the uptake."

"Doesn't it occur to you," I replied, "that a portrait of James Francis Edward, the King over the water, cherished secretly by a presumably loyal subject of His Majesty George the Fifth, tends to suggest highly improper political sentiments? I call it rank sedition."

"Oh, I see what you mean," said he, with an uneasy laugh, apparently relieved—and slightly annoyed—at my schoolboy jest, "but sedition of that kind is a trifle threadbare in these days."

He returned the jewel to its place in the drawer and carried the latter back to the safe. As he slid it in, he remarked:

"That's the last of the gem collection. The other drawers contain coins. You may as well see them, too."

I went through the coin collection and was rather surprised at its range, for it included ancient coins, Greek, Roman, Gaulish and British and English coins from the Middle Ages down to the late spade guineas. But all that remains in my memory concerning them is that the different periods seemed to be mixed up, with an almost total lack of order, and that there appeared to be an abnormal proportion of gold coins.

When the last of the drawers had been examined and returned and the safe and its enclosing cupboard had been closed and locked, I began once more to think of taking my leave. But my host pressed me to stay and take a cup of tea with him, and, when I had accepted his invitation, he conducted me back through the large gallery to the room into which I had first been shown. Here, the melancholy man-servant—who answered to the name of Kickweed—presently brought us tea and drew a couple of arm-chairs up to the table.

"This collection of yours," I remarked, as my host poured out the tea, "must represent a large amount of sunk capital."

"I hardly regard it as sunk," he replied, "seeing that I have the use and enjoyment of my treasures; but the collection is worth a lot of money—at least, I hope it is. It has cost a lot."

"So I should suppose," said I; "and it must cost you something quite substantial in the matter of insurance."

"Ah!" said he, "I am glad you raised that question. For the fact is that the collection is not insured at all. I have intended to go into the matter, but there are certain difficulties that have put me off. Now, I dare say you know a good deal about insurance."

"I know something about the legal aspects," I replied, "and such knowledge as I possess is at your disposal. You certainly ought to be secured against what might be a very heavy loss. What are the difficulties that you refer to?"

"Well," he answered in a low voice, leaning across the table, "I don't want to go about proclaiming myself as the owner of a priceless collection. Might arouse interest in the wrong quarter, you see. And as to the gems, as I told you, they are a secret hoard the existence of which I disclose to nobody excepting yourself. You are the only person to whom I have shown them."

"But," I protested, "somebody must have sold them to you and must be aware that you have them."

"They know that I have—or had—the individual jewels that they sold me, but they don't know that I have a great and valuable collection. And I don't want them to know; but that is the difficulty about the insurance. Before I could insure the collection, I should have to get it valued; and the valuer would have to see the gems; and then the cat would be out of the bag. At least, that is what I suppose. Perhaps I am wrong. Could I effect an insurance for a certain definite sum without calling in a valuer?"

"You mean," I replied, "on a declaration that you had certain property of a certain value? No. I think a Company would want evidence that the property insured actually existed and was of the value alleged; and in the event of a fire or a burglary, they certainly would not pay on property alleged to have been lost but which had never been proved to exist. But I think you are raising imaginary difficulties. You could stipulate that the valuation should be a strictly confidential transaction. Remember that the company's interests are the same as your own. If they insure you against burglary, they won't want you to be burgled."

"No, that is true," he admitted. "And you think I could rely on the secrecy of the valuer?"

"I have no doubt of it," I replied, "particularly if you made clear your reasons for insisting on secrecy."

"I am glad you think that," said he, "and I shall act on your advice without delay. I will put the case to the manager of the Society which has insured this house."

"I think you ought to do so at once," I urged. "There must be many thousands of pounds' worth of property in your collections and a fire or a burglary might sweep away the bulk of it in a night."

He repeated, with emphasis, his intention to attend to the matter without further delay, and the subject then dropped. After a little more desultory conversation, I rose to take my leave; and the lugubrious Kickweed, having presented me with my hat and stick, let me out at the street door with the air of admitting me to the family vault.

As I wended homewards I found ample matter for reflection in the incidents of my visit; but chiefly my thoughts concerned themselves with my eccentric host. Mr. Penrose was certainly a very strange man, and the more I thought about him, the less did I feel able to understand him. He had so many oddities, and each of them suggested problems to which I could find no solution. There was the collection, for instance. Including the gems and coins, it must have been of very great value, and its accumulation must have entailed a vast expenditure of time and effort, to say nothing of the prodigious sums of money that must have been spent. But with what object? He had none of the ordinary collector's expertness and enthusiasm. He had no special knowledge of any single class of objects, not even of the gems for which he professed so much affection. The motive force that impelled him to collect seemed to be simple acquisitiveness, the mere *cupiditas habendi*.

But the outstanding feature of his character was secretiveness. He was a secret man of the very deepest dye. His inveterate habit of secrecy coloured every word and action. The ridiculous jargon that he used, his silly circumlocutions and ellipses and paraphrases, were but phases of the tendency, as if he grudged to disclose the whole of his meaning. Even the preposterous catalogue revealed the same trait, for, while it seemed to have been made deliberately unintelligible, it was clear that the absurd entries held some hidden meaning which was intelligible to him.

It was not an endearing trait. None of us likes a secretive man. And very naturally. For secrecy implies distrust; and, moreover, we are apt—again very naturally—to assume some reason for the secrecy, and to suspect that it is a discreditable reason. Thus it was with me in the present case; and my general dislike of the secret habit of mind was aggravated by the fact that I had become involved in the secrecy. The promise that had been exacted from me in regard to the gems recurred to me with a certain distaste and resentment. I was committed to the concealment of a fact which was no concern of mine and of the bearings of which I knew nothing. The explanations that Penrose had given for keeping secret his precious hoard were not unreasonable. But suppose there were other reasons. The thing was possible. Some collectors are not over-scrupulous; and I recalled, not for the first time, the singular, startled expression with which he had looked at me when I made my foolish joke about the Jacobite jewel.

In short, I was not quite comfortable about that promise. There is something a little disturbing about a secret hoard of valuable gems; and, but for the fact that Penrose was obviously a man of ample means, my professional experiences might have caused me to ask myself whether this very odd collection might not cover some activities of a more questionable kind.

CHAPTER 3

EXIT MR. PENROSE

I did not see Penrose again for about a fortnight. Then, having occasion to call at Parrott's shop to inquire after a gate-leg table which I had purchased and which was undergoing some necessary restorations, I encountered him standing opposite to a lantern clock which had been fixed on a temporary bracket and was ticking cheerfully with every sign of robust health. Noting his evident interest in the venerable timepiece, I stopped to discuss it with him.

"You are looking at that clock, Mr. Penrose," said I, "as if you contemplated making an investment."

"I don't contemplate," he replied. "I investigated in it some time ago. It is a poor thing, but mine own."

"I shouldn't call it a poor thing," said I. "It is quite a good clock and it looks to me as if it were absolutely intact and in its original condition. Which is unusual in the case of lantern clocks. People will tinker at them and spoil them. You were lucky to find an untouched specimen."

"I didn't," said he. "When it came to me—through the usual psittacoid channel—it was a mere wreck. Some misbegotten Dædalus had eviscerated it and wrought havoc with its entrails. Thereupon I sought medicinal advice for the invalid and had it put under treatment."

"You sent it to a clockmaker?" I suggested.

"I did not," he replied. "It had had too much clockmaker already. I consulted the erudite and podophthalmate horologer, and behold! —it has renewed its youth like the eagle."

I must confess that this stumped me for the moment, until a flash of supernormal intelligence associated the word "podophthalmate" with Mr. Polton's protuberant eye-glass.

"I didn't know that Mr. Polton was a practical mechanic," I remarked.

"Oh, don't call him that!" Penrose protested. "He is a magician, a wizard, a worker of miracles. By the way, Mrs. Pettigrew, I rather expected to find him here. He promised to see this clock safely established in my gallery."

"He is here," replied Mrs. Pettigrew. "He is in the workshop, doing something to Mr. Tims's lathe. Would you like to walk across and let him know that you have arrived? You know the way. And perhaps, Mr. Lockhart, you would like to go and inspect your table? I think Tims wants you to see it."

I accepted the invitation and, following Penrose, passed out at the back of the shop and crossed a small paved yard to a wide doorway. Passing through this, I entered a roomy workshop, lighted by a skylight and littered with articles of ancient furniture in all stages of decay and dismemberment. There were three persons in the workshop. First, there was Mr. Tims, a tall, aged man, frail and decrepit of aspect—until he picked up a tool; when he seemed suddenly to develop fresh strength and vitality. Next, there was Mr. Polton in shirt-sleeves and an apron (which appeared by its length to have been borrowed from Tims), engaged at the moment in re-fixing the headstock of a wood-turner's lathe. The third person was Mr. Parrott, as I learned when Penrose greeted him; and, as this was the first time that I had encountered him in the flesh, I looked at him with some curiosity.

"Monsieur le Perroquet" was a somewhat unusual-looking man and not at all the type of a shopkeeper. Dark, clean-shaved and blue-jowled, he had rather the appearance of an actor; and this suggestion was heightened by a certain precision of speech and clearness of enunciation, and especially by a tendency to the use of studied and appropriate gestures. Obviously, he was not only an educated man but what one would call a gentleman; easy and pleasant in manner, with that combination of deference and dignity that is attainable only by a well-bred man.

When I had introduced myself, Mr. Tims produced the dismembered table and exhibited the repairs on the damaged leg.

"You see, sir," he explained, "I've cut out the worm-eaten part and let in a patch of sound oak. Do you think he'll do?"

"Do you propose to stain the patch?" I inquired.

"That's as you please," replied Tims. "I wouldn't. A mend's a mend, but a stained mend looks like a fake."

"I think Tims is right," said Parrott. "Better leave the patch to darken naturally."

To this I assented, and thereupon Mr. Tims proceeded to assemble the separated parts while Parrott and I looked on, and Penrose divided his attention between the table and Mr. Polton's operations on the lathe.

"By the way, Mr. Penrose," said I, suddenly remembering our last conversation, "how goes the insurance scheme? Have you solved the difficulty of the valuer?"

Penrose turned to me quickly with a look of annoyance, so that I was sorry I had spoken.

"There is nothing to report at present," he replied with unwonted shortness of manner; and, as if to close the subject, he stepped across to the lathe and manifested a sudden and not very intelligent interest in its mechanism. However, Mr. Polton's job was apparently completed, for, when he had replaced the band on the pulley, tested the centres and given the fly-wheel a trial spin, he proceeded to shed the apron and put on his coat, and was forthwith spirited away by Penrose.

I had noticed that when I spoke of the insurance Mr. Parrott had seemed to prick up his ears (which, perhaps, explained the annoyance of the secretive Penrose). But he made no remark while the latter was present, though he had evidently heard and noted what had been said, for, when Penrose had gone, he asked:

"Do I understand that Mr. Penrose has actually decided to insure his collection? I have repeatedly urged him to, but he has always agreed with me and then let the matter slide."

"I am afraid," said I, "that my experience is the same as yours. I advised him to insure without delay, but you heard what he said."

"I heard what he said," Parrott replied, "but it didn't convey much to me, excepting that he is still putting the business off. Which is rather foolish of him. His collection is of no great value, as collections go, but still, it represents a good deal of money, and he would suffer a substantial loss if he had a fire."

"Or a burglary," I suggested.

"There is not much risk of that," said he. "Burglars wouldn't be tempted by a collection of miscellaneous bric-à-brac, most of it identifiable and none of any considerable value. Burglars like more portable goods and things that are intrinsically valuable, such as precious metals and jewellery."

"You have seen his collection, of course?" said I.

"Yes. As a matter of fact, I supplied the greater part of it. And I gather that you have seen it, too?"

"Yes. He was good enough to show me his treasures. That was how I came to advise him about the insurance. It seemed to me very unsafe for valuable property like that to be quite unprotected."

"I shouldn't have called it very valuable property," said he. "But perhaps he has some things that I haven't seen. It would be like Mr. Penrose to keep his court-cards up his sleeve. Did he show you any really valuable pieces?"

Now, here was the very difficulty that I had foreseen. Obviously, Parrott was unaware of the existence of the hoard of jewels and coins, but he evidently suspected Penrose of possessing something more than he had disclosed. It was very unpleasant, but my promise of secrecy left me no choice. I must either lie or prevaricate.

"It is difficult for me to estimate values," said I, adopting the less objectionable alternative, "but some of the things that I saw must have been worth a good deal of money. There was a Saxon gold ornament, for instance. Wouldn't that be rather valuable?"

"Oh, certainly," he agreed, "but only in a modest way. I don't know what such a thing would fetch, say, at Christie's. But I think you said he was employing a valuer, and having some difficulty with him, apparently?"

"No," I replied. "His difficulty is that a regular valuation would have to be made, which would involve an inspection of his goods and the making of an inventory. He seems to object to having a valuer nosing round his premises."

"He would, naturally," said Parrott. "I have never met such an extraordinarily secretive man. But really, the valuer would not be necessary. I could draw up an estimate that would satisfy the Company—that is, if the property to be insured is only what I have seen. But, as I said, he may have some other things which he has not disclosed to me. Do you think he has?"

Here I must needs prevaricate again; but I kept as near to the truth as I could.

"It is impossible for me to guess what property he has," I said. "You know the man. I know only what he showed me."

Parrott looked dissatisfied with my answer, which was, indeed, pretty obviously evasive, and he seemed disposed to press the matter further; but, at this point, Mr. Tims, having completed the assembling of the parts of the table, offered the completed work for my inspection and approval. I looked it over quickly, and, having pronounced it satisfactory, took the opportunity to make my escape before Parrott should have time to propound any more questions.

As I re-entered the shop from the yard, Penrose and Polton were just passing out at the front door, the latter carrying the body of the clock and the former bearing a large parcel, which presumably contained the weights, the pendulum and the bracket. I went to the door and watched them receding down the street until they reached the corner, when Penrose, happening to glance back, observed me and greeted me with a flourish of his free hand. Then they turned the corner and disappeared from my sight; and thus, though I little guessed it at the time, did Mr. Penrose pass out of my ken for ever.

For I never saw him again. A few days later, I joined the South-Eastern circuit, and thenceforth, for the next few months, passed most of my time in the county towns in which the assizes were held; and when I came back, Mr. Penrose had disappeared.

The fact was communicated to me by Mrs. Pettigrew, who, in her kindly and discreet fashion, tried to minimize the abnormal features of the affair.

"Do you mean, Mrs. Pettigrew," I exclaimed, "that he has gone away from his home and left no address or indication as to where he is to be found?"

"So I understand," she replied, "but I don't really know any of the particulars."

"But," said I, "it is a very extraordinary affair."

"It would be," said she, "in the case of any ordinary man. But you know what Mr. Penrose is. It would be quite like him, if he had occasion, say, to go abroad, to go and keep his own counsel as to where he had gone to. I believe he has done it before, though not for so long a time. I understand that on more than one occasion he has gone out in his car and driven away into the country without saying anything to his servant as to his intentions—just gone out and returned after a few days, saying nothing to anybody as to where he had been."

"Amazing!" said I. "He can't be quite in his right mind. But this affair seems rather different from the other escapades. You say he has been gone for a couple of months. It looks very much as if he had gone for good."

"It does," she agreed; and then, after a pause, she continued: "It has been a great blow to Mr. Parrott, for Mr. Penrose was by far our best customer. He was really the mainstay of the business; and now that he has gone and that we have lost poor Mr. Tims, it is very doubtful if we can carry on."

"Why, what has happened to Tims?" I asked.

"He is dead, poor old thing," she replied. "He got influenza and went out like the snuff of a candle. He was very old and frail, you know. But he was invaluable to Mr. Parrott. He was such a wonderful workman."

"Still," I said, "I suppose he can be replaced."

"Mr. Parrott thinks not," said she, "and I am afraid he is right. It is very difficult to find a real cabinet-maker in these days. The few that are left are mostly old men, and even they don't understand old furniture as Mr. Tims did. But, without a skilled restorer, we can't get on at all. Mr. Parrott is an excellent judge, but he is no workman."

In short, what the absent Penrose would have called "the psittacoid emporium" was in a bad way. It had never been a very prosperous concern, I gathered, and indeed, I had seldom seen a stranger in the shop; but with the aid of Penrose's numerous purchases (or "investigations," as he would have described them) and the prestige of Tims's skilful restorations, it had just managed to keep afloat.

"I do hope," Mrs. Pettigrew said, rather dismally, "that we shall be able to struggle on. It will be an awful disaster for poor Joan and me if the business collapses. Of course, Mr. Parrott has not been in a position to pay me much of a salary, but Joan and I have the use of the rooms over the shop, and with her earnings as a secretary we have rubbed along quite comfortably. But it will be very different if I am earning nothing and we have only her little salary to live on, and rent to pay as well. And it will be so unfair to the poor girl, who ought to be considering her own future, to have to carry the burden of a superannuated mother."

I was very sorry for Mrs. Pettigrew and I tried to present a more hopeful picture of the financial possibilities. I also reminded her that she had my address and it was the address of a friend. And so we parted. A little way down the street—but on the opposite side— I met Miss Joan wending homewards and observed her with a new interest. With her short hair and short skirts, her horn-rimmed spectacles and her attaché case, she was the typical Miss Twentieth Century. But as she swung along manfully, she conveyed a pleasant impression of pluck and energy and buoyant spirits, with mighty little of the "poor girl" in her aspect or bearing; and, raising my hat in response to her friendly nod, I hoped that the gathering clouds might pass over her harmlessly.

But, when I next visited London the blow had fallen. I made my way to the dingy little street, only to find a gang of painters disfiguring the empty shop with garish adornments. The Tropic Bird had flown. The Popinjay was no more. The vacant window greeted me with a dull, unwelcoming stare. The pleasant little rendezvous had gone out, like poor Mr. Tims, with hardly a final flicker; and Mrs. Pettigrew and Joan and Penrose and the mysterious Mr. Polton seemed to have faded out of my life like the actors in a play when the curtain has fallen.

BOOK TWO

NARRATED BY CHRISTOPHER JERVIS, M.D.

CHAPTER 4

THE BURGLARY AT QUEEN SQUARE

My introduction to the strange and puzzling circumstances connected with the disappearance of Mr. Daniel Penrose occurred in a rather casual, almost accidental fashion. On a certain evening, at the close of the day's work in the Law Courts, I had walked up with my colleague, Dr. John Thorndyke, to New Square, Lincoln's Inn, to restore to our old friend, Mr. Brodribb, some documents which it had been necessary to produce in Court. Finding Mr. Brodribb in his office, apparently up to his eyes in business, we handed the documents to him, and when he had checked them, were about to depart when our friend laid down his pen, took off his spectacles and held up his hand to detain us.

"One moment, Thorndyke," said he. "Before you go, there is a little matter that I should like to take your opinion on. I'll just pop on my hat and walk with you to the corner of the Square. It is quite a trifling affair—at least—well, I'll tell you about it as we go."

He rose and, putting on the immaculate top hat which he invariably wore in defiance of modern fashions, stepped through into the outer office.

"I shall be back in a few minutes, Jarrett," said he, addressing his managing clerk, and with that he led the way out.

"The matter," he began, as we emerged on to the broad pavement of the Square, "relates to a burglary, or attempted burglary, at the house of a man whom I may call my client; a man named Daniel Penrose, though, actually, I am being consulted by his executor, a Mr. Horridge."

"Penrose, then, I take it, is deceased," said Thorndyke.

"No. Penrose is alive, but he is absent from his home and no one knows where he is at the moment. So Horridge is assuming that his position as executor authorizes him to take action in the absence of the testator."

"That doesn't seem a very sound position," Thorndyke remarked. "But what action does he propose to take?"

"I had better explain the circumstances," said Brodribb. "In the first place, the man Penrose, who has a biggish house in Queen Square, is the owner of a collection; a very miscellaneous collection, I understand; all sorts of trash from old clocks to china dogs. This stuff is kept in two large rooms on the ground floor, but adjoining the main rooms is a small room which contains nothing but a table, a chair and a large cupboard or armoire. This room is usually kept locked, but, by a fortunate chance, when Penrose went away he left the key in the door, and the butler, a man named Kickweed, finding it there, very properly took possession of it.

"Now, the alleged burglary occurred about ten days ago. It seems that Kickweed, making his morning round of the premises, unlocked the door of the small room to go in and inspect, when, to his astonishment, he found it bolted on the inside. Thereupon he took a pair of library steps round to the side of the house where the window of the small room looks on a narrow uncovered passage. On climbing up the steps he found the window unfastened and was able to slide it up and step over into the room. There he confirmed the fact that the door was bolted on the inside, but that, and the unfastened window, were the only signs of anything out of the ordinary. The cupboard was perfectly intact, with no traces whatever of its having been tampered with; and, although there were some scratches on the table by the window, as if some hard objects had been put on it and moved about, there was nothing to show when those marks had been made."

"The cupboard, I presume, was locked?" said Thorndyke.

"Yes, and with a Chubb lock."

"And what was in the cupboard?"

"Ah!" said Brodribb, "that is the problem. No one knows what it contained or whether it contained anything. But, having regard to the facts that Penrose is a collector, that he always kept this room locked and that the cupboard was fitted with a Chubb lock, the reasonable assumption is that it contained something of value."

"Yes," Thorndyke agreed, "that seems probable. But what does Mr. Horridge propose to do?"

"He would like, with my consent—I am co-executor—to have the lock picked and explore the inside of the cupboard."

"That plan seems to present difficulties," said Thorndyke. "To say nothing of the fact that a Chubb lock takes a good deal of picking, there is the objection that, as you don't know what was in the cupboard, you couldn't judge whether anything had been taken. Suppose you find it empty; you don't know that it was not empty previously. Suppose you find valuable property in it; you still don't know that nothing has been taken, and, by having forced the lock, you assume a slightly uncomfortable responsibility for the safety of the contents. Why not just seal the cupboard and let Penrose do the investigating when he returns?"

"Yes," said Brodribb, with a rather dissatisfied air, as he halted at the corner of the Square and looked up at the clock above the library. "But suppose he doesn't return?" He paused for a few moments and then burst out: "The fact is, Thorndyke, that this burglary is only an incident in a most complicated and puzzling affair. There is no time to go into it now, but I should very much like, some time when you have an hour or so to spare, to put the whole case before you and hear what you have to suggest."

"I shall have an hour or so to spare—for you—this evening," said Thorndyke, "if that will suit you."

Brodribb brightened visibly. "It will suit me admirably," said he. "I will get a bit of dinner and then I will trot along to King's Bench Walk."

"You needn't do that," said Thorndyke. "Jervis and I are dining at our chambers this evening. Come along and join us. Then we shall be able to get into our conversational stride with the aid of food and a glass of wine."

Brodribb accepted gleefully, and, when we had settled the time for him to arrive, he turned away towards his office. But suddenly he stopped, searching frantically in a bulging pocket-book.

"Here," said he, holding out a small piece of paper, "is something to occupy your mighty brains until we meet at dinner, when I will ask you to let me have it back."

As Thorndyke took the paper from him, he broke out into a broad smile, and, turning away once more, hurried off to relieve the waiting Jarrett. My colleague looked at the paper, considered for a few moments, turned it over to glance at the back, held it up to the light and passed it to me without comment. It was a small scrap of paper—about three inches square—apparently cut off a sheet with a paper-knife, and it bore three words untidily scribbled on it with a hard pencil: "Lobster (*Hortus petasatus*)."

"Well," I exclaimed, gazing at the paper with mild astonishment, "I suppose this has some meaning, but I'm hanged if I can make any sense of it. Can you?"

He shook his head, and, taking the little document from me, put it away carefully in his wallet.

"Do you suppose it is some sort of clue?" I asked.

"I don't suppose anything," he replied. "Let us wait and hear what Brodribb has to say about it. His expression suggested what school-boys call a leg-pull. But I suspect that he has something quite interesting to tell us about the absent Penrose."

Thorndyke's suspicion turned out to be correct, for when Mr. Brodribb arrived at our chambers, dressed immaculately and accompanied by a clerk carrying a brown-paper parcel, he gave us to understand that he had some rather surprising facts to communicate.

"But," he added, "I haven't come here just to eat your dinner and waste your time with idle talk. I want you to regard this as a professional consultation."

"We will consider that question later," said Thorndyke. "Our immediate purpose is to dine, but, meanwhile, I will return your rather cryptic document. I have kept a copy of it in case it may have a bearing on anything, and Jervis has made a minute study of its ostensible meaning."

"I am glad you say 'ostensible,' " chuckled Brodribb, as he stowed the document away in his pocket-book. "And what conclusions has the learned Jervis arrived at?"

"My conclusions," said I, "are not very illuminating. Broadly speaking, the inscription is damned nonsense."

"I am with you there," said Brodribb.

"Then, as to the ostensible meaning, I take it that the word 'Lobster' means—well, it means lobster—"

"I'll take my bible oath it doesn't," Brodribb interposed.

"And as to the Latin words, *hortus,* of course, is a garden and *petasatus,* according to the erudite Dr. William Smith, means 'having on a travelling-cap,' or, alternatively, in more general terms, 'dressed in readiness for a journey.' Which doesn't make any sort of sense. You can't imagine a garden wearing a travelling-cap or being dressed in readiness for a journey."

"Perhaps it was the lobster that wore the cap," Thorndyke suggested, regardless of syntax. "But what is the significance of this document? I presume that it has some connection with the burglary."

"Yes, it has," Brodribb replied; "and if we could only find out what the devil it means, it might be quite an important clue. The paper was found by Kickweed, when he was examining the small room, under the table by the window. He thinks that it came from inside the cupboard; and if he is right, it furnishes evidence that the cupboard had been opened. And if we could only make any sense of the damned thing, it might give us a hint as to what had been taken."

"Yes," Thorndyke agreed, "but this is all very hypothetical. There is no evidence as to when the paper was dropped. It is quite possible that it may have been dropped by Penrose himself. But as to this cryptic inscription. As Jervis says, it probably has some meaning. Does it convey anything at all to you?"

"As to meaning, most emphatically NO. But," Brodribb continued, grasping his wine-glass fiercely, "it impresses on me what I have always thought; that Daniel Penrose is an exasperating ass!"

At this outburst, Polton (our laboratory assistant and general factotum), who had just removed the covers and was in the act of re-filling Brodribb's glass, looked at the speaker with an expression of surprised interest. He even seemed disposed to linger; but as there was no excuse for his doing so, he retired slowly as if reluctant to go.

"Perhaps," Thorndyke suggested when Polton had withdrawn, "that statement might be amplified and its bearings explained. You seem to imply that the cryptic inscription was written by Penrose."

"Undoubtedly it was," Brodribb replied. "It is typical of the man. Let me explain to you what sort of fellow Penrose is; and I want you to bear his peculiarities in mind when I come to tell you my story, because they probably have an important bearing on it. Now, Penrose has two outstanding oddities of character. In the first place, he is an inveterate joker. He seems incapable of speaking seriously; and the form that his facetiousness takes is in calling everything by its wrong name. The tendency seems to have grown on him until it has become a fixed habit and now his conversation is a sort of ever-lasting cross-word puzzle. You have to cudgel your brains when he is speaking, to guess what he really means, and the only certainty that you have is that whatever he says, you know that he means something else."

"It sounds a bit confusing," said I. "But I suppose there is some method in his madness. Could you give us an illustrative example?"

"His method," replied Brodribb, "consists in using allusive phrases, equivalents in sound or sense, or distortions or perversions of words. He would not invest his money: he would investigate it. He would not call our friend John Thorndyke; he would probably describe him as Giovanni Brambleditch."

"I must bear that name in mind," said I, "for use on suitable occasions. But I think I grasp the principle. It is a sort of mixture of puns and metaphors."

"Yes," agreed Brodribb, "that is roughly what it amounts to. And now as to his other eccentricity. Penrose is an extraordinarily secretive man. I use the word 'extraordinarily' advisedly. We are all, as lawyers, in the habit of keeping our own counsel. But we don't make secrets of our common and simple doings. If Thorndyke wants to go to the Law Courts, he doesn't sneak out on tip-toe when there is nobody about and leave no information as to where he has gone. But that is what Penrose would do. His habit of secrecy is as inveterate as his habit of facetiousness. He has been known to set forth from his house in his car without giving any notice to his butler or anybody else, to drive away into the country and stay away for several days—probably rooting about for bargains for his collection—and come back without a word of explanation as to where he has been. I assure you that when I had to draft his will I had the greatest difficulty in extracting from him any intelligible particulars of the property that was to be disposed of."

"It is rather remarkable," said Thorndyke, "that he should have made a will at all."

"It is," agreed Brodribb. "Men of that type usually die intestate. And thereby hangs another part of the tale that I have to tell. But I repeat that it is most necessary to bear these oddities of character in mind in connection with what has happened. And now, I will drop Penrose for the present and let you finish your dinners in peace."

I think that Brodribb's resolution to change the subject occasioned some disappointment to Polton; for that cunning artificer developed an unprecedented degree of attentiveness, which caused him to make frequent incursions into the room for the ostensible purpose of filling wine-glasses and performing other unnecessary services. His obvious interest in our rather trivial conversation caused me some slight surprise at the time. But later events explained his curiosity.

When we had finished dinner, and before removing the debris, he drew the three easy chairs up to the fire, placed a small table by that which was assigned to Brodribb and deposited on it the invariable decanter of port and three wine-glasses. Then he proceeded to clear the table by small instalments and by methods strikingly at variance with his usual swift economy of time and labour. But his procrastination was all in vain; for, not until the table was cleared to the last vestige and Polton had made his final and reluctant disappearance, did Brodribb make the slightest allusion to the subject of our consultation.

Then, when the door had closed, the glasses had been filled and Thorndyke and I had produced our pipes, he extracted a slip of paper from his pocket-book and laid it on the table by his side, fortified himself with a sip of wine and opened the proceedings.

CHAPTER 5

MR. BRODRIBB PROPOUNDS A PROBLEM

"The circumstances connected with Penrose's disappearance," Mr. Brodribb began, "are so complicated that I hardly know in what order I should present them."

"Probably," suggested Thorndyke, "the simplest plan would be to deal with the events in their chronological sequence."

"Yes," Brodribb agreed, "that would probably be the best way. I can refer back to previous occurrences if necessary. Then we will begin with the seventeenth of last October, roughly three months ago. On that day, in the early afternoon, he started out from home in his car and, contrary to his usual practice, he told Kickweed that he did not expect to be back until rather late. He directed that no one should sit up for him, but that a cold supper should be left in the dining-room. As to where he was going or on what business, he naturally gave no hint, but we are justified in assuming that he started forth with the intention of returning that night.

But he did not return; and, so far as we know, he was never seen again by anybody who was acquainted with him."

"Your description," said Thorndyke, "seems to suggest that he is a bachelor."

"Yes," replied Brodribb, "he is a bachelor, and, with the exception of an aged father, to whom I shall refer presently, he seems to have no very near relations. Horridge, his executor, is a somewhat distant cousin, and a good deal younger man. Well, then, to repeat; on the day that I have mentioned, having given this very vague information to his butler, he went off to his garage, got his car out, closed up the garage and departed. Kickweed saw him drive away past the house; and that was the last that was seen of him by any person who knew him.

"His next appearance was in very remarkable circumstances. At midnight on that same day, or in the early hours of the next, a gentleman, a resident of Gravesend, who was returning home from Chatham in his car, saw a man lying face downwards on a heap of gravel by the roadside. The gentleman pulled up and got out to see what had happened; and as the man seemed to be either dead or unconscious, and there was nobody about excepting a rather squiffy labourer, he carefully lifted the man, with the labourer's assistance, put him into his car and conveyed him to the hospital at Gravesend, which was about a mile and a half from the place where he picked him up. At the hospital it was found that the man was alive though insensible, and on this the gentleman, a Mr. Barnaby, went away, leaving the hospital authorities to give information to the police.

"The injured man appeared to be suffering from concussion. He had evidently fallen on the gravel with great violence, for his face was a mass of bruises and both his eyes were completely closed by the swelling due to the contusions. There was a deep, ragged wound across his right eyebrow in which the house surgeon had to put a couple of stitches; and there were various other bruises about his person, suggesting that he had been knocked down by some passing vehicle, but there appeared to be no broken bones or other severe injuries. The visiting surgeon, however, seems to have suspected the existence of a fracture of the base of the skull, and, on this account, directed that the patient should be kept very quiet and not questioned or disturbed in any way.

"The next day he still appeared to be unconscious, or nearly so, though he took the small amount of nourishment that was offered. But he answered no questions, and, by reason of the suspected fracture, no particular attempts were made to rouse him. And so the day passed. On the following day, the nineteenth, he remained in much the same condition; speechless and somnolent, lying nearly motionless, taking no notice of anything that was occurring around him and giving no answers to questions.

"But about eight o'clock at night he roused quite suddenly and very completely, for he seemed at once to be in full possession of his senses. But what is more, he proceeded to get out of bed, and demanded his clothes, declaring that he was quite well and intended to leave the hospital and go about his business. As you may suppose, there was a mighty hubbub. The house surgeon absolutely forbade the patient to leave the hospital and at first refused to let him have his clothes. But the man persisted that he was going, clothes or no clothes. Well, of course, they had no power to detain him, so the end of it was that they produced his clothes, and when he had dressed himself they gave him a light meal and took the particulars of his name and address and what little he could tell them of the circumstances of the accident. But of this he knew practically nothing. All he could tell them was that some vehicle had come on him from behind and knocked him down, and he remembered no more.

"When he had finished his meal and made his statement, such as it was, he asked for his overcoat. But there was no overcoat with his clothes, though the ward sister remembered that he was wearing one when he was brought in. Apparently, a patient who had been discharged earlier in the evening must have taken it by mistake, for there was a spare overcoat of the same kind—the ordinary raincoat, such as you may see by the dozen in any street; and it was suggested that he should take this in exchange for his own. But he would not agree to this, and eventually, as it was a mild night, he was allowed to go as he was.

"Now, he had not been gone more than an hour when the man who had taken the wrong coat brought it back. He had discovered his mistake by finding in the pocket a motorist's driving license. But the odd thing was that the name and address on the license did not agree with those that the departed patient had given. And yet there seemed to be no doubt that it was the missing coat, for the night nurse remembered the daubs of mud that she had noticed on it when she had undressed the patient. Moreover, she now recalled that the collar which she had taken off him had borne the initials 'D.P.,' in Roman capitals, apparently written with a marking-ink pencil.

"But there was an evident discrepancy. The patient had given the name of Joseph Blewitt, with an address somewhere in Camden Town; but the name on the license was Daniel Penrose and the address was his address in Queen Square.

"It was certainly a facer. The coat had to be returned to its owner. But who was its owner? The secretary decided that it was not his business to solve that problem; and, moreover, as there seemed to be something a trifle queer about the affair, he thought it best to communicate with the police. But as it was rather late and there seemed to be no urgency in the matter, he put it off until the following morning; and when the morning came, the police saved him the trouble by calling to make inquiries. And then something still more queer came to light.

"That morning, early, a patrol had discovered an abandoned car backed into the bushes at the bottom of an unfrequented lane leading down to the marshes a mile or so outside Gravesend. On making inquiries, he learned that it had been there all the previous day, for it had been seen by some boys who had gone down to the marshes on their probably unlawful occasions. They had taken no special notice of it, assuming that the owner had gone off on some business into the village in the irresponsible way that motorists have of leaving their cars unattended. But the boys could not say when it had arrived, as they had not been to the marshes on the day before. However, when the patrol pushed his inquiries in the village, he heard of the accident and of the man who had been picked up on the road not very far away. Thereupon, he took possession of the car and brought it into the town, lodging it, for the time being, in the garage belonging to the police station. And then he came on to the hospital to interview the injured man. But the bird had flown and only the coat with the driving license remained.

"And then, once more, the plot thickened. For the name on the insurance certificate which was found in the car was the same as that on the license; and if—as seemed nearly certain—the coat belonged to the departed patient, then that patient had given a false name and address. And this turned out to be the fact. No such person as Joseph Blewitt was known at the Camden Town address; and on inquiring at Daniel Penrose's house, it was ascertained that the said Daniel had left home in his car in the early afternoon of the day on which the injured man had been brought into the hospital and had not since been seen or heard of.

"As to what had become of that injured man, all that they could discover was that he—or, at least, a man with two black eyes and generally answering to the description—had taken a first-class ticket to London shortly after the time at which the patient had left the hospital, and that a man, apparently the same, had got out at New Cross. But they could get no farther. From the time when he passed the barrier at New Cross all trace of him was lost."

"Did the police make any efforts to follow him up?" Thorndyke asked.

"At the moment, I don't think they did. Why should they? So far as they then knew, the man had committed no offence. He was no business of theirs. If he chose to vamoose, he was quite entitled to."

"I need not ask if you know of any reason that he may have had for disappearing?"

"Ah!" said Brodribb, "now we come to the inwardness of the affair. I have told the story in the actual order of events, and, at the time when he bolted from the hospital, there seemed no reason for his sneaking off and hiding himself. But, a day or two later, some other facts transpired which threw an entirely new light on his behaviour.

"It appeared that early in the morning of the eighteenth, the day after that on which he left home—and, incidentally, was picked up on the road—the dead body of an old woman was found in a dry ditch at the side of a by-road leading to the main road from Ashford to Maidstone. From the condition of the body as to rigor mortis and temperature, the police surgeon inferred that she had been dead about six hours; which, as the body was discovered at about five o'clock in the morning, roughly fixes the time of her death at eleven o'clock on the previous night. Of the cause of death there seemed to be no doubt. She had been knocked down by a motor, the driver of which had either been unaware of what had happened or had cleared off to avoid trouble. The latter seemed the more probable, for, not only must the force of the impact have been terrific to fling the poor old creature right across the grass verge into the ditch, but the tracks of a car, which were plainly visible in the lane, showed it to have been zigzagging wildly and to have actually struck the grass verge at the point where the accident must have occurred.

"At first, it looked as if the motorist had got away without leaving a recognizable trace. But when the police came to make inquiries, they picked up some important information from the attendant at a filling station at Maidstone. He recalled that, a little after eleven o'clock on the night of the old woman's death, a car had come to his establishment for a refill of petrol. It was apparently travelling from the direction of Ashford; and there were certain circumstances connected with the car and the driver which had attracted his attention. He had noticed, for instance, that the nearside mudguard was badly bent, and there was earth on the wheels, as if the car had been run over a ploughed field. He had also observed that the driver—who was alone in the car—looked rather pale and shaken, and seemed to be excited or agitated. Moreover, he smelt strongly of drink; and the man was of opinion that the liquor was not whisky, but smelt more like 'sherry wine.' These facts, taken together, made him suspect that the motorist had been in trouble and he very wisely made a note of the number of the car and had a good look at the driver. His description of the man is not very illuminating, excepting that he noticed the muddy state of the raincoat, which the nurse had mentioned. But the number of the car gave all the necessary information. It was that of Daniel Penrose's car; and, sure enough, in confirmation of the identity, was the fact that the left mud-guard of Penrose's car was badly bent and there was a quantity of earth on the wheels. And there is a bit of further evidence, for it appears that Penrose was stopped by a police patrol on the top of Bluebell Hill, on the Maidstone-Rochester Road, and asked to show his license; which explains how the license came to be in his raincoat pocket. When you consider the devil of a hurry that he was in, you can understand that he would just shove it into the nearest pocket.

"Well, the final phase of the affair—so far—was the inquest on the old woman. Naturally, when they had heard the evidence of the police and the man from the petrol-filling station, the jury found a verdict of manslaughter against some person unknown."

"Unknown!" I repeated. "Then they did not mention Penrose by name?"

"No," replied Brodribb. "The coroner knew his business better than many coroners do. He directed the jury to confine their finding to the facts that had been definitely proved and leave the identification of the offender to the police. But I need not say that the police are keeping a bright look-out for Daniel Penrose.

"So there, you see, we have an explanation of the initial disappearance. Perhaps, not a very reasonable one; but then Penrose is not a very reasonable man. But that explanation does not quite clear up the mystery. He disappeared about three months ago and since then has made no sign. Now, we can understand his bolting off in a panic, but it is less easy to understand his remaining in hiding. On reflection he must have seen that he was really in no great danger, even if he did actually knock the poor old woman down, which is by no means certainly the case. There were no witnesses of the accident. If he chose to deny that he was in any way concerned in it, it would be impossible to prove that he was. He might even have denied that he was ever on that particular road at all."

"You mentioned," said Thorndyke, "that there were distinct tracks of motor tires. Probably they would be identifiable."

"That would not be conclusive," Brodribb replied. "It would only prove that the tires were of the same make. But, even if he admitted that he had caused the old woman's death, still, in the absence of witnesses, he could give any account that he pleased of the disaster. Carelessness on the part of the pedestrian is usually quite satisfactory to a coroner or his jury."

"I don't think the matter is as simple as that," Thorndyke objected. "I agree with you that there has been a most amazing indifference to the value of human life since the coming of the motor car. But this was an exceptionally bad case. The man had been drinking; he must have known that he had knocked the woman down, but yet he drove on callously, leaving her to die uncared for, and did not even report the accident. Whatever the coroner's verdict might have been, the police would certainly have prosecuted, and the man would almost inevitably have been committed for trial. But at the assizes he would have had to deal with a judge; and judges, as a rule—to which there are, I admit, one or two remarkable exceptions—take a reasonable and legal view of the killing of a human being."

"Well, even so," Brodribb rejoined, "what does it amount to? Supposing he had been convicted of manslaughter? It might have been a matter of six months' hard labour, or even twelve. It could hardly have been more. Killing with a motor car is accepted as something different from any other kind of killing."

"But," said I, "he would not be particularly keen on twelve months' imprisonment with hard labour."

"No," Brodribb agreed, "but what is the alternative? To say nothing of the fact that he is pretty certain to be caught, sooner or later, what is his present condition? He—a well-to-do man, accustomed to every luxury, is a wanderer and a fugitive, hiding in obscure places by day and sneaking out in terror by night. It must be a dreadful existence; and how the devil he is living and what he is living on, is beyond my powers to imagine, seeing that, when he went off, he had, presumably, nothing more about him than the few pounds that he would ordinarily carry in his pockets."

"I suppose," Thorndyke said, reflectively, "it has not occurred to you to connect that fact with the burglary?"

Brodribb looked at him in evident surprise.

"I don't think," said he, "that I quite understand what you mean. What connection could there be?"

"I am only throwing out the suggestion," replied Thorndyke, "as a bare possibility. But the house seems undoubtedly to have been entered, and entered by a person who appears to have been acquainted with it. The entry was made into the small room; and that room was clearly the objective, as is proved by the fact that the door was bolted on the inside. Then the person who entered apparently knew what was in that room. But, so far as we know, the contents of that room were known only to Penrose. If the cupboard was opened, it was opened with a key; for it is practically impossible to pick a Chubb lock, and a burglar would not have tried. He would have used his jemmy and forced the door."

"By Jove, Thorndyke!" Brodribb exclaimed, slapping the table, at the risk of spilling the wine, "you have solved the mystery! It never occurred to me that the burglar might be Penrose himself. But your suggestion fits the case to a T. Here is poor old Penrose, penniless and perhaps starving. He knows that in that cupboard is portable property of very substantial value. He has the key of the cupboard in his pocket and he knows that he can get into the room easily by just slipping back the catch of the window with a knife. Of course it was Penrose. I was a damned blockhead not to have thought of it before. But you see, Thorndyke, I haven't got your criminal mind."

But Thorndyke, having made the suggestion, proceeded to sprinkle a little cold water on Brodribb's enthusiasm.

"It isn't a certainty," said he, "and we mustn't treat it as one. It is a reasonable and probable hypothesis, but we may think of others when we consider the matter further. However, the immediate question is what you want me to do."

"You can guess that," chuckled Brodribb, as I refilled his glass. "What do I always want you to do when I come here taking up your valuable time and drinking your excellent port? I want you to perform miracles and do impossibilities. It seems a pretty large order, I admit, even for you, seeing that the police are unable to locate Penrose, but I am going to ask you to exercise your remarkable power of resolving insoluble riddles and just tell us where he is."

"But why trouble to hunt him up?" Thorndyke objected. "He probably knows his own business best."

"I am not so sure that he does," Brodribb retorted. "But, in any case, it is not his business that is specially agitating me. There are some other people whose interests are affected and one of them is keeping me very effectively stirred up. However, I suppose I mustn't inflict on you details of the purely civil aspects of the case."

It was easy to gather from the apologetic tone of the concluding sentence and the wistful glance that he cast at Thorndyke, that he wanted very much to inflict those details, and I was not surprised when my colleague replied:

"It wouldn't be an affliction, Brodribb. On the contrary, it would be both interesting and helpful to have a complete picture of the case."

"I suspect," said Brodribb, "that you are only being beastly polite, but I will take you at your word. After all, the civil aspects are part of the problem and they may be more relevant than I realize. So here goes.

"I spoke just now of Daniel Penrose's aged father and I mentioned that there were no other near relations. Now, Penrose Senior, Oliver by name, is a very remarkable old gentleman. He is over ninety years of age, but surprisingly well preserved. Up to a week or two ago, he was, mentally and physically, the equal of an ordinary man of sixty. That was his condition at the time of Daniel's disappearance; lively and active, apparently going strong for his hundredth birthday.

"But, within the last fortnight, the old man has been taken ill—a slight touch of influenza, it appeared at first, that seemed to offer no particular cause for anxiety. But you know what these hale and robust nonagenarians are. They dodder along peacefully, looking as if they were going to live for ever, until, one fine day, something gives them a shake up and puts them out of their stride; and then they just quietly fade away. Well, that is what is happening to old Penrose. He doesn't seem particularly ill. But he shows no sign of recovering. Suddenly, the weight of his years seems to have descended on him and he is gradually fading out. It is practically certain that he will die within the next few weeks; and, when he does die, some very curious complications are going to arise.

"Oliver Penrose is what we humble professional people would call a rather rich man. Nothing on the commercial scale of wealth. Nothing of the millionaire order. But there will be an estate, mostly personal, of over a hundred and fifty thousand pounds. And, so far as we know, that estate is not disposed of by will. The old man was rather obstinate about it, though there was some reason in his contention that it was a waste of trouble to make a will leaving the estate to the next of kin, who would inherit without a will. However, that question is of no importance, for, in any case, Penrose junior would come into the property. If there is a will, he will be the principal beneficiary, and if there is no will, he is the next of kin, and, being the only child, will take the bulk of the estate.

"And now you see the difficulty. Daniel has made a will leaving a considerable proportion of his property to his cousin, Francis Horridge, who is also one of the executors and the residuary legatee. Daniel is not as rich as his father, but they are a well-to-do family and he has some fifty thousand pounds of his own. So Horridge will not do so badly if he should survive Daniel, which he is likely to do, as he is over twenty years younger. But he wants to do better. On the old man's death, the bulk of his property will, as I said, come to Daniel; and, as Daniel's will at present stands, it will fall into the residue of the estate and thus, eventually, come to Horridge.

"But there is a snag. Daniel has disappeared, but the old man is still alive. Now, suppose that Daniel elects to disappear for good. The thing is possible. He may have some resources that are unknown to us. It would be like him to have a secret banking account in a false name; and he may be in such a funk of criminal prosecution that he may never dare to come to the surface again. Well, suppose he remains in hiding. Suppose he has gone abroad or into some entirely new surroundings and has the means to go on living there; just see what a hideous mess will be created. In the first place, there will be an indefinite delay in distributing the old man's estate. Daniel is the next of kin (or else the principal beneficiary, if there should be a will). But his share cannot be allotted until it is proved that he is alive, and it cannot be otherwise disposed of until he is either proved or presumed to be dead. And, similarly, his own will cannot be administered so long as he is presumably alive."

"If he remains absent long enough," Thorndyke remarked, "the interested parties will probably apply for permission to presume his death."

"Well," retorted Brodribb, "they certainly wouldn't get it at present, or for a long time to come. If Daniel remains in hiding, the whole business may be hung up for years. But, even if they do, later, succeed in getting his death presumed, another and still worse complication will have to be dealt with. For, of course, the question of survivorship will be raised. Oliver's next of kin will naturally contend that Daniel died before the old man and that he could, therefore, not have inherited the old man's property; in which case, Horridge stands to lose the best part of a hundred and fifty thousand pounds. And that, I may say, is where I come in. Horridge is in a most frightful twitter for fear Daniel should slip away for good and perhaps die somewhere under a false name. He wants to find Daniel, or at least ascertain that he is alive; and he is prepared to spend untold gold on the search. He has tried to ginger up the police and induce them to set up a hue and cry, regardless of poor old Daniel's feelings. But the police are not enthusiastic, as they have no conclusive evidence against him, even if they were able to locate him. So he has fallen back on me, and I have fallen back on you. And now the question is, are you prepared to take up the case?"

I had expected that Thorndyke would return a prompt refusal, for there seemed absolutely nothing to go on. To my surprise, he replied with a qualified acceptance, though he was careful to point out the difficulties.

"It is not very clear to me," said he, "that I can give you much help. You must see for yourself that this is really a police case. For the tracing of a missing man, the police have all the facilities as well as the necessary knowledge and experience. I have no facilities at all. Any inquiries that I may wish to make I must make through them."

"Yes, I see that," said Brodribb, "and, of course, I am not really asking you to perform miracles. I don't expect you to go outside and put your nose down on the pavement and forthwith make a bee-line for Daniel's hiding-place. But it occurs to me that you may be able to approach the matter from a different direction and by different methods from those of the police."

"That is possible," Thorndyke admitted, "but even a medico-legal investigator cannot get on without evidence of some kind, and there seems to be practically nothing to lay hold of. Do you know where the car is?"

"In Daniel's garage. It was taken there and locked up as soon as the police had made their examination of it."

"Do you know whether anything was found in it?"

"I have heard of nothing excepting a large empty flask which had, apparently, once contained brown sherry."

"Do you know whether the car has been cleaned since it was returned?"

"I am pretty sure that it has not. Penrose was his own chauffeur and did all the cleaning himself."

"Then you spoke of a raincoat. What has become of that?"

"It is in the parcel that I brought with me and which I put on the table in the lobby. It was delivered at Daniel's house by the police when they had looked it over, and Kickweed handed it to Horridge, who at once locked it up, and later, at my request, transferred it to me. I knew you would want to see it."

"Was anything found in the pockets?"

"There was the driving license, as I told you. Beyond that there was nothing but the stump of a lead pencil, a wooden cigarette-holder and what looked like a fragment of a broken flower-pot. And I may say that those things are still in the pockets. So far as I know, the coat is in exactly the condition in which it was found."

"We will have a look at it presently," said Thorndyke, "though it doesn't seem likely that we shall extract much information from it."

"It certainly does not," I agreed, heartily, "and the little information it may yield can hardly have much bearing on what we want to know. It won't tell us what Penrose's intentions may have been, or where he is now."

"Oh, don't say that!" exclaimed Brodribb. "I had hoped that Thorndyke would practise some of his wizardry on that coat and make it tell us all that we want to know about Daniel. And I hope so still, notwithstanding your pessimism. At any rate," he added, glancing at my colleague, "you are going to give us a run for our money? You agree to that?"

"Yes," Thorndyke replied, "just as a forlorn hope. It is nothing more, and it is unlikely that I shall have more success than the police. Still, I will sort out the facts, such as they are, and see if they offer us any kind of opening for an investigation. I suppose I can see the car?"

"Certainly, you can. I will tell Kickweed to let you have the key of the garage and to give you any help that you may ask for. Is there anything that you will want me to do?"

"I think," replied Thorndyke, "that, as Penrose is quite unknown to me, I had better have a description of his person, and it should be as minute and exhaustive as possible; and if a photograph of him is available, I should like to have that, too."

"Very well," said Brodribb, "I will get a description of Daniel from Horridge and Kickweed, separately, and write out another from my own observations. I will let you have the three, so that you can compare them, and I will try to get you a photograph. And that," he concluded, emptying his glass with relish, and rising, "is all, for the present; and I may say that, despite Jervis's pessimism, you have taken a load of anxiety off my shoulders. Experience has taught me that when John Thorndyke starts an investigation, the problem is as good as solved."

CHAPTER 6

THORNDYKE EXAMINES THE RELICS

As we returned from the landing, to which we had escorted Mr. Brodribb, I took up the parcel from the lobby table and conveyed it to the sitting-room.

"Well, Thorndyke," I remarked, as I deposited it on the table under the electric light, "you seem to have let yourself in for a proper wild-goose chase."

He paused in the act of digging out his pipe to regard me with an approving smile.

"That is rather happily expressed, Jervis," said he, "having regard to the personal peculiarities of our quarry. But we are not actually committed to chasing him."

"I can't imagine why you undertook the case," I continued. "There is absolutely nothing to go on."

"That is how it strikes me," he agreed placidly, blowing through the pipe preparatory to refilling. "But we couldn't refuse Brodribb."

"The few facts that we have," I went on doggedly, "are all totally irrelevant. Our information stops short exactly at the point where the problem begins. Take this coat, for instance. Here is a fool— and a frightened, artful, secretive fool at that—who does a bolt and leaves his coat behind; and we are offered that coat as a guide to the particular bolt-hole that he has gone down. The thing is ridiculous. If it had been a question of where he had come from, the coat might have told us something. But obviously it can bear no traces of the place that he intended to go to."

"That is perfectly true," Thorndyke admitted, "but it might be worth while to find out whence he had come, if that were possible."

"I don't see why," I objected, adding hurriedly, to anticipate the inevitable reply: "Of course you will say that the significance of a fact cannot be judged until the fact is known; but still, I really cannot see any possible connection between the place whence he came and the place whither he went, especially as the circumstances had changed in the interval."

"Nor can I," said Thorndyke. "But yet it is possible that there may be some connection. It is evident that Penrose started out with a definite objective. He was going to a particular place with some defined purpose; and it seems to me at least conceivable that if we could discover whither he went and on what business, that knowledge might be helpful. Of course, it probably would not; but seeing that we know nothing of the habits and mode of life of this curious, eccentric and secretive man, our only course is to pick up any stray facts concerning him that may come within our reach."

"Yes," I agreed, without much conviction, "and I take it that what is in your mind is that when he bolted he probably made for some place that was known to him and where he believed that he could hide in safety."

"Exactly," Thorndyke agreed. "If we could discover some of his haunts, we might have a clue to a possible hiding-place."

"It may be so," I rejoined, "and if that is your view, I suppose you will begin by seeing what you can glean from this coat"; and with this I proceeded to untie the string and open the parcel.

The coat, when I lifted it out and unrolled it, was seen to be amazingly dirty. It was not merely splashed with mud. On the sleeves and around the bottom of the skirt were great daubs of thick dirt mingled with a number of whitish marks such as might have been produced by contact with wet chalk.

"It is extraordinary," said I, holding the coat up for Thorndyke's inspection. "The fellow seems to have been positively wallowing in the mire."

"Not exactly in the mire," said Thorndyke, looking closely at the great daubs. "This is not road dirt. It is earth; and the earth seems to have been mixed with particles of chalk. Perhaps we had better empty the pockets before we proceed with the examination of the coat."

I thrust my hand into the two pockets and drew out from one the driving license, crumpled, smeared, and marked with the prints of dirty fingers, and from the other a stump of lead pencil, a cigarette-holder and what looked like a fragment of a broken tile. But it was so encrusted with earth that it was difficult to see exactly what it was.

"Brodribb's description," said I, as I handed it to Thorndyke, "doesn't seem to fit. This is certainly not a fragment of a flower-pot.

It is too dark in colour. It looks to me more like part of a tile."

Thorndyke took it from me and examined it closely in the bright light of the electric lamp.

"I don't think it is a tile, Jervis," said he, "but we shall see better when we get it clean. The interesting point about it is that the earth in which it is embedded seems to be similar to that on the coat; a mixture of loam and small fragments of chalk—a sort of chalk rubble. We will brush off the earth when we have looked over the other things."

He laid it in a small cardboard tray and put it aside on the mantel-shelf. Then he turned his attention to the cigarette-tube which I held in my hand.

"There," said I, handing it to him, "is another example of excellent but quite irrelevant clues."

"How irrelevant?" he asked. "And irrelevant to what?"

"To the subject of our inquiry," I replied. "Here is a highly distinctive object, for it was certainly never bought at a shop. As evidence in a case of doubtful identity, it would be quite valuable. But it is of no use to us. It gives us no hint as to where its owner is at present hiding."

Thorndyke smiled indulgently. "We mustn't expect too much, Jervis," said he; "in fact, we have no reason to expect anything. We are just looking over this jetsam as a matter of routine to note any facts that it may seem to suggest, without regard to their apparent relevancy or irrelevancy to our inquiry. You cannot judge the relevancy of an isolated fact. Experience has taught me, and must have taught you, that the most trivial, commonplace and seemingly irrelevant facts have a way of suddenly assuming a crucial importance by connecting, explaining or filling in the detail of later discoveries.

"Take this cigarette-tube, for instance. It appears to be the property of Daniel Penrose. But how did he come by it? As you say, it was certainly not bought in the ordinary way at a shop. There is no suggestion of mass-production about it. It is an individual thing made by a particular person, and probably there is not another like it in the world. But if we look at it attentively, we can form some idea of the kind of person who made it and can suggest even the probable circumstances in which it was made. Thus, it is composed of a very hard, heavy, black wood, much like ebony in character but with a slight brownish tinge instead of the characteristic dead black. Probably it is African ebony. It is competently turned but with no special display of skill. The mouthpiece has been shaped with a chisel, whereas you or I would have used a file on such a very hard material. The suggestion is that the chisel was a tool to which the maker was accustomed and which he used with facility. Then the rather artless but quite pleasant decoration consists of a pattern of circular white spots, each an eighth of an inch in diameter, made, apparently, by boring holes—probably with a Morse drill—right through the half-finished piece and driving into them little dowels of holly or some other white hardwood, which would be cut off flush when the work was finished in the lathe. Then there is the suggestion that the tube was made from an odd scrap of wood, left over from some larger work."

"How do you arrive at that?" I asked.

"I think," he replied, "it is suggested by this little streak of sapwood. It is a distinct blemish, and one feels that it would have been avoided if a larger piece of wood had been available. So you see that the impression we get is of a workman who was handy with a paring-chisel but also had some skill as a turner; possibly a joiner or cabinet-maker who had a lathe in his workshop."

"Yes," I agreed, "he may have been, and, on the other hand, he may not. I don't see that it matters. He is not our pigeon. What seems to me of more interest—though mighty little at that — is that there is a good-sized stump of a cigarette still in the tube. It looks as if Penrose had dropped the holder in his pocket with a cigarette still alight; and if he did that—in a motor car, with plenty of petrol vapour about—he must have been either drunk or frightened out of his wits. What is the next proceeding?"

"I think," said he, as he deposited the license, the cigarette-tube and the stump of pencil provisionally in a cardboard box, "we had better collect as much earth as we can get off the coat to examine at our leisure. We shall want one or two photographic dishes, a clean toothbrush, a glass funnel, a wide-mouthed jar and a few filter-papers. Do you mind getting them while I damp the coat?"

I ran up to the laboratory and collected these articles, and when I returned with them I found Thorndyke with the coat spread out on the table, cautiously damping the larger mud-stains with a sponge; and we at once fell to work on the rather dirty and not very thrilling task of transferring the mud from the coat to one of the dishes, which I had partly filled with water. But the quantity that we collected by scraping with a paper-knife and brushing off into the water was quite surprising; and when, from the state of liquid mud in the dish, it was transformed into wet earth on a filter paper, it at once took on the character of a definite and recognizable type of soil.

"That," said Thorndyke as he carefully removed the filter-paper from the funnel and set it on a blotting-pad to drain, "we can examine later and, if necessary, with the aid of an expert geological opinion. It appears to be a rather fine reddish loam a little like the Thanet sands, with a few minute white particles, apparently chalk. But we shall see. And now let us take a look at Brodribb's alleged flower-pot."

He brought the tray from the mantelpiece and, taking out the fragment, cautiously wetted its surface. Then, having first carefully washed the toothbrush, he proceeded to brush the earth from the pottery fragment into a small dish until it was completely clean, and, having dried its surface with blotting-paper and his handkerchief, put it aside while he collected the detached earth on a filter-paper.

"You notice, Jervis, " said he as he opened out the filter-paper on the blotting pad, "that it seems to be the same soil as that on the coat. There are more chalk particles and they are larger; but that is what we should expect, as the larger particles would have less tendency to adhere to the coat. And now let us have your considered opinion of this fragment."

I took it from him and examined it with a decent pretence of interest (and an inward conviction that it didn't matter tuppence what it was).

"I still think," said I, "that it looks like a piece of tile. The material is as coarse as brick and it has a slight curvature like that of an old hand-made tile. But I don't quite understand what those marks are. They are evidently not accidental."

"No," he agreed, "and I think they exclude your diagnosis, and so does the definite thickening at the edge. But let us proceed systematically. I find it a help to a thorough examination of an object to describe it in detail as if one were preparing an entry in a museum catalogue."

I agreed warmly and invited him to go ahead.

"Very well," said he, "if you feel unequal to the effort, the task devolves upon me. We will take the physical properties in regular order, beginning with the general character.

"This is a fragment of pottery of excessively coarse and crude quality, consisting of a reddish buff matrix in which are embedded numerous angular white particles which have the appearance of burnt flint. The texture is somewhat porous and there is no trace of a glaze on either surface. On taking it in the hand, and allowing for the fact that it is wet, we find it noticeably heavy.

"Size and shape. The fragment forms an irregular oblong, approximately an inch and a half long by three-quarters wide. Of the four sides, three are fractured—recently, you notice—and the fourth —one of the long sides—is thickened into a definite flange or rim, roughly T-shaped in section. The thickness, as shown by the caliper gauge, varies from five thirty-seconds of an inch at the thinnest broken edge to eleven thirty-seconds on the thick unbroken edge.

"On the thick edge are five indented marks such as might have been made with a blunt knife on the soft clay, roughly a quarter of an inch apart; and on the convex surface, next to the long broken edge, are four similar linear indentations, roughly half an inch apart and at right angles to the thickened edge.

"The fragment is curved in both diameters, rather irregularly, but still quite definitely. Let us see, approximately, what those curvatures amount to."

He took a sheet of writing paper and placed the fragment on it, standing up on its thick edge, and, with a sharp pencil, carefully traced the outline. The tracing showed the curvature very distinctly; and it became still more obvious when he placed a straight-edge against the concave side and connected the two ends with a ruled line. Then he produced a pair of compasses furnished with a pencil, and, setting the pencil-point on one end of the ruled line, was able, after one or two trials, to strike an arc which passed through both ends of the line and followed the curve of the tracing. On measuring the distance from the centre to the arc, it was found to be three inches and an eighth.

"We see, then," said he, "that the curve has a radius of three inches and an eighth, so that it seems to be part of a circle, six inches and a quarter in diameter. Now, let us try the other curvature."

He stood the fragment up on one of its short ends and made a tracing as before. Measurement of this showed a curve with a radius of two inches and three-quarters.

"We can't take this last measurement very seriously," said he, "as the curve is so very short and irregular. But you see that we now have the material for a fairly reliable reconstruction of the object of which this fragment formed a part. It appears to have been an earthenware vessel of the very coarsest and crudest type, with curved sides—some kind of bowl or pot—approximately six inches across the top, or mouth, and possibly about three inches high. But the height is a matter of mere guess-work. The irregularity in the curvature of the mouth makes it pretty certain that the vessel was built by hand, not thrown on the wheel; and this suggestion is confirmed by the extremely crude and primitive decoration. The thickened rim of the mouth is ornamented by a series of linear markings about a quarter of an inch apart, made, apparently, by indenting with a blunt knife, or perhaps a long thumb nail, on the soft clay; and there is another series of similar markings, a little wider apart, which encircles the vessel about half an inch below the rim.

"There, Jervis, is a summary of the characteristics which enable us to form a reasonably exact picture of the object which yielded this fragment. Taking them together and in conjunction with the fact that the fragment was found in the pocket of a man who is known to be a collector of antiques, what conclusion do you arrive at?"

"Concerning the object? Well, I suppose we must conclude that the pot or bowl must have been an extremely ancient vessel, perhaps prehistoric. It would hardly be Roman."

"No," he agreed. "Roman pottery was the product of a developed industry with quite advanced technical methods. This was quite a primitive piece of work; certainly pre-Roman, I should say, and more probably neolithic than Bronze Age. But that is a question which we can easily settle by inquiries or reference to published work."

"Yes," said I; "and when you have settled it, you will be exactly where you are now, so far as the abiding-place of Daniel Penrose is concerned, and where you were before you carried out this very interesting little investigation. You will have established a fact that can have no possible bearing on the problem that you are asked to solve."

"Who knows?" he retorted. "We have learned that Penrose had in his pocket a fragment of ancient pottery. It is not likely that he picked it up by chance on the road; and if he did not, it is possible that we may have here a clue to the purpose with which he set out on his travels on the day when he disappeared."

"But," I persisted, "even if you knew that, you would be no more forward. He certainly did not set out with the purpose of killing an old woman and becoming a fugitive from the law. You would just have another irrelevant fact."

He smiled as he dropped the fragment into the box, together with the two filter-papers. "It is quite likely that you are right, Jervis," said he. "But we have already agreed that the relevancy of a fact often fails to be perceived until the appearance of some further facts brings its significance into view. It is always much easier to be wise after the event."

With this, he deposited the cardboard box in the drawer of a cabinet, while I hung the wet coat on a peg in the lobby. Then we disposed ourselves in our respective chairs to smoke the final pipe before turning in, and, dismissing the affairs of Daniel Penrose, chatted somewhat discursively on the morning's doings in court. But, in the intervals of our talk I found my thoughts drifting back to the cardboard box and to the occupations with which it was associated. And not only then but in the days that followed did that curious little investigation furnish me with matter for reflection.

Of course, Thorndyke was perfectly right in his contention. It is impossible to decide in advance whether a particular item of knowledge may or may not prove at some future time to be of value; and it was a fact that Thorndyke made a rule of acquiring every item of knowledge that was obtainable in connection with a case, without regard to its apparent relevancy. But, still, I had the feeling that, in this present case, he was not merely acting on this rather academic principle. The care and thoroughness and the appearance of interest with which he had made this examination conveyed to me the impression that the facts elicited meant more to him than they did to me.

Yet what could they mean? The disappearance of Penrose had the hospital as its starting-point, or, at the earliest, the accident to the old woman. But the mud and the pottery fragments were related to events that had occurred before the accident, and which were, therefore, totally unconnected with the disappearance. Then how could they possibly throw any light on the present whereabouts of the missing man, which was the problem that we had to solve?

That was the question that I asked myself again and again. But by no amount of cogitation could I find any answer.

CHAPTER 7

A VISIT OF INSPECTION

The dubious and slightly bewildered state of mind to which I have referred induced me to observe Thorndyke's proceedings with a little closer attention than was usual with me. Not that there was really any occasion, for Thorndyke appeared to go out of his way to make me a party to any doings connected with the Penrose case; which tended to increase my suspicion that I had missed some point of evidential importance.

It was some two or three days after Brodribb's visit to us, when we seemed to have a few hours at our disposal, that Thorndyke suggested a call at Queen Square to examine Penrose's car. I had been expecting this suggestion, and, with the hope of getting some new light on the purpose of his investigations, assented cheerfully. Accordingly, when Thorndyke had slipped a good-sized note-book and some other small necessaries into his pocket, we set forth on our quest.

I have always liked Queen Square, and have watched, regretfully, its gradual deterioration—or "improvement," as the optimistic modern phrase has it. When I first knew the place, it was nearly intact, with its satellites, Great Ormond Street, The Foundling Hospital and the group of other pleasant old squares adjacent. As we walked towards it we discussed the changes that the years had wrought. Thorndyke, as an old Londoner, sympathized warmly with my regrets.

"Yes," he agreed, "the works of man tell us more about him than we can gather from volumes of history. Every generation leaves, in the products of its activities, a faithful picture of its capabilities, its standard of taste and its outlook on life. The people who conceived and created these delightful, dignified haunts of peace and quiet, had never heard of town-planning and did not talk much about architecture. But they planned towns by instinctive taste and they built charming houses, the dismembered fragments of which we can now study in our museums. There is a beautiful wooden portico at South Kensington which I used to admire when it stood in Great Ormond Street."

"I remember it," said I. "But in the museum they have scraped off the paint and gilding to show the construction; which is all very interesting and instructive, but it is not quite what the architect had in view when he designed it. It is rather as if one should offer the anatomical exhibits in the Hunterian museum as illustrations of the beauty of the human figure. They might have restored the painting and gilding so that visitors could see what a fine London doorway was like in the time of Good Queen Anne."

As I spoke, we turned out of Great Ormond Street and crossed the square, passing the ancient pump with its surmounting lantern and its encircling posts, and directing our steps towards Penrose's house, which had been described as nearly opposite the statue of Queen Anne. As we approached the latter, Thorndyke remarked, continuing our discussion:

"There is another example of what is practically a lost art. It seems to me a pity that leadwork should have been allowed to fall into such a state of decay. Lead may not be an ideal material for statues, but it is imperishable, it is cheap and it is easy to work. In the eighteenth century, the Piccadilly foundries from which this statue probably came, turned out thousands of works—urns and vases, shepherds and shepherdesses and other rustic figures for use in parks and formal gardens or as architectural ornaments. But they have nearly all gone; melted down, I suppose, to form sheet lead or water pipes. This looks like the house, and a fine old house it is; one of the last survivors of its family."

We ascended to the broad door-step, enclosed by forged railings bearing a pair of link-extinguishers and the standard for an oil lamp, gave a tug at the old-fashioned bell-pull and executed a flourish on the handsome brass knocker. After a decent interval, the door was opened by a smart-looking maid-servant to whom Thorndyke communicated the purpose of our visit.

"We have called to see Mr. Kickweed on certain legal business. I think he is expecting a visit from me. I am Dr. Thorndyke."

On this the maid opened the door wide, and, inviting us to enter, conducted us to a small room adjacent to the hall, where she request-ed us to wait while she informed Mr. Kickweed of our arrival. When she had gone, I cast an inquisitive glance round the room, which contained a table, two chairs and a piece of furniture which might have been regarded either as a cupboard or as some kind of sideboard.

"This can hardly be the room in which the burglary took place," said I, "though it fits the description to some extent, but the window seems in the wrong place."

"Very much so," said Thorndyke, "as it looks out on the square and is over the area. And it is the wrong sort of cupboard with the wrong sort of lock. No, this is not the mysterious chamber."

Here the door opened slowly and discreetly to admit a pale-faced, rather unwholesome-looking elderly man who bowed deferentially and introduced himself by name as Mr. Kickweed; though the introduction was hardly necessary, for he might have served, in a museum of social anthropology, as a type specimen of the genus, upper manservant.

"Mr. Brodribb wrote to me, sir," he continued in a melancholy tone, "to say that you would probably call and instructing me to give you any assistance that I could. In what way can I have the pleasure of carrying out those instructions?"

"My immediate object," replied Thorndyke, "is to inspect Mr. Penrose's car. Has anything been done to it since it came back?"

"Nothing whatever, sir," Kickweed replied. "I suppose it ought to be cleaned, but I know nothing about cars. Mr. Penrose always attended to it himself excepting when it went out for repairs, and he always kept the garage locked up. In fact, it was locked when they brought the car back."

"Then how did you get the car in?" Thorndyke asked.

"The police officer, sir, who came with the car, fortunately had a few odd keys with him, and one of them happened to fit the lock. He was good enough to leave it with me, so I shall be able to let you in. If you would like to go round there now I will just get my hat and show you the way."

"Thank you," said Thorndyke. "If it is not troubling you—"

"It is no trouble at all, sir," interrupted Kickweed, and thereupon he stole out of the room with the light, noiseless tread that seems to be almost characteristic of heavy, bulky men. A few minutes later he reappeared in correct morning dress, including a slightly rusty top hat, and we set forth together. The garage was not far away, being situated in a sort of mews, approached from Guilford Street.

As we halted at the door and Kickweed produced the key, I noticed that Thorndyke cast an inquisitive glance at it, and I guessed what was in his mind, because it was also in mine. But we were both wrong. The key was not of the filed or skeleton variety but was just a normal warded key of a simple type. However, it turned in the lock, after a good deal of persuasion, and, the doors being flung open, we entered.

It was a roomy place and fairly well lighted by a wide window above the doors. The car stood in the middle, leaving ample space on either side and still more at the end, where a rough bench had been placed, with a vice and a number of rather rusty tools, together with various oddments in the way of bolts, nuts and miscellaneous scrap.

"I take it," said Thorndyke, glancing at the littered bench, "that Mr. Penrose is not a skilled mechanic."

"No, sir," Kickweed admitted. "I don't think he is much of a workman. And yet he used to spend a good deal of time here. I don't know what he would have been doing."

"You did not assist him, then?"

"No, sir. I have only been in here once or twice, and then only for a few minutes with Mr. Penrose. I never came here by myself, nor, I think, did anybody else. There was only one key, until I got this one, and Mr. Penrose kept that himself, and has it still."

"I suppose you don't know of any reason why he should have objected to your coming here alone?"

"No, sir. And I don't think there was any. It was just his way. He has rather a habit of making secrets of nothing."

"So I have understood," said Thorndyke, "and a very bad habit it is, leading to all sorts of unnecessary suspicions and surmises. However, we came here primarily to inspect the car, so perhaps we had better get on with that."

Accordingly, he proceeded to make a systematic and detailed survey of the vehicle, beginning with the bent mudguard, the leading edge of which he examined minutely with the aid of a lens. But, if there had ever been any fibres or other traces of the collision, they had been removed by the police. He then transferred his attention to the wheels, and, after a preliminary glance at them, produced one or two envelopes from his pocket and laid them on the bench.

"The dirt on the face of the tires," he remarked, "is of no interest to us, as it will have changed from moment to moment. But that on the inside and on the rims of the wheels is more significant. Its presence there suggests that, at one time, the car had been driven over quite soft earth; and that earth was a natural soil, not a road material; a reddish loam similar to that on the coat."

"Yes," I agreed, "it is evident that the wheels sank in pretty deep by the quantity of soil on the rims. And I think," I added, stooping low to look under the car, "that I can see a leaf sticking to the rim of the wheel."

With some difficulty I managed to reach in and pick it off together with the lump of dry loam in which it was embedded.

"A dead leaf," Thorndyke pronounced when I handed it to him; "I mean a last year's leaf, and it looks like a hornbeam. But we shall see better when we wet it and flatten it out."

He deposited the leaf and earth in an envelope, on which he wrote a brief memorandum of the source of the specimen, and then continued his examination. But there was nothing more to be seen from the outside excepting a general dirtiness, suggestive of a not very fastidious owner. Nor was there anything very significant to be seen when I opened the door. The interior showed no signs of anything unusual. The floor was moderately clean excepting that under the driver's seat, which was thickly plastered with loam. But this was what we should have expected; and the evidence that it furnished that there was almost certainly only one person in the car during that last drive, merely confirmed what we already knew. There were no loose articles in any of the pockets or receptacles other than the insurance certificate and the rather scanty outfit of tools. In fact, the only discovery—and a very modest one at that—was another dead leaf, apparently also hornbeam, trodden flat into the dirt by the driver's seat.

Having finished with the car, Thorndyke once more glanced round the garage and I could see that he was making a mental inventory of the various objects that it contained. But his next question reverted to the car.

"I understood," said he, "that the police found an empty flask in the car."

"Yes, sir," replied Kickweed. "I took that away to wash it and polish it up. It is a silver flask and it seemed a pity to leave it in the dirty state in which it was found. I have cleaned it thoroughly and put it away among the plate. Did you wish to see it?"

"No," replied Thorndyke, "but I should like a few particulars. About how much does it hold?"

"It holds the best part of a bottle. About an imperial pint."

"That is a large flask," Thorndyke remarked. "Did Mr. Penrose usually carry it in the car?"

"Do you know, sir, I really can't say. I have only seen it once before. That was about two years ago when I happened to be brushing Mr. Penrose's overcoat and found it in the pocket. But I have the impression that he usually carried it with him when he went away from home. He would be likely to because he is rather fastidious about his wine. He drinks nothing but Madeira and old brown sherry; and you can't get good Madeira or brown sherry at roadside inns."

"And as to quantity? It has been stated that when he was last seen he appeared to be under the influence of liquor. Was that at all usual?"

Kickweed shook his head emphatically. "No, sir," he replied. "That must have been a mistake. He may have smelt of sherry. He often does. But sherry has a very strong aroma and a little of it goes a long way in the matter of smell. But in all the years that I have known Mr. Penrose, I have never seen him in the slightest degree the worse for drink. He does certainly take a good deal, as I can judge by the wine merchant's deliveries and the empty bottles, but then he takes no beer or spirits or any other kind of wine. They must have been misled by the odour."

"That seems quite likely," said Thorndyke. "By the way, I notice a couple of hazel twigs hanging up there under that hat. Do you happen to know whether Mr. Penrose is a dowser?"

"A dowser, sir?" Kickweed repeated with a mystified air.

"A water-finder," Thorndyke explained. "That is what those forked twigs are used for." He took the hat from the peg and laid it on the bench, and, taking down one of the twigs, held it by its two ends and continued: "The specially gifted persons—known as dowsers—who search for underground streams or springs, hold the twig in this way and walk to and fro over the land where they expect to find water; and when they pass over a hidden spring—so it is stated—they become aware of the presence of underground water by a movement of the twig in their hands. It looks as if Mr. Penrose had practised the dowser's art."

"Ah!" exclaimed Kickweed, "I remember now that Mr. Penrose once showed me one of these things and told me about it. But I thought it was one of his little jokes; for it was not water that he professed to be able to find with it. He said that it was an infallible guide to buried treasure. It would show the treasure-seeker exactly where to dig. But I never supposed that he was speaking seriously. You see, sir, Mr. Penrose is rather a jocular gentleman and it is sometimes a little difficult to be quite sure what he really does mean."

"So I understand," said Thorndyke, "and he may have been joking in this case. But the idea of digging seems to have been in his mind. Now, so far as you know, did he ever engage in any sort of digging activities in his search for antiquities?"

"Well, sir," replied Kickweed, "it is rather difficult to say. He is so very facetious. But I have known him to bring home certain articles—lumps of flint and bits of crockery, they looked like to me— which were covered with earth and which I have helped him to scrub clean at the scullery sink. I supposed that he must have dug them up somewhere as he referred to them as 'Treasure Trove' and 'the resurrectionist's loot' and other similar expressions."

"Yes," Thorndyke agreed, "those expressions and the condition of the objects certainly suggest something in the way of excavations. But I don't see any tools suitable for the purpose; and I should suppose that if he had had any he would have kept them here. Do you happen to remember having seen any picks, shovels or similar tools here or elsewhere?"

Mr. Kickweed reflected as he ran an inquiring glance round the walls. "As I said, sir," he replied, "I have only been in here once or twice before Mr. Penrose went away. But I seem to remember a sort of pick—I think it is called a trenching tool—which I don't see now. And there was a small spade, pointed like the ace of hearts, with a leather case for the blade. But I don't see that either. It hung, I think, on one of those pegs. But that was over a year ago."

"It looks," I suggested, remembering the pottery fragment, "as if Mr. Penrose may have taken them with him when he left home. They were not in the car when it was found, but it had been lying unattended for a couple of days. Loose property has rather a way of disappearing from derelict cars."

"It is quite possible," said Thorndyke; and he then appeared to dismiss the subject, for he replaced the hazel twig on its peg and picked up the hat to return that also, but paused, looking with a faint smile into its dusty and decayed interior.

"Mr. Penrose," he remarked, "seems to have attached undue

value to this relic. But perhaps the marking was done when it was in a more presentable condition."

He exhibited the interior of the hat on the crown of which the name "D. Penrose" had been carefully printed with a rubber stamp.

"Yes, sir," said Kickweed, "the name was probably stamped when the hat was new. Not that that would have made any difference, for Mr. Penrose stamped his name on everything that he possessed; not only on his underclothing and handkerchiefs and the other things that are usually marked, but his hats, shoes, books, paper-knives—everything that was movable. It always seemed to me a little inconsistent."

"How inconsistent?" I asked.

"I mean," replied Kickweed, "he is in general a very secretive gentleman. He makes a secret of the most simple and ordinary things. And yet he prints his full name, not just his initials as most men do, inside his hat and his shoes and his waistcoat lining, and even on his pocket-knife. Now, if a stranger asked him his name he would probably avoid telling him; but yet, as soon as he takes his hat off, he discloses his identity to all the world."

"I take it," said Thorndyke, "that he usually does the stamping himself?"

"Lord bless you, yes, sir! That rubber stamp has always been kept under lock and key as if it had been the Koh-i-noor, or as if it could have been used for forging his signature. I have never even seen it. But, of course, that signifies nothing. It is just his way."

"Yes," said Thorndyke, "and you are a wise man to accept his harmless oddities and not let them worry you." He hung the hat on its peg and then, turning to Kickweed, opened a fresh subject.

"Mr. Brodribb consulted me about a burglary that occurred in your house a short time ago. There was a question of calling in the police and getting the cupboard opened. How does that suggestion strike you?"

"It strikes me," Kickweed replied severely, "as an improper and a foolish suggestion. It would be improper to tamper with Mr. Penrose's property in his absence and without his consent, sir, and it would be foolish because we should be none the wiser when we had opened the cupboard as we don't know what it contained, or whether it contained anything."

Here I interposed rather rashly.

"The suggestion has been made that it is just possible that the person who entered the room may have been Mr. Penrose, himself."

Kickweed looked, and professed to be, deeply shocked. But I had, nevertheless, a strong suspicion that that was his own opinion.

"But, you know, Mr. Kickweed," said I, "there is nothing immoral or even improper in a gentleman's entering his own house to take his own property if he happens to have need of it. Most men, it is true, would prefer to enter by the front door. But Mr. Penrose was not like most men; and if he preferred the window, he was entirely within his rights. It was his own window."

I had the feeling that my observations were received with approval and even with some relief. But Mr. Kickweed, if he secretly concurred, as I believed that he did, was not committing himself.

"No doubt, sir," said he, "you are perfectly right. But I couldn't imagine Mr. Penrose doing anything so undignified, especially as he had the key of the front door in his pocket. And," he added, with a pensive smile, "it was his own front door."

"You were saying just now," said Thorndyke, "that nothing is known as to the contents of that cupboard. Have you no idea at all as to what it contained, or contains?"

"I said knowledge, sir," replied Kickweed. "I know nothing at all as to what is, or has been, in that cupboard."

He spoke with an emphasis that gave us clearly to understand that he was not going beyond his actual knowledge. He was going to hazard no opinions.

"And it is the fact, Mr. Kickweed," Thorndyke pursued, "that there is no one in the world who knows, or could form any reasonable judgment as to what that cupboard did, does or might contain?"

Mr. Kickweed reflected, a trifle uneasily, I thought. But Thorndyke's question admitted of no evasion, and he at length replied with some reluctance:

"Well, sir, I wouldn't say that, for there is one person who may possibly know. I have not spoken of him to any one hitherto, because Mr. Penrose was very secretive about that room, and he is my employer and it is my duty to abide by his wishes, whether expressed or not. But you ask me a definite question and I suppose you are entitled to an answer. I think it possible that Mr. Penrose may have confided his secret to a certain friend of his; a gentleman named Lockhart."

"What makes you think that Mr. Lockhart may know what is or was, in the cupboard?" Thorndyke asked.

"The discovery—if it was one—" Kickweed replied, "was quite accidental. Mr. Lockhart came to the house by appointment to look over the collection, and Mr. Penrose took him into the great gallery. When they had been there some considerable time, I ventured to look in to ask if I should bring them up some tea. But when I entered the big gallery they were not there; but I could hear them talking, and the voices seemed to come from the small room, though the door of that room was shut. But they must have been in there because there was no other room that opened out of the great gallery. Now the small room contained nothing but the cupboard, so that if Mr. Penrose took Mr. Lockhart into that room, it could only have been to show him what was in the cupboard. And I did, in fact, hear sounds of movement in the room as if drawers were being pulled out. But, of course, as soon as I realized what was happening, I went away.

"But there was another circumstance that made me think that Mr. Penrose might have let Mr. Lockhart into the secret of the small room. When they had finished with the collection they went into the morning room—the little front room that you went into—and I took them up some tea; and there they were for quite a long time before Mr. Lockhart went away. Afterwards I learned from Mr. Penrose, himself, that Mr. Lockhart had been advising him about insuring the collection which made it seem likely that Mr. Lockhart had been shown all that there was to insure."

"Yes," said Thorndyke, "that seems a reasonable inference. Is Mr. Lockhart connected with insurance business?"

"No, sir. He is a legal gentleman, a barrister."

"Ah!" said Thorndyke. "Lockhart. Now I wonder if that would be—you don't happen to know what inn he belongs to?"

"Yes, sir. He belongs to Lincoln's Inn, at least, that is his address. I happen to know by having seen a card of his which Mr. Penrose left on his dressing-table."

"Is Mr. Lockhart an intimate friend of Mr. Penrose?"

"No, sir. Quite a recent acquaintance, I believe, though Mr. Penrose seemed to take to him more than he usually does to strangers. Still, I was rather surprised at his taking him into the small room. I have never known him to do such a thing before."

Thorndyke made no immediate rejoinder but stood, apparently considering this last statement and letting his glance travel about the place as if searching for some further objects of interest. But it seemed that he had squeezed both the garage and Mr. Kickweed dry, for he said, at length:

"Well, I think we have learned all that there is to learn here; and I must thank you, Mr. Kickweed, for having been so extremely helpful."

Kickweed smiled a somewhat dreary smile. "I hope I have not been too much so, sir," said he. "I am not a willing helper, though I feel bound to carry out Mr. Brodribb's instructions. I understand from him that you are trying to find out where Mr. Penrose has gone to; and, if you will pardon me for saying so, I hope you won't succeed."

Thorndyke smiled appreciatively. "Now, why do you say that?" he asked.

"Because, sir," Kickweed replied earnestly, "I feel that this pursuit is not justifiable. Mr. Penrose, as I understand, has had a little mishap and thinks it best to keep out of sight for a time. But if he thinks so, it is his own affair, and I don't consider it just or proper that other people, for their own purposes, should hunt him up and perhaps get him into difficulties."

I must confess that I sympathized heartily with Mr. Kickweed's sentiments, and so, apparently, did Thorndyke, for he replied:

"That is precisely what I pointed out to Mr. Brodribb. But there are legal reasons for ascertaining Mr. Penrose's whereabouts, though there are none for disclosing them to others. You may take it from me, Mr. Kickweed, that nothing which may come to my knowledge will be used in any way to his disadvantage."

"I am very relieved to hear you say that, sir," Kickweed rejoined with evident sincerity, "because I have felt that there are others who take a different view. Mr. Horridge, for instance, has, to my knowledge, been in communication with the police."

"Well," I said, as we retired from the garage and Kickweed locked the door, "I don't suppose he has done any harm if he has no more to tell them than we have been told."

As our way home led through Queen Square, we walked thither with Mr. Kickweed, and Thorndyke took the opportunity to ask a few questions concerning Mr. Penrose's collection.

"I don't know much about the things," said Kickweed, "excepting that there is a rare lot of them and that they take a terrible amount of dusting. I do most of it with a pair of bellows when Mr. Penrose is not about. But if you feel any interest in them, why not step in, as you are here, and have a look at them yourself?"

Now I have no doubt whatever that this was precisely what Thorndyke had intended to do, but, in his queer, secretive way, had preferred
that the inspection should seem to occur by chance. At any rate, he
accepted the invitation, and we followed Kickweed to the door of
the house and were by him admitted to the hall.

CHAPTER 8

MR. HORRIDGE

Mr. Kickweed, as has been mentioned, had a light tread, and his movements in general tended to be silent. Thus our entry into the hall of the old house and the subsequent closing of the door were almost noiseless. Nevertheless, our arrival was not unobserved; for, even as Kickweed was pocketing his latch-key, the door of the morning-room opened slowly and quietly and a large, distinctly fat gentleman appeared framed in the doorway.

There was something slightly odd and even ridiculous in the sudden and silent manner in which he became visible, and in the sly, inquisitive glance that he turned on us; as if he had been a plain-clothes officer and we a surprised party of burglars.

"How did you know I was here, Kickweed?" he demanded.

"I didn't sir," was the reply.

"Oh," rejoined the other. "I thought these gentlemen might have come on some business with me."

"No, sir. They have been inspecting the car. They are Dr. Thorndyke and Dr. Jervis."

The fat man bowed stiffly. "Ah!" said he, "they have inspected the car. And now?"

"Dr. Thorndyke thought he would like to take a look at the collection," Kickweed replied frigidly, evidently resentful of the other man's manner, "so I invited him to step in and look over it."

"Ha!" said the fat gentleman. "You thought it quite in order to do that? Well, if Dr. Thorndyke wants to see the collection, there is no reason why he should not. I will show him round the gallery, myself. My name," he added, turning to us, "is Horridge. You have probably heard of me. I am Mr. Penrose's executor, and, in his absence, am keeping an eye on his property."

Now, the tone of his remarks filled me with a burning desire to kick Mr. Horridge; but that being impracticable, I should certainly, if left to myself, have told him to go to the devil and forthwith walked out of the house. Thorndyke, however, was completely unruffled; and having once more thanked Kickweed, who was slinking away in dudgeon, he accepted the invitation with a suavity bordering on meekness (whereby I judged that he had definite reasons for wishing to see the collection).

"So," said Mr. Horridge, as he conducted us along the hall, "you have been examining the car. Now, what did you expect to find out from the car?"

"I did not expect anything," Thorndyke replied.

Horridge giggled. "And did your examination answer your expectations?" he inquired.

"Substantially," replied Thorndyke, "I may say that it did."

Horridge giggled again, and, throwing open a door which opened from the hall, invited us to enter. We accordingly passed in and found ourselves in an immense and lofty room communicating with another of similarly magnificent proportions by an opening from which the original folding doors had been removed.

I looked around me with surprise and extreme distaste, for the noble apartments had been degraded to the status of a mere lumber-room. Of the trim and orderly character of a museum there was not a trace. The walls were occupied by interminable ranges of open shelves and the floor was crowded with plain deal tables, coarsely stained and varnished to disguise their humble material; and shelves and tables were littered with a chaos of miscellaneous objects, all exposed baldly to the air and dust. There was not a single glazed case in the room and the only article of comely furniture was a lantern clock, perched on a bracket, which ticked sedately and actually showed the approximately correct time.

"This is a very singular collection," Thorndyke remarked, casting a puzzled glance over the shelves and tables. "One doesn't quite see what its purpose is; what it is intended to illustrate."

Horridge giggled again in his unpleasant way. "Whatever the intention is," said he, "it illustrates very perfectly poor old Pen's usual state of mind—muddle. But may I ask what is the object of this inspection? Is it just a matter of curiosity or is it connected with the inquiry into Pen's disappearance? Because I don't see how the inspection is going to help you."

"It is not very obvious, certainly," Thorndyke admitted. "But one never knows what light chance facts may throw on the problem. I think it will be worth while for me to see what things Mr. Penrose has collected and where he obtained them."

Horridge grinned—and the explanation of the grin was presently forthcoming. Meanwhile he rejoined:

"Well, cast your eye over the oddments and see what takes your fancy. Then you can go into the question of where they came from. What would you like to start with?"

Thorndyke glanced once more along the shelves and then announced his choice.

"I see there is a good deal of ancient pottery, mixed up with other exhibits. Perhaps it would be well to sort that out and see where the pieces were found. Now, here is a little dish of Gaulish red ware. The slip of paper that it rests on bears the number, 201. That, I presume, refers to a catalogue."

"It does," replied Horridge, giggling delightedly. "I will get you the catalogue and then you will be able to find out all about the specimen."

He went to a table near the end of the room and pulled out a drawer from which he extracted a stout quarto volume. This he brought to Thorndyke and, having handed it to him with something of a flourish, stood looking at him and giggling like a fool. But the reason for his merriment became apparent when Thorndyke opened the book and turned to the number. Observing the slow smile which spread over my colleague's face, I looked over his shoulder and read the entry, scrawled, not very legibly, in pencil:

201. Sammy. Pot Sand. Sinbad.

"This is not very illuminating," Thorndyke remarked; on which Horridge burst into a roar of laughter.

"Oh, don't say that!" he gurgled. "I understood from old Brodribb that you could see through a brick wall. Well, here's your chance. The whole catalogue is written in the same damn, silly sort of jargon. Of course, Pen knows what it means, but he doesn't intend that any one else shall. Perhaps you would like to note down a few examples to think over at your leisure."

Thorndyke instantly grasped the opportunity.

"Thank you," said he. "A most excellent suggestion. If you will be so very kind as to show Dr. Jervis the collection, I will make a few notes on the pottery and extract the entries from the catalogue. If we could identify some of the localities, we might get quite a useful hint."

This suggestion did not at all meet the views of Mr. Horridge, who was evidently as curious as to Thorndyke's proceedings as I was, myself. But he could not very well refuse; for Thorndyke, seeing a chance of carrying out his investigations—whatever they might be—uninterrupted by Horridge's chatter and free from his inquisitive observation, was quietly persistent and, of course, had his way, as he usually did.

"Very well," Horridge at length agreed, with a rather bad grace, "then I'll just take Dr. Jervis round the shelves and show him the curios. But I don't know much about them, and I don't suppose he cares much."

Accordingly, we set forth on a voyage of exploration round the crowded, disorderly shelves; and, realizing that my function was to keep Horridge's attention distracted from Thorndyke's activities, I plied him with questions about the exhibits and commented on their interest and beauty with the utmost prolixity and tediousness at my command. But it was a wretched make-believe on both sides; for, while Horridge was answering my questions (usually quite ignorantly and all wrong, as even I knew) he kept one eye cocked in Thorndyke's direction, and my own attention was similarly occupied.

But Thorndyke gave us but a poor entertainment. Drawing a chair up to a table near the window, he seated himself with his back to us and the catalogue before him. This he pored over for some time, making occasional entries in his note-book. Then he rose, and, having taken a survey of the shelves, began to select pieces of pottery, each of which he took in turn to the table where he examined it critically, compared it with the entry in the catalogue and copied the latter into his note-book. He began with the Roman pottery, but, from long acquaintance with his habits and methods, I suspected that this was only a tactical move to conceal from Horridge his actual purpose. For I knew that it was his invariable habit, when he had to work in the presence of inquisitive observers, to confuse the issues in their minds by actions which had no bearing on the matter in hand.

As to his real purpose, I had no doubt that it was in some way connected with the fragment which we had examined; and as Horridge conducted me round the loaded shelves, I kept a sharp look-out for pottery exhibits which might correspond to the hypothetical vessel which Thorndyke had sketched in his reconstruction. There were two pieces (in different places and among totally unrelated objects) which, so far as I could see without close inspection, answered the description; one, a largish, rather shallow bowl of which a large part was missing, and the other a deeper pot which had been broken and rather unskilfully mended and which was complete save for a small part of the rim. This pot corresponded very closely both in shape and size with Thorndyke's reconstruction, and it seemed to me, even, that the piece which was missing from the rim was about the size of our fragment. Accordingly, I gave that pot my special attention.

One after another Thorndyke gravely examined specimens of Roman, Saxon and Iron Age pottery in which I felt sure he could have no interest whatever. At last, after circling round, so to speak, he arrived at this pot, picked it up, and with a glance at the number on its paper, bore it over to the table. As he set it down and seated himself, I saw him take something from his pocket, but as his back was towards us I could not see what it was, or what he did with it. I assumed, however, that it was some measuring instrument and that he was ascertaining the dimensions of the piece that was missing. At any rate, his examination was quite brief, and, when he had copied the entry in the catalogue, he carried the pot back to its place and proceeded to look about for further objects for study.

By this time, however, Horridge had begun to be rather bored and was disposed to make no secret of the fact.

"I should think," said he, with an undisguised yawn, "that you've got enough material to occupy you for a month or two; and I'll wager that you don't make any sense of it then."

Thorndyke looked thoughtfully at his open note-book.

"Perhaps you are right," he agreed. "These entries will take a good deal of deciphering and probably will yield no information, after all. I don't think we need trespass on your patience any longer."

"Oh, that's all right," said Horridge, "but, before you go—if you've seen all that you want to see—perhaps you might as well have a look at the small room—the one that was broken into, you know. You heard about that burglary, I think? Old Brodribb said he was going to consult you about it."

"Mr. Brodribb did consult me," Thorndyke replied, "on the question of opening the cupboard by force or otherwise. I advised him that, in the absence of Mr. Penrose, it would not be proper to force the cupboard and that, as the contents of the cupboard were unknown, the proceeding would be useless as well as improper."

"But what about calling in the police?" Horridge suggested.

"I don't think the police would force a cupboard, without the owner's knowledge or consent, if it were locked and showed no signs of having been tampered with."

"Well," Horridge grumbled, "it's very unsatisfactory. Some one may have got away with a whole lot of valuable property and able to dispose of it at their leisure. However—if you have finished with the catalogue, do you mind putting it back in its drawer?"

As Thorndyke complied with this rather odd request, our host walked quickly up the long room to a door in the corner, and I had the impression that he inserted a key and turned it. But, as he stood half turned towards us and in front of the handle and keyhole, I could not see distinctly, nor did I give the matter any particular attention.

"It is odd," he remarked, still standing before the door, grasping the handle, "that Pen should have left the key in this door when he went away. He was always so deadly secret about Bluebeard's chamber, as he called it in his silly way. He never let me see into it. I always thought he had something very precious in it; and I'm inclined to think so still."

With this, he opened the door and we all entered the mysterious chamber; a smallish room and very bare of furniture, for it contained only a single chair, a mahogany table, placed under the window, and a massive cupboard, also of mahogany, with a pair of doors like a wardrobe.

"So this is the famous cupboard," said Thorndyke, standing before it and looking it over critically; "the repository of hidden treasure, as you believe. Well, looking at it, one would say that whatever precious things were once in it, are in it still. But one might be wrong."

Having made this rather ambiguous pronouncement, he proceeded to a more particular inspection. The escutcheon of the Chubb lock was examined with the aid of a lens, and the interior of the keyhole with the tiny electric lamp that he always carried. From the lock he transferred his attention to the cupboard itself, closely examining the sides, standing on the chair to inspect the top, and, finally, setting his shoulder to one corner and his foot against the skirting of the wall, tried to test its weight by tilting it. But beyond eliciting a complaining creak, he could make no impression on it.

"I've tried that," said Horridge. "It's like shoving against the

Eddystone lighthouse. The thing is a most ungodly weight, unless it is screwed to the floor. It can hardly be the stuff inside."

"Unless," I suggested, "Mr. Penrose indulged in the hobby of collecting gold ingots. But even a collection of plate can be pretty heavy if there is enough of it."

"At any rate," said Thorndyke, "one thing is clear. That cupboard has not been opened unless it was opened with its own key."

"Don't think the lock could have been picked?" said Horridge.

Thorndyke shook his head. "Burglars don't try to pick Chubb locks," said he. "They use the jemmy, or else cut the lock out with centre-bits."

Horridge grunted and then amplified the grunt with the remark: "Looks a bit as if our friend Kick had raised a false alarm."

"That can hardly be," Thorndyke objected. "I understood that he found the door bolted on the inside and had to enter through the window."

"Yes, that was what he said," Horridge admitted grudgingly in a tone that seemed to imply some scepticism as to the statement.

"It is conceivable," Thorndyke suggested, "that the visitor may have been disturbed, or that he gave up the attempt when he found it impossible to pick the lock. You see, there is no evidence that he was a skilled burglar. No difficulties were overcome. He simply opened the window and stepped in. The really astonishing thing is that Penrose should have left the place so insecure—that is, assuming that there actually was some valuable property here. The window, as you can see, has no shutters, or even screws or stops, and it looks on to an alley which I understand is invisible from the street. Let us see what that alley is like."

He moved the table away from the window, glancing at a number of parallel scratches on its polished surface, slid up the window and looked out.

"It is quite remarkable," said he. "The window is only a few feet from the ground and the alley is closed by a small wooden gate which has no bolt or latch and seems to be secured only by a lock; which is probably a simple builder's lock which could be easily opened with a skeleton key or a common pick-lock. There is no security whatever. That stout bolt on the room door is, of course, useless as it is on the inside; and the lock is probably a simple affair."

As he spoke, he opened the door and plucked out the key, which he held out for our inspection.

"You see," he said. "Just a plain warded lock which a skilled operator could turn with a bit of stiff wire. Penrose seems to have pinned his faith to the Chubb lock; and perhaps events have justified him."

He slipped the key back into the lock; and this seemed to bring the proceedings to an end. After a few perfunctory expressions of hope that our visit had satisfied us and that we had seen all that we wished to see, our host escorted us through the great gallery and the hall and finally launched us into the street.

CHAPTER 9

THORNDYKE TESTS A THEORY

As we took our way homeward I tried to arrange in my mind the rather confusing experiences of the last hour or two. Those hours, it seemed to me, had been virtually wasted, for we had learned nothing new that bore directly on our problem. This view I ventured to propound to Thorndyke, beginning, naturally, with Mr. Horridge, who had made a deep and disagreeable impression on me.

"Yes," Thorndyke agreed, "he is not a prepossessing person. A bad-mannered man and distinctly sly and suspicious. You probably noted his mental attitude towards Kickweed."

"Yes, distinctly hostile; and I gathered that he is inclined to suspect him of having faked that burglary for his own ends. I suppose, by the way, that it is not possible that he may be right?"

"It is not actually impossible," Thorndyke replied, "but there is nothing to support such a suspicion. Kickweed impressed me very favourably, especially by his loyalty to Penrose. If he is not a liar, the position with regard to the small room is this: some one entered that room; that some one either knew or thought he knew what it contained. He either failed to open that cupboard or he opened it with its own key. The only evidence that he did open it is the piece of paper that was found, which, you notice, was similar to the slips of paper under the specimens in the gallery, excepting that it bore no catalogue number but had an inscription similar to those in the catalogue. That paper strongly suggests that the cupboard had been opened, but is not conclusive, since it might have been dropped by Penrose on some other occasion. But, as I said, its presence is strongly suggestive of a hurried opening of the cupboard at night. There were one or two other points that probably did not escape you."

"You mean the extraordinary weight of the cupboard? That certainly impressed me as significant though I am not quite clear as to what it signifies. It might be due to some ponderous contents, but it seemed to me to suggest an iron safe inside."

"Yes," said Thorndyke, "that is undoubtedly the explanation. The cupboard is a mere wooden case enclosing a large iron safe. That was quite clear from the construction, which is very much like that of an organ case. The sides and top are fixed in position by large screws instead of being keyed in with proper cabinet-maker's joints. The wooden case was built on after the safe had been placed in position."

"Then," said I, "the Chubb lock is a mere hollow pretence."

"Exactly. The wooden case could have been taken off with a common screw-driver. You noticed the scratches on the table?"

"Yes. But, of course, there is no evidence as to when they were made."

"No," he agreed. "Probably they were made at various times. But they are of interest in relation to the arrangement of the cupboard. You must have noticed that they were in two groups, roughly two feet six inches apart and all approximately parallel. They looked like the scratches that would be made by the runners of drawers of that width; and comparing them with the cupboard, one saw that, allowing for the space taken up by the wooden case, there would just be room for a range of drawers of that width. The reasonable inference is that the iron safe houses a range of largish drawers and that these have been taken out from time to time and placed on the table so that their contents could be looked at by the light from the window."

I agreed that this appeared to be the case, but I could not see that it mattered very much whether it was so or not.

"It seems to me," I added, "that we are acquiring a lot of oddments of information none of which has the slightest bearing on the one question that we are asked to answer: Where is Penrose hiding at the present moment?"

"It would be safer," said he, "to say, 'seems to have.' I am picking up all the information that I can in the hope that some of it may turn out to have a bearing on our problem."

"By the way," said I, "why were you so keen on seeing the collection? You were, you know, or you would not have put up with Horridge's insolence. You had some definite point to clear up respecting that pottery fragment. What was it?"

"The point," he replied, "was this. To an archaeologist, that fragment alone would have been an object of interest, since, as you saw, it was possible to make from it a rough, but quite reliable reconstruction. But Penrose is not an archaeologist. He is, as we understood, a mere collector of curios. To such a man, a tiny fragment would be of no interest by itself.

"On the other hand, to an archaeologist, a broken pot is, practically, of the same scientific value as a complete pot. But to the mere collector, or curio-monger, the completeness of a specimen is a matter of cardinal importance. If he has an incomplete specimen, he will spare no trouble or expense to make it complete. He is not concerned with its scientific interest but with its value as a curio.

"Knowing, then, what we did of Penrose, it occurred to me as a bare possibility that this apparently worthless fragment that we found in his pocket might be the product of a definite search *ad hoc*. That he might have re-visited some place from which he had obtained an incomplete specimen with the express purpose of searching for the fragment which would make it complete. The edges of the fragment were freshly fractured. It had been broken off the pot in the course of digging it out. Therefore, the missing piece of the pot was still in the place where the digging had taken place and was certainly recoverable. It was just a speculative possibility, but it was worth testing as we are so short of data, so I decided to look over the collection when I got a chance."

"And I gather," said I, "that you obtained confirmation of your very ingenious theory?"

"I am hoping that I did," he replied; "but we shall see when we get home. If I have, we shall have some sort of clue to the place from which that disastrous homeward journey started."

I forebore to remark that it did not seem to me to matter two straws where it started from, since it was evident that he thought the information worth acquiring. So I merely asked what the clue amounted to.

"Unfortunately," he replied, "it amounts to very little. This is the entry in the catalogue corresponding to the pot which I examined."

He indicated the entry in his note-book, and I read: "Moulin à vent. Julie (Polly)."

"What a perfect and complete ass the fellow must be," I exclaimed, returning the note-book in disgust, "to write meaningless twaddle like that in what purports to be a museum catalogue!"

"I agree with you most warmly," he replied. "But the man's

oddities are an element in our problem. And, of course, these preposterous entries in the catalogue are not meaningless. They have a meaning which is deliberately concealed and which we have got to extract."

"In the case of this one," I asked, "can you make any sense of it? Can you, for instance, discover any connection between an earthen pot and a windmill?"

"Yes," he replied, "I think that is fairly clear, though it doesn't help us much. There is a place in Wiltshire, near Avebury, known as Windmill Hill, where a certain distinctive kind of neolithic pottery has been found and which has been named the Windmill Hill type. Probably, this pot is an example of that type, but that is a question that we can easily settle, though it doesn't seem to be an important one. The information that we want is probably contained in the other two words; and, at present, I can make nothing of them."

"No," I agreed, "they are pretty obscure. Who is Julie? What is she? And likewise: Who is Polly? Good God! What damned nonsense it is!"

He smiled at my exasperation. "You are quite right, Jervis," said he. "It is monstrous that two learned medical jurists should have to expend their time and intellect in solving a set of silly puzzles. But it is part of our present job."

"Do you find any method in this fellow's madness?" I asked. "I noticed you copying out a lot of this balderdash."

"There is a little method," he replied. "Not much. But this entry, relating to that little embossed red ware dish that you saw, will illustrate Penrose's method. You see, it reads: 'Sammy. Pot Sand. Sinbad.' Now, this Gaulish red ware is usually described as Samian ware, so we may take it that 'Sammy' means 'Samian.' The interpretation of 'Pot Sand' is also fairly obvious. There is a shoal in the Thames Estuary off Whitstable on which it is believed that a Roman ship, laden with pottery, went aground and broke up. From time immemorial, oyster dredgers working over that shoal have brought up quantities of Roman pottery, including Samian ware, whence the shoal has been named The Pan Sand, and is so marked on the Admiralty charts. Penrose's 'Pot Sand' is, therefore, presumably The Pan Sand; and as to Sinbad, we may assume him to have been a sailor, probably an oyster dredger or a whelk fisher."

"I have no doubt that you are right," said I, "but it is difficult to consider such childish twaddle with patience. I should like to kick the fellow."

"I should be delighted if you could," said he, "for, since you would have to catch him before you could kick him, that would mean that our problem would be solved. By the way, we shall have to contrive, somehow, to make the acquaintance of Mr. Lockhart. I wonder if Brodribb knows him."

"You think he could tell us what was in that small room. But I doubt if he would. Penrose would probably have sworn him to secrecy, and, in any case, it would be a matter of professional confidence. But it seems to me that the burglary is a side issue, though I know you will say that we can't judge which issues are side issues."

"At any rate," he retorted, "the burglary is not one. It is very material. For, if Penrose was the burglar, he must be in possession of property which he intends to dispose of, by which, if we knew what it was, we might be able to trace him. And if the burglar was not Penrose, we should very much like to know who he was."

I did not quite see why; but, as our discussion had now brought us to our doorstep, there was no opportunity to pursue the question; for, as I had expected, Thorndyke made straight for the laboratory, and I followed, with mild curiosity as to the test that I assumed to be in view. As we entered, the sound of Polton's lathe in the adjacent workshop informed us that he had some job on hand there, but his quick ear had noted our arrival and he came in at once to see if his services were required.

"I need not disturb you, Polton," said Thorndyke. "It is only a matter of a small plaster mould."

"You are not disturbing me, sir," replied Polton. "I am just turning up a few spare tool handles to pass the time. You would like the quick-setting plaster, I suppose?"

"If you please," Thorndyke replied; and as Polton retired to fetch the materials, he produced from his pocket a small tin box from which he tenderly shook out into his hand a slab of moulding wax. Looking at it as it lay on his palm, I saw that it was a "squeeze" of the edge of the pot, the gap in the broken rim being represented by a wart-like swelling of the shape of the missing piece. Noting the exact correspondence, I remarked:

"You hardly want the plaster. The shape of the squeeze is exact enough for comparison."

"Yes," he agreed, "but an actual measurement is always better than a judgment of resemblance."

Here, Polton returned with a jar of the special plaster, a rubber bowl, a jug of water and the other necessaries for the operation. Unobtrusively, but firmly taking possession of the squeeze, he laid it in one of the little paper trays that he used for making small moulds or casts, brushed it over lightly with a camel-hair brush containing a trace of oil, and then proceeded to mix the plaster. This had to be done quickly, since the special plaster set solid in about five minutes; and I could not but admire the calm, unhurried way in which Polton carried the process through its various stages. At exactly the right moment, the plaster was dropped on to the squeeze, blown with the breath into all the interstices, and then the remainder poured on until the little tray was full to the brim; and even as the last drops were being persuaded out of the bowl with a spoon, the change began which transformed the creamy liquid into a white solid like the "icing" on a wedding cake.

At this point Thorndyke retired to fetch the fragment and Polton and I took the opportunity to clean the bowl and spoon and spread on the bench a sheet of newspaper to receive the inevitable crumbs and scrapings; a most necessary precaution, for plaster, in spite of its delicate whiteness, is one of the dirtiest of materials. The particles which detach themselves from a cast seem to spread themselves over a whole room, with a special predilection for the soles of shoes, whence they distribute impressions on stairs and passages in the most surprising and unexpected fashion. But a sheet of paper collects the particles and enables them to be removed tidily before they have the opportunity to develop their diabolical tendencies.

When Thorndyke returned our labours were completed, and the little tray reposed on the paper with the plaster tools beside it.

"Is it hard enough to open?" Thorndyke asked.

Polton tested with his finger-nail the smooth, white mass that bulged up from the tray, and, having reported that it was "set as hard as stone," proceeded carefully to shell it out of the paper container. Then he scraped away the projecting edges until the wax was free all round. A little cautious persuading with the thumb induced the squeeze to separate from the plaster, when Polton laid them down side by side and looked expectantly at Thorndyke. The cast was now clearly recognizable as the replica of a portion of the outside surface of the pot, including the rim and the gap where a piece of the rim had been broken away.

Thorndyke now produced the fragment of pottery, and, holding it delicately between his finger and thumb—for the plaster was still moist and tender—very carefully inserted it into the gap; and as it dropped in, exactly filling the space, with a perfect fit at every point, he remarked:

"I think that settles the question of identity. This fragment is the piece that is missing from the museum pot."

"Yes," I agreed. "The proof is absolutely conclusive. What is not quite obvious to me is the importance of the fact which is proved. I see that it strongly supports your theory that the fragment was the product of a definite search, but it is not clear to me that even the confirmation of your theory has any particular value."

"It has now very little value," he replied. "The importance of the fact which this experiment has established is that it carries us out of the region of the unknown into that of the known. If this fragment was part of the museum pot, then the place from which that pot came is the place from which this fragment came."

"Yes," said I, "that is clear enough. And it is fair to assume that the place whence this fragment came is the place from which Penrose started on his homeward journey. But as we don't know where the pot came from, I can't see that we have got so very far from the unknown. We have simply connected one unknown with another unknown."

Thorndyke smiled indulgently. "You are a proper pessimist, Jervis," said he. "But you will, at least, admit that we have narrowed the unknown down to a very small area. We have got to find out where that pot came from; and I don't think we shall have very much difficulty. Probably the catalogue entry embodies some clue."

"But," I persisted, "even if you discover that, I don't see that you will be any further advanced. You will know where Penrose came from, but that knowledge will not help you to discover where he has gone to. At least, that is how it appears to me. But perhaps there is some point that I have overlooked."

"My impression is," Thorndyke replied, "that you have not given any serious consideration to this curious and puzzling case. If you would turn it over in your mind carefully and try to see the connections between the various facts that are known to us, you would realize that we have got to begin by re-tracing that last journey to its starting-point."

With this, he picked up the cast with the embedded fragment of pottery to put them into the box with the other "exhibits"; and, as he retired, Polton (who had been listening with a curious intentness to our conversation) gathered up the newspaper and the plaster appliances and went back to his lathe.

CHAPTER 10

INTRODUCES MR. CRABBE

Thorndyke's rather cryptic observation gave me considerable food for thought. But it was not very nourishing food, for no conclusion emerged. He was quite right in believing that I had given little serious consideration to the case of Daniel Penrose. It had not greatly interested me, and I had seen no practical method by which the problem could be approached. Nor did I now; and the only result of my cogitations was to confirm my previous opinion that I had missed some crucial point in the evidence and to make me suspect that there was in this case something more than met the eye.

This latter suspicion deepened when I reflected on Thorndyke's concluding statement: "You would realize that we have got to begin by re-tracing that last journey to its starting-point." But I did not realize anything of the sort. The problem, as I understood it, was to discover the present whereabouts of Daniel Penrose; and to this problem, the starting-point of his last known journey seemed completely irrelevant. But in that I knew that I must be wrong; a conviction which merely brought me back to the unsatisfactory conclusion that I had failed to take account of some vital element in the case.

But it was not only in respect of that disastrous return journey that I was puzzled by Thorndyke's proceedings. There was his unaccountable interest in the burglary at Queen Square. Apparently, he believed the burglar to have been Penrose himself; and in this I was disposed to concur. But suppose that we were able to establish the fact with certainty; what help would it give us in tracing Penrose to his hiding-place? So far as I could see, it would not help us at all; and Thorndyke's keenness in regard to the burglary only increased my bewilderment.

Naturally, then, I was all agog when, a few days later, Thorndyke announced that Mr. Lockhart was coming in to smoke a pipe with us on the following evening; for here seemed to be a chance of getting some fresh light on the subject. Lockhart was being lured to our chambers to be pumped, little as he probably suspected it, and if I listened attentively, I might catch some of the drippings.

"You haven't forgotten," said I, "that Miller is likely to call to-morrow evening?"

"No," he replied, "but we have no appointment so he may choose some other time. At any rate, we must take our chance; and it won't matter so very much if he does drop in."

It seemed to me that the superintendent would be very much in the way and I sincerely hoped that he would choose some other evening for his visit. But Thorndyke presumably knew his own business.

"How did you get hold of Lockhart?" I asked. "Did Brodribb know him?"

"I didn't ask him," Thorndyke replied. "I saw Lockhart's name in the list of cases at the Central Criminal Court so I dropped in there and introduced myself. When I told him that I was looking into Penrose's affairs, he was very ready to come in and hear all about the case."

I laughed aloud. "So," said I, "this poor deluded gentleman is coming with the belief that he is going to be the recipient of information. It is a rank imposition."

"Not at all," he protested. "We shall tell him what we know of the case, and no doubt we shall learn something from him in exchange. At least, I hope we shall."

"Then," said I, "you are an optimist. If he knows anything that you don't, you can be pretty certain that he learned it under the seal of the confessional."

Thorndyke agreed that I was probably right. "But," he added hopefully, "we shall see. It is sometimes possible to learn something from what a man refuses to disclose."

I made a mental note of this observation and kept it in mind when our visitor arrived on the following evening, for it suggested to me that Thorndyke's questions might be more illuminating than the answers that they might evoke, particularly if our friend should turn out to be uncommunicative. But this did not, at first, appear to be the case, for, after a little general conversation, he led up to the subject of Daniel Penrose of his own accord.

"I did not quite gather what it was," said he, "that your clients expected you to do. If it is a permissible question, what sort of inquiry are you engaged in?"

"It is a perfectly permissible question," replied Thorndyke. "I can tell you all about the case without any breach of professional confidence as the main facts are already in the public domain. What I am expected to do is to discover the place in which Mr. Penrose is at present hiding, or at least to locate him sufficiently to make it possible to produce him, if necessary."

"And apparently he doesn't want to be produced? But why not? Why has he gone into hiding? My very discreet informant told me that he had gone away from home and left no address, but she didn't mention any reasons for his disappearing. Are there any substantial reasons?"

"He thinks that there are," replied Thorndyke. "But, if you are interested, I will give you a sketch of the circumstances of his disappearance, so far as they are known to me."

"I am very much interested," said Lockhart. "Penrose is a queer fellow—the sort of fellow who might do queer things—and I don't know that I am so violently fond of him. But he always interested me as a human oddity, and I should like to hear what has happened to him."

Thereupon, Thorndyke embarked on a concise but detailed account of the strange circumstances which surrounded Penrose's disappearance from human ken; and I listened with almost as much attention as Lockhart himself. For Thorndyke's clear summary of the events in their due order was a useful refresher to my own memory. But, what specially amused and delighted me was the masterly tactical approach to the cross-examination which I felt pretty sure was to follow. Thorndyke's perfectly open and unreserved narrative, treating the whole affair as one generally known, in respect of which there was not the slightest occasion for secrecy, was an admirable preparation for a few discreet questions. It would be difficult for Lockhart to adopt a reticent attitude after being treated with such complete confidence.

"Well," said Lockhart, when the story was told, "it is a queer affair, but, as I remarked, Penrose is a queer fellow. Still, there are some points that rather surprise me."

"For instance?" Thorndyke suggested.

"It is a small matter," replied Lockhart, "and I may be mistaken in the man, but I shouldn't have expected him to be the worse for liquor. You seemed to imply that he was definitely squiffy."

"It is only hearsay," Thorndyke reminded him, "and an inexpert opinion at that. The report may have been exaggerated. But, in your experience of him, should you say that he is a strictly temperate man?"

"I wouldn't go so far as that," said Lockhart. "He is most uncommonly fond of what he calls 'the vintages of the Fortunate Isles' and the 'elderly and fuscous wine of Jerez,' and I should think that he gets through a fair amount of them, but he impressed me as a man who would take a glass, or two or three glasses, of sherry or Madeira pretty often, but not a great quantity at once. Your regular nipper, especially of wine, doesn't often get drunk."

"No," Thorndyke agreed, "though sherry and Madeira are strong wines. What were the other points?"

"Well," replied Lockhart, "doesn't it strike you that the actions of Penrose are rather disproportionate to the cause? He seems to have been abnormally funky. After all, it was only a motor accident, and there isn't any clear evidence that it was his car. He could have denied that he was there. And, in any case, it doesn't seem worth his while to bolt off and abandon his home and all his worldly possessions. If he had committed a murder or arson or something really serious, it would have been different."

"It was manslaughter," I remarked; "and a rather bad case. And the vintages of the Fortunate Isles didn't make it any less culpable. He might have got a longish term of hard labour, even if he escaped penal servitude."

"I don't think it was as bad as that," said Lockhart. "At any rate, if I had been in his place, I would have stayed and faced the music; and I would have left it to the prosecution to prove that I was on that road."

"That," said Thorndyke, "is a matter of temperament. From your knowledge of Penrose, should you have taken him for a nervous, panicky man?"

Lockhart reflected for a few moments. "You speak," said he, "of my knowledge of Penrose. But, really, I hardly know him at all. I made his acquaintance quite recently, and I have not met him half a dozen times."

"You don't know his people, then?"

"No. I know nothing about his family affairs. Our acquaintance arose out of a chance meeting at a curio shop in Soho. We walked away from the shop together, discussing collecting and antiques, and he then invited me to go and inspect his treasures. Which I did;

and that is the only occasion on which I was ever in his house. But I must say that it was a memorable experience."

"In what way?" Thorndyke asked.

"Well," replied Lockhart, "there was the man, himself; one of the oddest fishes that I have ever encountered. But I dare say you have heard about his peculiarities."

"I understand that he is a most inconveniently secretive gentleman, and also that he has an inveterate habit of calling things by their wrong names."

"Yes," said Lockhart, "that is what I mean. He speaks, not in parables, but in a sort of cross-word puzzle, leaving you to make out his meaning by the exercise of your wits. You can imagine what it was like to be shown round a collection by a man who called all the specimens by utterly and ridiculously inappropriate names."

"Yes," said Thorndyke; "rather confusing, I should suppose. But you did see the collection; and perhaps he showed you the catalogue too?"

"He did. In fact, he made a point of letting me see it in order, I think, to enjoy my astonishment. What an amazing document it is! If ever he should have to plead insanity, I should think that the production of that catalogue would make medical testimony unnecessary. I take it that you have seen it and the collection, too?"

"Yes," said Thorndyke, "I examined the catalogue and made a few extracts with notes of the pieces to which they referred. And I was shown round the collection by Mr. Horridge, Penrose's executor. But I have an idea that he did not show us the whole collection. We saw only the collection in the great gallery; but probably you were more favoured, as you were shown round by the proprietor?"

The question was very adroitly thrown out; but, at this point, Mr. Lockhart, as I had expected, developed a sudden evasiveness.

"It is impossible for me to say," he replied; "as I don't know what the whole collection consisted of. I assumed that he had shown me all that there was to see."

"Probably you were right," said Thorndyke; and then, coming boldly to the real issue, he asked: "Did he show you the contents of the small room?"

For some moments Lockhart did not reply, but sat looking profoundly uncomfortable. At length, he answered in an apologetic tone: "It's a ridiculous situation, but you know what sort of man

Penrose is. The fact is that when he showed me his collection, he made it a condition that I should regard the transaction as a strictly confidential one and that I should not discuss his possessions or communicate their nature or amount to any person whatsoever. It is an absurd condition, but I accepted it and consequently I am not in a position to tell you what he did actually show me. But I don't suppose that it is of any consequence. I take it that you have no special interest in his collection."

"On the contrary," said Thorndyke, "we have a very special interest in the collection, and particularly that part of it which was kept in the small room. Since Penrose went away, there has been a burglary—or a suspected burglary—at his house. The small room was undoubtedly entered one night, and there is a suspicion that the big cupboard was opened. But, if it was, it was opened with a key, as there was no trace of any injury to the doors. On the other hand, it is possible that the burglar failed to pick the lock and was disturbed. But Penrose has the only key of the cupboard, so there are no means of ascertaining, without picking the lock or forcing the door, whether there has or has not been a robbery; and we have decided that it would not be admissible to do either in Penrose's absence. Nevertheless, it is important for us to know what was in that cupboard."

"I don't see why," said Lockhart. "If it is not admissible to force the door—and I entirely agree with you that it is not—I don't see that it would help you to know what was in the cupboard—or whether it contained anything at all. Supposing that it had certain contents, you cannot ascertain, without opening it, whether those contents are still there or whether they have been stolen. But, if you say that the lock has not been picked nor the door forced, and Penrose has the only key, doesn't that prove pretty conclusively that no burglary has taken place?"

At this moment, a familiar sound came to justify my fears of an interruption. I had taken the precaution to shut the outer oak door when Lockhart had entered. But the light from our windows must have been visible from without. At any rate, the well-known six taps from a walking-stick—in three pairs, like the strokes of a ship's bell—spelled out the name of the visitor who stood on our threshold. Accordingly, I rose and threw open the doors, closing them again as the superintendent walked in.

"Now, don't let me disturb any one," exclaimed Miller, observing that, at his entrance, Lockhart had risen with the air of taking his departure. "I am only a bird of passage. I have just dropped in to collect those documents and hear if the doctor has any remarks to make on them."

Thorndyke walked over to a cabinet, and, unlocking it, took out a small bundle of papers which he handed to the superintendent.

"I can't give a very decided opinion on them," said he. "It is really a case for a handwriting expert. All that I can say is that there are none of the regular signs of forgery; no indications of tracing or of very deliberate writing. The separate words seem to have been written quickly and freely. But I got the impression—it is only an impression—that there is a slight lack of continuity, as if each word had been executed as a separate act."

"I don't quite follow that," Miller said.

"I mean," Thorndyke explained, "that—assuming it, for the moment, to be a forgery—the forger's method might have been, instead of copying words continuously from an original, to take one word, copy it two or three times so as to get to know it thoroughly, then write it quickly on the document and go on to the next word. Written in that way, the words would not form such completely continuous lines as if the whole were written at a single operation. But you had better get the opinion of a first-class expert."

"Very well," said Miller, "I will; and I will tell him what you have suggested. And now, I had better take myself off and leave you to your conference."

"You need not run away, Miller," Thorndyke protested, very much to my surprise. "There is no conference. Fill up a glass of grog and light a cigar like a Christian."

He indicated the whisky decanter and siphon and the box of cigars, which had been offered to, and declined by, Lockhart, and drew up a chair.

"Well," said Miller, seating himself and selecting a cigar, "if you are sure that I am not breaking in on a consultation, I shall be delighted to spend half an hour or so in your intellectual society." He thoughtfully mixed himself a temperate whisky and soda, and then, with a quizzical glance at Thorndyke inquired: "Was there any little item of information that you were requiring?"

"Really, Miller," Thorndyke protested, "you underestimate your personal charms. When I ask for the pleasure of your society, need you look for an ulterior motive?"

Miller regarded me with a crafty smile and solemnly closed one eye. "I'm not looking for one," he replied. "I merely asked a question."

"And I am glad you did," said Thorndyke, "because you have reminded me that there was a little matter that I wanted to ask you about."

Miller grinned at me again. "Ah," he chuckled. "Now we are coming to it. What was the question?"

"It was concerned with a man named Crabbe. Jonathan Crabbe of Hatton Garden. Do you know him?"

"He is not a personal friend," Miller replied. "And he is not Mr. Crabbe of Hatton Garden just at present. He is Mr. Crabbe of Maidstone Jail. What did you want to know about him?"

"Anything that you can tell me. And you needn't mind Mr. Lockhart. He is one of the Devil's own, like the rest of us."

"I know Mr. Lockhart very well by sight and by reputation," said the superintendent. "Now, with regard to this man Crabbe. He had a place, as you say, in Hatton Garden where he professed to carry on the business of a diamond broker and dealer in precious stones. I don't know anything about the diamond brokery, but he was a dealer in precious stones all right. That's why he is at Maidstone. He got two years for receiving."

"Do you remember when he was convicted?"

"I can't give you the exact date off hand," replied Miller. "It wasn't my case. I was only an interested onlooker. But it was somewhere about the end of last September. Is that near enough?"

"Quite near enough for my purpose," Thorndyke replied. "Do you know anything more about him? Is he an old hand?"

"There," replied Miller, "you are asking me a question that I can't answer with certainty. There were no previous convictions against him, but it was clear that he had been carrying on as a fence for a considerable time. There was definite evidence of that. But there was another little affair which never got beyond suspicion. I looked into that myself; and I may say that I was half inclined then to collar the worthy Jonathan. But when we came to talk the case over, we came to the conclusion that there was not enough evidence and no chance of getting any more. So we put our notes of the case into cold storage in the hope that something fresh might turn up some day. And I still hope that it may, for it was an important case and we got considerable discredit for not being able to spot the chappies who did the job."

"Is there any reason why you should not tell us about the case?" Thorndyke asked.

"Well, you know," Miller replied, "it was only a case of suspicion, though, in my own mind, I feel pretty cock-sure that our suspicions were justified. Still, I don't think there would be any harm in my just giving you an outline of the case, on the understanding that this is in strict confidence."

"I think you can take that for granted," said Thorndyke. "We are all lawyers and used to keeping our own counsel."

"Then," said Miller, "I will give you a sketch of the case; what we know and what I think. It's just possible that you may remember the case as it made a good deal of stir at the time. The papers referred to it as 'The Billington Jewel Robbery.'"

"I have just a faint recollection of the affair," Thorndyke replied; "but I can't recall any of the details."

"It was a remarkable case in some respects," Miller proceeded, "and the most remarkable feature was the ridiculous softness of the job. Billington was a silly fool. He had an important collection of jewellery, which is a stupid thing in itself. No man ought to keep in a private house a collection of property of such value—and portable property, too—as to offer a continual temptation to the criminal class. But he did; and what is more, he kept the whole lot of jewels in a set of mahogany cabinets that you could have opened with a pen-knife. It is astonishing that he went on so long without a burglary.

"However, he got what he deserved at last. He had gone across to Paris, to buy some more of the stuff, I believe, when, some fine night, some cracksmen dropped in and did the job. It was perfectly simple. They just let themselves in, prised the drawers open with a jemmy, cleared them out and went off quietly with the whole collection. Nobody knew anything about it until the servants came down in the morning and found the drawers all gaping open.

"Then, of course, there was a rare philaloo. The police were called in and our people made a careful inspection of the premises. But it had been such an easy job that anybody might have done it. There was nothing that was characteristic of any known burglar. But, on taking impressions of the jemmy-marks and a few other trifles, we were inclined to connect it with one or two other jobs of a similar type in which jewels had been taken. But we had not been able to fix those cases on any particular crooks, though we had a growing suspicion of two men who were also suspected of receiving. Of those two men, one was Jonathan Crabbe and the other was a man named Wingate. So we kept those two gentlemen under pretty close observation and made a few discreet inquiries. But it was a long time before we could get anything definite; and when, at last, we did manage to drop on Mr. Crabbe, it was only on a charge of receiving. The Billington job still remained in the air. And that's where it is still."

"And what about Wingate?" asked Thorndyke.

"Oh, he disappeared. Apparently, he rumbled the fact that he was getting a bit of attention from the police, and didn't like it. So he cut his connection with Crabbe and went away."

"And have you lost sight of him?" Thorndyke asked.

"Yes. You see, we never had anything against him but his association with Crabbe, and that may have been a perfectly innocent business connection. And our inquiries seemed to show that he belonged to quite a respectable family, and the man, himself, was of a decidedly superior type; a smart, dressy sort of fellow with a waxed moustache and an eye-glass. Quite a toff, in fact. The only thing about him that seemed at all fishy was the fact that he was using an assumed name. But there was not so very much even in that, for we ascertained that he had been on the stage for a time, and he had probably taken the name of Wingate in preference to his family name, which was rather an odd one—Deodatus Pettigrew."

"You never traced any of the proceeds of the robbery?" Thorndyke suggested.

"No. Of course, jewellery is often difficult to trace if the stones are taken out of their settings and the mounts melted down. But these jewels of Billington's ought to have been easier than most to trace, as a good many of them were quite unusual and could only have been disguised by re-cutting, which would have brought down their value a lot. And there was one that couldn't have been disguised at all. I remember the description of it quite well. It was rather a famous piece, known as the Jacobite Jewel. It consisted principally of a lump of black opal matrix with a fire opal in the centre, and on this fire opal was carved a portrait of the Old Pretender, who called himself James the Third. I believe there was quite a little history attached to it. But the whole collection was rather famous. Billington was particularly keen on opals, and I believe that his collection of them was one of the finest known."

"Had you any inkling as to what had become of this loot?" Thorndyke asked. "The thieves could hardly have been able to afford to put the whole of it away into storage for an indefinite time."

"No," agreed Miller. "They would have had to get rid of the stuff somehow. We thought it just possible that there might be some collector behind the affair."

"But," I objected, "a collector would probably know all about the specimens in other collections and particularly a famous piece like this Jacobite Jewel. And he would be almost certain to have heard of the robbery. It would be a matter of special interest to him."

"Yes, I know," said Miller. "But collectors are queer people. Some of them are mighty unscrupulous. When a man has got the itch to possess, there is no saying what he will not do to gratify it. Some of the rich Americans who have made their fortunes by pretty sharp practice, are not above a little sharp practice in spending them. And your millionaire collector is dead keen on getting something that is unique; something of which he can say that it is the only one of its kind in the world. And if it has a history attached to it, so much the better. I shouldn't be at all surprised if that Jacobite Jewel had been smuggled out of the country together with the great collection of opals. It is even possible that Crabbe had negotiated the sale before the robbery was committed; but, of course, it is also possible that I may be mistaken and that Crabbe may have had nothing to do with the robbery. We are all liable to make mistakes."

Here the superintendent, having come to the end of his story, emptied his glass, re-lit his cigar and looked at his watch.

"Dear me!" he exclaimed, "how the time does go when you are enjoying intellectual conversation—especially if it is your own. It's time I made a move. No, thank you; not another drop. But, well, yes, I will take another of these excellent cigars. You have listened very attentively to my yarn, and I hope you have picked up something useful from my chatter."

"I always pick up something useful from your chatter, as you call it," replied Thorndyke, rising as the superintendent rose to depart; "but on this occasion you have given me quite a lot to think about."

He walked to the door with Miller and even escorted him out on to the landing; and meanwhile, I occupied myself in restraining, with exaggerated hospitality, a strong tendency on the part of our guest to rise and follow the superintendent. For I could not let him go until I had seen what Thorndyke's next move was to be.

The superintendent's narrative had given me a very curious experience, in respect of its effect on Lockhart. At first, he had listened with lively interest, probably comparing the Billington collection with that of Penrose. But presently he began to look distinctly uncomfortable and to steal furtive glances at Thorndyke and me. I kept him unobtrusively under observation, and Thorndyke, I know, was watching him narrowly, though no one who did not know him would have suspected it, and we both observed the change of manner. But when Miller mentioned the Jacobite Jewel and went on to describe its appearance, the expression on Lockhart's face was unmistakable. It was that of a man who has suffered a severe shock.

Having seen the last of the superintendent, Thorndyke closed both the doors and went back to his chair.

"That was a queer story of Miller's," he remarked, addressing Lockhart. "One does not often hear of a receiver including burglary in his accomplishments. I am disposed to think that Miller's surmise as to the destination of the swag from the Billington robbery is about correct. What do you think, Lockhart?"

"You mean," the latter replied, "that it was smuggled out of the country."

"No," said Thorndyke, "I don't mean that, Lockhart, and you know I don't. What I am suggesting is that the Billington opals, including the Jacobite Jewel, are, or were, in Penrose's possession; that they were in the cupboard in the small room and that you saw them there."

Lockhart flushed hotly, but he kept his temper, replying with mild facetiousness:

"Now you know, Thorndyke, it's of no use for you to try the suggesting dodge on me. I am a practising barrister, and I have used it too often myself. I have told you that I gave an undertaking to Penrose not to discuss his collection with anybody; and I intend to honour that undertaking to the letter and in the spirit."

"Very well, Lockhart," Thorndyke rejoined, "we will leave it at that. Probably, I should adopt the same attitude if I were in your position, though I doubt if I should have given the undertaking. We will let the collection go, unless you would consider it admissible to discuss the source of some of the things in the big room, which we all saw. The question as to where he got some of those things has a direct bearing on the further question as to where he is lurking at the present moment."

"I don't see the connection," said Lockhart, "but if you do, that is all that matters. What is it that you want to know?"

"I should like to know," Thorndyke replied, "what his methods of collection are. Has he been in the habit of attending farmhouse auctions, or prowling about in labourers' cottages? Or did he get his pieces through regular dealers?"

"As to that," said Lockhart, "I can only tell you what he told me. He professed to have discovered many of his treasures in cottage parlours and in country inns and elsewhere, and to have practised on quite an extensive scale what he called 'resurrectionist activities,' but he was mighty secret about the actual localities. My impression is that his explorations were largely bunkum. I suspect that the bulk of his collection came from the dealers, and particularly from the antique shop that I mentioned to you. In fact, he almost admitted as much, for he told me that when his explorations drew a blank, he was accustomed to fall back on the Popinjay."

"The Popinjay?" I repeated.

"The proprietor of the antique shop was a man named Parrott, but I need not say that Penrose never referred to him by that name. He was always 'our psittacoid friend,' or 'Monsieur le Perroquet' or 'the Popinjay.' You will even find him referred to in those terms in the catalogue."

"That is useful to know," said Thorndyke. "I met with some entries containing the words, 'Psitt,' 'Perro' and 'Pop' and could make nothing of them. Now I realize that they represented purchases from Mr. Parrott. And there was an entry, 'Sweeney's resurrection.' That, I suppose, had a similar meaning. Do you know who Sweeney is?"

Lockhart laughed as he replied: "No, I have never heard of him, though I remember the entry. The only thing that I feel sure of is that his name is not Sweeney. Possibly it is Todd; and he is probably a dealer in antiquities. The piece, I remember, is an Anglo-Saxon brooch; and we may guess that Mr. Sweeney Todd got it from a Saxon burial ground in the course of some unauthorized excavations."

"That seems likely," said Thorndyke. "I must look up the list of dealers in antiquities in the directory and see if I can find out who he is."

"But does it matter who he is?" asked Lockhart. "If you are trying to discover the whereabouts of our elusive friend, I don't quite follow your methods."

"My dear Lockhart," Thorndyke replied, "my methods are of the utmost simplicity. I know practically nothing about Penrose, his habits and his customs, and I am out to pick up any items of information on the subject that I can gather, in the hope that some of them may prove to have some bearing on my quest. After all, it is only the ordinary legal method which you, yourself, are in the habit of practising."

"I suppose it is," Lockhart admitted. "But, fortunately for me, I have never had a problem of this kind to deal with. I can't imagine a more hopeless task than trying to find a very artful, secretive man who doesn't mean to be found."

At this moment, I heard the sound of a key being inserted in the outer door. Then the inner door opened and Polton entered with an apologetic crinkle.

"I have just looked in, sir," he announced, "to see if there is anything that you wanted before I go out. I shall be away about a couple of hours."

"Thank you, Polton," Thorndyke replied. "No, there is nothing that I shall want that I can't get for myself."

As Thorndyke spoke, Lockhart looked round quickly and then stood up, holding out his hand.

"This is a very unexpected pleasure, Mr. Polton," said he. "I didn't know that you were a denizen of the Temple; and I was afraid that I had lost sight of you for good, now that Parrott's is no more." He shook hands heartily with our ingenious friend and explained to us: "Mr. Polton and I are quite old acquaintances. He, also, was a frequenter of Parrott's establishment, and the leading authority on clocks, watches, hall-marks and other recondite matters."

"You speak of Parrott's shop," said Thorndyke, "as a thing of the past. Is our psittacoid friend deceased, or has he gone out of business?"

"Parrott is still to the good, so far as I know," replied Lockhart, "but the business is defunct. I suspect that it was never more than half alive. Then poor Parrott had a double misfortune. Penrose, who was by far his best customer, disappeared; and then his cabinet-maker—a remarkably clever old man named Tims—died and could not be replaced. So there was no one left to do the restorations which were the mainstay of the business. I was sorry to find the shop closed when I came back from my travels on circuit. It was quite a loss, wasn't it, Mr. Polton?"

"It was to me," replied Polton, regretfully. "Many a pleasant and profitable hour have I spent in the workshop. To a man who uses his hands, it was a liberal education to watch Mr. Tims at work. I have never seen any man use wood-working tools as he did."

With this, Polton wished our guests "Good evening!" and took himself off. As the outer door closed, Lockhart asked:

"If this is not an impertinent question, what is Mr. Polton's connection with this establishment? He has always been rather a mystery to me."

"He is rather a mystery to me," Thorndyke replied, with a laugh. "He says that he is my servant. I say that he is my faithful friend and Jervis's. Nominally, he is our laboratory assistant and artificer. Actually, since he can do or make anything and insists on doing everything that is to be done, he is a sort of universal fairy godmother to us both. And I can assure you that he is not unappreciated."

"I am glad to know that," said Lockhart. "We all—the frequenters of Parrott's I mean—held him in the greatest respect, and none more so than Penrose."

"Oh, he knew Penrose, did he?" said I, suddenly enlightened as to Polton's interest in our conversations respecting the missing man. "He has never mentioned the fact."

"Perhaps you have never given him an opening," Lockhart suggested, not unreasonably. "But they were quite well acquainted; in fact, the very last time that I saw Penrose, he and Mr. Polton were walking away from the shop together, carrying a lantern clock that Mr. Polton had been restoring."

We continued for some time to discuss Polton's remarkable personality and his versatile gifts and abilities, in which Lockhart appeared to be deeply interested. At length the latter glanced at his watch and rose.

"I have made an unconscionably long visit," said he, as he prepared to depart; "but it is your fault for making the time pass so agreeably."

"You certainly have not out-stayed your welcome," Thorndyke replied, "and I hope you will stay longer next time."

With this exchange of civilities, we escorted our guest out to the landing, and, having wished him "Good night!" returned to our chamber to discuss the events of the evening.

CHAPTER II

RE-ENTER MR. KICKWEED

When I had closed the door and drifted back towards my chair, I cast an expectant glance at Thorndyke; but, as he maintained a placidly reflective air, and thoughtfully re-filled his pipe in silence, I ventured to open the inevitable discussion.

"May I take it that my revered senior is satisfied with the evening's entertainment?"

"Eminently so," he replied; "in fact, considerably beyond my most sanguine expectations. We have made appreciable progress."

"In what direction?" I asked. "Does Miller's story throw any light on the case?"

"I think so," he answered. "What he told us, in conjunction with what Lockhart refused to tell us, seems to help us to this extent; that it appears to disclose a motive for the burglary, or the attempt."

"Do you mean that it establishes the probability that there was something there worth stealing and that somebody besides Penrose knew of it?"

"No," he replied, "though that also is true. But, what is in my mind is this: When Penrose disappeared, either for good or for some considerable time, there arose the probability that, sooner or later, the cupboard in the small room would be opened for inspection by Horridge or some other person claiming authority. But if that cupboard contained—as I have no doubt it did—a quantity of stolen property, the identifiable proceeds of a known robbery, a very awkward situation would be created."

"Yes," I agreed, "it would be awkward for Penrose when Miller caught the scent. There would be a hue and cry with a vengeance. And it might be unpleasant for Mr. Crabbe if any connection could be traced between him and Penrose. I suppose there can be no doubt that the stuff was really there?"

"It is only an inference," Thorndyke replied, "but I am convinced that the Billington jewels were in that cupboard and that Lockhart saw them there. Everything points to that conclusion. You saw how intensely uncomfortable Lockhart looked when Miller described the stolen jewels; and you must have noticed that he was perfectly willing to discuss the general collection. From which we may reasonably infer that his promise of secrecy referred only to the contents of the small room. Besides, if the stolen jewels had not been there, or he had not seen them, he would certainly have said so when I challenged him. The denial would have been no breach of his promise."

"No," I agreed, "I think you are right in assuming that he saw them, though how Penrose could have been such an idiot as to show them at all is beyond my comprehension—that is, if he knew that they were stolen goods, which I gather is your opinion."

"It is not by any means certain that he did," said Thorndyke. "Evidently he is quite ignorant of the things that he collects. The promise may have been only a manifestation of his habitual secrecy, accentuated by the knowledge that he had acquired the jewels from some rather shady dealer. The evidence seems a little contradictory."

"At any rate," said I, "it was a lucky chance that Miller happened to drop in this evening. Or wasn't it a chance at all? There was just a suspicion of arrangement in the way things fell out. Did you know that Miller would select this evening for his call?"

"In effect, I may say that I did. I had good reason to believe that he would call this evening, and, as you suggest, I made my arrangements accordingly. But those arrangements did not work out according to plan, for I knew nothing of the Billington robbery. Miller's disclosure was a windfall and it made the rest of my plan unnecessary."

"Then what had you proposed to do?"

"My intention was," Thorndyke replied, "to demonstrate to Lockhart that there had been transactions between Crabbe and Penrose. Of course, I could have done this without Miller's help, but I thought that if he heard of Crabbe's misdeeds from a police officer he would be more impressed and, therefore, more amenable to questions. But, as I said, Miller's story did all that was necessary."

"Then," said I, "there was a connection between Crabbe and Penrose, and that connection was known to you. How did you find that out? And, by the way, how did you come by your knowledge of Mr. Crabbe? I had never heard of him until you mentioned his name."

Thorndyke chuckled in his exasperating way. "My learned friend is forgetting," said he. "Are we not decipherers of cross-word puzzles and interpreters of dark sayings?"

"I am not," said I. "So you may as well come straight to the point."

"You have not forgotten the scrap of paper with the cryptic inscription which was found in the small room?"

"Ha!" I exclaimed, suddenly recalling the ridiculous inscription, "I begin, as Miller would say, to 'rumble you.' But not very completely. The inscription read: 'Lobster: *hortus petasatus.*' But I still don't see how you arrived at it. Crabs are not the only crustaceans— besides lobsters."

"Very true, Jervis," said he. "Lobster is ambiguous as to its possible alternatives. Evidently, the more specific character was contained in the other term, '*hortus petasatus.*' Now, the learned Dr. Smith translates *petasatus* as 'wearing, or having on, a travelling-cap; ready for a journey.' But the word *petasus* means either a cap or a hat, so the adjective, *petasatus*, may be rendered as 'hatted' or 'having a hat on.' "

"Yes, I see," said I, with a sour grin. "So *hortus petasatus* would be a hat-on garden. But what puerile balderdash it is. That man, Penrose, ought to be certified."

"Still," said Thorndyke, "you see that it was worth while to study his jargon, for, when I had deciphered the inscription so far, the rest of the inquiry was perfectly simple. I looked up Hatton Garden in the directory and ran through the names of occupants in search of one that seemed related to the term 'lobster.' Among them I found the name of Jonathan Crabbe (the only one, in fact, who answered the description); and, as he was described as a diamond broker and dealer in precious stones, I decided that he was probably the man referred to by Penrose. Accordingly, I paid a visit to Hatton Garden and made a few discreet inquiries, which elicited the fact that Mr. Crabbe was absent from his premises and was in some sort of trouble in connection with a charge of receiving. Whereupon I made arrangements to give Lockhart a shock."

"And very completely you succeeded," said I. "He is in a deuce of a twitter, and well he may be, knowing quite well that he is making himself an accessory after the fact."

"Yes," Thorndyke agreed, "he is in a very unpleasant dilemma. But I don't think we can interfere, at least for the present. He is a lawyer and knows exactly what his position is; and, meanwhile, his reticence suits us well enough. I don't want a premature hue and cry raised."

Here the discussion appeared to have petered out; but it seemed that the evening's experiences were not yet finished, for, in the silence which followed Thorndyke's rejoinder, there came to my ear the sound of soft and rather stealthy footsteps ascending the stairs, and at the same moment I suddenly remembered that I had not shut the outer door when we came in after seeing Lockhart off.

The steps continued slowly to ascend. Then they crossed the landing and paused opposite our door. There was a brief interval followed by a very elaborate flourish, softly and skilfully executed, on the little brass knocker of the inner door, very much in the style of the old-fashioned footman's knock. I rose, and, striding across the room, threw open the door, when my astonished gaze encountered no less a person than Mr. Kickweed. He broke out at once into profuse apologies for disturbing us at so untimely an hour. "But," he explained, "the matter seemed to me of some importance, and I thought it best not to call in the daytime in case you might not wish my visit to become known."

This sounded rather mysterious, so, in accordance with his hint, I closed both the doors before ushering him across the room to the chair lately vacated by Miller.

"You needn't be apologetic, Mr. Kickweed," said Thorndyke, as he shook his visitor's hand. "It is very good of you to turn out at night to come and see us. Sit down and mix yourself a whisky and soda. Will you light a cigar as an aid to business discussion?"

Kickweed declined the refreshments but was obviously gratified by the manner of his reception; and, having expressed his thanks, he came at once to the object of his visit.

"I am the bearer of news, sir, which I think you will be glad to hear. I have received a letter from Mr. Penrose."

There did not, to me, appear to be anything particularly surprising in this statement. But it was evidently otherwise with Thorndyke, for he received the announcement with more astonishment than I had ever known him to show; though, even so, it needed my expert and accustomed eye to detect his surprise.

"When did you receive the letter?" he asked.

"It came by the first post this morning," Kickweed replied. "I thought you would like to know about it, and, perhaps, like to see it, so I have brought it along for your inspection."

He produced from his pocket a bulging letter-case from which he extracted a letter in its envelope and handed it to Thorndyke, who took out the letter, opened it and read it through. When he had finished the reading, he proceeded, according to his invariable custom when dealing with strange letters, to scrutinize its various parts, especially the signature and the date, to examine the paper, holding it up to the light, and, finally, to make a minute inspection of the envelope.

"The letter, I see," said he, "is dated with yesterday's date but gives no address; but the postmark is Canterbury and is dated yesterday afternoon. Do you suppose Mr. Penrose is staying at Canterbury?"

"Well, no, sir," replied Kickweed, "I do not, though he used rather frequently to stay there. But, from my knowledge of Mr. Penrose, I don't think he would have posted the letter in the town where he was staying. Still, he can hardly be far away from there. I think he knows that neighbourhood rather well."

"Does any one else know about this letter?"

"No, sir. I took it from the letter-box myself, and I have not spoken of it to anybody."

"I think," said Thorndyke, "that Mr. Brodribb ought to be told. In fact I think that the letter ought—with your consent—to be handed to him for safe keeping. You probably realize that it may become of considerable legal importance."

"Yes, sir, I realize that and that it ought to be taken great care of. What I proposed was to hand it to you, if you will take custody of it. Of course, you will dispose of it as you think best, but I brought it to you because you seemed to take a more sympathetic view of poor Mr. Penrose than any one else has done. And I may say, sir, that I should be more happy if you would keep it in your possession for the present. I shouldn't like it to be used to help the police to worry Mr. Penrose by searching in his neighbourhood."

"Very well, Mr. Kickweed," said Thorndyke. "I will keep the letter for the present on the understanding that it shall be produced only if circumstances should arise which would make its production necessary in the interests of justice. Do you agree to that?"

"Oh, certainly, sir," replied Kickweed. "You will, of course, make any use of it that you think proper and necessary, other than the one I mentioned."

"You may take it," said Thorndyke, "that no attempt will be made by me, or with my connivance, to harass Mr. Penrose, and that you may safely leave the letter in my custody. And I may say that I am greatly obliged to you for letting me have it and for having taken the trouble to report the matter to me."

Kickweed mildly deprecated these acknowledgments, and Thorndyke continued: "On reading this letter I am struck by certain peculiarities on which I should like to hear your opinion. It is a rather odd letter."

"It is," Kickweed admitted, "but then you know, sir, Mr. Penrose is a rather odd man, if I may venture to say so."

Here Thorndyke handed me the document and I rapidly read it through. It was certainly a very odd letter. Secretly, I pronounced it the letter of a born fool or a lunatic, but I made no audible comments. Its precious contents were as follows:

"26th March, 1935.

"CERASTIUM VULGATUM, ESQ.

"RESPECTED CER,

"These presents are to inform you that, some time after my departure from Her Deceased Majesty's Equilateral Rectangle, I discovered that the key of the small room was not in my pocket. Thereupon I reflected, and after profound cogitation decided that it must be somewhere else. Peradventure, when I sarahed forth on that infelicitous occasion, I may have left it in the door, where it may have presented itself to your penetrating vision and been taken into protective custardy. This is my surmise; and if I have reason and you are now seised or possessed of the said key, I will ask you to convey the same to my bank and deliver it into the hand of the manager, in my name, to have and to hold until such time as I shall demand it from him. But first, fasten the window and lock the door. The room contains nothing but a few unconsidered trifles of merely scentimental value, but I wish it to remain undisturbed until I shall return carrying my sheaves and ready to do justice to the obese calf.

"Hoping that you are in your usual boisterous spirits,

"Yours in saecula saeculorum,

"DANIEL PENROSE."

"You will agree with me, Jervis," said Thorndyke, when I returned the document, "that this is a very odd letter?"

I agreed with him in the most emphatic and unmistakable terms.

"We are all, by now," he continued, "accustomed to Mr. Penrose's oddities of speech. But this seems to go rather beyond even his usual eccentricity. What do you think, Mr. Kickweed?"

"I am disposed to think you are right, sir," replied Kickweed a little to my surprise; for the letter contained just the sort of twaddle that I should have expected from Penrose.

"I think," said Thorndyke, "that you mentioned, when we last met, having noticed a gradual change in Mr. Penrose; a growing tendency to oddity and obscurity of speech."

"I think I did say," replied Kickweed, "that the habit of jocularity had been growing and becoming more confirmed. But habits usually do tend to grow, and I don't know that he was changed in any other respect. And as to this letter, we must bear the circumstances in mind. He is probably very much upset and he may have been a little more facetious than usual by way of keeping up his spirits."

"Yes," said Thorndyke, "that has to be considered. But a tendency to increasing eccentricity is a very significant thing, especially in the case of a man who has rather unaccountably disappeared. Any recent change in Mr. Penrose's mental condition might have an important bearing on his recent conduct, and I am inclined to believe that there has been some such change. Now, take this letter. Is it the kind of letter that you have been in the habit of receiving from him?"

"Well, no, sir," Kickweed admitted. "He did not often have occasion to write to me, and when he did, his letters were usually quite short and to the point. They were not written in a jocular vein."

"In this letter," Thorndyke continued, "he addresses you by the style and title of Cerastium Vulgatum, Esq. Has he ever done that before?"

"No, sir; and it doesn't convey much to me now."

"Cerastium vulgatum," said Thorndyke, "is the botanical name of the common chickweed."

"Oh, indeed," said Kickweed, with a sad and rather disapproving smile. "I supposed it was some kind of a joke, but I did not connect it with my somewhat unfortunate name."

"Has Mr. Penrose ever before made any kind of joke on your surname?" Thorndyke asked.

"No, sir," Kickweed replied, promptly and emphatically. "Mr. Penrose has his oddities, but he is a gentleman, and in all his dealings with me he has always been scrupulously correct and courteous. I am almost disposed to think that you may be right, sir, after all, in believing that his troubles have affected his mind."

Evidently, the botanical joke had produced a profoundly un-favourable impression.

"By the way," said Thorndyke, "have you delivered the key to the bank manager?"

"Not yet," replied Kickweed. "Of course, I must carry out Mr. Penrose's instructions, but I don't at all like the idea of having a locked room—possibly containing valuable property—with no means of access in case of an emergency."

"No," said Thorndyke, "it is a bad and unsafe arrangement. I suppose you have kept the key in your own possession?"

"Always," was the reply, "excepting on one occasion when I let Mr. Horridge have it for a few minutes to examine the window of the room. I was just going out to post a letter when he asked for it, and he gave it back to me when I returned from the post."

"I certainly think," said Thorndyke, "that you ought to have the means of access to that room. Do you happen to have the key about you?"

By way of reply, Kickweed thrust his fingers into his waistcoat pocket and withdrew them holding a key, which he held out to Thorn-dyke, who took it from him and inspected it.

"An extraordinarily simple key," he remarked, "for the lock of so important a room. It looks very like the key of my office cupboard. Would you mind if I tried it in the lock?"

"Not in the least," replied Kickweed; whereupon Thorndyke bore the key away to the office, the door of which he closed after him; a proceeding that somehow associated itself in my mind with the idea of moulding wax. In a couple of minutes he returned, and, handing the key back to Kickweed, announced:

"It fits the lock quite fairly; which is not surprising as it is of quite a common pattern. But it is a fortunate circumstance, for now, if the need should arise, I could supply you with a key that would open the small room door."

"That is very kind of you, sir," said Kickweed, "and I will bear your offer in mind. And now I mustn't detain you any longer. It is exceedingly good of you to have given me so much of your time."

With this he rose, and once more declining our offer of refresh-ment, took up his hat and stick and was duly escorted out on to the landing. When he had gone, and we were once more within closed doors, I delivered myself of a matter that had rather puzzled me.

"There seems to be something a little queer about that key. You haven't forgotten that Horridge had it—or a duplicate—in his possession when he showed us the small room?"

"I remember that he had a key," replied Thorndyke; "and the feeble and clumsy efforts that he made to keep it out of sight made me suspect that it was a duplicate. Now we know that it was."

"I presume that you took a squeeze of Kickweed's key?"

"Yes," he replied, "and I shall ask Polton to make a key from the pattern. If it is good enough for Horridge to have a duplicate, it is good enough for us to have one, too."

"Why do you suppose Horridge had his made?"

"It is difficult to say. Horridge, as you observed, is convinced that the mysterious cupboard contains something of enormous value— which it undoubtedly did at one time, and may still—and he is highly suspicious of Kickweed. He may want to try the cupboard lock at his leisure, or he may simply want to see that Kickweed does not. I doubt whether he has any very definite purpose."

"You seem," said I, "to be pretty confident that the Billington jewels were in that cupboard and that they are not there now. Have you formed an opinion as to who the burglar was?"

"We haven't much to go on," he replied. "We know that Crabbe could not have been the man, as he was in prison when the burglary occurred; and we know—or may fairly assume—that the Chubb key was in Penrose's possession. Those are all the facts that we have, and they lead to no certain conclusion. But now we have another problem to consider."

"You mean that idiot Penrose's letter. But what is its importance, apart from the internal evidence that the writer is certainly a fool and possibly a lunatic?"

"That is precisely what we have to discover. How important is it? Perhaps we had better begin with the obituary columns of *The Times*."

We did not keep a complete file of *The Times* on account of its enormous bulk, but it was our custom to retain our copies for three months, which usually answered our purpose. And it did on this occasion; for, on opening the file and scanning the obituary columns, we presently came upon a notice announcing that Oliver Penrose passed away peacefully in his sleep on the 16th of March, a few days before his ninetieth birthday.

"There," said Thorndyke, carefully replacing the papers and closing the file, "you have the answer to our question. Penrose's letter is dated—and was posted—ten days after his father's death. That is a fact of cardinal importance. It anticipates any possible question of survivorship. If Penrose should never be heard of again; if he should die and neither the time nor place of his death should ever be known, this letter could be produced as decisive proof that he was alive ten days after his father's death. Its immediate effect is to enable Brodribb to deal with Oliver's estate. If there is a will, it can be proved and administered; if there is no will, the intestacy proceedings can be set going."

"Yes," I said, "it is a mighty important letter in spite of its ridiculous contents, and its arrival will be hailed with profound relief by Brodribb. But it is a remarkably opportune letter, too. Doesn't it strike you as rather singularly opportune?"

"It does," he replied. "That is what immediately impresses one. So much so that one asks oneself whether its arrival can be no more than a coincidence."

"To me," said I, "it suggests that Penrose is not such a fool as his letter would imply. He has been keeping his eye on the obituary columns of *The Times,* and, when he read the notice of the old gentleman's death, he made a pretext to write to Kickweed and thus put it on record that he was alive. That is how it strikes me. And that view is supported by the letter, itself. It was a perfectly unnecessary letter. Kickweed had had the key for months and there was no reason why he should not have continued to keep it, and every reason why he should. It looks as if the key had been a mere pretext for writing a letter. Don't you agree with me?"

"I do," he replied, "so far as the character of the letter is concerned. But we have to remember that when Penrose went away, his father was quite well, so that there was no need for him to watch the obituary columns. However, this is all rather speculative. The material fact is that the letter has arrived, and that fact will have to be communicated to Brodribb. I shall take the letter round and show it to him to-morrow morning."

CHAPTER 12

MR. ELMHURST

Between Thorndyke and me there existed a rather queer convention, which the reader of this narrative may have noticed. In the cases on which we worked together, he was always most scrupulous in keeping me informed as to the facts, and making me, if possible, a partner in the investigation by which they were ascertained. But he expected me to make my own inferences. Any attempt of mine to elicit from him a statement of opinion, or of his interpretation of the facts that were known to us both, met with the inevitable response: "My dear fellow, you know as much about the case as I do, and you have only to make use of your excellent reasoning faculties to extract the significance of what is known to us." The convention had been established when I first joined Thorndyke as his partner or understudy, as part of my training in the art and science of medico-legal investigation. But, apparently, my education was to continue indefinitely, for Thorndyke's attitude continued unchanged. He would tell me everything that he knew, but he was uncommunicative, even to secretiveness, as to what he thought.

But a habit of secretiveness sets up certain natural reactions. If Thorndyke would not tell me what he thought, it was admissible for me to find out, if I could; and I occasionally got quite a useful hint by observing the books that he was reading. For, unlike most lawyers, he dealt comparatively little in legal literature. His peculiar type of practice demanded a wide range of knowledge other than legal; and frequently it happened that his knowledge required amplification on some particular point. But, by observing the direction in which he was seeking to enlarge his knowledge, I was able, at least, to judge which of the facts seemed to him the most significant.

Now, I had noticed, of late, the appearance in our chambers of a number of books on prehistoric archæology, a subject in which, so far as I knew, Thorndyke was not specially interested. There was, for instance, Jessup's *Archæology of Kent,* into which I dipped lightly; and there was a copy of the *Archæological Journal,* containing a paper by Stuart Piggott on the "Neolithic Pottery of the British Isles." In this a slip of paper had been inserted as a bookmark, and, on opening it, I found that it was marked at the section headed "Pottery of the Windmill Hill Type," and opposite, a page of drawings representing the characteristic forms of vessels and their decorative markings. And there were others of different characters, but all agreeing in giving descriptions and illustrations of neolithic pottery.

From these facts it was evident to me that Thorndyke's attention was still occupied by the ridiculous fragment of pottery that we had found in the pocket of Penrose's raincoat; and the object of his researches was, I had no doubt, the discovery of some likely place from which that fragment might have come. But why he wished to discover that place or what light it would throw, if found, on the present whereabouts of Daniel Penrose, I was utterly unable to imagine. That the question was one of importance I did not doubt for a moment. Thorndyke was not in the least addicted to the finding of mares' nests or the pursuit of that interesting phenomenon, the Will-of-the-Wisp. He wanted to discover that place which had been the starting-point of that wild journey in the motor car. Therefore, the identity of that place had some profound significance; and for several days I continued, at intervals, to cudgel my brains in a vain effort to reason out its bearing on our quest.

About a week after the receipt of the mysterious letter from Mr. Penrose, our inquiry entered on a new stage. Hitherto, Thorndyke's attitude had been mainly that of a passive observer. The visit to Queen Square, the examination of the coat and the pottery fragment, and the unearthing of Mr. Crabbe were the only instances of anything like active investigation. Otherwise, he had listened to the reports from Brodribb, Miller and Lockhart, and, while he had, no doubt, turned them over thoroughly in his mind, had made no positive move. But now he showed signs of a kind of activity which I associated, by the light of experience, with a definite objective.

I became aware of the change when, on a certain evening, coming home after a long day's work, I found a visitor seated by the fire, apparently in close consultation with Thorndyke. A glance at the little table with the decanter, wine glasses and box of cigars told me that he was certainly a welcome and probably an invited guest;

and a sheet of the six-inch ordnance map, on which lay the pottery fragment, hinted at the nature of the consultation.

The visitor, who rose as I entered, was a young man of grave and studious aspect, whose face—adorned with an impressive pair of tortoise-shell rimmed spectacles—seemed familiar, but yet I could not place him until Thorndyke came to my aid.

"You haven't forgotten Mr. Elmhurst, surely, Jervis?" said he.

"Of course, I haven't," I replied, as we shook hands. "You are the dene hole gentleman and the discoverer of headless corpses."

Mr. Elmhurst did not repudiate the dene hole, but protested that he had not actually made a habit of discovering headless corpses, at least in the recent state. "The corpses that come my way," he explained, "are usually prehistoric corpses, in which the presence or absence of the head is of no special significance."

"In short," said Thorndyke, "Mr. Elmhurst is an archæologist who is kindly allowing us to benefit by his special knowledge, as we did in the case of the dene hole."

"That," said Elmhurst, "is very nicely put, but it gives me undeserved credit. I am not an altruist at all. I am agreeing to do something that I have long wanted to do, but have been deterred by the cost. But now Dr. Thorndyke wants this thing done and is prepared to bear the expense, or at least part of it. You see, it is a case of enlightened self-interest on both sides."

"And what is this job?" I asked. "Something in the resurrection line, I suspect."

"Yes," said Elmhurst, "it is an excavation. The doctor has here a fragment of what seems to have been a neolithic pot of the Windmill Hill type, as it is usually described. He thinks it possible that this fragment was found in a certain long barrow in Kent. I don't know why he thinks so, but it is not improbable that he is right. At any rate, if that barrow contains any pottery, it is pretty certain to be of this type."

"That doesn't carry you very far," said I. "Supposing you found some pottery of this kind in the barrow, would that enable you to say that this fragment must have come from that barrow?"

"No," he replied, "It would only enable one to say that this fragment was of the same type as that found in the barrow."

"But you know that already," said I.

"Believe," Elmhurst corrected.

"You said it was pretty certain to be of this type; and if you would repeat that on oath in the witness-box, I should think it would be sufficient. The excavation seems to be unnecessary."

"Oh, don't say that!" exclaimed Elmhurst. "You would degrade me from the rank of an investigator to that of a mere expert witness."

"My learned friend," said Thorndyke, "in spite of his great experience in court, seems to fail to appreciate the vast difference, in their effects on a jury, between an expert opinion—and a qualified one at that—and a pair of exhibits which the expert can declare, and the jury can see for themselves, are identically similar."

"Still," I persisted, "even if you could prove them to be identically similar, that would not be evidence that they came from the same barrow. You admit that, Elmhurst?"

"I admit nothing," he replied. "You know more about evidence than I do. But Dr. Thorndyke wants that barrow excavated and I want to do the excavation. And I may say that all the necessary preliminaries have been arranged. As the barrow is scheduled as an ancient monument, I have had to apply for, and have been granted by the Office of Works, a permit authorizing me to excavate and examine the interior of the tumulus situated by the river Stour near Chilham in Kent and commonly known as Julliberrie's Grave."

"Whose grave?" I demanded with suddenly-aroused interest; for as he pronounced the name there flashed instantly into my mind the words of Penrose's ridiculous entry: "Moulin-à-vent; Julie: Polly."

Elmhurst cast a quick, inquisitive glance at me and then proceeded to explain:

"Julliberrie's. There is a local tradition that the mound is the burial-place of a more or less mythical person named Jul Laber, or Julaber, said to have been either a witch or a giant. If he was a giant we may be able to confirm that tradition, but I am afraid that a witch—in the fossil state—would defy diagnosis."

"And has this mound never been excavated, so far as you know?" I asked.

"It was excavated tentatively," he replied, "in 1702 by Heneage Finch, whose report is extant; but it appears that nothing was found beyond a few animal bones. Then an aerial photograph, taken only a week or two ago, shows signs of some more recent disturbance on the surface. Apparently some one has been doing a little unauthorized digging, which may account for this fragment of the doctor's. But still, we hope to find the burial chamber intact."

I reflected on the possible means by which Thorndyke had

managed to locate this barrow and once more speculated on his inexplicable interest in this locality. And then suddenly I recalled Penrose's mysterious letter and the postmark on it. ·

"You say," said I, "that this mound is near Chilham. Isn't that somewhere in the Canterbury district?"

"Yes," he replied. "Quite near. Not more than half a dozen miles from Canterbury."

This began to be a little more understandable, though I was still unable to make out exactly what was in Thorndyke's mind. But I now had something like a clue which I could consider at my leisure; and meanwhile I returned to the subject of the excavation.

"I gather," said I, "that you are practically ready to begin operations. Is the date of the expedition fixed?"

"That is what we were discussing when you came in," replied Elmhurst. "Of course, there is no need for the doctor or you to attend the function. I can let you know if any pottery is found, and produce it for your inspection. But I hope you will both be able to come at least once while the work is in progress. One doesn't often get the chance of seeing a complete excavation of a virtually intact long barrow. If you can only make one visit, I would recommend you to wait until we are ready to expose the burial chamber. That is the most thrilling moment."

"It sounds like quite a big job," I remarked. "How long do you think it will take?"

"I should say from three to four weeks," he replied.

"My word!" I exclaimed. "Four weeks! Why, it will cost a small fortune. Of course, you will have to employ a gang of labourers."

"We shall want five men," said he, "in addition to the volunteers, and I reckon that sixty pounds will cover it easily."

I whistled. "I suspect, Thorndyke," said I, "that you will have to find that sixty pounds yourself. You won't get Brodribb to include archæological researches in the costs. But do you tell me, Elmhurst, that this colossal work is necessary just to find out what sort of pottery there is in the barrow?"

"Perhaps not," he replied. "But, you see, the position is this: Julliberrie's Grave is scheduled as an Ancient Monument. No one may—lawfully—disturb it without a permit from the Office of Works. Now, they are perfectly willing to grant a permit to genuine archæologists who are known to them as such, but subject to very rigorous conditions. They won't grant permits for mere casual digging. Their conditions are that, if you want to excavate, you must excavate completely and exhaustively so that the mound need never be touched again. All finds must be preserved and labelled and a detailed account of the excavation must be published; and when the work is finished, the barrow must be restored completely to its original condition. I explained all this to the doctor."

I must confess that I was staggered. The means seemed to be so disproportionate to the end. But Thorndyke seemed quite satisfied to pay sixty pounds for a few specimens of pottery and Elmhurst made no secret of his unholy joy at the prospect of a first-class "dig."

"Are you proposing to take part in this super-resurrection, Thorndyke?" I asked sourly.

"I am not proposing to join the diggers," he replied, "but I shall take the opportunity to see how a thorough excavation is done. I want to see the burial chamber opened, but I am also rather curious to see how the work is begun, and what the barrow looks like when the turf is removed and the mound exposed as it appeared when it was newly made. When do you reckon that you will have the barrow uncovered?

"I expect," Elmhurst replied, "that we shall begin skinning off the turf on Thursday. We start operations, as I told you, on Tuesday morning, and there will be a full two days' work on the preliminaries—pegging out the site, putting up an enclosing fence and preparing the dumps. I think, if you come down on Thursday—not too early—I can promise you that you will see the barrow as its builders saw it. I could, if you liked, meet you at Maidstone or Canterbury and personally conduct you to the scene of the operations."

"That isn't necessary," said Thorndyke. "We have the map, and you will want to be early at work. Moreover, I think I shall take the opportunity to do some prospecting on my way and I may be a little late in arriving at the barrow."

"That will be all to the good," said Elmhurst. "The later you arrive the more we shall have ready to show you."

This brought the discussion on ways and means to an end; and shortly afterwards our guest, having a train to catch, rose and took his leave.

During the week that intervened, very little was said either by Thorndyke or me on the subject of the expedition. Not that I was not keenly interested; for Thorndyke's reference to his "prospecting" intentions made it clear to me that he had something in his mind beyond the mere search for pottery. It seemed that now, for the first time, he was going to take some active measures to locate the elusive Penrose. But I asked no questions. I was going to take part in the prospecting operations and I hoped that their nature would throw some light on the methods by which Thorndyke proposed to attempt what looked like an impossibility.

One discovery I made, however; which was that Polton had in some way managed to attach himself to the expeditionary force. The fact was revealed to me when I found him in the act of pasting a couple of sheets of the six-inch ordnance map on thin mounting board. Observing that one of them included Chilham and our tumulus on Julliberrie Downs, I ventured to make inquiries.

"Why are you mounting them, Polton?" I asked. "You are not proposing to frame them and hang them on the wall?"

"No, sir," he replied. "When they are dry, I am going to cut them up into sections nine inches by six, that is four sections to a sheet. Then I shall number them and make a case to carry them in. You see, sir, a map is awkward to carry, even if you fold it, and most inconvenient to use out of doors if there is any wind. But by this method you can just take out the one or two sections that you are using, and the whole lot will go easily into my poacher's pocket, or the doctor's either, for that matter. I'm getting them ready for our little trip next Thursday."

"Oh!" said I, "you are coming with us, are you?"

"Yes, sir," he replied, with a complacent crinkle. "The doctor mentioned to me that he was going down into Kent on some sort of exploring job, so I persuaded him to let me come and lend a hand. I understood him to say that they were going to dig up that old grave that is marked on the map—Julliberrie's Grave."

"That is quite correct, Polton," I assured him.

"Ah!" said he, with a crinkle of ghoulish satisfaction. "That will be very interesting. Do you happen to know when the party was buried?"

"I understand," I replied, "that the burial took place at some time from four to ten thousand years ago."

"Good gracious!" exclaimed Polton. "Ten thousand years! Well, well! I should have thought that if he has been there as long as that they might have let him stay there. There can't be much of him left."

"That is what we are going to find out," said I; and with this I retired, leaving him to his pasting and his reflections.

CHAPTER 13

THE TRACK OF THE FUGITIVE

In the course of my long association with Thorndyke, I had often been impressed by the number of things that he appeared to carry in his pockets. He reminded me somewhat of The White Knight. But there was this essential difference; that whereas that unstable equestrian was visibly encumbered with a raffle of things that he could never possibly want, Thorndyke was invisibly provided with the things that he did want. If the need arose for any instrument, appliance or material, forthwith the desiderated object was produced from his pocket even as the parlour magician produces the required guinea-pig or goldfish. So, after all, the appearances may have been illusory; they may have been due, not to the gross quantity of things carried, but to an accurate prevision of the probable requirements.

The matter is recalled to my mind by the astonishing stowage capacity that Polton developed on the morning of our expedition to Chilham. Not only did the special outfit for the day's work—six-inch map, one-inch map, prismatic compass, telescope, surveyor's tape and other oddments, laid out for Thorndyke's inspection—vanish into unsuspected pockets, leaving no trace, but, as appeared later, his lading included a substantial meal, a big flask of sherry and a nest of aluminium drinking cups. And even then he didn't bulge perceptibly.

Of the details of our travels on that day I have but a confused recollection. It was all very well for Thorndyke, who had apparently transferred the six-inch map bodily to his consciousness; he knew exactly where he was at any given moment. But to me, when once we had left the plain high road, all sense of direction was lost and I was aware only of a bewildering succession of abominably steep lanes, cart-tracks and footpaths, which we scrambled up or stumbled down until we became finally and hopelessly submerged in a wood.

However, I will make an effort to give an intelligible account of this "prospecting" expedition, with apologies in advance for the somewhat nebulous topography. From Charing Cross we proceeded uneventfully to Ashford, where we got out of the train and took our places in a motor omnibus which was lurking in the vicinity and which was bound for Canterbury. Apparently it had been awaiting the arrival of the train, for as soon as we and one or two other train passengers had settled ourselves, the conductor, having taken a last fond look at the station, gave the signal to the driver, who thereupon started the vehicle with a triumphant hoot.

We rumbled along the main road for about six miles (as I afterwards ascertained) and then, shortly after crossing a small river, drew up at a village which the conductor announced as Godmersham. Here we got out and walked forward until we came to the cross-roads beyond the village, where Thorndyke turned to the right and led the way along the by-road. Presently we passed under a railway line and then, as the road made a sharp turn to the right, followed it along the bottom of a valley nearly parallel to the railway. About half a mile farther on, another by-road led off to the left, and, as Thorndyke turned off into it, my sense of direction began to get somewhat confused. It was quite a good road and fairly level, but its windings made it difficult to keep a "dead reckoning," and when, half a mile along it, yet another by-road led off from it to the left at right angles—into which Thorndyke turned confidently —and then made a right-angle turn to the right, I abandoned all attempts to keep count of our direction.

Along this road we trudged for three-quarters of a mile, still keeping fairly on the level, but then the ground began to rise sharply and the road zig-zagged more than ever. A mile or so farther on we passed through a village, and I found myself casting a slightly wistful glance at a couple of rustics who were seated on a bench outside the inn, sustaining themselves with beer and conversation. But Thorndyke plodded on relentlessly, and when, a few hundred yards beyond the village, we came to yet another cross-roads, he finished me off by taking the turning to the left.

"I suppose, Thorndyke," said I, when we had toiled up this road for about half a mile and he halted to look around, "you know where you are?"

"Oh, yes," he replied. "That village that we passed through just now is Sole Street. I will show you on the map where we are. Let us have the six-inch, Polton."

The latter dived into the interior of his clothing, whence he produced the case of mounted sections and handed it to his principal.

"Here we are," said Thorndyke, when he had picked out the appropriate card. "That is the village at the bottom and this is the road we are on. You see that it peters out, more or less, when it enters the wood."

I compared the section of map with the visible objects and was able to identify a farm-house across the fields on our right and a considerable wood which we were approaching.

"Yes," I said, "it is clear enough so far, though it doesn't mean much to me. What is the significance of that pencilled cross by the roadside?"

"That," he replied, "marks the spot, as nearly as I could locate it from the evidence at the inquest, where the old woman was killed."

"Indeed!" I exclaimed. "So this is where the chapter of accidents began, or, at least, a few yards farther up. Then I may assume that the purpose of this prospecting expedition is to retrace the route of Penrose's car?"

"That is so," he admitted; "and presently we must begin to look for traces. At the moment, we don't need them, as there seems to be no doubt that the car came down this road. It was seen—or, at least, a car was seen—to come flying round the corner into the village and past the inn. Of course, it may not have been Penrose's car. But the time, the outrageous speed, and the wild manner in which it was being driven, all seem to connect it with the disaster."

"But," I objected, "even if it was the car that killed the woman, that is no evidence that it was Penrose's car. It seems to me that the argument against Penrose moves in a circle. Penrose is proved to have killed the old woman by the fact that he was on the road where she was killed; and he is proved to have been on that road by the fact that he killed the old woman. I respectfully suggest that my learned senior may possibly be tracing, laboriously and with characteristic skill, the movements of a motor car in which we are not interested at all."

Thorndyke chuckled appreciatively. "Admirably argued, Jervis; and the point that you make is clearly realized by the police. There is very little doubt that it was Penrose's car, but there is no positive evidence that it was. And the police know, and we know, that you can't secure a conviction on mere probabilities. That is a further purpose of the prospecting expedition; not only to ascertain which way, and from whence, the car was travelling, but also, if possible, to establish what car it was."

As we continued to toil upwards towards the wood, I cogitated on this statement with considerable surprise. It seemed inconsistent with what I had supposed to be Thorndyke's object and especially with his assurance to Kickweed that no action was contemplated which might compromise Penrose or menace his safety. Yet, here he was, by his own admission, industriously searching for the one missing item of evidence which could secure Penrose's conviction. Unless, indeed, he had any reason to believe that the wrong car had been identified; which his words did not in the least suggest. Incidentally, I was utterly unable to imagine how he proposed to identify a car which had passed down the road months ago, or even pick up its tracks. The road was extraordinarily unfrequented. We had met not a single car, and only one farm cart, since we had passed under the railway. But still it was a metalled road, showing only slight traces of the carts and wagons that had passed over it; and obviously none of those traces had anything to tell us.

When we entered the wood, I noticed that Thorndyke kept a close watch on the borders of the road though he did not slacken his pace.

"I presume," said I, "that you are looking for the tracks of the car. But isn't that rather hopeless, seeing that it is about six months since Penrose passed down this road—if he ever did actually pass down it?"

"Of course," he replied, "it would be futile to look for tracks on the road, or even on the margins. But what I am looking for—though I don't expect to find it here—is some sign of a car having driven or backed off the road into the wood and along one of the footpaths. The marks made by a car entering the wood over the soft soil would be deep and they would remain visible for years. Moreover, they would be unique. They would not be confused with other tracks, as in the case of any kind of road."

"You have reasons, then, for believing that Penrose backed his car into the wood?"

"*We* have reasons, Jervis," he replied. "You saw the car and the dead leaves and earth on the wheels; and you will remember that the earth was of the same type as the surface soil here; a loam of the Thanet Sands type. Besides, there is the fact that, if Penrose was engaged, as the evidence suggests, in digging in the barrow, he must have left the car somewhere. But it appeared at the inquest that nobody had seen the car until it passed through Sole Street."

"There isn't much in that," said I. "We seem to have this tract of country all to ourselves. A car might remain parked by the side of this road for hours without being noticed."

He admitted the truth of this, "but," he added, "don't forget the state of the car, or the fact that Penrose was engaged in an unlawful act."

"And have you any idea," I asked, "where the car was probably left?"

"I have settled on a spot which seems likely," he replied. "But it is little more than a guess; and if I am wrong we shall have to give up the quest. We can't search the whole area of woodland."

Half a mile farther on, we came to a fork in the road, the left-hand branch being little more than a cart-track. Into this Thorndyke turned unhesitatingly; and by the care with which he scrutinized the margins, I judged that we were approaching the "likely spot." But the issue was rather confused by the fact that the rough, un-metalled road was fairly deeply rutted, having evidently been used by various carts and wagons. This road, however, after crossing a considerable open space, took a sharp, right-angle turn to the left opposite a pair of cottages, but its original direction was continued by a broad footpath. Thorndyke first followed the road in its new direction where it entered and crossed a narrow strip of wood, but, after a careful examination of the ruts in the wood, he came back and explored the footpath. And here it was that we struck the first trace of what might have been a car-track.

The footpath passed along the front of the cottages, still in the open, but presently it skirted the edge of the wood. It was an old path, never disturbed by the plough, and its surface was trodden down hard by years of use. Moreover, its margins showed faint impressions of wheels, which had been nearly obliterated by the feet of the wayfarers who had walked over them.

"They don't look to me like the tracks of a car," I remarked as we all stooped to examine them.

"No," he agreed, taking a rough measurement with his stick. "The gauge is much too wide. Probably they are the tracks of some woodman's cart or timber-carriage. But a hard path like this would scarcely show an impression of a pneumatic tire excepting after heavy rain."

We continued our progress slowly for another hundred yards, keeping a close watch on the faint ruts beside the path. Then we all halted simultaneously. For here we could see the faint, but clearly distinguishable, tracks of some wheeled vehicle which had turned off the path on to the rough turf of the open field.

"This looks more likely," I remarked; and Polton supported me with the opinion that "the Doctor's got him this time, as I knew he would."

Thorndyke made no comment, but, producing from his pocket a steel tape, carefully measured the space between the wheel-marks.

"The measurement is correct," he announced, "but that is only an agreement. It would apply to thousands of other cars. However, we will see whither these tracks lead us."

We followed the tracks, not without difficulty, across the wide meadow until we reached another belt of woodland. Here the tracks entered the wood by a footpath and were easy enough to follow on the soft earth. The path continued for about a furlong and then emerged into the open, where it crossed a small grass-covered space; and, following it, we were still able to distinguish the wheel-tracks by its sides. When it reached the edge of the wood, the footpath turned sharply to the right, keeping in the open. But here the tracks left the path and plunged straight into the wood, which was fairly free from undergrowth. Following the comparatively deep ruts which the wheels had made in the soft leaf-mould, we advanced by a rather tortuous route about a couple of hundred yards into the wood. And then, once more, we halted; for we had apparently come to the end of the tracks.

There seemed to be no doubt about it; but, as the last year's leaves lay here more deeply, and the undergrowth had suddenly grown denser, I went on a few yards to make sure that the tracks did not reappear beyond the place where they had seemed to end. With difficulty I forced my way through the bushes and was further impeded by the brambles and spreading roots; and I had not gone more than a few yards when my foot was caught by some hard, angular object—obviously not a root or a bramble—whereby, after staggering forward a pace or two, I fell sprawling among the tangle of vegetation.

At the sound of the fall, and the accompanying pious ejaculations, Thorndyke hurried towards me to see what had happened. I picked myself up, and, having wiped my hands, proceeded to search for the object which had tripped me up. Cautiously probing with my foot in a clump of nettles, I brought to light what looked like the haft of an axe; but, when I seized it and drew it out, it proved to be a trenching tool.

It was at this moment, as I stood with it in my hand, trying to connect it with some vague stirring of memory, that Thorndyke appeared through the bushes.

"I hope you are not hurt, Jervis," he said, anxiously. "That would be a nasty thing to fall upon."

I assured him that I had come to no harm beyond a few scratches. "But," I added, "I am not quite clear about the significance of this thing. I have a vague idea that something was said by somebody about a trenching tool, but I can't remember what or who it was."

"The somebody," he replied, "was Kickweed. Don't you remember our interview in the garage when he told us, among other items, that he had a vague recollection of having seen a trenching tool there?"

"Yes, of course, I remember now. Then it is quite possible that this is the very tool he was speaking of?"

By way of answer, he took the tool from me, and, having run his eye along the handle and turned it over, placed his finger on a spot near to the blade and held it out to me. Looking at it closely, I was able to make out in very faded lettering the name "D. Penrose," apparently printed with a rubber stamp.

I must confess that I was profoundly impressed. Once more Thorndyke had achieved what had seemed to me an impossibility. Not only had he traced the route that the car had followed, but he had clearly established the identity of the car. Moreover, he had settled the place from which the car started in a country which he had never seen, working by inference and aided only by the map. It was a remarkable performance even for Thorndyke.

But here my reflections were interrupted by a hail from Polton in a tone of high excitement. For he, too, had been "prospecting"; and as we returned to the end of the track, he met us, fairly bubbling with exultation and carrying his treasure trove in the form of a small spade and a leather case.

"Here is an astonishing thing, sir!" he exclaimed. "I found these in the bushes, and they've both got Mr. Penrose's name stamped on them. I could hardly believe my eyes. But there," he added, "I don't suppose, sir, that you are surprised at all. I expect you knew they were there before we started from home."

Thorndyke smilingly disclaimed the omniscience with which his admiring henchman credited him (though, in fact, Polton was not very wide of the mark), and taking from him the spade and case, looked them over and verified the marks of ownership.

"You notice, Jervis," said he, "that these things correspond exactly with Kickweed's description; a small, light spade, pointed at the end, and a leather sheath or case to protect the point. The spade and the trenching tool appear to have been Penrose's equipment for his clandestine digging expeditions."

"Yes," I said, "and their presence here demonstrates that you were right in your inference as to the place where he parked his car. By the way, how did you arrive at it?"

"I can hardly say that I arrived at it," he replied. "As I said, it was little more than a guess. I started with the hypothesis—a very well-supported one—that Penrose went forth that day with the intention of digging in Julliberrie's Grave, and that he did dig there. If that were so, he would park his car as near to the place as possible; and the more so since he knew that he was committing an unlawful act and might have to clear out of the neighbourhood in a hurry. For the same reason he would wish to leave his car where it would not be seen. But examination of the map showed this excellent place of concealment, less than half a mile from the barrow."

"Yes," I said, "it looks perfectly simple and obvious now that you have explained matters. But these tools, thrown away into the bushes, seem to suggest that the contingency that you mentioned did actually arise. Apparently, he did have to clear out of the neighbourhood in a hurry. Probably he was spotted in the act of digging and had to do a bolt, which would account for his having got rid of the incriminating tools. At any rate, it looks as if the panic had started here and not after the accident."

"Exactly," Thorndyke agreed. "The killing of the old woman was not the cause but the consequence of the panic. And now, as we have finished this part of our quest, we may as well move on and see how Elmhurst is progressing—unless there is anything more that you would like to see."

"There is," I replied with emphasis. "What I should like to see, above all other things in the world, is a good hospitable pub with oceans of beer and mountains of bread and cheese. As you seem to have memorized the whole neighbourhood, perhaps you know where one is to be found."

"I am afraid," said Thorndyke, "that there is nothing nearer than the Wool-pack at Chilham."

But here Polton, crinkling ecstatically, proceeded to unbutton his coat.

"No need for a pub, sir," said he. "We're provided. And we can do something better than bread and cheese and beer."

With this he fished out of his inexhaustible pockets a flat parcel—found to contain a veal and ham pie—a large flask of sherry, a nest of three aluminium drinking-cups and a shoe-maker's knife in a leather sheath wherewith to carve the pie. There were no forks, but the need of them was not felt as the thickness of the flat pie had been thoughtfully adapted to the dimensions of a moderately-opened human mouth. Joyfully, we selected a place as free as possible from brambles and nettles and there seated ourselves on the ground; and while Polton, by his unerring craftsman's eye, divided the pie into three equal parts, Thorndyke and I filled our cups and toasted the giver of the feast.

When the banquet was finished and the empty flask, the cups and the knife had vanished into the receptacles whence they came, Polton thriftily utilized the wrapping-paper to disguise the naked form of the trenching tool. Then, with the aid of the compass, Thorndyke led the way through the wood and presently brought us out on to a stretch of rough pasture where, some three hundred yards away, we could see the excavators at work.

CHAPTER 14

JULLIBERRIE'S GRAVE

The scene on which I looked as we came out of the wood rather took me by surprise; though, to be sure, Elmhurst's lucid and detailed account of the proposed operations ought to have prepared me. But to an uninformed person like myself, excavation is just a matter of digging, and I had hardly taken in the elaborate preliminaries that exact scientific procedure demands.

Looking along the brow of the steep hill-side, one could see the barrow—a long, oval, grassy mound about fifty yards in length—standing out plainly against a background of trees that were just about to burst into leaf. Past it, to the left, down in the river valley, rose the tall white shape of Chilham Mill, while farther to the left and more distant was the town or village of Chilham. At ordinary times it must have been a rather desolate and solitary place, for no habitation was visible nearer than the distant mill, but now it was a scene of strenuous activity, peopled by busy workers.

The preparatory operations had apparently been nearly completed. The barrow was surrounded by a substantial spile fence—evidently new—which marked off a rectangular enclosure. Inside this, two rows of surveying pegs had been driven into the ground and a theodolite stand set up over one of them suggested a survey in progress. Outside the enclosure was a methodically spread dump of turf, and a trackway of planks was being laid to another spot, apparently the site of a dump for the chalk and earth which would be removed from the mound as the excavation proceeded. There was also a stack of half a dozen metal wheelbarrows, and, hard by, a small shepherd's hut, in which a stoutly-built gentleman, apparently the surveyor, was at the moment depositing what looked like a theodolite case; which he did carefully, with a proper respect for the instrument, and then, having shut the door of the hut, strode away briskly down the hill towards the village.

We seemed to have timed our arrival rather fortunately, for the work of uncovering the barrow had already commenced. Within the fenced enclosure two parties of workers were engaged, from opposite sides, in cutting out strips of turf and rolling them up like lengths of stair carpet. Of the two parties, one consisted of four labourers, who went about their work with the leisurely ease born of long experience, while the other party was, with the exception of one labourer, evidently composed of volunteers, among whom I distinguished, with some difficulty, our friend Elmhurst, transformed into the likeness of a coal-miner with leanings towards tennis.

We halted near the edge of the wood to observe the procedure without interrupting the work. Presently Elmhurst, having accumulated a goodly heap of turf-rolls, loaded them into a wheelbarrow, which was promptly seized by one of his two assistants—a fairhaired young viking in a blue jersey and a pair of the most magnificent orange-red trousers of the kind known by fishermen as "fear-noughts"—who trundled it off through an opening in the fence and unloaded it neatly on to the turf dump on top of the already considerable stack that occupied it. Then he returned at a brisk trot, and, having set down the empty wheelbarrow, picked up his spade and fell to work again on the cutting out of a fresh load.

It was at this moment that Elmhurst, happening to glance in our direction, not only observed our presence but evidently recognized us, for he laid down his spade and began to walk towards us; whereupon we hurried forward to meet him. As we approached, I noticed that he cast an inquisitive eye on the tools which Polton was carrying, and, as soon as we had exchanged greetings, he inquired:

"Are you proposing to take an active part in the proceedings? I see that you are provided with the necessary implements."

"The appearance is illusory," Thorndyke replied. "We did not bring these tools with us. They are the products of our prospecting activities in the wood hard by. And they are not going to be used on this occasion. It seems advisable to preserve them in the condition in which they were found."

Elmhurst regarded the tools with intelligent interest and, I thought, with some disfavour.

"I see," he said reflectively; "you connect those tools with the piece of pottery that you showed me?"

Thorndyke admitted that the connection seemed to be a reasonable one.

"Yes," said Elmhurst. "A pick and a spade do certainly seem to connect themselves with traces of unlawful digging in the neighbourhood. And they are quite workmanlike tools, especially the spade. I only hope that your friends have not been too workmanlike. In one respect they certainly have not. They have made a very poor job of replacing the turf."

"Then," said Thorndyke, "you have found evidence that the mound has really been dug into?"

"Yes," was the reply. "There is no doubt whatever. But they seem only to have made a short, irregular trench, and, as they were nowhere near the burial chamber, I am still hopeful of finding that intact. But we shall see better how far they went when we get the turf off. As you see, we have got all the margin unturfed and we are just starting on the mound itself. We shall soon get that done with eight workers besides myself; and, meanwhile, I can take you round and show you the arrangements for excavating a barrow."

"You mustn't let us waste your time," said Thorndyke, "and leave your colleagues to do all the work; though I must say, they seem to enjoy it."

"Yes, by Jove!" I agreed. "They are proper enthusiasts. I have been watching that sea rover in the decorative trousers and wondering what those labourers think of him. But perhaps they are not Union men."

Elmhurst smiled a cryptic smile but expressed complete satisfaction both with the labourers and his volunteer assistants. "I think," he added, "that my friends would like to make the acquaintance of the benefactor who has given us this very great pleasure."

Accordingly we proceeded towards the fenced enclosure and entered it by one of the openings left for the wheelbarrows to pass in and out.

"You notice," said Elmhurst, "that we have driven in a row of pegs all round the tumulus to define its edges. Those are for use in marking our plan and to guide us when we come to rebuild the mound. It has to be restored exactly to its original shape and size."

"You speak of rebuilding the mound," said I. "You don't mean that you are going to move the entire structure?"

"Certainly we are," he replied. "The essence of a complete excavation is in the thorough examination of every part of it. The whole of it will be moved excepting a narrow longitudinal wall, or spine, along the middle, which has to be left to preserve the contour and serve as a guide to build up to. We shall move one half at a time and the earth—or chalk rubble, as it will be in this case—that we take out will be carefully deposited in one of those dumps. Each dump will have a revetment of chalk blocks to prevent the piled earth from slipping away and getting scattered."

"Yes," said Thorndyke, "it is all very thorough and methodical; a very different thing from the slovenly methods of the casual digger. By the way, which side do you propose to begin with?"

"The right-hand side," replied Elmhurst. "That is the side on which your friends operated, and we are rather anxious to settle once for all what they really did in the way of excavation and how much damage they have done. My colleagues are now beginning to peel off the turf from that side of the mound."

As he spoke, we rounded the end of the barrow and came in sight of the two volunteers and the labourer, all busily engaged in cutting lines in the turf with implements like cheese-cutters set on long handles. As we approached, the owner of the fear-noughts looked up and rather disconcerted me by disclosing an extremely comely feminine countenance; which accounted for Elmhurst's cryptic smile and caused me hurriedly to reexamine the other "gentleman," only to discover that the breeches which I had innocently accepted as diagnostic of masculinity, appertained to a lady.

The introductions, effected by Elmhurst with a ceremonious bow and a grin of malicious satisfaction, informed us that the two ladies were, respectively, Miss Stirling—the wearer of the nautical garments —and Miss Bidborough, and that both were qualified and enthusiastic archæologists (this was Elmhurst's statement, and neither denied it on behalf of the other); and that both were profoundly grateful to Thorndyke.

"It is the chance of a life-time," said Miss Stirling, "to carry out a complete excavation of a neolithic barrow; and such a famous one, too. I have often come here and looked at Julliberrie's Grave and thought how interesting it would be to turn it out thoroughly and see what it really contained. But we are in an awful twitter about those tomb-robbers who have been hacking at the mound. It will be a tragedy if they have reached the important part of the barrow."

"Yes," Miss Bidborough agreed, severely. "These clandestine diggers are the bane of scientific archæology. They confuse all the issues by disturbing the stratification, they break or damage valuable relics, and, worst of all, they sneak off secretly with things of priceless scientific value and never record what they have found. Do you happen to know who these people were, Dr. Thorndyke, who broke into this barrow?"

"The only person," replied Thorndyke, "known to me as being under suspicion is an amateur—a very amateur—collector of antiques."

"They usually are," said Elmhurst, gloomily; "and this fellow must have been worse than usual. Just look at the way he put the turf back!"

He pointed indignantly to an irregular area on the side of the mound in which even my inexpert eye could detect the ragged lines which marked the untidy replacement. From my knowledge of the man (and my distinct prejudice against him) it was just what I should have expected; and I was indiscreet enough to say so.

"By the way," said Miss Bidborough, addressing Elmhurst, "I am in hopes that we shall have a visit from Theophilus. He has to come down to Canterbury today, and I think he intends to come on here and see how we are getting on with the work. I hope he will. I know he would like to meet Dr. Thorndyke."

Thorndyke looked inquiringly at Elmhurst. "Do I know Mr. Theophilus?" he asked.

"His name isn't really Theophilus," Elmhurst explained. "That is only a term of affection among his friends. He is actually Professor Templeton."

"Then I do know him, at least by repute," said Thorndyke. "And now I suggest that we move on and let these ladies proceed with their work and see what enormities the unauthorized diggers have committed."

With this we bowed to the fair excavators, and as they picked up their cheese-cutters to renew their assault on the turf, we resumed our personally conducted tour, passing round the head of the mound (where Elmhurst pointed out to us the probable position of the burial chamber) to inspect the works on the other side. As we came out on to the lower side, whence we could see the whole hill-side and the river valley below, we observed a figure in the distance striding up the steep ascent with a purposeful air suggesting a definite objective.

"Here is Theophilus, himself," remarked Elmhurst (whose power of recognizing distant persons did credit to his spectacles). "We may as well go down and meet him and get the introductions over before we come to the scene of the operations."

Accordingly, we proceeded down the hill-side, but at a leisurely pace, as we had to come up again, and, in due course, came within hail of the visitor, who viewed us with undisguised interest; which, indeed, was mutual; for a man who gets called by an affectionate nickname by his juniors probably merits respectful consideration. And this gentleman—a tall, athletic, eminently good-looking man, very unlike the popular conception of a professor—made a definitely pleasant impression.

When we at length met, he shook hands cordially with Elmhurst and then looked at Thorndyke.

"I think," said he, "that I can diagnose the giver of the archæological feast. You are Dr. Thorndyke, aren't you?"

Thorndyke admitted his identity, but protested:

"I am really getting a great deal of undeserved credit for this excavation. Actually, I am greatly indebted to Elmhurst for all the trouble that he is taking, since I am hoping to get some useful information from the opening of the barrow."

Professor Templeton looked at him somewhat curiously.

"Of course," said he, "you know your own business—uncommonly well, as I understand—but I can't imagine what information you expect to get by the excavation that we couldn't have given you without it."

"Probably you are right," Thorndyke admitted, "at least in a scientific sense. But in legal practice, and in relation to a particular set of circumstances, an ascertained fact is usually of more weight than even the most authoritative opinion."

"Yes," said the professor, "I appreciate that. But when Elmhurst told me about the project, I wondered—and am still wondering—whether there might not be some—what shall we say?—some *arrière-pensée,* some expectation that the digging operations might yield some extra-archæological facts. You see, your reputation has preceded you."

He smiled genially, and Thorndyke was evidently in no-wise disconcerted by the implied suspicions; and I was just beginning to wonder, for my part, whether there might not be some justice in those suspicions when my colleague addressed Elmhurst.

"I think," said he, "your presence is required at the diggings. Some rather urgent signals are being made."

We all looked up towards the barrow, and there, sure enough, was a picturesque, red-trousered figure standing on the summit of the mound, beckoning excitedly; and, even as we looked, a labourer came down the hill at a heavy trot, and, when he had arrived within earshot, announced that Miss Stirling asked Mr. Elmhurst to return at once.

In compliance with this unmistakably urgent summons, Elmhurst immediately started up the hill at something between a walk and a trot, and we turned and followed at a more convenient pace.

"Those girls have apparently found something out of the common," the professor remarked. "I wonder what it can be. They can't have struck the burial chamber, for they have only begun peeling the turf off; and you don't look for anything important so near the surface."

We watched Elmhurst run round the end of the mound, where he disappeared for the moment. But in a very short time he reappeared, hurrying in our direction; and, as we, thereupon, quickened our pace, we met within a short distance of the mound.

"My colleagues," he announced in his usual sedate, self-contained manner, though a little breathlessly, "have found something, Doctor, which is rather more in your line than in ours. Apparently, there is some one buried just under the surface in the place where the unauthorized digging has been carried out."

"You say 'apparently,'" said Thorndyke. "Then I take it that you have not uncovered the body?"

"No," replied Elmhurst, as we turned to accompany him back. "What happened was this: Miss Stirling was rolling up a strip of turf when she saw what looked like the toe of a boot showing through the surface soil. So she scraped away some of the soil with her spade and uncovered the greater part of a boot; and then the toe of a second boot came into view; whereupon she ran up the mound and signalled for me to come."

"You are sure that they are not just a pair of empty boots?" Thorndyke asked.

"Quite sure," was the reply. "I scraped away the earth enough to see the bottoms of a pair of trousers and then came on to report. But there is no doubt that there are feet in those boots."

Nothing more was said as we walked quickly up the hill, but I caught a significant glance from the professor's eye, and I noticed that Polton had developed a new and lively interest in the proceedings. As to Thorndyke, it was impossible to judge whether the discovery had occasioned him any surprise; but I suspected—and so, evidently, did the professor—that the possibility had been in his mind. Indeed, I began to ask myself if this gruesome "find" did not represent the actual purpose of the excavation.

On arriving at the barrow, we passed round the foot end and came in sight of the scene of the discovery where a broad patch of the chalky soil had been uncovered by the removal of the turf. The two ladies stood close by it, backed by the gang of labourers who had been attracted to the spot by the report of the discovery; and the eyes of them all were riveted on a shallow depression at the bottom of which a pair of whitened boots projected through the chalk rubble.

"Would you like me to get the body out?" Thorndyke asked. "As you said, it is more in my line than yours."

"I didn't mean that," replied Elmhurst. "I'll dig it out. But, as I have had no experience of the exhumation of recent remains, you had better see that I go about it in the right way."

With this, he selected a suitable pick and spade, and, having placed a wheelbarrow close by to receive the soil, fell to work.

We watched him cautiously and skilfully pick away the clammy chalk rubble in which the corpse was embedded, and, as each new part became disclosed, attention and curiosity quickened. First the legs, looking almost as if modelled in chalk, then the skirt of a raincoat, and one whitened, repulsive-looking hand. Then, partly covered by the body, an object was seen, the nature of which was not at first obvious; but when Elmhurst had carefully disengaged it from the soil and drawn it out, it appeared as the whitened and shapeless remains of a felt hat, which was at once handed to Thorndyke; who restored it, as far as possible, to a recognizable shape, wiped its exterior with a bunch of turf, glanced into its interior, and then put it down on the side of the mound.

Gradually the corpse was uncovered and disengaged from its chalky bed until, at length, it lay revealed as the body of a stoutish man who, so far as could be judged, was on the shady side of middle age. Naturally, six months of burial in the clammy chalk had left uncomely traces and obscured the characteristics of the face; but when Thorndyke had gently cleaned the latter with a wisp of turf, the chalk-smeared, sodden features still retained enough of their original character to render identification possible by one who had known the man. In fact, it was not only possible. It was actually achieved. For, as Thorndyke stood up and threw away the wisp of turf, Polton, who had watched the procedure with fascinated eyes, suddenly stooped and gazed with the utmost astonishment into the dead man's face.

"Why!" he exclaimed, "it looks like Mr. Penrose!"

"You think it does?" said Thorndyke, without the slightest trace of surprise.

"Of course, sir," replied Polton, "I couldn't be positive. He's so very much changed. But he looks to me like Mr. Penrose; and I feel pretty certain that that is who he is."

"I have no doubt that you are right, Polton," said Thorndyke. "The hat is certainly his hat; and the fact that you recognized the body seems to settle the question of identity. And now another question arises. How is the body to be disposed of? The correct procedure would be to leave it where it is and notify the police. What do you say to that, Elmhurst?"

"You know best what the legal position is," was the reply. "But it won't be very comfortable carrying on the work with that gruesome object staring us in the face. Is there any legal objection to its being moved?"

"No, I think not," replied Thorndyke. "There are competent witnesses as to the circumstances of the discovery, and the soil is going to be thoroughly examined, so that any objects connected with the body are certain to be found."

"Quite certain," said Elmhurst. "The soil will not only be examined. That from this part will be sifted. And, of course, any objects found will be carefully preserved and reported. Still, we don't want to do anything irregular."

"I will take the responsibility for moving the body," said Thorndyke, "if you will find the means. But I think it would be as well to send a messenger in advance to the police so that they may be prepared."

"Very well," Elmhurst agreed. "Then I will send a man off at once and, if Mr. Polton will come and lend me a hand, we can rig up an extemporized stretcher from some of the spare fencing material."

With this he went off, accompanied by Polton, in search of the necessary material; the ladies migrated to the farther end of the mound, where they resumed their turf-cutting operations, and the labourers returned to their tasks.

When we were alone, the professor stood for a while looking

thoughtfully at the ghastly figure, lying at the bottom of its trench. Presently he turned to Thorndyke and asked:

"Has it occurred to you, Doctor—I expect it has—that the person who buried this poor creature showed very considerable foresight?"

"You mean in selecting a scheduled monument as a burial-place?"

"Yes—but I see that you have considered the point. It is rather subtle. According to ordinary probabilities, a scheduled tumulus should be the safest of all places in which to dispose of a dead body. It is actually secured by law against any disturbance of the soil. But for your intervention, this place might have remained untouched for a century."

"Very true," Thorndyke agreed, "but, of course, there is the converse aspect. If suspicion arises in respect of a given locality, the very security of a barrow from chance disturbance makes it the likeliest place for a suspected burial."

"I suppose," the professor ventured, "that an ordinary exhumation order would not have answered your purpose?"

"It would not have been practicable," Thorndyke replied. "I did not know that the body was here. I did not even know for certain that there was a dead body; and I don't suppose that either the Home Office or the Office of Works would have agreed to the excavation of a scheduled tumulus to search for a corpse whose existence was purely hypothetical. The only practicable method was a regular excavation by competent archæologists; which would not only settle the question whether the body was there or not, but, in the event of a negative result, would not have raised any troublesome issues or disclosed any suspicions which might possibly turn out to be unfounded."

"Yes," the professor agreed. "I admire your tact and discretion. You have done a valuable service to archæology and you have managed very neatly to harness the unsuspecting Elmhurst to your legal chariot."

"I am not sure," said I, "that Elmhurst was quite so unsuspecting as you think. But he also is a discreet gentleman. He wanted to excavate the barrow and was willing to do it and ask no questions. But I fancy that he expected to find something more significant than neolithic pottery."

Here our discussion was brought to an end by the arrival of Elmhurst and Polton bearing a sort of elongated hurdle formed very neatly by lashing together a number of stout rods. This they deposited opposite the place where the body was lying in readiness to receive its melancholy burden.

"I think, Jervis," said Thorndyke, "that the next proceeding devolves upon us. Will you lend us a hand, Polton? The body ought to be lifted as evenly as possible to avoid any disturbance of the joints."

Accordingly, we placed ourselves by the side of the trench, Thorndyke taking the head and shoulders, I taking the middle, while Polton supported the legs and feet. At the word from Thorndyke, we all very carefully lifted the limp, sagging figure and carried it to the hurdle on which we gently lowered it. As we rose and stood looking down at the poor shabby heap of mortality, Polton, who appeared to be deeply moved, moralized sadly.

"Dear, dear!" he exclaimed, "what a dreadful and grievous thing it is. To think that that miserable, dirty mass of rags and carrion is all that is left of a fine, jovial, happy gentleman, full of energy and enjoying every moment of his life. There is a heavy debt against somebody, and I hope, sir, that you will see that it is paid to the uttermost farthing."

"I hope so, too, Polton," said Thorndyke. "That, you know, is what we are here for. Can we find anything to cover the body? It is a rather gruesome object to carry down into the village."

As he spoke, the four labourers who had volunteered as bearers approached carrying a bundle of sacks; and with these, laid across the hurdle, the wretched, unseemly remains were decently covered up. Then the four men lifted the hurdle (which, with its wasted burden, must have been quite light) and moved away round the foot of the barrow, watched, not without evident relief, by Elmhurst and his two colleagues.

"I suppose," said Elmhurst, as we prepared to follow, "you won't be coming back here?"

"Not to-day," replied Thorndyke. "But we shall have to attend the inquest, either as witnesses or to watch the proceedings, so we shall have an opportunity to see your work in a more advanced stage. Don't think that our interest in it is extinct because we are no longer concerned with neolithic pottery."

With this we took leave of our friends and, starting off down the hill-side, soon overtook and passed the bearers and made our way to the foot-bridge over the river near the mill. A few yards farther on, we met our messenger returning in company with a police sergeant, and halted to give the latter the necessary particulars.

"I suppose," he remarked, "you ought, properly, to have left the body where it was and reported to us. Still, as you say, there's nothing in it as the witnesses are available. I'll just note your addresses and those of any other persons that you know of who may be wanted at the inquest."

We accordingly gave our own names and addresses (at which I noticed that the sergeant seemed to prick up his ears), and Thorndyke gave those of Brodribb, Horridge and Kickweed. And this concluded the day's business. Of the spade and the trenching tool Thorndyke said nothing, evidently intending to examine them at his leisure before handing them over to the police.

I may say that the discovery had given me one of the greatest surprises of my life. The idea that Penrose might be dead had never occurred to me. And yet, as soon as the discovery had been made, I began to realize how all the facts that were known to us pointed in this direction, and I also began to see the drift of the many hints that Thorndyke had given me. But, although, over a very substantial tea at the Wool-pack Inn, we discussed the various and stirring events of the day, I did not think it expedient to enter into the details of the case in Polton's presence. Not that, in these days, we had many secrets from Polton. But there were certain other matters, as yet undisclosed, that it seemed better to reserve for discussion when we should be alone.

CHAPTER 15

WHAT BEFELL AT THE WOOL-PACK

The inquest on the body of Daniel Penrose yielded nothing that was new to us. The coroner had been provided by Thorndyke with a brief synopsis of the known facts of the case (which my colleague had, apparently, prepared in advance) to serve as a guide in conducting the inquiry; but he was a discreet man who understood his business and avoided extending the proceedings beyond the proper scope of a coroner's inquest. Nor had we been able to increase our knowledge of the case; for neither the spade nor the trenching tool furnished any information whatever. All our attempts to develop finger-prints failed utterly, and the most minute examination of the tools for traces of hair or blood was equally fruitless. Which was not surprising; for even if such traces had originally existed, six months' exposure to the weather would naturally have dissipated them.

But if the coroner was not disposed to go beyond the facts connected with the discovery, there was another person who was. We had put up for the night at the Wool-pack in Chilham in order to be present at the post-mortem (by the coroner's invitation), and were just finishing a leisurely breakfast when the coffee-room door opened to admit no less a person than Mr. Superintendent Miller. He had come down by an early train for the express purpose of getting an outline of the case from Thorndyke to assist him in following the proceedings at the inquest.

"Well, Doctor," he said, cheerfully, seating himself without ceremony at our table, "here we are, and both on the same errand, I take it."

"We are," Thorndyke replied, "if you have come to attend the inquest on poor Penrose."

"Exactly," rejoined Miller. "We have a common purpose—which isn't always the case. Lord, Doctor! What a pleasure it is to find myself, for once in a way, on the same side of the board with you, playing the same game against the same opponent! You won't mind if I ask a few questions?"

"Not at all," replied Thorndyke. "But the first question is, have you had breakfast?"

"Well, I have, you know," said Miller, "but it was a long time ago. I think I could pick a morsel, since you mention the matter."

Accordingly, Thorndyke rang the bell, and, having given an order for a morsel in the form of a gammon rasher and a pot of coffee, prepared himself for the superintendent's assault.

"Now, Doctor," the latter began, in his best cross-examining manner, "it is perfectly clear to me that you know all about this case."

"I wish it were as clear to me," said Thorndyke.

"There, now, Dr. Jervis," exclaimed Miller, "just listen to that. Isn't he an aggravating man? He has got all the facts of the case up his sleeve, as he usually has, and now he is going to pretend—as he usually does—that he doesn't know anything about it. But it won't do, Doctor. The facts speak for themselves. Here were our men trapesing up and down the country, looking for Daniel Penrose to execute a warrant on him, and all the time you knew perfectly well that he was safely tucked away in a barrow—though why the deuce they call the thing a barrow when it is obviously just a mound of earth, I can't imagine."

"That is a wild exaggeration, you know, Miller," Thorndyke protested. "After six months' study of the case, I came to the conclusion that Penrose was probably buried in this barrow. But I was so far from certainty that I had to take this roundabout way of settling the question whether I was or was not mistaken. It happened that my conclusion was correct."

"It usually does," said Miller. "And I expect you have formed some conclusions as to who planted that body in the barrow. And I expect those conclusions will happen to be right, too. And I should very much like to know what they are."

"Really, Miller," I exclaimed, "I am surprised at you. Have you known Thorndyke all these years without discovering that he never lets the cat out of the bag until he can let her right out? No protruding heads or tails for him. But, when everything is finished and the course is clear, out she comes."

"Yes, I know," said Miller, gloomily, "I know his beastly secret ways. I think that, in some previous state of existence, he must have been an oyster. Still, Doctor, you needn't be so close with an old friend."

"But my dear Miller," protested Thorndyke, "you are entirely mistaken. I am withholding nothing that I could properly tell you. What Jervis has said, though crudely put, is the strict truth. If I knew who had committed this crime, of course I should tell you. But I don't know. And if I have any half-formed suspicions, I am going to keep them to myself until I am able to test them. In short Miller, I will tell you all I know. But I tell nobody what I think. So now ask me any questions you please."

I must admit that it was not very encouraging for Miller. My experience of Thorndyke was fairly expressed in what he had just said. He would tell you all the facts (which you usually knew already and which were more or less common property) but the general truths which were implicit in those facts he would leave you to discover for yourself; which you never did until the final conclusions emerged; when it was surprising how obvious they were.

"Well, to begin with," said Miller. "There was that chappie at the hospital whom we all supposed to be Penrose. Have you any idea who he really was? You obviously spotted the fact that he was not Penrose."

"No," replied Thorndyke, "I have no idea who he was. My suspicion that he was not Penrose was based on his behaviour, especially on the fact that he appeared particularly anxious to avoid being seen or recognized by any one who knew Penrose. As a matter of fact, he was not then recognizable at all, and nobody knows what he was really like. But I don't think that there is any utility in going into details of the case at that stage. Remember that my investigations were then concerned with the questions: Is Penrose alive or dead? And, if he is dead, what has become of his body? Now, I have settled those questions and their solution has evolved the further questions: Was he murdered? And, if so, who murdered him? The first question will be answered at the inquest—pretty certainly in the affirmative; and we shall then address ourselves to the second. And as you say, we have a common purpose and shall try to be mutually helpful.

"Now, I have given the coroner a synopsis of the case from the beginning, and I have a copy of it which I am going to hand to you. I suggest that you study it, and then, if anything occurs to you in connection with it, and you like to ask me any questions on matters of fact, I will give you all the information that I possess. How will that do for you?"

I suspected that it was not at all what Miller would have liked; but he saw clearly, as I did, that Thorndyke was not going to disclose any theories that he might have formed as to where we might look for the possible murderer. Accordingly, he accepted the position with as good a grace as he could, and, when he had finished a very substantial breakfast, he demanded the synopsis, which Thorndyke fetched from his room and placed in his hands.

"Are you coming to watch the post-mortem, Jervis?" my colleague asked.

"No," I replied. "I shall hear all about it at the inquest, so I think I shall improve the shining hour by taking a walk up to the barrow to see how the work is progressing."

"Ha!" said Miller. "Then perhaps you wouldn't mind my walking with you. I have never seen a barrow. Never heard of one until I read the report in the paper."

Of course, I had to agree; not unwillingly, in fact, for I liked our old friend. But I knew quite well what the proposal meant. As nothing was to be got out of Thorndyke, Miller intended to apply a gentle squeeze to me. And to this also I had no objection, for I was still in the dark as to how Thorndyke had reached his very definite conclusions and was quite willing to have my memories of the investigation stirred up.

The process began as soon as we were fairly outside the inn.

"Now, look here, Dr. Jervis," said the superintendent, "it's all very well for the doctor to pretend that he hasn't anything to go on, but there are certain obvious questions that arise when a well-to-do man like Penrose gets murdered. The first is: Who benefits by his death?"

"The answer to that," I replied, "is quite simple. Penrose made a will by which practically the whole of his property goes to a man named Horridge."

"Then," said Miller, "it will be worth while to give a little attention to Mr. Horridge. Do you know anything about him?"

"Not very much," I replied. "But I know this much; that he is about the most unlikely man in the world to have murdered Penrose."

"Why do you say that?" demanded Miller.

"Because, if Penrose died when we believe he did, Horridge stands to lose something like a hundred and fifty thousand pounds by his death. Penrose was the principal heir of his father, who was quite a rich man. But when Penrose died—if he did die on the date which we are assuming—his father was alive and consequently the father's estate would not pass to him. But Horridge was Penrose's heir and would have inherited the father's property, as well as Penrose's, under the latter's will. So it didn't suit Horridge at all for Penrose to die when he did."

"And is the old man still alive?"

"No. He died quite recently."

"Ha!" said Miller. "Then somebody else benefits by Penrose's death. Do you happen to know who that will be?"

"No," I replied. "I understand, but do not know for certain, that the old man died intestate. In that case, the next of kin will benefit. They will benefit very considerably, as their expectations would have been quite small if Penrose had been alive when his father died. But I have no idea who they are."

"Well, we shall have to find that out," said Miller. "It seems that somebody had a perfectly understandable motive for getting rid of Penrose while the old man was still alive."

As Miller continued his interrogations, asking uncommonly shrewd questions and making equally shrewd comments, I began to feel an unwonted sympathy with Thorndyke in respect of his habitual reticence and secretiveness. For his approach to a criminal problem was quite different from Miller's, and there might easily arise some conflict between the two. Miller was evidently on the look-out for a suspect, and he was considering the problem in terms of persons; whereas Thorndyke's practice was to watch, unseen and unsuspected, while he collected and sifted the evidence, and, above all, to avoid alarming the suspected persons until he was ready to make the final move.

But our arrival at the top of Julliberrie Downs put an end, for the time being, to Miller's bombardment; for here we came in sight of the barrow, now stripped of its turf and presenting the smooth, white, rounded shape on which its builders had looked a couple of thousand years or more before the coming of the Romans. I explained its nature and its great antiquity to Miller, who was deeply impressed, but who, nevertheless, showed a strong inclination to "cut the cackle and get back to the case." But as we approached, the eagle-eyed Elmhurst observed us and came forward to do the honours of the excavation.

Under his guidance we went round to the farther side of the mound which was in the process of being cut away like a gigantic cheese, and the chalk rubble, stored in the dump, was mounting to the magnitude of a considerable hill. At this point, the superintendent's interest in the barrow awakened surprisingly, for an excavation was more or less in his line, and he took the opportunity to pick up a few technical tips. He was particularly impressed by a builder's sieve which had been set up at the dump.

"I see," he remarked to Elmhurst, "that you don't mean to miss anything. I shall bear your methods in mind the next time I have to direct a search. And speaking of a search, have you turned up anything that seems to be connected with the body that you found?"

"Yes," replied Elmhurst. "We found, near the place where the body was lying, quite an interesting thing, and, I should say, decidedly connected with that body—a small bronze pestle, apparently belonging to an ancient drug-mortar. I'll show it to you. Miss Stirling, have you got that pestle?"

As the lady addressed turned round and greeted me with a friendly nod, the superintendent whispered to me in an awe-stricken tone:

"Good gracious! That young person in the fisherman's trousers is a female! And I believe the other one is, too. Well, I never!"

"You would hardly expect them to wear evening dress for a job like this," I remarked; to which the superintendent assented, but continued to watch the ladies furtively and with fascinated eyes.

The pestle was presently produced from the shepherd's hut and offered for our inspection; a smallish pestle of bronze—now covered with a thick green patina—with a bulbous end and a rather elaborately decorated handle surmounted by a bearded head of the classical type which I assumed to represent Æsculapius. Attached to it was a small tie-on label on which was written a note of its precise "find-spot" in the mound.

Miller took it in his hand and executed a warlike flourish with it, by way of testing its weight.

"It's of no great size," he remarked, "but it is quite a formidable weapon. Uncommonly handy, too, and as portable as a life-preserver. Perhaps I had better take charge of it."

He was about to slip it into his pocket when Elmhurst interposed firmly.

"I think I must keep it for the present. I am summoned to give evidence at the inquest and I shall have to produce this. Besides, I am personally responsible to the Office of Works for all objects found during the excavation."

With this he quietly resumed possession of the pestle, which Miller reluctantly surrendered, and as the latter had no further interest in the excavation, and made no secret of the fact, we presently took our leave and resumed our perambulations, with a running accompaniment of interrogation on the part of the super-intendent which caused me to hail the luncheon hour with a certain sense of relief.

The superintendent, of course, lunched with us, and even at the table he continued his quest for knowledge, beginning, naturally, with inquiries as to the result of the post-mortem.

"The cause of death is obvious enough," said Thorndyke. "There is a depressed fracture of the skull at the left side and towards the back; not very large, but deep, and suggesting a very violent blow. The shape of the depression—a fairly regular oval concavity—implies a blunt weapon of a smooth, rounded shape."

"Such as a pestle, for instance," Miller suggested.

"Yes," Thorndyke replied, "a pestle would agree with the conditions. But why do you suggest a pestle?"

"Because your excavating friends have found one; a bronze pestle; quite a handy little weapon, and portable enough to go quite easily into an ordinary pocket."

Here he gave a very excellent and concise description of the weapon, to which Thorndyke listened with deep interest.

"So you see," Miller concluded, "that it is a thing that ought to be quite easy to identify by any one who had ever seen it. Dr. Jervis thinks that it would not be likely to be the property of a chemist or apothecary. What do you say to that?"

"I agree with him," Thorndyke replied. "That is to say, it does not definitely suggest an apothecary as would have been the case if it had been a Wedgwood pestle. Bronze mortars and pestles are not now in general use; and this is pretty evidently an ancient pestle."

"A sort of curio, in fact," said Miller, "and rather suggestive of a collector or curio monger?"

Thorndyke agreed that this was so, but he made no further comment, though the connection of a curio with the late Daniel Penrose was fairly significant. But my recent experiences of Miller's eager and persistent cross-examinations enabled me to understand the sort of defensive reticence that they tended to engender. Moreover, the connection, though significant, was not very clear as to its bearing. It would have been more obvious if Penrose had been the murderer.

The inquest was held in a large room at the inn, normally reserved for gatherings of a more festive character, and when we entered and took our places the preliminaries of swearing in the jury and viewing the body had already been disposed of. I looked round the room and noted that in the seats set apart for the witnesses, not only Elmhurst and his two coadjutors were present but also Kickweed and Horridge. Both of the latter showed evident signs of distress, but more especially Horridge. Which rather surprised me. The grief of the lugubrious, red-eyed Kickweed was understandable enough; for not only had he manifested a genuine affection and loyalty towards his dead master, but the death of Penrose was a very material loss to him. But I could not reconcile Horridge's condition with the callous selfishness that he had shown previously. It is true that the apparent date of the death put an end to his hopes of inheriting the fortune of the lately deceased Penrose senior, but, on the other hand, he stood to gain forthwith the very respectable sum of fifty thousand pounds, for which he might reasonably have expected to wait for years. Nevertheless, he was obviously extremely upset, and it was evident from his pale, haggard face and his restless movements, that this sudden, unforeseen catastrophe had come on him as an overwhelming shock.

The first witness called was Miss Stirling, who gave a brief, matter-of-fact description of her discovery, to which the jury listened with absorbed interest. She was followed by Elmhurst, who amplified her statement and described his disinterment of the body and the appearance and position of the latter. He also explained the methods of excavation and the procedure after the body had been removed.

"In the soil which was taken away after the removal of the body," the coroner inquired, "did you find any objects that seemed to be connected with it?"

"Yes," replied Elmhurst. "I found this pestle, which could certainly not have been among the original contents of the barrow."

Here he produced the pestle wrapped in a handkerchief and, having removed the latter, handed the "find" to the coroner, who inspected it curiously and then passed it on to the foreman of the jury.

"This," he remarked, "does not look like a modern pestle. As you are an authority on antiquities, Mr. Elmhurst, perhaps you can tell us something about it."

"I am not much of an authority on recent antiquities," Elmhurst disclaimed modestly, "but I should judge that this pestle belonged to a bronze drug-mortar of the kind that was in use in the seventeenth or early eighteenth century."

"You would not regard it as probably part of the outfit of a chemist's shop?"

"No," replied Elmhurst. "I understand that, since the introduction of grinding machinery, the practice of grinding hard drugs in metal mortars is quite extinct."

"Can you form any idea how long this object has been buried?"

"I could not judge the exact time; but, assuming it to have been bright, or at least clean, when it was buried, I should say that it must have been lying in the ground for several months."

That concluded Elmhurst's evidence, and, as he retired to his seat, the name of the medical witness was called.

"You have made an examination of the body of the deceased?" the coroner began, when the preliminaries had been disposed of. "Can you give any opinion as to how long deceased has been dead?"

"My examination," the witness replied, "led me to the belief that he had been dead at least six months."

"Did you arrive at any conclusion as to the cause of death?"

"The cause of death was an injury to the brain occasioned by a heavy blow on the head. There is a small but deep depressed fracture of the skull on the left side just above and behind the ear, which appears to have been produced by a blunt, smooth weapon with a rounded end."

"Please look at this pestle, which you have heard was found near the place where the body had been lying. Could the injuries which you found have been produced by this?"

The doctor examined the pestle and gave it as his opinion that it corresponded completely with the shape of the fracture.

"I suppose that it is a mere formality to ask whether the injuries could have been self-inflicted or due to an accident?" the coroner suggested.

"They certainly could not have been self-inflicted," the witness replied. "As to an accident, one doesn't like to use the word impossible, but I cannot imagine any kind of accident which could have produced the injuries that were found."

This completed the medical evidence proper, but Thorndyke was called to give confirmatory testimony.

"You have heard the evidence of the doctor. Have you any observations to make on it?"

"No," replied Thorndyke. "I am in complete agreement with everything that my colleague has said."

"We may take it," said the coroner, "that you know more about this affair than anybody else. Can you throw any light on the actual circumstances in which the tragedy occurred?"

"No," Thorndyke replied. "My investigations have been concerned with the question whether Daniel Penrose was alive or dead; and, if he was dead, when and where his death occurred. I can make no suggestion as to the identity of the person who killed him."

"As to the date of his death; have you arrived at any conclusion on that point?"

"Yes. I have no doubt that deceased met his death at some time in the evening of the seventeenth of last October. I base that conclusion principally on the fact that his car was seen coming away from the neighbourhood of the place where his body was found, and that it was evidently being driven by some other person."

"And have you formed any opinion as to who that other person may have been?"

"I have not. At present I have no evidence pointing to any particular person."

"Well," said the coroner. "I hope you will now take up this further question, and that your efforts will be as successful in this as in the problem which you have solved in such a remarkable manner. Is there any question that any member of the jury would like to ask?"

Apparently there was not. Accordingly Thorndyke returned to his seat and the name of Francis Horridge was called. And, as he walked up to the table, I was once more impressed by his extraordinarily agitated and shaken condition. It was noticed also by the coroner, who, before beginning his examination, offered a few words of sympathy.

"This, Mr. Horridge," said he, "must be a very painful and distressing experience for you, as an intimate friend of the deceased."

"It is," replied Horridge. "I had not the faintest suspicion that my old friend was not alive and well. It has been a terrible shock."

"It must have been," the coroner agreed, "and I am sorry to have to trouble you with questions. But we have to solve this dreadful mystery if we can, or at least find out as much as possible about it. You have seen the body of deceased. Could you identify it?"

"Yes. It is the body of Daniel Penrose."

"Yes," said the coroner, "there seems to be no doubt as to the identity of the body. Now, Mr. Horridge, the medical evidence makes it clear that deceased met his death by the act of some unknown person. It is very necessary to discover, if possible, who that person is. You were an intimate friend of deceased and must know a good deal about his personal affairs. Do you know of anything that might throw any light on the circumstances surrounding his death?"

"No," was the reply. "But I did not know so very much about his personal habits or his friends and acquaintances."

"I understand that deceased had made a will. Do you know anything about that?"

"Yes. I am the executor of his will."

"Then you can tell us whether there was anything in connection with it which might give rise to trouble or enmity. In rough, general terms, what are the provisions of the will?"

"They are quite simple. There is a handsome, but well-deserved legacy to his butler, Kickweed, amounting to two thousand pounds. Beyond that, the bulk of the property is devised and bequeathed to me."

"So you and Mr. Kickweed are the persons who benefit most in a pecuniary sense by the death of deceased?"

"Yes; and I am sure we should both very gladly forgo the benefit to have our friend back again."

"I am sure you would," said the coroner. "But can you tell us if there are any other persons who would benefit materially in any way by the death of deceased?"

"Yes, there are," replied Horridge. "Quite recently, deceased's father died and left a considerable fortune. If deceased had been alive at that time, the bulk of that fortune would have come to him. As it is, it will be distributed among his next of kin. Consequently, those persons will benefit very considerably by deceased's death if that death occurred on the date given by Dr. Thorndyke. I do not know who they are; and, of course, I do not suspect any of them of being concerned in this crime."

"Certainly not," the coroner agreed. "But one naturally looks round for some persons who might have had a motive for making away with deceased. But you know of no such persons? You do not know of any one with whom deceased was on terms of enmity or who had any sort of grudge against him?"

"No. So far as I know, he had no enemies whatever. He was not likely to have any. He was a kindly man and on pleasant terms with every one with whom he came in contact."

"May the same be said of us all when our time comes," the coroner moralized. "But there is another motive that we ought to consider. That of robbery. Do you know whether deceased was in the habit of carrying about with him—on his person I mean—property of any considerable value?"

"I have no idea," replied Horridge. "He must have done so at times, for he was a great collector and was in the habit of going about the country making purchases. I had supposed that his last journey was made with that object, and I am disposed to think so still. He used to come down to this neighbourhood to visit a dealer named Todd who has a shop at Canterbury."

"You say that he was a collector. What kind of things did he collect?"

"It was a very miscellaneous collection, but I have always believed that, in addition to the oddments that were displayed in the main gallery, he had a collection of jewels of much more considerable value which were kept in a small room. That room was always kept locked, and deceased would never say definitely what it contained."

Here Horridge gave a description of the small room as we had seen it on the occasion of our visit of inspection, and he also gave an account of the supposed burglary, to which the coroner—and Superintendent Miller—listened with profound interest.

"This," said the former, "seems to be a matter of some importance. What is the precise date on which the supposed burglary took place?"

"The second of last January."

"That," said the coroner, "would be nearly three months after the death of deceased, if Dr. Thorndyke is correct as to the date on which the death occurred. And you say that, if the cupboard was opened, it must have been opened with its own proper key, since the lock is unpickable and the cupboard had not been broken open.

Is there any reason to believe that the cupboard was actually opened?"

"I think there is," replied Horridge. "It is certain that some one entered the room on that night, and it is practically certain that he entered the premises by the side gate, as there is no other way of approaching the window. But that gate was always kept locked, and it was found to be locked on the morning after the supposed burglary. So it seems that the burglar must have had the key of the gate, at least."

"And who usually had possession of that key?"

"Mr. Penrose. It seems that he sometimes used that gate and he kept the key in his own possession. There was no duplicate."

"When you went to the mortuary to identify the body, did you look over the effects of deceased which had been taken from the pockets?"

"No; but I asked the coroner's officer if any keys had been found and he told me that there had not."

The coroner nodded gravely and Miller remarked to me in a whisper that we were beginning to see daylight.

"It is unfortunate," the former observed, "that we have no clear evidence as to whether a burglary did or did not take place. However, that is really a matter for the police. But the question is highly significant in relation to the problem of the motive for killing deceased. Do you know whether, apart from this burglary, there were any attempts to rob deceased?"

"Yes," replied Horridge; "but I think it was only a chance affair. Deceased told me on one occasion that his car had been stopped on a rather solitary road by a gang of men who were armed with revolvers and who made him deliver up what money he had about him. But, apparently, his loss was only trifling as he had nothing of value with him at the time."

This concluded Horridge's evidence; and when the coroner's officer, who turned out to be the police sergeant whom I had met, had deposed to having examined the contents of deceased's pockets and found no keys among them, the name of Edward Kickweed was called.

CHAPTER 16

MR. KICKWEED SURPRISES THE CORONER

The evidence given by our friend, Horridge, had been listened to with keen interest, not only by the coroner and the jury, but especially by Superintendent Miller. For, though it comprised nothing that we did not already know, it had elicited the important fact that the body of Penrose had apparently been rifled of his keys. But striking and significant as this fact was, it was left to Kickweed to contribute the really sensational item of evidence.

But this came later. The early part of his evidence seemed to be little more than a series of formalities, confirming what had already been proved. When he took his place at the table, his lugubrious aspect drew from the coroner a kindly expression of sympathy similar to that with which he had greeted Horridge, after which he proceeded with his examination.

"You have seen the body which is lying in the mortuary, Mr. Kickweed. Were you able to identify it?"

"Yes," groaned Kickweed. "It is the body of my esteemed and beloved employer, Mr. Daniel Penrose."

"How long had you known deceased?"

"I have known him practically all his life. I was in his father's service and when he grew up and took a house of his own, he asked me to come to him as butler. So I came gladly, and have been with him ever since."

"Then you probably know a good deal about his manner of life and the people he knew. Can you tell us whether there was any one who might have had any feelings of enmity towards him?"

"There was not," Kickweed replied confidently. "Deceased was a rather self-contained man, but he was a kind, courteous and generous man and I am sure that he had not an enemy in the world."

"You confirm Mr. Horridge's estimate," said the coroner, "and a very satisfactory one it is; and it seems to dispose of revenge or malice as the motive for killing him. By the way, it is not of much consequence, but do you recognize these objects?"

Here he took from behind his chair the spade and trenching tool which we had found in the wood and laid them on the table for Kickweed's inspection.

"Yes," said the witness, "they belonged to deceased. He used to keep them in the garage. I am not quite sure what he used them for, but I know that he occasionally took them with him when he went out in the country in his car."

"Were you aware that he had taken them with him when he last left home?"

"I was not. But afterwards, when I saw that they were not in their usual place, I assumed that he had taken them with him."

The coroner entered this not very illuminating statement in the depositions, and then, noting that the witness's eyes were fixed on the pestle which lay on the table, he picked it up, and, holding it towards him, said:

"I suppose it is needless to ask you if you recognize this object?"

"I do," was the totally unexpected reply. "It belongs to a small bronze mortar which forms part of Mr. Penrose's collection."

"This is very extraordinary!" the coroner exclaimed. "You are sure that you recognize it?"

"Perfectly sure," replied Kickweed. "The pestle and mortar stood together on a shelf in the great gallery and I have often, when dusting the things in the collection, given this pestle and the mortar a rub with the cloth. I know it very well indeed."

"Well," the coroner exclaimed, "this is indeed a surprise! The weapon is actually the property of the deceased!"

There was a short interval of silence, in which I could hear Miller cursing softly under his breath.

"There," he muttered, "is another promising clue gone west!"

Then the coroner, recovering from his astonishment, resumed his examination of the witness.

"Can you explain by what extraordinary chance deceased came to have this thing with him on the day when he was killed?"

"Yes. It was his usual custom, when he went out in his car and was likely to be on the road late, to slip the pestle in his pocket before he started. The custom arose after he had been stopped on the road by robbers, as Mr. Horridge has mentioned. I urged him to get a revolver or some other means of defending himself. But he had a great dislike to fire-arms, so I suggested a life-preserver. But then he happened to see me polishing this pestle, and it occurred to him that it would do as well as the life-preserver, and, as he said, would be a more interesting thing to carry. So he used to take it with him, and he did on this occasion, as I discovered a few days after he had gone, when I saw the mortar on the shelf without the pestle."

"Well," said the coroner, "there is evidently no doubt that this pestle really belonged to deceased, and that fact may have a rather important bearing on the case."

He paused, and, having entered Kickweed's last statement in the depositions, turned to him once more.

"Apparently, Mr. Kickweed, of all the persons who knew deceased you are the one who last saw him alive. Can you recall the circumstances of his departure from his home?"

"Yes," the witness replied, "very clearly. At lunchtime on the seventeenth of last October, deceased informed me that he should presently be starting for a run in the country in his car. He was not sure about the time when he would return, but he thought he might be rather late; and he directed that no one should sit up for him, but that a cold supper should be left for him in the dining-room. He left the house a little before three to go to the garage, and, about a quarter of an hour later, I saw him drive past the house in his car. That would be about three o'clock."

"And after that, did you ever see him again?"

"I never saw him again. I sat up until past midnight, but, of course, he never came home."

"Did you then suspect that any mischance had befallen him?"

"I was rather uneasy," Kickweed replied, "because he had apparently intended to come home. Otherwise, I should not have been, as he often stayed away from home without notice."

"When did you first learn that there was something wrong?"

"It was in the afternoon of the twentieth of October. Mr. Horridge had called to see him, and we were just discussing the possible reasons for his staying away when a police officer arrived, carrying deceased's raincoat, and told us that deceased had apparently absconded from the hospital at Gravesend. And that was all that I ever knew of the matter until I heard Dr. Thorndyke's evidence."

"Then," said the coroner, "to repeat; you saw him drive away on the seventeenth of October and you never saw him, or had any knowledge of him, again. Is that not so?"

"I never saw him again. But as to having any further knowledge of him, I am rather doubtful. I received a letter from him."

"You received a letter from him!" the coroner repeated in evident surprise. "When did you receive that letter?"

"It was delivered on the morning of the twenty-seventh of last March."

A murmur of astonishment arose from the jury and the coroner exclaimed in a tone of amazement:

"Last March! Why, the man had been dead for months!"

"So it appears," Kickweed admitted; "and I am glad to believe that the letter was not really written by him."

"Why do you say that?"

"Because," Kickweed replied, "it was not a very creditable letter for a gentleman of Mr. Penrose's character. It was a foolish letter and not as polite as it should have been."

"Have you that letter about you?"

"No. I handed it to Dr. Thorndyke, and I believe he has it still. But I can remember the substance of its contents. It directed me to lock up the small room and deposit the key at Mr. Penrose's bank."

"And did you do so?"

"Certainly, I did, though Dr. Thorndyke seemed rather opposed to my doing so. But, at the time, I supposed it to be a genuine letter from my employer and, of course, I had no choice but to carry out his instructions."

"Have you formed any opinion as to who might have written that letter?"

"No, I have not the faintest idea. Until I heard Dr. Thorndyke's evidence, I still supposed it to be a genuine letter from deceased."

"Well," said the coroner, "it is a most extraordinary affair. I think we had better recall Dr. Thorndyke and hear what he can tell us about it."

Accordingly, as Kickweed had apparently given all the information that he had to give, and no one wished to ask him any questions, he was allowed to return to his seat and Thorndyke was recalled.

"Will you tell us what you know about this very remarkable letter that Mr. Kickweed received?" the coroner asked.

"I first heard of that letter when Mr. Kickweed called at my chambers late in the evening of the twenty-seventh of last March.

He then informed me that he had received that letter and gave it to me to read. I read and examined it and at once came to the conclusion that it was a forgery. I took a photograph of it—of which I have a copy here—and carried the original to Mr. Brodribb, deceased's solicitor, to whom I handed it for safe custody and to whom I stated my opinion that it was a forgery."

"You decided at once that the letter was a forgery. What led you to that decision?"

"My decision was based on the circumstances and on the character of the letter itself. As to the circumstances, I had by that time formed the very definite opinion that Daniel Penrose was dead and that he had died on the seventeenth of the previous October. The letter itself presented several suspicious features. The matter of it was quite unreasonable and inadequate. The room was already locked up and the key was in the very safe custody of deceased's trusted and responsible servant, and had been for months. The directions in the letter appeared to be merely a pretext for writing and suggested some ulterior purpose. Then the manner of the letter was quite out of character with that of the supposed writer—a gentleman addressing his confidential servant. It was written in a tone of coarse, jocular familiarity with a most ill-mannered caricature of Mr. Kickweed's name. It impressed me as a grotesque, overdone attempt to imitate deceased's habitually facetious manner of speech. And, on questioning Mr. Kickweed, who was obviously hurt and surprised by the rudeness of this letter, I learned that deceased had always been in the habit of addressing him in a strictly correct and courteous fashion."

"Apart from these inferences, was there anything visible that marked this letter as a forgery?"

"I did not discover anything. Of the handwriting I could not judge as I was not familiar with deceased's writing. But there were no signs of tracing or other gross indications of forgery. But I may say that Mr. Brodribb was of the opinion that the writing did not look, to him, like that of deceased."

"You say that the matter of this letter suggested to you that a mere pretext had been made for writing and that there was some ulterior purpose. Can you suggest what that ulterior purpose might have been?"

"I suggest that its purpose was to make it appear that deceased was alive."

"That seems to imply that the unknown writer of the letter knew that he was dead, though no one but yourself had any suspicion that he was not still alive. There would seem to be no object in trying to prove that a man was alive when nobody supposed that he was dead. Don't you agree?"

"Yes," replied Thorndyke; "that seems to be the natural inference."

"I suppose you cannot offer any suggestion as to who the writer of the letter may have been?"

"I cannot. It seems clear that whoever he may have been, he must have been well acquainted with deceased, for the phraseology of the letter, although greatly exaggerated, was a recognizable imitation of deceased's rather odd manner of expressing himself. But I cannot give him a name."

"There was one matter that we overlooked when you were giving your evidence. You ascertained in some mysterious manner that deceased was buried in Julliberrie's Grave. But is that the place where he met his death, or was his body brought from some other place?"

"I should say that there is no doubt that he was killed close to the place where his body was found. The implements which we found in the wood and which have been identified as his property suggest very strongly that he came to Julliberrie's Grave of his own accord with the intention of searching for antiquities for his collection. Probably he had actually done some excavation in the mound and the cavity that he had dug offered the facilities for disposing of his body. And the finding of the weapon with which he was apparently killed, near to the body, supports this view."

"Yes," said the coroner, "I think you have made it clear that the death occurred in the neighbourhood of the barrow and that the body was not brought there from a distance. And that, I think, gives us all the evidence that we need."

He bowed to Thorndyke, and, as the latter returned to his seat, he began a brief and very sensible summing up.

"The disappearance of Mr. Daniel Penrose involves a long and complicated story. But with that story we are not concerned. This is a coroner's inquest; and the function of such an inquiry is to answer certain questions relating to a dead body which has been found within our jurisdiction. Those questions are: Who is the dead person? and where, when and by what means did deceased meet with his death? We are not concerned with the person, if any, who caused the death of deceased unless such person should be plainly and evidently in view. We have to decide whether or not a crime has been committed, but it is not our function to bring that crime home to any particular person. That duty appertains to the police.

"Now, in respect of those questions which I have mentioned, we have no difficulty. The evidence which we have heard enables us to answer them quite confidently. The body has been identified as that of a gentleman named Daniel Penrose; and it has been clearly proved that he met his death at a place called Julliberrie's Grave on the seventeenth of last October and that his death was caused by violence inflicted by some unknown person. These are matters of fact which have been proved; and the only question which you have to decide is that of the nature of the act by which the death was caused. Deceased was killed by a heavy blow on the head inflicted with a bronze pestle. The person who struck that blow killed deceased and, therefore, undeniably committed an act of homicide. But there are many kinds of homicide, varying in their degree of culpability. A man may justifiably kill another in defence of his own life. Then there is no crime. Or he may kill another quite accidentally, when, again, there is no crime. Or he may kill another in the course of a struggle, by violence which was not intended to cause death. Here the act of homicide amounts only to manslaughter; and the degree of criminality will depend on the particular circumstances. Again, a man may kill another with the deliberate and considered intention of killing him—that is with what the law calls malice. Such deliberate and premeditated killing constitutes wilful murder.

"Now, in the present case, we have to consider the circumstances in which the death of deceased occurred; and of those circumstances we have very imperfect knowledge. A striking fact is that the weapon with which deceased was killed was his own property and must, apparently, have been brought to the place by himself. We have learned, also, that he habitually carried this weapon for the purpose of self-defence. There is thus the suggestion that he may have so used it on the occasion when he was killed. That is to say, there is a distinct suggestion of a struggle, and the actual possibility that deceased may have been the aggressor, killed by the unknown in self-defence.

"On the other hand, the unknown, having killed deceased, buried the body secretly and hurried away from the place—incidentally

killing another person on his way—and has since given no information and made no sign, unless we assume that the very mysterious
letter that Mr. Kickweed received emanated from him. And it is,
perhaps, worth while to give that letter a brief consideration, as it
seems to have some bearing on the question which we are trying to
decide.

"Who was the writer of that letter and for what purpose was the
letter written? From Dr. Thorndyke we learn that the writer must
have been some person who was well acquainted with deceased.
That is an important matter, but we are not concerned with the
actual identity of the writer. We are concerned with his connection
with the death of deceased; and that connection seems to be suggested by the purpose of the letter. That purpose seems to be indicated
quite clearly by Dr. Thorndyke. It was to create the belief that
deceased was still alive. But nobody—excepting the doctor—had
any doubt that he was alive. No suggestion had been made by anybody that he might be dead. Then why should the writer of this
letter have sought to create a belief which was already universally
held? The only possible answer seems to be that he, himself, knew
that deceased was dead and he wished, in the interests of his own
safety, to forestall any suspicions that might arise that deceased
might be dead.

"Thus the consideration of this letter suggests to us, first, that
the writer knew that deceased was dead, and, second, that he had
reasons for desiring that the fact of the death should not become
known or suspected. But the fact of the death could have been
known only to the person who killed deceased; and his anxiety to
conceal the fact suggests strongly that he had no reasonable defence
if he should be charged with the murder of deceased.

"That, I think, is all that I need say. Deceased was evidently killed
by some unknown person; and it is for you to decide whether the
circumstances, so far as they are known to us, suggest excusable
homicide, accidental homicide, manslaughter, or wilful murder."

On the conclusion of the summing up, the jury consulted together
for a few minutes. Then the foreman announced that they had agreed
on their finding.

"And what decision have you arrived at?" the coroner asked.

"We find that the deceased was murdered by some person
unknown."

"Yes," said the coroner, "I think that it is the only reasonable conclusion at which you could have arrived. I will record a verdict of wilful murder by some person unknown, and we may hope that the police will presently be able to discover who that unknown person is and bring him to justice."

He entered the verdict in the depositions and this brought the proceedings to an end.

CHAPTER 17

THORNDYKE RETRACES THE TRAIL

As the court rose and we all stood up, Miller turned on me fiercely.

"You never told me about that letter," he exclaimed; "and there was not a word about it in the synopsis that the doctor gave me."

"As to me," said I, "there is no question of reservations. I did not refer to it because I had not regarded it as having any particular bearing on the case."

"No bearing!" exclaimed Miller. "Why, it hits you in the face. But if you think it has no bearing, I'll warrant that is not the doctor's view."

"Naturally," I replied, "I don't know what his views are, but he is here and can answer for himself."

"Well," said Miller, "what about it, Doctor? You knew about that letter and you must know quite well who wrote it and why he wrote it."

"Now, Miller," said Thorndyke, "don't let us misuse words. We don't know who wrote that letter. We may have our opinions, and they may be right—or wrong. But in any case they will be pretty difficult to turn into evidence."

"I suspect you have done that already," grumbled Miller, "and you are keeping that evidence to yourself."

"You are quite wrong," Thorndyke replied. "I have no evidence beyond the facts which are known to you. Actually, I have given very little attention to the letter. It threw no light on the problem which I was trying to solve; whether Penrose was alive or dead, and, if he was dead, where we might look for his body."

"I should have thought it was highly relevant," Miller objected. "If it was good enough for some one to forge a letter to prove that Penrose was alive, when nobody supposed otherwise, that would suggest pretty strongly that the forger knew he was dead."

"So it would," Thorndyke agreed, "but that was of no use to me.

I was not out for opinions or beliefs but for demonstrable facts."

"Well," said Miller, "you have produced your demonstrable facts all right, and you have solved your problem. And now, I suppose, you are going on to the next problem: Who murdered Daniel Penrose? And the solution of that problem is to be found in that letter; and as we are both working to the same end, I think you ought to put me in possession of any facts that are known to you."

"But, my dear Miller," Thorndyke protested, "I have no facts respecting this letter that are not known to you. I will hand you the photograph, and you can have an enlargement if you want to employ handwriting experts, or you can have the original. That is all I can do for you."

He produced his letter-case, and, taking the photograph of the forged letter from it, handed it to Miller, who slipped it into his wallet and buried the latter in the depths of an internal pocket. As he did so, he looked round sharply and exclaimed:

"What is the matter, Mr. Horridge? Are you not feeling well, sir?"

I looked at our friend, who seemed to be groping his way towards the door, and certainly the inquiry was justified. His aspect was ghastly. His face was blanched to a tallowy white, his hands trembled visibly, and he had the dazed, bewildered appearance suggestive of a severe mental shock.

"No," he replied unsteadily. "I am not feeling at all well. This awful affair has been too much for me. It was all so horrible and so unexpected."

"Yes," Miller agreed sympathetically. "I expect it has given you a bad shake-up. Better come along with me to the bar and have a good stiff whisky. Don't you think so, Doctor?"

"I think," replied Thorndyke, "that a hot meal and a glass of wine would be better, if Mr. Horridge is returning to town this evening."

"I am," said Horridge, "but I couldn't look at food just now. Besides, my train is due in less than half an hour."

"Well, then," urged Miller, "come along to the bar and have a good, stiff drink. That will pick you up and fit you for the journey home. I happen to be going by that train, myself, so I can see you safely to Charing Cross, and into a cab if necessary."

I think Horridge would sooner have been without the proffered escort, but Miller left him no choice, and he accordingly allowed himself passively to be led away in the direction of the bar.

Thorndyke watched the two men disapprovingly as they passed out, and when they had disappeared, he remarked:

"I am afraid Miller is going to be a nuisance to us. His activity is premature."

"Yes," I agreed, "he is in full cry after Horridge and he thinks that he is on a hot trail. Obviously, he is convinced that Horridge wrote that letter, and I think he is right."

"I have no doubt that he is," said Thorndyke. "The obvious purpose of that letter was to create evidence that Penrose was alive after Oliver's death, and so would inherit his property. But it would be impossible to prove that Horridge wrote it."

"So it may be," said I. "But Miller has got him at a disadvantage, and he is going to push his opportunity for all that it is worth. If he lets on that he is a police officer, Horridge will probably collapse altogether. He is in a fearful state of panic."

"And well he may be," Thorndyke rejoined, "if he wrote that letter. For, quite apart from the suggestion of guilty knowledge that it offers, the mere writing and uttering of that letter is a serious crime. It is a forgery in the fullest sense. It was done with intent to deceive, and the purpose of the deception was grossly fraudulent. If Miller can frighten him into an admission of having written the letter, he will be absolutely certain of securing a conviction."

"On the charge of forgery," said I. "But that is not Miller's objective. You heard what he said. He is all out on the capital charge."

"Yes, I realize that," said Thorndyke. "Which is why I say that he is going to be a nuisance to us. Because he won't be able to prove his case and he will have set up a disturbance just at the moment when what is needed is a little masterly inactivity combined with careful observation. It is a pity that Miller will not trust us more. He will butt in when the case is not ready for police methods. However, I am glad he is not travelling up with us. His eagerness to acquire knowledge becomes rather fatiguing."

"We are not going up by that train, then?"

"No. We may as well have a little early dinner and take the motor omnibus to Canterbury."

We adopted this plan, and, after a comfortable and restful meal, caught the omnibus and were duly deposited in the main street of Canterbury, not far from the cathedral. As we proceeded thence towards the station, we noticed an "antique" shop, the fascia of which bore the single word "Todd."

"This," I remarked, halting to glance at the antiquities—mostly of the prehistoric type—which were displayed in the window, "seems to be the shop that Horridge referred to as a favourite resort of poor Penrose. Probably some of the things that we saw in the collection came from here."

"One of them almost certainly did," said Thorndyke. "Don't you remember that Saxon brooch? The entry in the catalogue noted its origin as 'Sweeney's Resurrection.' "

"I remember the entry, now you mention it. Lockhart suggested that 'Sweeney' probably meant Todd, and apparently he was right."

We went on our way, discussing the late Daniel Penrose and his harmless oddities, of which I had been so intolerant, and eventually reached the station in time to select our compartment at our leisure. There were few passengers besides ourselves, so that we were able to secure a first-class smoking-compartment of which we were the sole occupants, a matter to which I attended with some anxiety. For the train ran through to Charing Cross without a stop, and the long, uninterrupted journey would afford an opportunity for certain explanations which I felt were now overdue. With this view Thorndyke apparently agreed, for, when I presently opened my examination with a tentative question, he replied quite freely, without a sign of his customary reticence and evasiveness.

"Of course," I began, "when Penrose's body was found, I realized at once, in general terms, how I had managed to miss the essential points of the case. The possibility that Penrose might be dead never occurred to me; and it ought. It looks obvious enough now. But still I don't quite see how you contrived to establish the fact of his death—which you evidently did—and locate the place of his burial."

"It was all very hypothetical," he replied, "even up to the last stage. Until Elmhurst reported the discovery I was not certain that my theory of the course of events might not contain some fallacy that I had overlooked. Hence my rather elaborate provisions to cover up a possible failure. But to come back to your own case; the initial mistake that you made was in disregarding the good old Spencerian principle that when certain facts are presented as proving a particular thesis, we should consider, not only that which is presented, but that, also, which is not presented. In other words, we should at once separate fact from inference.

"Now, when Brodribb gave us his narrative of the disappearance of Penrose, he honestly believed that his story was a recital of facts;

whereas it was really a mixture of fact and inference. It had not occurred to him that the hospital patient might be some person other than Penrose, and he accordingly presented that patient as Penrose. And you accepted that presentation as a statement of fact, whereas it was only an inference. Hence you made a false start and got on the wrong track from the beginning.

"I was fortunate enough to avoid this pitfall; for even while Brodribb was telling us his story, I made a mental note that the identity of the patient had been taken for granted, and that it would have to be considered, before any action could be taken. But as soon as I began to consider the question, it became clear to me that the balance of probability was against the patient's being Penrose."

"Did it really?" I exclaimed. "Now, I should have said that all the known facts pointed to his being Penrose. And so it seems to me still."

"Then," said Thorndyke, "let us argue the question. We will take two hypotheses: A, that the patient was Penrose; and B, that he was some other person, and examine the evidence in support of each.

"Let us begin with hypothesis A. What evidence was there that the patient was Daniel Penrose?

"There were five principal items of evidence. 1. The car was certainly Penrose's car. 2. The patient had been in possession of that car. 3. The coat, which was undeniably the patient's coat, had Penrose's driving license in its pocket. 4. The initials on the patient's collar were Penrose's initials. 5. A fragment of an ancient object was found in the pocket of the patient's coat. But Penrose was a collector of antiquities and there was reason to believe that he had gone out that day for the purpose of acquiring some such objects.

"Now, you will notice that the first three items are what we may call extrinsic. They afford no evidence of personal identity. They merely prove that the patient was in possession of Penrose's property and they are thus of very little weight. The other two items we may call intrinsic. They are connected with the actual personality of the patient.

"Of these, the initials on the collar furnished by far the more weighty evidence of identity."

"I should have assumed them to be quite conclusive," said I.

"Then you would have been wrong," he replied, "for you would have been assuming that Penrose was the only man in the world whose initials were D. P. Still, the fact that the patient's initials were D. P. established a very high probability that he was Daniel Penrose."

"I should have put it higher than that," said I. "It would have seemed to me as nearly as possible a certainty. For if he were not Penrose the coincidence would be, as it was, such an amazing one."

"I think you exaggerate the abnormality," he rejoined. "It was a very remarkable coincidence; but there are two things that we should bear in mind. First, the adverse chances were not so enormous as you seem to imply. There are great numbers of men whose initials are D. P. And, secondly, that the laws of probability relate to large numbers. They must be applied with great caution to particular cases. The tendency to assume that because a thing is improbable it will not happen is a mistake. Improbabilities and coincidences are constantly occurring, and we have to allow for that fact.

"Nevertheless, it had to be admitted that those initials made it, in a very high degree, probable that the patient was Daniel Penrose. But now let us take the alternative hypothesis and see what the probabilities were on the other side. And first, consider the conduct of the patient. Owing to his black eyes and contused face, he was completely unrecognizable. Nobody could form any idea what he was like. But when his injuries cleared up he would have been recognizable; and the extraordinary and determined way in which he absconded from the hospital at a carefully-chosen time, is very suggestive. Evidently, during his simulated unconsciousness, he had been watching for an opportunity to get away at night when his odd appearance would be less observed. His behaviour was like that of a man who sought to escape before recognition should be possible.

"Then, there was the man's previous behaviour. Apparently he had abandoned his car. But a car which is abandoned is usually a stolen car. Again, the car which killed the old woman was being driven wildly and furiously. We knew then of no reason why Penrose should have been driving in that manner. But a stranger in unlawful possession of a car would probably have sufficient reasons; and in fact, persons who steal cars usually do drive furiously. Then, if Penrose had knocked down the old woman he would probably have stopped and reported the accident. He was a responsible, decent gentleman and there was no reason why he should not have stopped. But a stranger, in possession of a stolen car—in effect, a fugitive— could not afford to stop and be interviewed.

"Furthermore, if this man had been in unlawful possession of a car, something must have happened to the owner of that car at some place. The stranger would have good reasons for getting away from that neighbourhood as quickly as possible. Thus, the furious driving both before and after the accident would be sufficiently explained.

"So, looking at the case as a whole, you will see that, on the assumption that the patient was Penrose, his conduct was utterly unreasonable and inexplicable; on the assumption that he was not Penrose, his behaviour was in every respect exactly what we should have expected it to be. For if he was not Penrose, he was under strong suspicion of having made away with Penrose for the reasons: 1. That Penrose had unaccountably disappeared, and; 2. That the stranger was in possession of Penrose's car and his driving license. Taking all the facts together, I came to the conclusion that, in spite of the initials, the balance of probability was against his being Penrose.

"Nevertheless, those initials presented a formidable objection to the view that I was disposed to adopt, and I decided that the question whether they were Penrose's initials or those of some other person must be settled before any further investigation would be worth while. It was not a difficult question to dispose of, and it turned out to be easier than I had expected. You remember how we obtained the answer?"

"Indeed, I don't," I replied. "I never knew that the question had been raised."

"You never followed this case very closely, for some reason," said Thorndyke, "but if you will recall our visit to the garage, you will remember that I was able, quite easily, to extract a statement from Kickweed which settled the question definitely. We learned from him that Penrose was in the habit of marking all his portable property, including his collars and handkerchiefs, with his name, D. Penrose, by means of a rubber stamp."

I grinned rather sheepishly. "I remember quite well now you mention it, but I am afraid that, at the time, I merely wondered, like a fool, why you were going into such trivialities at such length."

"Well," said Thorndyke, "you will now see that our conversation with Kickweed cleared up all our difficulties. Penrose's collars were marked 'D. Penrose' with a rubber stamp; the patient's collar was marked 'D. P.' with a marking-ink pencil. Therefore, the evidence of the collar supported all the other evidence; it went to prove that the patient was not Penrose.

"Then, at once, arose two other questions: If he was not Penrose, who was he? And what had become of Penrose? The first question had to be left until we had answered the second. Penrose had disappeared. What had happened to him? Was he alive or dead?

"Now, having regard to the strange and sinister circumstances: the disappearance of one man, the appearance of another man in possession of his property and the anxiety of that other man to escape without being identified, there was only one reasonable conclusion that we could come to. The overwhelming probability was that Penrose was dead and that his body had been concealed by burial or otherwise.

"Adopting this view, as I did, the next questions were: Where did Penrose meet his death? And where was his body concealed? The latter question was the more important, but the answer to both was probably the same. And both questions were contained in the further question: From what place did the car start on that wild journey home?

"Now, in regard to this problem—the starting-point of the car's journey—we had two clues, and they were both very imperfect. The place where the woman was killed was in the Canterbury district and the car was travelling via Maidstone towards Gravesend. But the speed at which it was travelling made it difficult to judge how far it might have come, especially as we had no exact information as to the time at which it started. All that we knew was that the car advanced towards the Canterbury-Ashford road from some place to the south and east.

"The other clue was the very distinctive pottery fragment. But this also was a very ambiguous clue. The pocket in which we found it was not Penrose's pocket; and we did not know how long it had been in that pocket. However, when we came to examine these difficulties, they did not appear insuperable. Thus notwithstanding that the fragment was in another man's possession, I was disposed to associate it with Penrose for two reasons; first, that Penrose was a collector of antiquities, and, second, that, when he started from home, he took with him—as we learned from Kickweed—two digging tools and was, apparently, intending to do some sort of excavation. As to the second difficulty, the earth in which the fragment was embedded was of the same kind as that which we scraped from the coat and that which we found later on the car. So it appeared practically certain that the fragment was the product of that day's digging.

"The next question was: Whence had that fragment come? That was a vitally important question; for there could be little doubt that the place where that fragment was dug up was the place where Penrose had met his death and where his body was concealed. But how was that question to be answered? It seemed that the only possible method was that which I had adopted in regard to the other questions; to form a working hypothesis and see whither it led. Now, the broken edges of the fragment showed fresh fractures. It had been broken off the pot at the time of the excavation; and as the digging had probably been done after dark, by a very imperfect light, the fragment had apparently been overlooked, the new fracture of the pot being mistaken for an ancient one. It followed that, somewhere, there was a broken pot with a space in it corresponding to this fragment, by which it could infallibly be recognized. If we could find that pot it would probably be possible to ascertain where it had been dug up.

"But where were we to look for that pot? The only possible place known to us was Penrose's collection; and circumstances created an initial probability that it was there. But, further, I had a theory, as I mentioned to you, that the expedition on which Penrose had embarked that day possibly had the express purpose of recovering this fragment to make the imperfect pot complete. Accordingly, I took an opportunity of inspecting the collection, and I took with me my invaluable box of moulding wax.

"You know the result. The pot was there, easily recognizable at sight and conclusively identified by the wax squeeze. There was also a catalogue entry, presumably describing the piece and recording the source whence it had been obtained. But the wording of the entry was so obscure as to present a fresh puzzle. Nevertheless, it was a great advance; for the information was there, if we could only extract the meaning of the words.

"Those words were, you will remember: "Moulin à vent; Julie: Polly.' Now, the first term was obvious enough; the piece was a 'Windmill Hill' pot. By the study of other entries in the catalogue, I reached the conclusion that 'Julie' probably represented the locality, and 'Polly' the person from whom the pot was obtained. Accordingly, the first thing to be done was to ascertain, if possible, the meaning of the word 'Julie.'

"To this end, I procured and read various works dealing with neolithic pottery; and, since our pot had almost certainly been dug out of a long barrow, I gave attention to those also. But the result, for a time, was very disappointing. I read through quite a large number of books and papers on barrows and pottery without meeting with any name resembling 'Julie.' At last, I struck the clue in Jessup's *Archæology of Kent*. There, in the chapter dealing with neolithic remains, I found a reference to a long barrow known as Julliberrie's Grave, in the neighbourhood of Chilham. Looking it up on the ordnance map, I saw at once that its situation fitted the circumstances exactly, for it was quite close to the known track of the car. Thereupon I decided that Julliberrie's Grave was almost certainly the place for which I had been searching; the starting-point of the car's wild career and the place in which the body of Daniel Penrose was probably reposing.

"The question then arose: What was to be done? I had not a particle of definite evidence to support my belief. My whole case was just a train of hypothetical reasoning—guess-work, if you will; and guess-work was not good enough either for the Home Office or the Office of Works. Besides, as you acutely observed, I didn't want to let the cat out of the bag prematurely. Yet it was impossible to get any further in the investigation until the barrow had been explored.

"There was only one thing to do—to organize a scientific excavation of the barrow by skilled and trained archæologists. That would ensure an absolutely exhaustive exploration without injury to the barrow and without any disclosure of my suspicions if they should prove to be unfounded. Accordingly, I looked up our invaluable friend, Elmhurst, and, to my great satisfaction, found that he had both the means and the will to carry out the excavation if I were prepared to finance the work.

"You know the rest. Everything went according to plan and the first stage of our investigation was brought to a triumphant conclusion. I only hope that the second stage will go as well. It ought to; for we have now a solid foundation of established fact to build on."

"Yes," I agreed. "We know that Penrose is dead and that somebody killed him. But I don't see much of a lead towards the conclusion as to who that somebody may have been. But I expect that you do. Perhaps the word 'Polly,' in that ridiculous catalogue entry, suggests something to you. Apparently, it refers to a person, though it is hardly safe to say even that. The only thing that is certain is that it doesn't mean Polly."

"The meaning of that word," he replied, "really belongs to the second stage of our inquiry, on which we are now embarking; the identification of the person whom we may call 'the murderer'—though the fact of murder is not established. Penrose was killed with his own weapon, which, as the coroner justly observed, suggests a struggle or conflict. But as to the identity of that person, I have not yet formed a definite opinion. There is one essential question that has to be settled before we begin to theorize. We have got to know whether the alleged burglary at Queen Square was an actual burglary and whether the cupboard in the small room was actually opened."

"You mean," said I, "that, if the cupboard was opened, it must have been opened with Penrose's keys, as you have always maintained, and that, therefore, the person who opened it must have been the murderer."

"I would hardly go as far as that," he replied. "If some person did actually enter that room and open the cupboard, he must have opened it with Penrose's keys or with duplicates made from them. That would suggest that he was either the murderer or in league with the murderer. But even if he opened the cupboard, that would not be conclusive evidence that he stole the jewels. He might have found the cupboard empty. That is not probable, but it has to be borne in mind. And then we have to remember that the only evidence of the room's having been entered is the unsupported statement of one person."

"Yes," said I, "and not an entirely unsuspected person. Our friend, Horridge, seems to have had considerable misgivings as to the discreet and melancholy Kickweed; but I didn't think that you had any suspicions in that direction."

"I don't say that I have," replied Thorndyke, "or that I entertain seriously the various possibilities that I have mentioned. I am merely pointing out that we have got a good many eggs in our basket. A sensible man keeps in his mind all the possibilities, no matter how remote; but he also gives his special attention, in the first place, to those that are least remote. And, meanwhile, we have got to begin our quest by settling definitely whether that cupboard has or has not been opened. We have very little doubt as to what was in it when Penrose was alive, and Lockhart will now have to make an explicit statement. If the things are not there, we shall have a definite fact and can consider what follows from it; and if we find the collection intact—well, I shall be very much surprised."

CHAPTER 18

THE OPENING OF THE SAFE

On suitable occasions, Thorndyke could lie remarkably low and exhibit a most masterly inactivity. But also, on suitable occasions he could act with surprising promptitude. And the matter of the alleged burglary at Queen Square presented such an occasion. Armed with an authority from Mr. Brodribb, as joint executor, he proceeded to call on Chubbs and make all necessary arrangements for the opening of the safe in the small room; and then, as I gathered, he had an interview with Lockhart. What passed at that interview I did not learn, but I suspect that there was some rather plain speaking. Not that it should have been necessary, for Lockhart was a lawyer and knew in what a very questionable position he stood. But whatever passed on that occasion, he was quite amenable. He frankly admitted that he had seen in the small room a collection of jewels which were almost certainly the Billington jewels, and he gave Thorndyke a written statement to that effect. Further, he wrote a letter to Miller, in somewhat ambiguous terms, referring him to Thorndyke for fuller particulars, and agreed to be present when the safe was opened.

Naturally, this letter brought Miller, hotfoot, to our chambers, and a preliminary discussion was unavoidable in spite of Thorndyke's efforts to stave it off.

"Now, Doctor," the superintendent began a little truculently, "this is the sort of thing that I was complaining of. You knew those jewels were there, but you didn't let on the faintest hint to me."

"I did not know," Thorndyke protested. "I only suspected; and I don't profess to communicate mere suspicions."

"Well," rejoined Miller, "there they were, at any rate, and we can take it as a certainty that they are not there now."

"I expect you are right," said Thorndyke, "but why not leave the discussion until we know?"

"For all practical purposes, we do know," replied Miller. "We can take it that there was either a real or a pretended burglary, and in either case the stuff is pretty certainly gone; and the question is, who lifted it?"

"You remember," said Thorndyke, "that the keys were stolen from Penrose's body. Presumably, they were taken for the purpose of being used; and they could have been used only by entering the premises. Moreover, if the cupboard was opened, it could have been opened only with Penrose's keys."

"Yes, that's a fact," Miller agreed. "But suppose the murderer did enter the premises, how do we know that he found the stuff there? Or, for that matter, how do we know that the place was ever entered? We have got only one man's word for it. And, to an experienced eye, it looks a bit like an indoor job."

"I don't quite see what is in your mind," said Thorndyke. "You are not letting your thoughts run on Horridge?"

Miller grinned sourly. "No," he replied, "though I must admit that I did suspect him very considerably in connection with the murder. But I have squeezed him pretty dry—and I can tell you he didn't like being squeezed. But in the end, he was able to produce an undeniable alibi—a club dinner that he attended on the seventeenth of October at which all the members signed their names. So Horridge is now out of the picture."

"He was never in," said Thorndyke. "The proceedings at the inquest made that perfectly clear."

"What proceedings do you mean?" Miller demanded.

"I am referring to Kickweed's evidence," Thorndyke replied. "If you had not been so preoccupied with the forged letter, you would have seen that it excluded Horridge from any possible suspicion in regard to the murder. Kickweed deposed that on the twentieth of October, three days after the murder, and the very day after the flight of the presumed murderer from Gravesend Hospital, Horridge called at Queen Square to see Penrose; and the two of them, Horridge and Kickweed, interviewed a police officer who had come to bring the coat that was assumed to belong to Penrose. Now, if Horridge had been the murderer, he must also have been the hospital patient. But the patient had two very bad black eyes and a severe wound across his right eyebrow. Obviously, he would have been in no condition for paying calls; and you will remember that the police officer was looking for a man with two black eyes and a cut across his right eyebrow."

"Yes," Miller admitted, "I had overlooked that. But it did look as if Horridge had written that letter. Have you any idea who did write it? We have got to find that out."

"My dear Miller," Thorndyke said, a little impatiently, "you had better forget that letter. It is a criminal matter, but it has no bearing on the crime which we are investigating. But if you have dropped Horridge, what do you mean by suggesting that this burglary may have been an indoor job?"

"Well, you know," replied Miller, "this burglary rests on the story told by Mr. Kickweed; and Mr. Kickweed strikes me as a decidedly downy bird."

"He couldn't have been the murderer, you know," said Thorndyke. "But it was presumably the murderer who had the keys."

"I know," rejoined Miller. "But he was in the house; and there is such a thing as wax."

"You can take it," said Thorndyke, "that Penrose was not in the habit of leaving his keys about."

"No, probably not," Miller agreed, "but I suppose he had a bath sometimes, and I don't suppose he took his clothes into the bathroom with him."

Thorndyke smiled indulgently at the superintendent and admonished him in mock solemn tones:

"Now, my dear Miller, let me urge you to beware of obsessions. At the inquest you allowed yourself to become letter-minded, and so you missed a vitally important item of evidence. And now you seem inclined to let yourself become Kickweed-minded. Why not leave Kickweed alone and address yourself to the more obvious lines of inquiry?"

"Still, you know, Doctor," Miller persisted, "somebody must have known that those jewels were there."

"There is not a particle of evidence that Kickweed did. You must remember that Penrose kept their existence absolutely secret from everybody excepting Lockhart; and he swore him to secrecy before he showed them. So far as we know, their existence was known only to two persons; Lockhart, and the man, whoever he was, who supplied them."

"Yes," said Miller, "the chappie who supplied them to Penrose certainly knew that they were there. It would be interesting, quite apart from the murder business, to know who he was. I wonder if it could have been Crabbe, after all."

"You needn't wonder, Miller," said Thorndyke. "It was Crabbe. I think there can be no doubt about that."

Miller sat up in his chair and turned a rather startled face to my colleague.

"Hallo, Doctor!" he exclaimed. "You seem to know a mighty lot about it. And how did you manage to dig up Mr. Crabbe? I've been wondering about that ever since that evening when you asked me about him."

"There was a document," replied Thorndyke; "a scrap of paper, apparently a descriptive label, which was found in the small room, on the morning after the alleged burglary. That was what enabled me to connect Crabbe with Penrose's collection."

"Then," Miller exclaimed excitedly, "we have got actual, tangible evidence against Crabbe. Who has got that scrap of paper?"

"Brodribb has the original, but I kept a copy. You shall see it"; and, with this, he rose and went to the cabinet in which the Penrose dossier was kept. Taking out from the collection of notes and papers the copy of Mr. Penrose's cryptogram, he brought it over and gravely handed it to Miller, who stared at it aghast while I watched him with unholy glee.

"I can't make anything of this," the superintendent grumbled. "'Lobster: *hortus petasatus*.' It doesn't make sense. Besides, a lobster isn't a crab; and what in creation is a *hortus petasatus?*"

Thorndyke expounded the meaning of the inscription, explaining the late Mr. Penrose's peculiarities of speech, and Miller listened with incredulous astonishment.

"Well, Doctor," he commented. "I take off my hat to you. That thing would have conveyed nothing to me. It's like some damn' silly puzzle game. And you might have passed it all round the C.I.D. and no one would have been an atom the wiser. But I am afraid it wouldn't do as evidence in a court of law."

"Possibly not," Thorndyke admitted; "but I am not concerned with the robbery charge against Crabbe. I am investigating the murder of Daniel Penrose; and I am assuming that there was a burglary, that the burglar was in possession of Penrose's keys and that he knew what the cupboard in the small room contained. Of course, if we find the jewels still in the cupboard, we shall know that those assumptions were wrong."

"Yes," Miller agreed, "but we shan't. Burglary or no burglary, those jewels have been pinched. I'd lay my bottom dollar to that.

But you realize, Doctor, that, even if there was a burglary, the burglar couldn't have been Crabbe. He was in chokee at the time when it was supposed to have occurred."

"Yes," said Thorndyke, "I had noted that fact; so we shall have to look round for some other person who knew that the jewels were there. And no such person is actually known to us, if we except Lockhart, and I suppose we can hardly suspect him."

Miller grinned faintly at the suggestion and then became thoughtful. After a few moments of profound reflection he remarked:

"Those locksmiths will make hay with poor old Penrose's safe. Are you going to be present to see how the job is done?"

I was instantly struck by this abrupt change of subject and I could see that it was also noticed by Thorndyke, who, however, followed the superintendent's lead.

"No," he replied. "I shall not turn up until they have had time to get the job finished. But Polton will be there to watch the proceedings and pick up a few tips on the correct method of opening a safe."

"Ah!" said Miller, "I shall have to keep an eye on Mr. Polton if he is going to qualify as an expert safe-breaker. He is mighty handy already in the matter of locks and skeleton keys and housebreaker's tools."

He pursued this facetious and quite irrelevant topic at considerable length and with no tendency whatever to revert to the subject of the Queen Square burglary. And then he pulled out his watch and, having bestowed on it a single startled glance, sprang up, declaring that, if he didn't look sharp, he would be late for an important appointment. And with this he took his departure hurriedly and with a distinctly purposive air.

"Miller has got a bright idea of some kind," I remarked when he had gone.

"Yes," Thorndyke agreed, "and he thinks he has got it all to himself. You noticed his sudden anxiety to switch the conversation off the subject of Mr. Crabbe. Well, it is all to the good if he doesn't get busy prematurely. I suppose you are coming to swell the multitude at Queen Square to-morrow?"

"If there is room," I replied, "I should like to see the fateful question decided. But it will be a bit of an anti-climax if the stuff is there after all, though I don't suppose Horridge will complain."

"He will have a bad disappointment," said Thorndyke, "if we

find the jewels there and he is then told that they are stolen property. However, there is no use in speculating. To-morrow we shall know whether they were or were not stolen, and until we know that, neither Miller nor I can decide on the next move."

When, on the following morning, we arrived at the house in Queen Square and were admitted by Kickweed, we learned from him that the locksmiths had started their work on the safe about an hour previously and that the operations were still in progress. Our friend shook his head despondently as he showed us into the morning-room and remarked that it was a dreadful business and very disturbing.

"Would you like to wait here until they are ready," he asked, "or will you join the—er—assembly in the great gallery?"

We elected to join the assembly, whereupon he ushered us into the gallery, announcing us with due solemnity as he threw open the door. The word "assembly" appeared to represent Mr. Kickweed's state of mind rather than the actual facts, for there were only three persons present; Lockhart, Miller and Horridge, the latter very subdued, care-worn and decidedly gloomy. The cause of his depressed state was made evident presently when he took us apart, leaving Lockhart and Miller amicably discussing the legal position of an accessory after the fact.

"This is a nice state of affairs," Horridge complained. "Do you know that this detective fellow actually accused me, in so many words, of having murdered poor old Pen? Me, his old and trusted friend and an executor of his will! And, if I hadn't had a conclusive alibi, I believe he would have run me in. And now he tells me that even if we find the jewels intact, it will be of no advantage to me because they are all stolen property; which I don't believe. I ask you, is it likely that a man of Pen's character would have been guilty of trafficking in stolen goods?"

"I should say, certainly not," replied Thorndyke, "if he knew that the goods were stolen. But the point is hardly worth discussing if the goods in question have disappeared."

Here our conversation was interrupted by Polton who entered to announce that the work on the lock was completed and that the safe door was free and ready to be opened. Thereupon we followed him into the small room where we found two very superior artificers standing on guard over the remains of a large iron safe, the massive door of which was disclosed by the opening of the wooden case.

Miller's prognostications had certainly not over-stated the results of the locksmiths' activities. To say nothing of the wooden door with its shattered detector lock, those artificers had undoubtedly "made hay with" the safe, itself.

"Now, Mr. Horridge," said Miller, "you, as executor, are the proper person to open the safe."

Horridge, however, deputed his functions to one of the workmen who accordingly took hold of the battered door and swung it wide open, disclosing a range of shallow drawers like those of an entomo-logical cabinet.

"Are these drawers in the condition in which you saw them when Mr. Penrose showed you his collection?" Thorndyke asked.

"Yes, so far as I can see," Lockhart replied. "He took them out, one by one, in their proper order from above downwards, and carried each over to that table by the window so that we could see the contents better."

"Then," said Thorndyke, "we had better do the same."

But it was not necessary; for when the top drawer was pulled out it was seen to be undeniably empty. Horridge exhibited its vacant interior to the assembled company, turned it upside-down and shook it, and glumly returned it to its place. The case was the same with the second drawer and also with the third, excepting that when it was inverted some small object was heard to fall out on to the floor. Miller picked it up and exhibited it in the palm of his hand, when it was seen to be a small opal and was dropped back into the drawer. But that little opal was the solitary occupant of the cabinet. Apart from it and a plentiful covering of dust, the whole range of drawers from top to bottom was empty.

"That burglar," Lockhart commented as the last of the drawers was slid back into its place, "was pretty thorough in his methods. He made a clean sweep of the whole collection; not only the gems but the coins as well. And he must have been fairly heavily laden when he went away, for most of the coins were gold and I should say there were some hundreds of them."

"I don't fancy those coins were gold," said Miller. "I think I know where they came from, and, if I am right, they were electros —copper, gilt. Still, even copper electros weigh something. But it's surprising what a lot of coins and jewellery you can stow away about your person if you have the right sort of pockets. And it's pretty certain that he had an overcoat as well."

"Do you remember, Lockhart," Thorndyke asked, "whether, when you saw the jewels, there were any labels attached to them?"

"Not attached," Lockhart replied. "There were no fixed labels; only slips of paper like those on the shelves of the gallery."

"Did you notice what was written on those slips of paper? Were they descriptive labels?"

Lockhart grinned. "You know what Penrose's descriptions were like," he replied, "and you have seen the catalogue. So far as I could make out, the descriptions on the labels were similar to those in the catalogue; apparently, unintelligible nonsense."

"You can't recall any of them?" Thorndyke asked.

"I remember one, because I tried to puzzle out what it could mean, and failed utterly. It was 'Decapod; *jardin à chapeau.*' Does that convey anything to you?"

"It does to me, thanks to the doctor's explanations," said Miller, who had been listening eagerly to the questions and answers. "I don't know what a decapod is but I've got enough French to infer that *jardin à chapeau* is much the same as *hortus petasatus*. And the doctor can tell you what that means."

"What does it mean?" Lockhart demanded; and Thorndyke— not very willingly, I thought—gave the required explanation.

"Yes," Lockhart chuckled, "I see now, though I hadn't your ingenuity. Poor old Penrose! What nonsense he did write and speak! But I think I also see the point of your questions."

"And an uncommonly good point it is," said Miller. "That chappie was careful to take away the labels as well as the goods, and if he hadn't dropped one of them we should know a good deal less than we do. It's a very significant point, indeed."

"And now," said Thorndyke, "as we have done what we came to do, perhaps we had better leave Mr. Horridge to discuss the question of repairs. Are you walking in our direction, Miller?"

The superintendent was not. He was proposing, he said, to make a slight survey of the premises to elucidate the circumstances of the burglary, but I suspected that he was unwilling to run the risk of an interrogation by Thorndyke. So we left him to his survey, and, having once more condoled with Horridge, we set forth in company with Lockhart, leaving Polton to spy on the superintendent and worm out any trifles in the way of technical tips and trade secrets that he could from the locksmiths.

CHAPTER 19

THORNDYKE'S DILEMMA

I have referred more than once to Thorndyke's habitual unwillingness to discuss uncompleted cases, excepting in relation to questions
of fact, or to disclose any opinions or theories that he had built on
the facts which were known to us both. I had come to accept this
reticence as a condition of our friendship and usually refrained
from any attempts to discover what lines his thoughts were pursuing
or what inferences he had drawn. But when we met at our chambers
in the evening after our visit to Queen Square, I found him in a mood
of unwonted expansiveness, apparently ready to discuss our present
case without any reservations.

The discussion opened with a question that I put tentatively, half
expecting the usual invitation to exercise my own admirable faculty
of deduction.

"I noticed that you and Miller seemed to attach great importance
to the circumstance that the burglar had carefully removed all the
labels from the drawers. I don't quite see why. Would not a burglar
ordinarily take away any labels that might furnish a clue to what
had been stolen?"

"I don't see why he should," Thorndyke replied. "An ordinary
burglar would assume that the contents of the drawers were known,
so that the labels would give no additional information. But these
were not ordinary descriptive labels. They gave very definite
information as to the person who had supplied the jewels; and
as those jewels were the proceeds of a robbery which was known
to the police, the information would be very dangerous to the
person named. But that would not concern an ordinary burglar.
The labels would furnish no clue to his identity. Of course, we
know that he was not an ordinary, casual burglar, since he had
Penrose's keys. But the point is that, whoever he was, he seemed
to consider it a matter of importance that the identity of the

person who sold the jewels to Penrose should not become known."

"But the jewels were sold to Penrose by Crabbe."

"Yes."

"But Crabbe could not have been the burglar. He was in prison at the time."

"Exactly," Thorndyke rejoined. "That is the importance of the discovery. The labels implicated Crabbe. But Crabbe could not have been the burglar. It seems to follow that they implicated some one besides Crabbe; and as the burglar was in possession of Penrose's keys and would thus appear to have been either the murderer or an accessory to the murder, it would be very interesting to know whom those labels could have implicated. I fancy that Miller has a very definite opinion on the subject; and I am disposed to think that he is right."

"The deuce you are!" I exclaimed. "Then it seems to me that you have got the investigation much farther advanced than I had imagined. I had supposed that the search for the murderer had still to be begun. But it seems that there is already a definite suspect. Is that so?"

He reflected for a few moments and then replied:

"The word 'suspect' is perhaps a little too strong. My conclusions as to the possible identity of the murderer are at present on an entirely hypothetical plane. I have considered the whole complex of circumstances connected with the murder and have noted the persons who seem to have made any sort of contact with those circumstances; and I have considered each of those persons in relation to the questions whether he could possibly be the murderer and whether his known characteristics agree with those of the murderer."

"But," I demanded, "what do we know of the characteristics of the murderer?"

"Very little," he replied, "but still enough to enable us to apply at least a negative test in conjunction with the other considerations. Thus we can exclude Kickweed and Horridge because, although they make certain contacts, neither could have been present at the place and time of the murder. But let us take a glance at the positive aspects.

"We begin with the justifiable assumption that the hospital patient was the murderer. Now, what do we know about him? Of his personal characteristics we have no description whatever. All that we know is that his collar bore the letters, D. P., which were presumably the initial letters of his name, and that he had a deep wound crossing his right eyebrow which must have left a rather conspicuous permanent scar. So you see that, little as we know, we have the means of excluding or accepting any given individual. If his characteristics agree with those of the patient, he is a possible suspect; if they do not agree, he is not possible."

"And do you know of any person whose characteristics do agree with those of the patient?"

"Up to a certain point," he replied. "The ascertainment of the scar would involve a personal examination. That will have to come later as a final test. For the present, we must be content with agreement so far as is known."

"But you have some such person in view?"

Again he reflected for a few moments. At length, he replied:

"I am in a rather odd dilemma. I have two theoretically possible suspects and I can make no sort of choice between them."

"And do the names of both of them begin with D. P.?" I asked, imagining that I was putting a poser.

"But," he exclaimed, "that is the extraordinary thing. They do. There is a coincidence for you if you like. It was a striking coincidence that the murderer should have the same initials as the victim. But this is more than striking. It is almost incredible."

"I suppose we name no names," I suggested humbly.

"I don't know why not," he replied. "We keep our own counsel until we can turn hypothesis into proof. Well, my two possible suspects are Deodatus Pettigrew and David Parrott."

"Parrott!" I exclaimed in astonishment. "I don't see where he comes into it; or Pettigrew either for that matter."

"It is just a question of the contacts that they make with the circumstances of the murder," he replied. "Let us take them separately and see what those contacts are. The odd and confusing thing is that their contacts are entirely separate and from different sides."

"Is it possible that they were both concerned in the murder?" I suggested; "that they may have been confederates?"

"I have considered that," he answered. "It is possible, but, I think, unlikely. The crime has all the appearances of a one-man job. Moreover, I can find no evidence of any contact between these two men. So far as I know, they were strangers to each other and they persistently remain completely separate. So we will consider them separately.

"Now, as to Parrott. The hospital patient had in his pocket a fragment of pottery which almost certainly came from Julliberrie's Grave. That fragment had been broken off a pot which was in Penrose's museum and which had come from Julliberrie's Grave. The entry in the catalogue relating to that pot consisted of the usual three terms; the description of the piece—'*Moulin à vent*'—the place whence it came—'Julie'—and a third term—'Polly'—which presumably indicated the person who supplied it."

"Yes," I agreed, "that seems to have been Penrose's custom. So now the question is: Who is Polly? What is she? Have you found an answer to it?"

"I infer, having regard to Penrose's cryptic terminology, that 'Polly' indicates Mr. Parrott."

"Of course," I exclaimed. "I ought to have spotted that. Poll parrot. Pretty Polly. But still, you know, Thorndyke, it is only a guess, after all."

"It is a little more than that," he objected. "Parrott is referred to frequently in the catalogue, and always by some allusive name, such as Perroquet, Psittacus, or Popinjay. Penrose may well have tried to find a new variant. But I admit your objection. This is not proof; it is only hypothesis. That is all I claim. At present we are only looking for some one whom it would be possible to suspect, as a guide to further investigation. Parrott is such a person, and so is Pettigrew, whose case is equally hypothetical. But you will note that Parrott agrees with the hospital patient in the initials of his name and that we have reason to believe that he knew Julliberrie's Grave and had actually dug into it.

"Now let us consider Pettigrew. He does not appear to be in any way connected with Julliberrie's Grave, or, so far as I know, with Penrose. But there are reasons for connecting him with the burglary. The burglar knew of the existence of the Billington jewels and apparently knew where they were kept. Moreover, he was at pains to take away the labels which contained evidence that the jewels had been supplied by Crabbe. Apparently, he was anxious that Crabbe's guilt should not be revealed. But why? He certainly was not Crabbe himself. What was his interest in the matter?

"You remember that Miller strongly suspected Crabbe of the Billington robbery. And it was not mere suspicion. He had enough evidence to make him consider seriously the possibility of a prosecution, though he decided that the evidence was not sufficient.

The difficulty was that the jewels had disappeared and could not be traced. But now they have been traced and are known to have been sold to Penrose by Crabbe. So there is probably a complete case against the latter. But you will also remember that Miller's case against Crabbe included Pettigrew, for the reason—and no other—that Pettigrew was associated with Crabbe at the time of the robbery.

"Now, that robbery was committed by Crabbe, or by his agents—but almost certainly by Crabbe himself. Whether Pettigrew did or did not take part in the robbery, we don't know. But we do know that he was associated with Crabbe at the time, that that association put him under suspicion, and that if Crabbe should be proved guilty, he, Crabbe's associate, would certainly be implicated. You see, therefore, that Pettigrew agrees completely with the special characteristics that we have assigned to the burglar, and we know of no one else who does.

"But that burglar was in possession of Penrose's keys and was, therefore, either the murderer himself or a confederate of the murderer."

"Yes," I agreed, "it is a very complete case so far as it goes. But it is only a string of hypotheses, after all."

"Not entirely," he replied. "The association of Crabbe and Pettigrew is a fact, if we accept Miller's statement. There is really a definite case of suspicion against Pettigrew, at least that is my opinion; and it is certainly Miller's. If I am not greatly mistaken, the superintendent is in full cry after Deodatus. But you see the curious dilemma that we are in. Here are two men of whom each agrees in certain respects with the characters of the murderer. But the characters with which they agree are not the same. Parrott is connected with Julliberrie's Grave but seems to have no connection with the burglary. Pettigrew is connected with the burglary but seems to have no connection with Julliberrie's Grave. But the murderer must have been connected with both."

"It almost seems," said I, "that you will have to accept—at least provisionally—the idea of confederacy. The assumption that both men were concerned in the murder would release you from your dilemma."

"That is quite true," he replied. "But it would be a gratuitous assumption. There is nothing to support it. The two men are separate and there is no apparent connection between them; nothing to suggest that they were even acquainted. And again I must say that I have the strongest feeling that the murder was the work of one man absolutely alone."

"It certainly has that appearance," I admitted, "but still—"

I paused as the sound of footsteps on our landing caught my ear. A moment later, an old-fashioned flourish on the little brass knocker of our inner door at once announced the arrival of a visitor and declared his identity. I rose, and, crossing the room, threw open the door; whereupon Mr. Brodribb bounced in, looking, with his glossy silk hat and his faultless morning dress, as if he had just bounced out of a band-box.

"Now," said he, holding up his hand, "don't let me create any disturbance. I am only a bird of passage. Off again in two or three minutes."

"But why?" said Thorndyke. "Polton will be bringing in our dinner by that time. Why not stay and season the feast with your illustrious presence?"

"Very good of you," replied Brodribb, "and very nicely put. I should love to. But I have got a confounded engagement. However, I will sit down for a minute or two and say what I have to say. It isn't very important."

He placed his hat tenderly on the table and then continued:

"My principal object in calling, I don't mind admitting, is to bespeak the good offices of the incomparable Polton. I've got a fine old bracket clock—belonged to my grandfather; made for him by Earnshaw, and I set considerable store by it. Now, something has gone wrong with its strike and I don't like to trust it to a common clock-jobber. So I thought I would ask Polton to have a look at it. Probably he can do all that is necessary, and, if he can't, he will be able to give me the name of one of his Clerkenwell friends who is equal to dealing with a fine bracket clock."

"Very well," said Thorndyke, "I will undertake the commission on his behalf. He will be delighted, I am sure, to do what he can for pure love of a good clock, to say nothing of his love of the owner."

"Does he love me?" asked Brodribb. "Well, I hope he does, for I have the greatest admiration and regard for him. Then that is settled. And now to the other matter. I thought you would be interested to know that I have got the intestacy proceedings *in re* Penrose well under way."

"You haven't lost much time," I remarked in some surprise.

"Oh, I don't mean that I have got it settled," said he. "That will be a work of months, at least. But I have got the essentials in train. As soon as I got your note informing me that Daniel Penrose was dead and that he died on the seventeenth of October, I set the machinery going. Seemed a bit callous, with the body still above ground, but I don't believe in wasting time. None of the law's delay for me if I can help it. So I put out the necessary advertisements at once. You see, it was pretty plain sailing as I had a copy of the Penrose pedigree. That told me at once who the principal next of kin were, though, of course, I didn't know where to find them. But I was able to give names and particulars which were likely to catch the attention of interested parties. And they did. As a matter of fact, there are only two persons who matter and I have got into touch with them both. They are descendants of a certain Elizabeth Penrose, an aunt of Oliver's, who married a man named John Pettigrew. What their exact relationship is to each other, I have forgotten, but they are both named Pettigrew. One of them is a young lady named Joan; a nice girl, poor as a church mouse but very independent and industrious. Works for her living and supports her mother—secretary to some professor fellow. And the mother is quite a nice lady. She had a job as manageress of some sort of antique shop, but the proprietor went bust and she lost the billet. It is pleasant to think of these two worthy ladies coming in for a bit of luck."

"You have seen them, apparently," said Thorndyke.

"Yes, they turned up two days after the advertisement appeared, and I liked the look of both of them. The girl, Joan, is very much on the spot and very modern—short skirts, head like a mop, you know the sort of thing. But I like her. She's a good girl and she has evidently been a good daughter."

"And the other person?" Thorndyke asked.

"The other is a man, Deodatus Pettigrew. Quaint name, isn't it? I hope he will justify it, but I have my doubts. Joan and her mother knew him, but they were mighty reticent about him. Rather evasive, in fact. Made me suspect that he might be a sheep of the brunette type. But we shall see. In any case, his personal character is no concern of mine."

"You haven't met him yet?" Thorndyke suggested.

"No. He didn't seem keen on an interview. Joan and her mother turned up in person, but he just wrote and seemed to want to do the whole business by correspondence. Of course, I couldn't have that in the case of a big estate like this. Must know the people I am dealing with."

"What do you reckon these two persons are likely to receive?" Thorndyke asked.

"The whole estate is about a hundred and fifty thousand pounds, and, as there are practically no other claimants, they can hardly get less than fifty thousand apiece."

"Fifty thousand pounds," I remarked, "ought to be worth the trouble of an interview."

"So I told him," said Brodribb, "and, in effect, he agreed. So he is coming up to see me to-morrow."

"At what time?" Thorndyke asked.

"The appointment is for twelve o'clock, noon, sharp. But why do you ask that?"

"Because I rather want to see Mr. Pettigrew."

"Ho, ha!" said Brodribb. "So you know something about him."

"Not very much," replied Thorndyke. "I am interested. I should like to have a look at him in a good light to see if he agrees with a description that I had of a person of that name. Can you manage that?"

"I can and I will. Would you like an introduction?"

"No," replied Thorndyke. "I don't want to know him and I don't wish him to know who I am. I just want to have a good look at his face."

"Ha!" exclaimed Brodribb. "I scent a mystery. But I ask no questions. You will bear me out in that, Jervis. I ask no questions though I am bursting with curiosity. I just do what I am asked to do. I shall arrange for you to be shown into the waiting-room—where, by the way, the clock is. Pettigrew will come to the clerk's office, but when he goes away I shall let him out through the waiting-room. So, if you sit or stand close to the outer door, which is by the window, you will have a good view of him in an excellent light. I wonder why the devil you want to see him. But I don't ask. No, not at all. I know my place."

Here Brodribb consulted a fat gold watch. Then, as he sprang up and seized his hat, he concluded:

"Now I must really be off. To-morrow at noon; and don't forget to tell Polton about the clock."

When he had gone, I reopened our previous discussion with the inevitable comment.

"This communication of Brodribb's throws a fresh and lurid light on the case and lets you out of your dilemma. It looks as if Parrott might be dismissed from the role of suspect."

"It does," Thorndyke agreed. "But we mustn't exaggerate the significance of these new facts. Because a man stands to benefit by another man's death, it doesn't follow that he is prepared to murder that other man."

"True," I replied. "But that is not quite the position. It is not merely a case of a man standing to benefit by the death of another. The benefit was actually created by the murder. If Penrose had not been murdered, he would have taken practically the whole estate and the others would have received nothing. There is no blinking the fact that the murder of Daniel Penrose was worth fifty thousand pounds to Pettigrew, and that without the murder he would have got nothing. I should say that you might pretty safely forget Parrott."

"You may be right, Jervis," he rejoined. "You are, certainly, in regard to the reality of the motive. But that motive is no answer to the positive evidence that seems to implicate Parrott."

Here Polton stole silently into the room (having let himself in with his key), bearing the advance guard of the materials for dinner, and the discussion was necessarily suspended. Thorndyke lapsed into silence, and, as his invaluable henchman laid the table in his quietly efficient fashion, he watched him thoughtfully as if noting his noiseless, unhurried dexterity. As Polton retired to fetch a fresh consignment, he rose, and, stepping over to the cabinet, pulled out a drawer and took from it the cardboard box in which the pottery fragment and its mould and the other objects from the pocket of the hospital patient had been deposited. From the box he picked out the cigarette-tube—the existence of which I had forgotten—turned it over in his fingers, looking at it curiously, and replaced the box in the drawer. Then he walked over to the table, and, having laid the tube on the white cloth, went back to his chair.

I watched the proceeding with a good deal of curiosity but I made no comment. For the immediate purpose was plain enough and it remained only to await the further developments. And I had not long to wait. Presently Polton returned with the remainder of the materials for our meal on a tray. The latter he set down on the table and was about to begin unloading it when the cigarette-tube caught

his eye. He looked at it very hard and with evident surprise for a
few moments and then picked it up and turned it over as Thorndyke
had done, examining every part of it with the minutest scrutiny.

"Well, Polton," said Thorndyke, "what do you think of it?"

Polton looked at him with a cunning and crinkly smile and replied
comprehensively in a single word: "Tims."

"Tims," I repeated. "What on earth are Tims?"

"Mr. Tims, sir," he explained, "now deceased. Mr. Parrott's
cabinet-maker."

"You think it once belonged to Mr. Tims?" Thorndyke suggested.

"I don't think," Polton replied. "I know. I saw him make it.
The way it came about was this; there was a little cabinet of African
ebony sent to the workshop for some repairs, and the owner of it
sent with it a piece of the same wood that he had managed to get
hold of—queer-looking stuff of a sort of brownish-black, rather like
a lump of pitch, with a streak of grey sapwood running through
it.

"Well, Tims did the repairs and he was mighty economical with
the wood because there was none too much of it. However, when the
job was finished, there was a small bit left over, mostly sap-wood.
But Tims cut most of that away and then put the piece in the lathe
and turned up this tube, finishing the mouthpiece with a paring
chisel; and he made these white dots by drilling holes and driving
little holly-wood dowels into them before he finished the turning.
He was quite pleased with it when it was done."

"Did he keep it for his own use?" Thorndyke asked, "or did he
sell it?"

"That I can't say, sir. But he would hardly have kept it, because
he didn't smoke cigarettes. I supposed at the time that he had made
it to give to Mr. Parrott, who smoked cigarettes a lot and always
used a tube; and the one that he had was burned to a stump. Still,
Tims may have given it or sold it to some one else. Might I ask, sir,
how it came into your hands?"

"We found it," Thorndyke replied, "in the pocket of a raincoat
that was left by the unknown man who was in possession of Mr.
Penrose's car."

"Oh, dear!" said Polton. "Then I am afraid it has been in bad
company."

He laid it down on the table and resumed the business of unloading the tray. Then, having removed the covers, he made a

little bow to intimate that dinner was served, and retired, apparently wrapped in profound thought.

"There, Jervis," said Thorndyke, picking up the tube and restoring it to its abiding-place, "you see how the evidence oscillates back and forth and still keeps a rough balance. Here we are, back in the old dilemma. First comes Brodribb and weights the balance heavily against Pettigrew; so heavily that you are disposed to drop Parrott overboard. But then comes Polton and weights the balance heavily against Parrott—and, by the way, I think he has his own suspicions of the Popinjay. He looked mighty thoughtful after I had answered his question."

"Yes," said I, "it seemed to me that your answer had given him something to think about. But with regard to this tube. There is not a particle of evidence that it was ever in Parrott's possession."

"Not of direct evidence," he admitted. "But just look at the *prima facie* appearances as a whole. Here was a man who was evidently intimately acquainted with Penrose, for they had been digging together in the barrow. He had in his pocket an object which had been dug up in that barrow and which was part of another object, dug up from the same barrow, and almost certainly dug up by Parrott and sold by him to Penrose. That, at least, suggests the possibility—even a probability—that the man was Parrott. Now we find in that same man's pocket an object that was certainly made in Parrott's workshop. That is a very striking fact. It makes, at least, another connection between Parrott and the hospital patient. And then there is the very strong probability that Tims made the thing as a gift to his employer; that it was actually Parrott's property. By the ordinary rules of circumstantial evidence, all these agreements create a very definite probability that the man was Parrott."

I had to admit the truth of this. "But," I objected, "this suspicion of Parrott is no answer to the positive evidence against Pettigrew. If you refuse to entertain the idea of a joint crime by two confederates —which still seems to me the only way out—you are left in a hopeless dilemma. You have got evidence suggesting that Tweedledum is the guilty party and evidence that Tweedledee committed the crime; and yet—on your one-man theory—they can't both be guilty. I don't quite see how you are going to resolve the puzzle."

"Don't forget, Jervis," said he, "that there are certain final tests which, if we can only apply them, will carry us out of the region of inference into that of demonstrable fact. If our inferences are correct, one of these men is pretty certainly in possession of the Billington jewels. And there are other confirmatory tests equally conclusive. The purpose of our hypothetical reasoning is to discover the persons to whom the tests may be applied."

CHAPTER 20

THE DILEMMA RESOLVED

It wanted some minutes to the appointed time when Thorndyke and
I, accompanied by Polton and a burglarious-looking handbag,
arrived at Mr. Brodribb's premises in New Square, Lincoln's Inn.
The visitor, we learned from the chief clerk, had not yet made his
appearance, and we were shown at once into the private office,
where we found Brodribb seated at his writing-table sorting out a
heap of letters and documents. He rose as we were announced, and,
taking off his spectacles, proceeded to the business on which we had
come.

"You had better come out into the ante-room at once," said he,
"as Pettigrew will come in through the clerk's office. I don't think
you will have so very long to wait. The interview needn't be a very
protracted affair as there isn't much to discuss. It is really only a
matter of my making his acquaintance."

He opened a small, light door and ushered us through into the
ante-room, a rather long, narrow chamber, lighted by a large
window at one end which was close to the door of exit. A large
office table occupied a good deal of the floor space and extended
to the neighbourhood of the window, leaving a space just sufficient
for a couple of chairs.

"There," said Brodribb, indicating the latter, "if you take those
chairs you will be close to the window and the door. He will have to
pass quite near to you and you will be able to inspect him in an
excellent light. And I think this table will do for you, Polton. There
is your patient on the mantelpiece. He is ticking away all right but,
when he tries to strike, he makes a most ungodly noise."

Polton walked round to the mantelpiece and surveyed the clock
with a friendly and appreciative crinkle.

"It's a noble old timepiece," said he. "They don't make clocks
like that nowadays. Don't want 'em, I suppose, now that you

can get the time by counting the hiccups from a loud-speaker."

He listened for a few moments, with his ear close to the dial, and then lifted the clock, cautiously and with loving care, on to the table. The keys were in the front and back doors, and, when he had unlocked and opened them, he placed his bag on the table and began to discharge its cargo of tools and appliances. First, he took out a roll of clean, white paper, which he spread on the table, weighting it with one or two tools and a couple of lignum-vitæ bowls. Then he started the strike, which was accompanied by the most horrid asthmatical wheezing, and having listened critically to these abnormal sounds, he took off the pendulum and fell to work with a screwdriver to such effect that, in a jiffy, the clock was out of its case and lying on its back on the sheet of paper.

At this point a clerk appeared at the door of the private office and announced that Mr. Pettigrew had arrived; whereupon Mr. Brodribb directed him to show the visitor in, and, after a last, anxious glance at the clock, went back into his office and shut the communicating door.

But the latter, as I have said, was by no means a massive structure, and, in fact, hardly seemed to meet the requirements of a lawyer's office in the matter of privacy. Brodribb's voice, indeed, was hardly audible, but I heard quite distinctly the visitor's reply: "Yes, sir. I am Mr. Pettigrew."

But I was not the only person who heard that reply. As Pettigrew spoke, I noticed that Polton seemed to pause for an instant in his operations and listened with a rather odd expression of interest and attention. And so, as the interview proceeded, each time that Pettigrew spoke, Polton's movements were arrested and he sat with his mouth slightly open, listening, without any disguise, to the voice that penetrated the door.

It was a rather peculiar voice, resonant, penetrating and clear; and its quality was reinforced by the deliberate manner and distinct enunciation. The disjointed sentences that came through the door might have been spoken by an actor or by a man making a set speech. But I think that Brodribb must have done most of the talking, for the sounds that came through took the form, generally, of an indistinct rumble which certainly did not proceed from Pettigrew.

The interview was not a long one, but to me the inaction, coupled with an ill-defined expectancy, made the time pass slowly and tediously. Thorndyke relieved the tedium of waiting by following Polton's operations and discussing—almost in a whisper—the construction of the striking mechanism and the symptoms of its disorder. The latter did not appear to be very serious, for, presently, Polton began to reassemble the dismembered parts of the movement, applying here and there, with a pointed style, a delicate touch of oil.

He had got the greater part of the striking movement together when the sound, from the private office, of a chair being drawn back seemed to herald the termination of the interview. Thereupon Thorndyke went back to his chair and Polton, softly laying down a pair of flat-nosed pliers, suddenly became immobile and watchful. Then the door opened an inch or two and Brodribb's voice became audible.

"Very well, Mr. Pettigrew," he said, "you shall not be troubled with unnecessary journeys. I shall let you know, from time to time, how matters are progressing and not ask for your personal attendance unless it is absolutely necessary."

With this he threw open the door and ushered his client into the ante-room, filling up the doorway with his own rather bulky person as if to prevent any retreat. I glanced with natural curiosity at Pettigrew and saw a rather large man, dark-complexioned and wearing a full beard and moustache, the latter turned up fiercely at the ends in a fashion slightly suggestive of wax. Apparently, he had supposed the room to be empty, for he looked round with quick, uneasy surprise. And then his glance fell on Polton; and I could see at once that he recognized him and was rather disconcerted by the recognition. But he made no sign after the first startled glance, walking straight up the room in the narrow space between the table and the fireplace, looking neither to the right nor left. But just as he had advanced midway, Polton rose suddenly and exclaimed:

"Why, it's Mr. Parrott! Bless me, sir, I hardly knew you with that beard."

Pettigrew cast a malignant glance at the speaker and replied gruffly:

"My name is Pettigrew."

"Ah!" said Polton, "I suppose Parrott was the business name."

Pettigrew made no reply, but stalked up the room until he passed between our chairs and the table to reach the door. And then he suddenly clapped on his hat. But not soon enough. For I had already noted—and so certainly had Thorndyke—an irregular, rather recent, scar crossing his right eyebrow. And when I saw that, I realized what Thorndyke had meant by the "final tests."

As Pettigrew grasped the handle of the door, he cast a swift, apprehensive glance at my colleague. Then he opened the door quickly, and, when he had passed out, shut it after him. Instantly, Thorndyke rose and followed him, and, of course, I followed Thorndyke; and so we came out in a sort of procession into the Square.

As we emerged from the house, I became aware of a man loitering on the pavement at its northern end. He was a stranger to me, but I diagnosed him at once as a plain-clothes police officer. So perhaps had Pettigrew, for he turned in the other direction, towards the Searle Street gate. But that path also was guarded, and by no less a person than Superintendent Miller. When I first saw him, he was standing in the middle of the pavement, apparently studying a document. But as we turned in his direction, Thorndyke took off his hat; whereupon Miller hastily pocketed the paper and waited the approach of his quarry.

It was evident that Pettigrew viewed the superintendent with suspicion for he turned and crossed the road to the railings of the garden; and when the superintendent also crossed the road, with the evident purpose of intercepting him, the position was unmistakable. Pettigrew paused for a moment irresolutely, thrusting his hand into his pocket. Then, as Miller rushed towards him, he drew out a revolver and fired at him nearly point-blank. The superintendent staggered back a couple of paces but did not fall; and when Pettigrew, having fired his shot, dodged across to the pavement and broke into a run, he clapped his hand to his thigh and followed as well as he could.

The swift succession of events has left an indelible impression on my memory. Even now I can see vividly with my mind's eye that strange picture of hurry and confusion that disturbed the peace and repose of New Square: the terrified fugitive, racing furiously down the pavement with Thorndyke and me in hot pursuit; the plain-clothes man clattering noisily behind; and the superintendent hobbling after us with a blood-stained hand grasping his thigh.

But it was a short chase. For hardly had Pettigrew—running like a hare and gaining on us all—covered half the distance to the gate when suddenly he halted, flung away his revolver and sank to the ground, rolling over on to his back and then lying motionless. When we reached him and looked down at the prostrate figure, his aspect—wretch as he was—could not but evoke some feelings of pity and compunction. The ghastly face, the staring, terrified eyes, the retracted lips, and the hands, clutching at the breast, presented the typical picture of *angina pectoris*.

But this, too, was a passing phase. Before any measures of relief could be thought of, it was over. The staring eyes relaxed, the mouth fell open, and the hands slipped from the breast and dropped limply to the ground.

The superintendent, hobbling up, still grasping his wounded thigh, looked down gloomily at his prisoner.

"Well," he commented, "he made a game try, and he has given us the slip, sure enough. It's a pity, but it's no one's fault. We couldn't have got him any sooner. Hadn't we better move him indoors before a crowd collects?"

It did seem desirable; for the pistol shot and the sounds of hurrying feet had brought startled faces to office windows and now began to bring curious spectators from office doorways.

"Do you mind if we carry him into your ante-room?" Thorndyke asked, turning to Brodribb, who had just come up with Polton.

"No, no," Brodribb replied. "Take the poor creature in, of course. Is he badly hurt?"

"He is dead," Thorndyke announced as I hastened with the assistance of the plain-clothes officer to lift the body.

"Dead!" exclaimed Brodribb, turning as pale as his complexion would permit. "Good God! What a shocking thing! Just as he was coming into a fortune too. How perfectly appalling!"

He followed the gruesome procession as the officer and I, now aided by Thorndyke, bore the corpse back along the pavement to the doorway from which we had emerged but a minute or two previously and finally laid it down on the ante-room floor; and he stole softly into the room and shrank away with a horrified glance at the ghastly figure. And his agitation was natural enough. There was something very dreadful in the suddenness of the catastrophe. I was sensible of it myself as I rose from laying down the corpse and my glance lighted on the clock and the litter of tools on the table, lying just as the dead man had seen them when he passed to the door.

"I think," said Thorndyke, "that we had better telephone for

an ambulance to take away the body and convey the superintendent
to the hospital. Where is he?" he added anxiously.

The question was answered by Miller in person, who limped into
the room, his gory hand still grasping his wound and a trickle of
blood running across his boot.

"My God, Miller!" exclaimed Brodribb, gazing at him in consternation, "you too! But aren't you going to do something for him,
Thorndyke?"

"We had better see what the damage is," said I, "and at least
control the bleeding."

"I don't think it is anything that matters," said Miller, "excepting
to Mr. Brodribb's carpet. However, you may as well have a look at it."

I made a rapid examination of the wound and was relieved to
find that his estimate was correct. The bullet had passed through
the outer side of the thigh leaving an almost imperceptible entrance
wound but a rather ragged wound of exit which was bleeding somewhat freely.

"You haven't any bandages or dressing material, I suppose?"
said I.

"I have not," replied Brodribb, "but I can produce some clean
handkerchiefs, if they will do. But bring him into my private office.
I can't bear the sight of that poor creature lying on the floor."

We accordingly moved off to the private office where, with
Brodribb's handkerchiefs, I contrived a temporary dressing which
restrained the bleeding.

"There," said I, "that will serve until the ambulance comes.
Some one has telephoned, I suppose?"

"Yes," replied Brodribb, "the police officer sent a message. And
now tell me what it is all about. I heard a pistol shot. Who was it
that fired?"

"Pettigrew," Thorndyke answered. "The position is this: the
superintendent came here on my information to arrest Pettigrew and
charge him with the murder of Daniel Penrose, and Pettigrew fired
at Miller in the hope of getting away."

Brodribb was horrified. "You astound me, Thorndyke!" he
exclaimed. "I have actually been conferring with poor Penrose's
murderer. And not only that. I have been aiding and abetting him
in getting possession of the plunder. But I don't understand how
he comes to be dead. What killed him?"

"It was a heart attack," Thorndyke replied, "angina, brought

about by the excitement and the intense physical effort. But I think
I hear the ambulance men in the ante-room. That sounded like a
stretcher being put down."

He opened the door and we looked out. At the table Polton was
seated, apparently engrossed in his work upon the clock and
watched with grim amusement by the plain-clothes officer, while the
ambulance men, having lifted the body on to the stretcher, were
preparing to carry it away. I was about to help Miller to rise from
his chair when Thorndyke interposed.

"Before you go, Miller," said he, "there is one little matter to be
attended to. You had better get Pettigrew's address from Mr.
Brodribb; and you had better lose no time in sending some capable officer there with a search warrant. You understand what
I mean?"

"Perfectly," replied Miller. "But there isn't going to be any
sending. I shall make that search myself, if I have to go down in
an ambulance."

"Very well, Miller," Thorndyke rejoined. "But remember that
you have got only two legs and that you can't afford to part with
either of them."

With this warning he assisted the superintendent to rise; and
when the latter had received and carefully pocketed the slip of
paper on which Brodribb had written Pettigrew's address, we escorted him out to the ambulance and saw him duly dispatched en
route for Charing Cross Hospital.

As we turned to re-enter the house, our ears were saluted by the
cheerful striking of a clock; and passing into the ante-room, we
found Polton, still seated at the table, surveying with an admiring
and crinkly smile the venerable timepiece, now completely reconstructed and restored to its case.

"He's all right now, sir," he announced triumphantly. "Just listen
to his strike."

He moved the minute hand round, and, having paused a moment
for the "warning," set it at the hour and listened ecstatically as the
hammer struck out six silvery notes.

"Clear as the day he was born," he remarked complacently; and
forthwith moved the hand round to the next hour.

"You must stop that noise," exclaimed Brodribb. "I can't bear
it. Have you no sense of decency, to be making that uproar in the
house of death, you—you callous, indifferent little villain?"

Polton regarded him with a surprised and apologetic crinkle (and moved the hand round to the next hour).

"But, sir," he protested, "you can't set a striking clock to time any other way, unless you take the gong off. Shall I do that?"

"No, no," replied Brodribb. "I'll go outside until you've finished. And I apologize for calling you a villain. My nerves are rather upset."

We accompanied him out into the Square and walked up and down the pavement for a few minutes giving him some further explanations of the recent events. Presently Polton made his appearance, carrying his bag, and announced that the clock was now set to time and established in its place on the mantelpiece. Brodribb thanked him profusely and apologized still more profusely for his outburst.

"You must forgive me, Polton," he said. "My nerves are not equal to this sort of thing. You understand, don't you?"

"I understand, sir," replied Polton, "and I suppose I *was* callous. But he was a bad man, not worth troubling about, and the world is the better without him. I never liked him and I always suspected him of fleecing poor Mr. Penrose."

"Probably you were right," rejoined Brodribb, "but we must talk about that when I am more myself. And now I will get back to my business and try to forget these horrors."

He shook hands with us and retired into his entry, while we turned away and set a course for the Temple.

"I suppose, Thorndyke," I said presently, "you were not surprised by our friend's recognition of Parrott. I am judging by the fact that you took the opportunity of having Polton with us."

"No," he replied, "I was not. The assumption that Parrott and Pettigrew were one and the same person seemed to offer the only way out of my dilemma if I rejected—as I certainly did—the idea of confederacy. There were the two men, making separate appearances. Each of them seemed, by the evidence, to be the murderer. But there was only one murderer. The only solution of the problem was the assumption that they were the same man. That was a perfectly reasonable assumption and there was nothing against it."

"Nothing at all," I admitted. "In fact, it is rather obvious—when once it is suggested. But I have found this case rather confusing from the first; it has seemed to me a bewildering mass of disjointed facts."

"That is a mistake, Jervis," said he. "The facts form a perfectly coherent sequence. Some time, we will go over the ground again, and then I think you will see that your confusion was principally due to your having made a false start."

CHAPTER 21

AFTERTHOUGHTS

"It seems to me," Lockhart suggested, "that this case is, to a certain extent, left in the air. The essential facts, in a legal sense, are perfectly clear. But there is a lot that we don't know, and, I suppose never shall know."

The remark—which fairly expressed my own view—was made on the occasion of a little dinner-party at our chambers, arranged partly to celebrate the completion of the case, and partly to enable Lockhart—who had developed unexpected archæological sympathies—to make the acquaintance of Elmhurst. The dinner was supplied by the staff of a neighbouring tavern, an arrangement which not only relieved Polton of culinary labours but included him in the festivities; for he was enabled thereby to entertain, in his own apartments adjacent to the laboratory, no less a person than Mr. Kickweed.

Both of our guests had been, in a sense, parties to the case; but each had made contact with it at only a single point. It was natural, then, that when the meal had reached its more leisurely and less manducatory stage, the desultory conversation should have subsided into a more definite discussion, with a demand from both for a complete exposition of the investigation. And it was then, when Thorndyke readily complied with the demand, that I was able, for the first time, to realize how clearly he had grasped the essentials of the problem from the very beginning and how steadily and directly he had proceeded, point by point, to unravel the tangle of false appearances.

I need not report his exposition. It contained nothing but what is recorded in the foregoing narrative of the events. It consisted, in fact, of a condensed summary of that narrative with the events presented in their actual sequence with a running accompaniment of argument demonstrating their logical connections. When he had come to the end of the story with an account of its tragic climax, he paused to push round the decanters and then proceeded reflectively to fill his pipe; and it was then that Lockhart made the observation which I have recorded above.

"That is quite true," Thorndyke agreed. "For legal purposes— for the purpose of framing an indictment and securing a conviction— the case was as complete as it could well be. But the death of Pettigrew has left us in the dark on a number of points on which we should probably have been enlightened if he had been brought to trial and had made a statement in his defence. At present, the circumstances surrounding the murder—if it was a murder—and the motive—if there was a clear-cut motive—are more or less wrapped in mystery."

"Are they?" Elmhurst exclaimed in evident surprise. "To me it looks like a simple murder, deliberately planned in cold blood, for the plain purpose of getting possession of a very large sum of money. Fifty thousand pounds would seem to furnish a very sufficient motive to a man of Pettigrew's type. But you don't take that view?"

"No," replied Thorndyke, "I do not. I am even inclined to doubt whether the money was a factor in the case at all. We must not lose sight of the conditions prevailing at the time. When Penrose left home, that is to say on the day of his death, his father was alive and well and the question of the disposition of his property had not arisen. At that time, the only persons who knew the state of affairs were Penrose, Horridge and Brodribb; and even they knew it very imperfectly. Brodribb, himself, was not certain whether there was or was not a will. As to Pettigrew, there is no evidence, or any reason for believing, that he had any knowledge, or even suspicion, that Oliver's estate was not duly disposed of by a will."

"Penrose knew, more or less, how matters stood," said Lockhart, "and he may have 'let on' to Pettigrew."

"That is possible," Thorndyke admitted. "though it would be rather unlike the secretive Penrose to babble about his private affairs to a comparative stranger. For it seems pretty certain that he had no idea as to who Parrott was. Mrs. Pettigrew almost certainly knew who he was, but she must have been sworn to secrecy, and she kept the secret loyally. Still, we must admit the possibility of Penrose having made some unguarded statements to Parrott, unlikely as it seems."

"Then," said Lockhart, "if you reject the money as the impelling motive, what is there left? What other motive do you suggest?"

"I am not in a position to make any definite suggestion," replied Thorndyke, "but I have a vague feeling that there may have been a motive of another kind; a motive that would fit in better with the circumstances of the murder—or homicide—in so far as they are known to us."

"I am not sure that I quite follow you," said Lockhart.

"I mean," Thorndyke explained, "that the money theory of motive would imply a deliberate, planned, unconditional murder with carefully prepared means of execution; and the method would involve the necessary detail of taking the victim unaware and fore-stalling any possibility of resistance. But that is not what happened. The weapon with which Penrose was killed was not brought there by his assailant. It was his own weapon. So that the method of homicide actually used must have been improvised. And Penrose must have been either on the defensive or offensive. There was an encounter. But it was a deadly encounter, as we can judge by the formidable weapon used, not a mere chance 'scrap.' And the deadliness of that encounter implies something more than a sudden disagreement. There is a suggestion of something involving a fierce and bitter enmity. Perhaps it is possible to imagine some cause of deadly strife between these two men. But I knew very little of either of them; and before I offer even a tentative suggestion, I would ask you, Lockhart, who at least knew them better than I did, if anything occurs to you."

"They were both practically strangers to me," said Lockhart. "I knew nothing of their relations except as buyer and seller. But could you put your question a little more definitely?"

"I will put it quite definitely," Thorndyke replied. "Looking back on your relations with these two men, and considering them by the light of what we now know, does it appear to you that there was anything that might have been the occasion of enmity between them or that might have caused one of them to go in fear of the other?"

Lockhart looked at Thorndyke in evident surprise, but he did not reply immediately. He appeared to be turning the question over in his mind and considering its bearing. And then a little frown appeared on his brow as if some new and rather surprising idea had occurred to him.

"I think I see what is in your mind, Thorndyke," he replied, at length; "and I am not sure that you aren't right. The idea had never occurred to me before; but now, looking back as you say, by the light of what we know, I am disposed to think that there may have been some occasion of enmity, and especially of fear. But you don't want my opinions. I had better relate the actual experiences that I am thinking of.

"I have told you about my visit to Penrose when he showed me his collection of jewels, which we now know to have been the stolen Billington collection."

"Do you think," Thorndyke asked, "that Penrose knew they were stolen property?"

"I can hardly think that," Lockhart replied, "or he would surely never have let me see them. But I do think that he had some uneasy suspicions that there may have been something a little fishy about them. I have told you how startled he seemed when I jocosely suggested that the Jacobite Jewel was a rather incriminating possession. My impression is that he may have got the collection comparatively cheap, on the condition that no questions were to be asked."

"Which," I remarked, "usually means that the goods are stolen property."

"Yes," Lockhart admitted, "that is so. But I am afraid that your really acquisitive collector is not always extremely scrupulous. However, there the things were, obviously property of considerable value, and I naturally raised the question of insurance. Penrose was quite alive to the desirability of insuring the jewels. But he was in a difficulty. Before they could be insured, they would have to be valued; and he had an apparently unaccountable objection to their being seen by a valuer. I put this down to his inveterate habit of secrecy. Now, of course, we know that he was doubtful of the safety of letting a stranger—and an expert stranger, too—see what they were. But he agreed in principle and promised to think over the problem of the valuer.

"Now, on the only occasion when I met Parrott in the flesh, it happened that Penrose was present. The meeting occurred in Parrott's workshop when I was waiting for a table that poor Tims had been repairing and Penrose was waiting for Mr. Polton. By way of making conversation, I rather foolishly asked Penrose what he was doing about the valuer. I saw instantly that I had made a *faux pas* in referring to the matter before Parrott, for Penrose— usually a most suave and amiable man—snapped out a very short answer and was obviously extremely annoyed.

"At the moment, Parrott made no comment and seemed not to have noticed what had passed. But as soon as Penrose had gone, he opened the subject of the insurance and the valuer; and as I, having been sworn to secrecy, was necessarily evasive in my answers, he pressed the matter more closely and went on to question me in the most searching and persistent fashion as to what I had seen and whether Penrose had shown me anything more than the contents of the large gallery. It was very awkward as I could not give him a straight answer, and eventually I had to cut the interrogation short by making a hasty retreat.

"Looking back on this interview, I now see a new significance in it. Parrott was undoubtedly angry. He was quiet and restrained, but I detected an undercurrent of deep resentment, the occasion of which I entirely misunderstood, putting it down to mere pique on his part that Penrose should have contemplated employing a strange valuer when he, Parrott, could have managed the business quite competently. And I also misunderstood the drift of his questions, for I assumed that he knew nothing of the jewels and was merely curious as to whether Penrose had any things of value which had been obtained through some other dealer. Now I see that he suspected Penrose of having shown me the jewels and was trying to find out definitely whether he had or had not. And I think that my evasive answers must have convinced him that I had seen the jewels."

"Yes," said Thorndyke, "I think you are right. And what do you infer from that?"

"Well," replied Lockhart, "by the light of what we now know, certain conclusions seem to emerge. The jewels were sold to Penrose by Crabbe, but I think we are agreed that Parrott—I will still call him Parrott as that is the name by which I knew him—was the go-between who actually negotiated the deal. Now, as these jewels were a complete collection, instantly identifiable by any one who had seen them, and of which the police had a full description, I think it follows that they must have been sold to Penrose with the condition that he should maintain inviolable secrecy as to their being in his possession and that he should neither show them nor disclose their existence to anybody. Do you agree?"

"I do, certainly," Thorndyke replied. "It seems impossible that they could have been sold on any other conditions."

"Moreover," Lockhart continued, "there is nothing improbable in such a condition. Penrose wanted the things, not for display, but for the purpose of gloating over in secret. In consideration of a low price, he would be quite willing to accept the condition of secrecy. Very well, then; we are agreed that Penrose must have been bound by a promise of secrecy to Parrott, on the faithful performance of which Parrott's safety depended. Consequently, when it appeared to Parrott that Penrose had broken his promise by showing me the jewels and that he was actually contemplating their disclosure to a valuer (who would almost certainly recognize them), he would suddenly see himself placed in a position of great and imminent danger. Penrose's indiscretion threatened to send him to penal servitude. In your own phrase, Parrott must thenceforth have gone in fear of Penrose. But when a man of a criminal type like Parrott goes in fear of another, there has arisen a fairly adequate motive for the murder of that other. I think that answers your question."

"It does, very completely," said Thorndyke. "It brings into view exactly the kind of motive for which I have been looking. The money motive, even if Pettigrew had known about the intestacy, would have seemed hardly sufficient. Deliberate, planned murder for the purpose of pecuniary profit is rare. But murder planned and committed for the purpose of removing some person whose existence is a menace to the safety of the murderer, is relatively common. The motive of fear is understandable, and, in a sense, reasonable. It may even be, in certain circumstances, justifiable. But in any case, it is a strong and urgent motive, impelling to immediate action and making it worth while to take risks. You don't remember the date of your interview with Parrott, I suppose?"

"I don't," replied Lockhart, "but it must have been quite a short time before Penrose's disappearance, for, when I came back to London, he had been absent for a month or two. It looks as if the murder had followed pretty closely on that interview."

"And now, Thorndyke," said I, "that you have heard Lockhart's story, what is your final conclusion? Apparently you exclude the money motive altogether."

"I would hardly say that," he replied, "because, after all, we have no certain knowledge. But I see no reason to suppose that Pettigrew knew anything about his position as next of kin until he saw Brodribb's advertisement. On the other hand, from the moment when he became a party to the sale of the jewels, he was at Penrose's mercy; and as soon as he formed the definite suspicion that Penrose was not keeping faith with him, he had a perfectly understandable motive for making away with Penrose."

"Then," said I, "you think it was a deliberate, premeditated murder?"

"I think that is the conclusion that we are driven to," he replied. "At any rate, we must conclude that Pettigrew lured Penrose to that place with the idea of murder in his mind. The intention may have been conditional on what happened there; on whether, for instance, Penrose could or would clear himself of the charge of bad faith. But the remarkable suitability of the time and place, both for the murder, itself, and for the secure disposal of the body, seems to imply a careful selection and a considered intention."

"What makes you suggest that the intention may have been conditional?" Lockhart asked.

"There are two facts," Thorndyke replied, "which seem to offer that suggestion. The piece of pottery that we found in Pettigrew's pocket shows clearly that an excavation was actually carried out by the two men. There would certainly have been no collecting of pottery after the murder. Then the fact that Penrose was killed with his own weapon suggests a quarrel, and a pretty violent one, for Penrose must, himself, have produced his weapon. But when Pettigrew had got possession of that weapon, his behaviour was unmistakable. He struck to kill. It was no mere tap on the head. It was a murderous blow into which the assailant put his whole strength.

"So, taking all the facts into account, I think our verdict must be wilful murder, not only in the legal sense—which it obviously was—but in the sense in which ordinary men use the words. But it is an impressive and disturbing thought that only by a hair's-breadth did he miss escaping completely. He had abandoned and hidden the car and was sneaking off in the darkness to disappear for ever, unknown and unsuspected. But for the incalculable chance of his being knocked down by that unknown car or lorry, he would have got away without leaving a trace, and we should still be looking for the missing Penrose."

There was a short interval of silence when Thorndyke had concluded. Then Elmhurst remarked:

"It is rather a gruesome thought, that of the two men digging away amicably into the barrow when one of them must have known that the other was almost certainly digging his own grave."

"It is," I agreed. "But Thorndyke's interpretation of the facts suggests some other strange and gruesome pictures; that, for instance, of the murderer reading Brodribb's advertisement and realizing that his murderous blow had been worth fifty thousand pounds; and his visit to New Square to collect his earnings."

"Yes, indeed," moralized Elmhurst, "and he collected them truly enough. It is a satisfaction to think of that moment of disillusionment when he saw his ill-gotten fortune turn to dust and ashes and realized that, for him as for others, the wages of sin was death."

A CATALOGUE OF
SELECTED DOVER BOOKS
IN ALL FIELDS OF INTEREST

A CATALOGUE OF SELECTED DOVER BOOKS IN ALL FIELDS OF INTEREST

CELESTIAL OBJECTS FOR COMMON TELESCOPES, T. W. Webb. The most used book in amateur astronomy: inestimable aid for locating and identifying nearly 4,000 celestial objects. Edited, updated by Margaret W. Mayall. 77 illustrations. Total of 645pp. 5⅜ x 8½.
20917-2, 20918-0 Pa., Two-vol. set $9.00

HISTORICAL STUDIES IN THE LANGUAGE OF CHEMISTRY, M. P. Crosland. The important part language has played in the development of chemistry from the symbolism of alchemy to the adoption of systematic nomenclature in 1892. ". . . wholeheartedly recommended,"—Science. 15 illustrations. 416pp. of text. 5⅝ x 8¼. 63702-6 Pa. $6.00

BURNHAM'S CELESTIAL HANDBOOK, Robert Burnham, Jr. Thorough, readable guide to the stars beyond our solar system. Exhaustive treatment, fully illustrated. Breakdown is alphabetical by constellation: Andromeda to Cetus in Vol. 1; Chamaeleon to Orion in Vol. 2; and Pavo to Vulpecula in Vol. 3. Hundreds of illustrations. Total of about 2000pp. 6⅛ x 9¼.
23567-X, 23568-8, 23673-0 Pa., Three-vol. set $26.85

THEORY OF WING SECTIONS: INCLUDING A SUMMARY OF AIRFOIL DATA, Ira H. Abbott and A. E. von Doenhoff. Concise compilation of subatomic aerodynamic characteristics of modern NASA wing sections, plus description of theory. 350pp. of tables. 693pp. 5⅜ x 8½.
60586-8 Pa. $7.00

DE RE METALLICA, Georgius Agricola. Translated by Herbert C. Hoover and Lou H. Hoover. The famous Hoover translation of greatest treatise on technological chemistry, engineering, geology, mining of early modern times (1556). All 289 original woodcuts. 638pp. 6¾ x 11.
60006-8 Clothbd. $17.50

THE ORIGIN OF CONTINENTS AND OCEANS, Alfred Wegener. One of the most influential, most controversial books in science, the classic statement for continental drift. Full 1966 translation of Wegener's final (1929) version. 64 illustrations. 246pp. 5⅜ x 8½. 61708-4 Pa. $3.00

THE PRINCIPLES OF PSYCHOLOGY, William James. Famous long course complete, unabridged. Stream of thought, time perception, memory, experimental methods; great work decades ahead of its time. Still valid, useful; read in many classes. 94 figures. Total of 1391pp. 5⅜ x 8½.
20381-6, 20382-4 Pa., Two-vol. set $13.00

YUCATAN BEFORE AND AFTER THE CONQUEST, Diego de Landa. First English translation of basic book in Maya studies, the only significant account of Yucatan written in the early post-Conquest era. Translated by distinguished Maya scholar William Gates. Appendices, introduction, 4 maps and over 120 illustrations added by translator. 162pp. 5⅜ x 8½.
23622-6 Pa. $3.00

THE MALAY ARCHIPELAGO, Alfred R. Wallace. Spirited travel account by one of founders of modern biology. Touches on zoology, botany, ethnography, geography, and geology. 62 illustrations, maps. 515pp. 5⅜ x 8½.
20187-2 Pa. $6.95

THE DISCOVERY OF THE TOMB OF TUTANKHAMEN, Howard Carter, A. C. Mace. Accompany Carter in the thrill of discovery, as ruined passage suddenly reveals unique, untouched, fabulously rich tomb. Fascinating account, with 106 illustrations. New introduction by J. M. White. Total of 382pp. 5⅜ x 8½. (Available in U.S. only)   23500-9 Pa. $4.00

THE WORLD'S GREATEST SPEECHES, edited by Lewis Copeland and Lawrence W. Lamm. Vast collection of 278 speeches from Greeks up to present. Powerful and effective models; unique look at history. Revised to 1970. Indices. 842pp. 5⅜ x 8½.   20468-5 Pa. $8.95

THE 100 GREATEST ADVERTISEMENTS, Julian Watkins. The priceless ingredient; His master's voice; 99 44/100% pure; over 100 others. How they were written, their impact, etc. Remarkable record. 130 illustrations. 233pp. 7⅞ x 10 3/5.   20540-1 Pa. $5.00

CRUICKSHANK PRINTS FOR HAND COLORING, George Cruickshank. 18 illustrations, one side of a page, on fine-quality paper suitable for watercolors. Caricatures of people in society (c. 1820) full of trenchant wit. Very large format. 32pp. 11 x 16.   23684-6 Pa. $5.00

THIRTY-TWO COLOR POSTCARDS OF TWENTIETH-CENTURY AMERICAN ART, Whitney Museum of American Art. Reproduced in full color in postcard form are 31 art works and one shot of the museum. Calder, Hopper, Rauschenberg, others. Detachable. 16pp. 8¼ x 11.
23629-3 Pa. $2.50

MUSIC OF THE SPHERES: THE MATERIAL UNIVERSE FROM ATOM TO QUASAR SIMPLY EXPLAINED, Guy Murchie. Planets, stars, geology, atoms, radiation, relativity, quantum theory, light, antimatter, similar topics. 319 figures. 664pp. 5⅜ x 8½.
21809-0, 21810-4 Pa., Two-vol. set $10.00

EINSTEIN'S THEORY OF RELATIVITY, Max Born. Finest semi-technical account; covers Einstein, Lorentz, Minkowski, and others, with much detail, much explanation of ideas and math not readily available elsewhere on this level. For student, non-specialist. 376pp. 5⅜ x 8½.
60769-0 Pa. $4.00

THE COMPLETE BOOK OF DOLL MAKING AND COLLECTING, Catherine Christopher. Instructions, patterns for dozens of dolls, from rag doll on up to elaborate, historically accurate figures. Mould faces, sew clothing, make doll houses, etc. Also collecting information. Many illustrations. 288pp. 6 x 9. 22066-4 Pa. $4.00

THE DAGUERREOTYPE IN AMERICA, Beaumont Newhall. Wonderful portraits, 1850's townscapes, landscapes; full text plus 104 photographs. The basic book. Enlarged 1976 edition. 272pp. 8¼ x 11¼. 23322-7 Pa. $6.00

CRAFTSMAN HOMES, Gustav Stickley. 296 architectural drawings, floor plans, and photographs illustrate 40 different kinds of "Mission-style" homes from *The Craftsman* (1901-16), voice of American style of simplicity and organic harmony. Thorough coverage of Craftsman idea in text and picture, now collector's item. 224pp. 8⅛ x 11. 23791-5 Pa. $6.00

PEWTER-WORKING: INSTRUCTIONS AND PROJECTS, Burl N. Osborn. & Gordon O. Wilber. Introduction to pewter-working for amateur craftsman. History and characteristics of pewter; tools, materials, step-by-step instructions. Photos, line drawings, diagrams. Total of 160pp. 7⅞ x 10¾. 23786-9 Pa. $3.50

THE GREAT CHICAGO FIRE, edited by David Lowe. 10 dramatic, eye-witness accounts of the 1871 disaster, including one of the aftermath and rebuilding, plus 70 contemporary photographs and illustrations of the ruins—courthouse, Palmer House, Great Central Depot, etc. Introduction by David Lowe. 87pp. 8¼ x 11. 23771-0 Pa. $4.00

SILHOUETTES: A PICTORIAL ARCHIVE OF VARIED ILLUSTRATIONS, edited by Carol Belanger Grafton. Over 600 silhouettes from the 18th to 20th centuries include profiles and full figures of men and women, children, birds and animals, groups and scenes, nature, ships, an alphabet. Dozens of uses for commercial artists and craftspeople. 144pp. 8⅜ x 11¼. 23781-8 Pa. $4.00

ANIMALS: 1,419 COPYRIGHT-FREE ILLUSTRATIONS OF MAMMALS, BIRDS, FISH, INSECTS, ETC., edited by Jim Harter. Clear wood engravings present, in extremely lifelike poses, over 1,000 species of animals. One of the most extensive copyright-free pictorial sourcebooks of its kind. Captions. Index. 284pp. 9 x 12. 23766-4 Pa. $7.50

INDIAN DESIGNS FROM ANCIENT ECUADOR, Frederick W. Shaffer. 282 original designs by pre-Columbian Indians of Ecuador (500-1500 A.D.). Designs include people, mammals, birds, reptiles, fish, plants, heads, geometric designs. Use as is or alter for advertising, textiles, leathercraft, etc. Introduction. 95pp. 8¾ x 11¼. 23764-8 Pa. $3.50

SZIGETI ON THE VIOLIN, Joseph Szigeti. Genial, loosely structured tour by premier violinist, featuring a pleasant mixture of reminiscences, insights into great music and musicians, innumerable tips for practicing violinists. 385 musical passages. 256pp. 5⅝ x 8¼. 23763-X Pa. $3.50

TONE POEMS, SERIES II: TILL EULENSPIEGELS LUSTIGE STREICHE, ALSO SPRACH ZARATHUSTRA, AND EIN HELDEN-LEBEN, Richard Strauss. Three important orchestral works, including very popular *Till Eulenspiegel's Marry Pranks,* reproduced in full score from original editions. Study score. 315pp. 9⅜ x 12¼. (Available in U.S. only)
23755-9 Pa. $7.50

TONE POEMS, SERIES I: DON JUAN, TOD UND VERKLARUNG AND DON QUIXOTE, Richard Strauss. Three of the most often performed and recorded works in entire orchestral repertoire, reproduced in full score from original editions. Study score. 286pp. 9⅜ x 12¼. (Available in U.S. only)
23754-0 Pa. $7.50

11 LATE STRING QUARTETS, Franz Joseph Haydn. The form which Haydn defined and "brought to perfection." *(Grove's).* 11 string quartets in complete score, his last and his best. The first in a projected series of the complete Haydn string quartets. Reliable modern Eulenberg edition, otherwise difficult to obtain. 320pp. 8⅜ x 11¼. (Available in U.S. only)
23753-2 Pa. $6.95

FOURTH, FIFTH AND SIXTH SYMPHONIES IN FULL SCORE, Peter Ilyitch Tchaikovsky. Complete orchestral scores of Symphony No. 4 in F Minor, Op. 36; Symphony No. 5 in E Minor, Op. 64; Symphony No. 6 in B Minor, "Pathetique," Op. 74. Bretikopf & Hartel eds. Study score. 480pp. 9⅜ x 12¼.
23861-X Pa. $10.95

THE MARRIAGE OF FIGARO: COMPLETE SCORE, Wolfgang A. Mozart. Finest comic opera ever written. Full score, not to be confused with piano renderings. Peters edition. Study score. 448pp. 9⅜ x 12¼. (Available in U.S. only)
23751-6 Pa. $11.95

"IMAGE" ON THE ART AND EVOLUTION OF THE FILM, edited by Marshall Deutelbaum. Pioneering book brings together for first time 38 groundbreaking articles on early silent films from *Image* and 263 illustrations newly shot from rare prints in the collection of the International Museum of Photography. A landmark work. Index. 256pp. 8¼ x 11.
23777-X Pa. $8.95

AROUND-THE-WORLD COOKY BOOK, Lois Lintner Sumption and Marguerite Lintner Ashbrook. 373 cooky and frosting recipes from 28 countries (America, Austria, China, Russia, Italy, etc.) include Viennese kisses, rice wafers, London strips, lady fingers, hony, sugar spice, maple cookies, etc. Clear instructions. All tested. 38 drawings. 182pp. 5⅜ x 8.
23802-4 Pa. $2.50

THE ART NOUVEAU STYLE, edited by Roberta Waddell. 579 rare photographs, not available elsewhere, of works in jewelry, metalwork, glass, ceramics, textiles, architecture and furniture by 175 artists—Mucha, Seguy, Lalique, Tiffany, Gaudin, Hohlwein, Saarinen, and many others. 288pp. 8⅜ x 11¼.
23515-7 Pa. $6.95

THE AMERICAN SENATOR, Anthony Trollope. Little known, long unavailable Trollope novel on a grand scale. Here are humorous comment on American vs. English culture, and stunning portrayal of a heroine/villainess. Superb evocation of Victorian village life. 561pp. 5⅜ x 8½.
23801-6 Pa. $6.00

WAS IT MURDER? James Hilton. The author of *Lost Horizon* and *Goodbye, Mr. Chips* wrote one detective novel (under a pen-name) which was quickly forgotten and virtually lost, even at the height of Hilton's fame. This edition brings it back—a finely crafted public school puzzle resplendent with Hilton's stylish atmosphere. A thoroughly English thriller by the creator of Shangri-la. 252pp. 5⅜ x 8. (Available in U.S. only)
23774-5 Pa. $3.00

CENTRAL PARK: A PHOTOGRAPHIC GUIDE, Victor Laredo and Henry Hope Reed. 121 superb photographs show dramatic views of Central Park: Bethesda Fountain, Cleopatra's Needle, Sheep Meadow, the Blockhouse, plus people engaged in many park activities: ice skating, bike riding, etc. Captions by former Curator of Central Park, Henry Hope Reed, provide historical view, changes, etc. Also photos of N.Y. landmarks on park's periphery. 96pp. 8½ x 11. 23750-8 Pa. $4.50

NANTUCKET IN THE NINETEENTH CENTURY, Clay Lancaster. 180 rare photographs, stereographs, maps, drawings and floor plans recreate unique American island society. Authentic scenes of shipwreck, lighthouses, streets, homes are arranged in geographic sequence to provide walking-tour guide to old Nantucket existing today. Introduction, captions. 160pp. 8⅞ x 11¾. 23747-8 Pa. $6.95

STONE AND MAN: A PHOTOGRAPHIC EXPLORATION, Andreas Feininger. 106 photographs by *Life* photographer Feininger portray man's deep passion for stone through the ages. Stonehenge-like megaliths, fortified towns, sculpted marble and crumbling tenements show textures, beauties, fascination. 128pp. 9¼ x 10¾. 23756-7 Pa. $5.95

CIRCLES, A MATHEMATICAL VIEW, D. Pedoe. Fundamental aspects of college geometry, non-Euclidean geometry, and other branches of mathematics: representing circle by point. Poincare model, isoperimetric property, etc. Stimulating recreational reading. 66 figures. 96pp. 5⅝ x 8¼.
63698-4 Pa. $2.75

THE DISCOVERY OF NEPTUNE, Morton Grosser. Dramatic scientific history of the investigations leading up to the actual discovery of the eighth planet of our solar system. Lucid, well-researched book by well-known historian of science. 172pp. 5⅜ x 8½. 23726-5 Pa. $3.00

THE DEVIL'S DICTIONARY. Ambrose Bierce. Barbed, bitter, brilliant witticisms in the form of a dictionary. Best, most ferocious satire America has produced. 145pp. 5⅜ x 8½. 20487-1 Pa. $1.75

HISTORY OF BACTERIOLOGY, William Bulloch. The only comprehensive history of bacteriology from the beginnings through the 19th century. Special emphasis is given to biography-Leeuwenhoek, etc. Brief accounts of 350 bacteriologists form a separate section. No clearer, fuller study, suitable to scientists and general readers, has yet been written. 52 illustrations. 448pp. 5⅝ x 8¼. 23761-3 Pa. $6.50

THE COMPLETE NONSENSE OF EDWARD LEAR, Edward Lear. All nonsense limericks, zany alphabets, Owl and Pussycat, songs, nonsense botany, etc., illustrated by Lear. Total of 321pp. 5⅜ x 8½. (Available in U.S. only) 20167-8 Pa. $3.00

INGENIOUS MATHEMATICAL PROBLEMS AND METHODS, Louis A. Graham. Sophisticated material from Graham *Dial*, applied and pure; stresses solution methods. Logic, number theory, networks, inversions, etc. 237pp. 5⅜ x 8½. 20545-2 Pa. $3.50

BEST MATHEMATICAL PUZZLES OF SAM LOYD, edited by Martin Gardner. Bizarre, original, whimsical puzzles by America's greatest puzzler. From fabulously rare *Cyclopedia*, including famous 14-15 puzzles, the Horse of a Different Color, 115 more. Elementary math. 150 illustrations. 167pp. 5⅜ x 8½. 20498-7 Pa. $2.50

THE BASIS OF COMBINATION IN CHESS, J. du Mont. Easy-to-follow, instructive book on elements of combination play, with chapters on each piece and every powerful combination team—two knights, bishop and knight, rook and bishop, etc. 250 diagrams. 218pp. 5⅜ x 8½. (Available in U.S. only) 23644-7 Pa. $3.50

MODERN CHESS STRATEGY, Ludek Pachman. The use of the queen, the active king, exchanges, pawn play, the center, weak squares, etc. Section on rook alone worth price of the book. Stress on the moderns. Often considered the most important book on strategy. 314pp. 5⅜ x 8½. 20290-9 Pa. $3.50

LASKER'S MANUAL OF CHESS, Dr. Emanuel Lasker. Great world champion offers very thorough coverage of all aspects of chess. Combinations, position play, openings, end game, aesthetics of chess, philosophy of struggle, much more. Filled with analyzed games. 390pp. 5⅜ x 8½. 20640-8 Pa. $4.00

500 MASTER GAMES OF CHESS, S. Tartakower, J. du Mont. Vast collection of great chess games from 1798-1938, with much material nowhere else readily available. Fully annotated, arranged by opening for easier study. 664pp. 5⅜ x 8½. 23208-5 Pa. $6.00

A GUIDE TO CHESS ENDINGS, Dr. Max Euwe, David Hooper. One of the finest modern works on chess endings. Thorough analysis of the most frequently encountered endings by former world champion. 331 examples, each with diagram. 248pp. 5⅜ x 8½. 23332-4 Pa. $3.50

SECOND PIATIGORSKY CUP, edited by Isaac Kashdan. One of the greatest tournament books ever produced in the English language. All 90 games of the 1966 tournament, annotated by players, most annotated by both players. Features Petrosian, Spassky, Fischer, Larsen, six others. 228pp. 5⅜ x 8½.   23572-6 Pa. $3.50

ENCYCLOPEDIA OF CARD TRICKS, revised and edited by Jean Hugard. How to perform over 600 card tricks, devised by the world's greatest magicians: impromptus, spelling tricks, key cards, using special packs, much, much more. Additional chapter on card technique. 66 illustrations. 402pp. 5⅜ x 8½. (Available in U.S. only)   21252-1 Pa. $3.95

MAGIC: STAGE ILLUSIONS, SPECIAL EFFECTS AND TRICK PHOTOGRAPHY, Albert A. Hopkins, Henry R. Evans. One of the great classics; fullest, most authorative explanation of vanishing lady, levitations, scores of other great stage effects. Also small magic, automata, stunts. 446 illustrations. 556pp. 5⅜ x 8½.   23344-8 Pa. $5.00

THE SECRETS OF HOUDINI, J. C. Cannell. Classic study of Houdini's incredible magic, exposing closely-kept professional secrets and revealing, in general terms, the whole art of stage magic. 67 illustrations. 279pp. 5⅜ x 8½.   22913-0 Pa. $3.00

HOFFMANN'S MODERN MAGIC, Professor Hoffmann. One of the best, and best-known, magicians' manuals of the past century. Hundreds of tricks from card tricks and simple sleight of hand to elaborate illusions involving construction of complicated machinery. 332 illustrations. 563pp. 5⅜ x 8½.   23623-4 Pa. $6.00

MADAME PRUNIER'S FISH COOKERY BOOK, Mme. S. B. Prunier. More than 1000 recipes from world famous Prunier's of Paris and London, specially adapted here for American kitchen. Grilled tournedos with anchovy butter, Lobster a la Bordelaise, Prunier's prized desserts, more. Glossary. 340pp. 5⅜ x 8½. (Available in U.S. only)   22679-4 Pa. $3.00

FRENCH COUNTRY COOKING FOR AMERICANS, Louis Diat. 500 easy-to-make, authentic provincial recipes compiled by former head chef at New York's Fitz-Carlton Hotel: onion soup, lamb stew, potato pie, more. 309pp. 5⅜ x 8½.   23665-X Pa. $3.95

SAUCES, FRENCH AND FAMOUS, Louis Diat. Complete book gives over 200 specific recipes: bechamel, Bordelaise, hollandaise, Cumberland, apricot, etc. Author was one of this century's finest chefs, originator of vichyssoise and many other dishes. Index. 156pp. 5⅜ x 8.
23663-3 Pa. $2.50

TOLL HOUSE TRIED AND TRUE RECIPES, Ruth Graves Wakefield. Authentic recipes from the famous Mass. restaurant: popovers, veal and ham loaf, Toll House baked beans, chocolate cake crumb pudding, much more. Many helpful hints. Nearly 700 recipes. Index. 376pp. 5⅜ x 8½.
23560-2 Pa. $4.00

"OSCAR" OF THE WALDORF'S COOKBOOK, Oscar Tschirky. Famous American chef reveals 3455 recipes that made Waldorf great; cream of French, German, American cooking, in all categories. Full instructions, easy home use. 1896 edition. 907pp. 6⅝ x 9⅜.   20790-0 Clothbd. $15.00

COOKING WITH BEER, Carole Fahy. Beer has as superb an effect on food as wine, and at fraction of cost. Over 250 recipes for appetizers, soups, main dishes, desserts, breads, etc. Index. 144pp. 5⅜ x 8½. (Available in U.S. only)   23661-7 Pa. $2.50

STEWS AND RAGOUTS, Kay Shaw Nelson. This international cookbook offers wide range of 108 recipes perfect for everyday, special occasions, meals-in-themselves, main dishes. Economical, nutritious, easy-to-prepare: goulash, Irish stew, boeuf bourguignon, etc. Index. 134pp. 5⅜ x 8½.
                                                            23662-5 Pa. $2.50

DELICIOUS MAIN COURSE DISHES, Marian Tracy. Main courses are the most important part of any meal. These 200 nutritious, economical recipes from around the world make every meal a delight. "I . . . have found it so useful in my own household,"—N.Y. Times. Index. 219pp. 5⅜ x 8½.   23664-1 Pa. $3.00

FIVE ACRES AND INDEPENDENCE, Maurice G. Kains. Great back-to-the-land classic explains basics of self-sufficient farming: economics, plants, crops, animals, orchards, soils, land selection, host of other necessary things. Do not confuse with skimpy faddist literature; Kains was one of America's greatest agriculturalists. 95 illustrations. 397pp. 5⅜ x 8½.
                                                            20974-1 Pa. $3.95

A PRACTICAL GUIDE FOR THE BEGINNING FARMER, Herbert Jacobs. Basic, extremely useful first book for anyone thinking about moving to the country and starting a farm. Simpler than Kains, with greater emphasis on country living in general. 246pp. 5⅜ x 8½.
                                                            23675-7 Pa. $3.50

A GARDEN OF PLEASANT FLOWERS (PARADISI IN SOLE: PARADISUS TERRESTRIS), John Parkinson. Complete, unabridged reprint of first (1629) edition of earliest great English book on gardens and gardening. More than 1000 plants & flowers of Elizabethan, Jacobean garden fully described, most with woodcut illustrations. Botanically very reliable, a "speaking garden" of exceeding charm. 812 illustrations. 628pp. 8½ x 12¼.   23392-8 Clothbd. $25.00

ACKERMANN'S COSTUME PLATES, Rudolph Ackermann. Selection of 96 plates from the Repository of Arts, best published source of costume for English fashion during the early 19th century. 12 plates also in color. Captions, glossary and introduction by editor Stella Blum. Total of 120pp. 8⅜ x 11¼.   23690-0 Pa. $4.50

MUSHROOMS, EDIBLE AND OTHERWISE, Miron E. Hard. Profusely illustrated, very useful guide to over 500 species of mushrooms growing in the Midwest and East. Nomenclature updated to 1976. 505 illustrations. 628pp. 6½ x 9¼.   23309-X Pa. $7.95

AN ILLUSTRATED FLORA OF THE NORTHERN UNITED STATES AND CANADA, Nathaniel L. Britton, Addison Brown. Encyclopedic work covers 4666 species, ferns on up. Everything. Full botanical information, illustration for each. This earlier edition is preferred by many to more recent revisions. 1913 edition. Over 4000 illustrations, total of 2087pp. 6⅛ x 9¼.   22642-5, 22643-3, 22644-1 Pa., Three-vol. set $24.00

MANUAL OF THE GRASSES OF THE UNITED STATES, A. S. Hitchcock, U.S. Dept. of Agriculture. The basic study of American grasses, both indigenous and escapes, cultivated and wild. Over 1400 species. Full descriptions, information. Over 1100 maps, illustrations. Total of 1051pp. 5⅜ x 8½.   22717-0, 22718-9 Pa., Two-vol. set $12.00

THE CACTACEAE,, Nathaniel L. Britton, John N. Rose. Exhaustive, definitive. Every cactus in the world. Full botanical descriptions. Thorough statement of nomenclatures, habitat, detailed finding keys. The one book needed by every cactus enthusiast. Over 1275 illustrations. Total of 1080pp. 8 x 10¼.   21191-6, 21192-4 Clothbd., Two-vol. set $35.00

AMERICAN MEDICINAL PLANTS, Charles F. Millspaugh. Full descriptions, 180 plants covered: history; physical description; methods of preparation with all chemical constituents extracted; all claimed curative or adverse effects. 180 full-page plates. Classification table. 804pp. 6½ x 9¼.
23034-1 Pa. $10.00

A MODERN HERBAL, Margaret Grieve. Much the fullest, most exact, most useful compilation of herbal material. Gigantic alphabetical encyclopedia, from aconite to zedoary, gives botanical information, medical properties, folklore, economic uses, and much else. Indispensable to serious reader. 161 illustrations. 888pp. 6½ x 9¼. (Available in U.S. only)
22798-7, 22799-5 Pa., Two-vol. set $11.00

THE HERBAL or GENERAL HISTORY OF PLANTS, John Gerard. The 1633 edition revised and enlarged by Thomas Johnson. Containing almost 2850 plant descriptions and 2705 superb illustrations, Gerard's *Herbal* is a monumental work, the book all modern English herbals are derived from, the one herbal every serious enthusiast should have in its entirety. Original editions are worth perhaps $750. 1678pp. 8½ x 12¼.
23147-X Clothbd. $50.00

MANUAL OF THE TREES OF NORTH AMERICA, Charles S. Sargent. The basic survey of every native tree and tree-like shrub, 717 species in all. Extremely full descriptions, information on habitat, growth, locales, economics, etc. Necessary to every serious tree lover. Over 100 finding keys. 783 illustrations. Total of 986pp. 5⅜ x 8½.
20277-1, 20278-X Pa., Two-vol. set $10.00

AMERICAN BIRD ENGRAVINGS, Alexander Wilson et al. All 76 plates. from Wilson's *American Ornithology* (1808-14), most important ornithological work before Audubon, plus 27 plates from the supplement (1825-33) by Charles Bonaparte. Over 250 birds portrayed. 8 plates also reproduced in full color. 111pp. 9⅜ x 12½. 23195-X Pa. $6.00

CRUICKSHANK'S PHOTOGRAPHS OF BIRDS OF AMERICA, Allan D. Cruickshank. Great ornithologist, photographer presents 177 closeups, groupings, panoramas, flightings, etc., of about 150 different birds. Expanded *Wings in the Wilderness*. Introduction by Helen G. Cruickshank. 191pp. 8¼ x 11. 23497-5 Pa. $6.00

AMERICAN WILDLIFE AND PLANTS, A. C. Martin, et al. Describes food habits of more than 1000 species of mammals, birds, fish. Special treatment of important food plants. Over 300 illustrations. 500pp. 5⅜ x 8½. 20793-5 Pa. $4.95

THE PEOPLE CALLED SHAKERS, Edward D. Andrews. Lifetime of research, definitive study of Shakers: origins, beliefs, practices, dances, social organization, furniture and crafts, impact on 19th-century USA, present heritage. Indispensable to student of American history, collector. 33 illustrations. 351pp. 5⅜ x 8½. 21081-2 Pa. $4.00

OLD NEW YORK IN EARLY PHOTOGRAPHS, Mary Black. New York City as it was in 1853-1901, through 196 wonderful photographs from N.-Y. Historical Society. Great Blizzard, Lincoln's funeral procession, great buildings. 228pp. 9 x 12. 22907-6 Pa. $7.95

MR. LINCOLN'S CAMERA MAN: MATHEW BRADY, Roy Meredith. Over 300 Brady photos reproduced directly from original negatives, photos. Jackson, Webster, Grant, Lee, Carnegie, Barnum; Lincoln; Battle Smoke, Death of Rebel Sniper, Atlanta Just After Capture. Lively commentary. 368pp. 8⅜ x 11¼. 23021-X Pa. $8.95

TRAVELS OF WILLIAM BARTRAM, William Bartram. From 1773-8, Bartram explored Northern Florida, Georgia, Carolinas, and reported on wild life, plants, Indians, early settlers. Basic account for period, entertaining reading. Edited by Mark Van Doren. 13 illustrations. 141pp. 5⅜ x 8½. 20013-2 Pa. $4.50

THE GENTLEMAN AND CABINET MAKER'S DIRECTOR, Thomas Chippendale. Full reprint, 1762 style book, most influential of all time; chairs, tables, sofas, mirrors, cabinets, etc. 200 plates, plus 24 photographs of surviving pieces. 249pp. 9⅞ x 12¾. 21601-2 Pa. $6.50

AMERICAN CARRIAGES, SLEIGHS, SULKIES AND CARTS, edited by Don H. Berkebile. 168 Victorian illustrations from catalogues, trade journals, fully captioned. Useful for artists. Author is Assoc. Curator, Div. of Transportation of Smithsonian Institution. 168pp. 8½ x 9½. 23328-6 Pa. $5.00

THE SENSE OF BEAUTY, George Santayana. Masterfully written discussion of nature of beauty, materials of beauty, form, expression; art, literature, social sciences all involved. 168pp. 5⅜ x 8½. 20238-0 Pa. $2.50

ON THE IMPROVEMENT OF THE UNDERSTANDING, Benedict Spinoza. Also contains *Ethics, Correspondence*, all in excellent R. Elwes translation. Basic works on entry to philosophy, pantheism, exchange of ideas with great contemporaries. 402pp. 5⅜ x 8½. 20250-X Pa. $4.50

THE TRAGIC SENSE OF LIFE, Miguel de Unamuno. Acknowledged masterpiece of existential literature, one of most important books of 20th century. Introduction by Madariaga. 367pp. 5⅜ x 8½.
20257-7 Pa. $3.50

THE GUIDE FOR THE PERPLEXED, Moses Maimonides. Great classic of medieval Judaism attempts to reconcile revealed religion (Pentateuch, commentaries) with Aristotelian philosophy. Important historically, still relevant in problems. Unabridged Friedlander translation. Total of 473pp. 5⅜ x 8½. 20351-4 Pa. $5.00

THE I CHING (THE BOOK OF CHANGES), translated by James Legge. Complete translation of basic text plus appendices by Confucius, and Chinese commentary of most penetrating divination manual ever prepared. Indispensable to study of early Oriental civilizations, to modern inquiring reader. 448pp. 5⅜ x 8½. 21062-6 Pa. $4.00

THE EGYPTIAN BOOK OF THE DEAD, E. A. Wallis Budge. Complete reproduction of Ani's papyrus, finest ever found. Full hieroglyphic text, interlinear transliteration, word for word translation, smooth translation. Basic work, for Egyptology, for modern study of psychic matters. Total of 533pp. 6½ x 9¼. (Available in U.S. only) 21866-X Pa. $4.95

THE GODS OF THE EGYPTIANS, E. A. Wallis Budge. Never excelled for richness, fullness: all gods, goddesses, demons, mythical figures of Ancient Egypt; their legends, rites, incarnations, variations, powers, etc. Many hieroglyphic texts cited. Over 225 illustrations, plus 6 color plates. Total of 988pp. 6⅛ x 9¼. (Available in U.S. only)
22055-9, 22056-7 Pa., Two-vol. set $12.00

THE ENGLISH AND SCOTTISH POPULAR BALLADS, Francis J. Child. Monumental, still unsuperseded; all known variants of Child ballads, commentary on origins, literary references, Continental parallels, other features. Added: papers by G. L. Kittredge, W. M. Hart. Total of 2761pp. 6½ x 9¼.
21409-5, 21410-9, 21411-7, 21412-5, 21413-3 Pa., Five-vol. set $37.50

CORAL GARDENS AND THEIR MAGIC, Bronsilaw Malinowski. Classic study of the methods of tilling the soil and of agricultural rites in the Trobriand Islands of Melanesia. Author is one of the most important figures in the field of modern social anthropology. 143 illustrations. Indexes. Total of 911pp. of text. 5⅝ x 8¼. (Available in U.S. only)
23597-1 Pa. $12.95

THE PHILOSOPHY OF HISTORY, Georg W. Hegel. Great classic of Western thought develops concept that history is not chance but a rational process, the evolution of freedom. 457pp. 5⅜ x 8½. 20112-0 Pa. $4.50

LANGUAGE, TRUTH AND LOGIC, Alfred J. Ayer. Famous, clear introduction to Vienna, Cambridge schools of Logical Positivism. Role of philosophy, elimination of metaphysics, nature of analysis, etc. 160pp. 5⅜ x 8½. (Available in U.S. only) 20010-8 Pa. $1.75

A PREFACE TO LOGIC, Morris R. Cohen. Great City College teacher in renowned, easily followed exposition of formal logic, probability, values, logic and world order and similar topics; no previous background needed. 209pp. 5⅜ x 8½. 23517-3 Pa. $3.50

REASON AND NATURE, Morris R. Cohen. Brilliant analysis of reason and its multitudinous ramifications by charismatic teacher. Interdisciplinary, synthesizing work widely praised when it first appeared in 1931. Second (1953) edition. Indexes. 496pp. 5⅜ x 8½. 23633-1 Pa. $6.00

AN ESSAY CONCERNING HUMAN UNDERSTANDING, John Locke. The only complete edition of enormously important classic, with authoritative editorial material by A. C. Fraser. Total of 1176pp. 5⅜ x 8½. 20530-4, 20531-2 Pa., Two-vol. set $14.00

HANDBOOK OF MATHEMATICAL FUNCTIONS WITH FORMULAS, GRAPHS, AND MATHEMATICAL TABLES, edited by Milton Abramowitz and Irene A. Stegun. Vast compendium: 29 sets of tables, some to as high as 20 places. 1,046pp. 8 x 10½. 61272-4 Pa. $14.95

MATHEMATICS FOR THE PHYSICAL SCIENCES, Herbert S. Wilf. Highly acclaimed work offers clear presentations of vector spaces and matrices, orthogonal functions, roots of polynomial equations, conformal mapping, calculus of variations, etc. Knowledge of theory of functions of real and complex variables is assumed. Exercises and solutions. Index. 284pp. 5⅝ x 8¼. 63635-6 Pa. $4.50

THE PRINCIPLE OF RELATIVITY, Albert Einstein et al. Eleven most important original papers on special and general theories. Seven by Einstein, two by Lorentz, one each by Minkowski and Weyl. All translated, unabridged. 216pp. 5⅜ x 8½. 60081-5 Pa. $3.00

THERMODYNAMICS, Enrico Fermi. A classic of modern science. Clear, organized treatment of systems, first and second laws, entropy, thermodynamic potentials, gaseous reactions, dilute solutions, entropy constant. No math beyond calculus required. Problems. 160pp. 5⅜ x 8½. 60361-X Pa. $2.75

ELEMENTARY MECHANICS OF FLUIDS, Hunter Rouse. Classic undergraduate text widely considered to be far better than many later books. Ranges from fluid velocity and acceleration to role of compressibility in fluid motion. Numerous examples, questions, problems. 224 illustrations. 376pp. 5⅝ x 8¼. 63699-2 Pa. $5.00

AN AUTOBIOGRAPHY, Margaret Sanger. Exciting personal account of hard-fought battle for woman's right to birth control, against prejudice, church, law. Foremost feminist document. 504pp. 5⅜ x 8½.
20470-7 Pa. $5.50

MY BONDAGE AND MY FREEDOM, Frederick Douglass. Born as a slave, Douglass became outspoken force in antislavery movement. The best of Douglass's autobiographies. Graphic description of slave life. Introduction by P. Foner. 464pp. 5⅜ x 8½.
22457-0 Pa. $5.00

LIVING MY LIFE, Emma Goldman. Candid, no holds barred account by foremost American anarchist: her own life, anarchist movement, famous contemporaries, ideas and their impact. Struggles and confrontations in America, plus deportation to U.S.S.R. Shocking inside account of persecution of anarchists under Lenin. 13 plates. Total of 944pp. 5⅜ x 8½.
22543-7, 22544-5 Pa., Two-vol. set $9.00

LETTERS AND NOTES ON THE MANNERS, CUSTOMS AND CONDITIONS OF THE NORTH AMERICAN INDIANS, George Catlin. Classic account of life among Plains Indians: ceremonies, hunt, warfare, etc. Dover edition reproduces for first time all original paintings. 312 plates. 572pp. of text. 6⅛ x 9¼.
22118-0, 22119-9 Pa.. Two-vol. set $10.00

THE MAYA AND THEIR NEIGHBORS, edited by Clarence L. Hay, others. Synoptic view of Maya civilization in broadest sense, together with Northern, Southern neighbors. Integrates much background, valuable detail not elsewhere. Prepared by greatest scholars: Kroeber, Morley, Thompson, Spinden, Vaillant, many others. Sometimes called Tozzer Memorial Volume. 60 illustrations, linguistic map. 634pp. 5⅜ x 8½.
23510-6 Pa. $7.50

HANDBOOK OF THE INDIANS OF CALIFORNIA, A. L. Kroeber. Foremost American anthropologist offers complete ethnographic study of each group. Monumental classic. 459 illustrations, maps. 995pp. 5⅜ x 8½.
23368-5 Pa. $10.00

SHAKTI AND SHAKTA, Arthur Avalon. First book to give clear, cohesive analysis of Shakta doctrine, Shakta ritual and Kundalini Shakti (yoga). Important work by one of world's foremost students of Shaktic and Tantric thought. 732pp. 5⅜ x 8½. (Available in U.S. only)
23645-5 Pa. $7.95

AN INTRODUCTION TO THE STUDY OF THE MAYA HIEROGLYPHS, Syvanus Griswold Morley. Classic study by one of the truly great figures in hieroglyph research. Still the best introduction for the student for reading Maya hieroglyphs. New introduction by J. Eric S. Thompson. 117 illustrations. 284pp. 5⅜ x 8½.
23108-9 Pa. $4.00

A STUDY OF MAYA ART, Herbert J. Spinden. Landmark classic interprets Maya symbolism, estimates styles, covers ceramics, architecture, murals, stone carvings as artforms. Still a basic book in area. New introduction by J. Eric Thompson. Over 750 illustrations. 341pp. 8⅜ x 11¼.
21235-1 Pa. $6.95

CATALOGUE OF DOVER BOOKS

THE STANDARD BOOK OF QUILT MAKING AND COLLECTING, Marguerite Ickis. Full information, full-sized patterns for making 46 traditional quilts, also 150 other patterns. Quilted cloths, lame, satin quilts, etc. 483 illustrations. 273pp. 6⅞ x 9⅝. 20582-7 Pa. $4.50

ENCYCLOPEDIA OF VICTORIAN NEEDLEWORK, S. Caulfield, Blanche Saward. Simply inexhaustible gigantic alphabetical coverage of every traditional needlecraft—stitches, materials, methods, tools, types of work; definitions, many projects to be made. 1200 illustrations; double-columned text. 697pp. 8⅛ x 11. 22800-2, 22801-0 Pa., Two-vol. set $12.00

MECHANICK EXERCISES ON THE WHOLE ART OF PRINTING, Joseph Moxon. First complete book (1683-4) ever written about typography, a compendium of everything known about printing at the latter part of 17th century. Reprint of 2nd (1962) Oxford Univ. Press edition. 74 illustrations. Total of 550pp. 6⅛ x 9¼. 23617-X Pa. $7.95

PAPERMAKING, Dard Hunter. Definitive book on the subject by the foremost authority in the field. Chapters dealing with every aspect of history of craft in every part of the world. Over 320 illustrations. 2nd, revised and enlarged (1947) edition. 672pp. 5⅜ x 8½. 23619-6 Pa. $7.95

THE ART DECO STYLE, edited by Theodore Menten. Furniture, jewelry, metalwork, ceramics, fabrics, lighting fixtures, interior decors, exteriors, graphics from pure French sources. Best sampling around. Over 400 photographs. 183pp. 8⅜ x 11¼. 22824-X Pa. $5.00

Prices subject to change without notice.

Available at your book dealer or write for free catalogue to Dept. GI, Dover Publications, Inc., 180 Varick St., N.Y., N.Y. 10014. Dover publishes more than 175 books each year on science, elementary and advanced mathematics, biology, music, art, literary history, social sciences and other areas.